MY NERDY VALENTINE

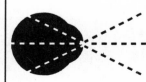

My Nerdy Valentine

Vicki Lewis Thompson

WHEELER PUBLISHING
An imprint of Thomson Gale, a part of The Thomson Corporation

Detroit • New York • San Francisco • New Haven, Conn. • Waterville, Maine • London

LIBRARY OF CONGRESS CATALOGING-IN-PUBLICATION DATA

Thompson, Vicki Lewis.
  My nerdy valentine / by Vicki Lewis Thompson.
    p. cm.
  ISBN-13: 978-1-59722-555-7 (pbk. : alk. paper)
  ISBN-10: 1-59722-555-X (pbk. : alk. paper)
  1. Sex therapists — Fiction. 2. Stockbrokers — Fiction. 3. Stalkers —
Fiction. 4. Large type books. I. Title.
PS3620.H73M9 2007
813'.6—dc22   2007012639

Published in 2007 by arrangement with St. Martin's Press, LLC.

Printed in the United States of America on permanent paper
10 9 8 7 6 5 4 3 2 1

For Carly Phillips, who scored the first romance book pick on national television (*The Bachelor,* debuting on Kelly Ripa's Book Club in 2002), and paved the way for *Nerd in Shining Armor* to be chosen by Kelly a year later. Carly, you're a true pioneer, and I cherish your support, advice, and friendship more than I can say.

ACKNOWLEDGMENTS

Although I may do the typing, I couldn't write a chapter, let alone an entire book, without the aid and comfort of some very special people. Thanks to Audrey Sharpe for locating a research tool essential to my creativity: a Barmaster Deluxe. Audrey and my husband Larry made the supreme sacrifice of helping me try it out in an actual bar. Their dedication to the cause will not be forgotten. The evening was pretty much a blur, but their dedication will shine forever.

Many thanks to Jennifer Enderlin for giving such attention to the book, and to Kim Cardascia for being my go-to person at St. Martin's. You're both consummate pros, and I've learned so much!

As always, I treasure the enthusiasm of my son and daughter-in-law, Nathan and Lauri Thompson. I'm also blessed by many talented and intelligent friends who keep me humble. And finally, I'm grateful to NovelTalk for hooking me up with some of the funniest people I know. To the NovelTalk chatters, thanks bunches for the giggles and the attagirls. You're the best.

ONE

The paper bag crammed with sex toys began to rip as Amanda Rykowsky trudged up the marble staircase to her boss's second-floor office. Clamping her gloved hand over the tear, she shoved the protruding red vibrator out of sight. The cold drizzle falling outside must have weakened the bag.

She should have asked for plastic instead, but paper concealed the contents better. She was always afraid she'd run into someone she knew on the way back to the office, and her reputation as the Girl Who Doesn't Date would be shot if anyone caught her with these goodies. How ironic that she was constantly surrounded by sex at a time when she'd sworn off the activity completely.

"Need some help with that?"

She glanced over her shoulder. Coming up the steps behind her was a tall guy wearing a tan trench coat and a hat with earflaps.

Those earflaps would stand straight out from his head if he discovered what she had in the bag.

"Thanks. I've got it." No sooner were the words out of her mouth than the bag self-destructed. Various colors and models of vibrators clattered down the marble steps, along with an array of X-rated videos. The feathers, velvet ropes, and soft handcuffs made less noise, but no less of an impression.

At least, Amanda assumed it was shock and awe widening the guy's green eyes to the approximate size of a traffic light. His mouth opened, closed, opened again. He stared at the items scattered around him. The fire-engine red, penis-sized vibrator lay across the laces of his brown oxfords. "Um . . . I . . ."

Amanda's cheeks grew hot. She shouldn't care what this guy thought, but she did, anyway. Her explanation came out in a rush. "My boss is Gloria Tredway and she's a sex therapist and she asked me to buy these on my lunch break."

"Uh, that . . . that makes sense. I guess."

"I'll just gather up everything and be on my way." She'd pretend the sex toys were groceries she'd dropped. And she wouldn't look at him while she did that. With a

10

decent dose of luck, she'd never see him again. She reached for a space-age silver vibrator that gleamed in contrast to the worn marble steps.

"I'll help." He pulled a pair of horn-rimmed glasses out of his coat pocket and put them on.

"That's okay. No problem." Unzipping her parka partway, she tucked the vibrator inside. Then she grabbed feathers and velvet handcuffs, stuffing them into her small shoulder purse.

They didn't quite fit, but maybe they'd stay long enough for her to escape up the stairs and duck into Gloria's office. She moved down a step and snatched up two videos — *Bareback and Bare: Lady Godiva Fantasies* and *Hotter than a Pistol-Packin' Momma*.

About the time she put those inside her parka, the vibrator fell out of the bottom. The elasticized hem used to fit tighter around her hips, but lately she'd been working hard and skipping meals. Apparently she'd lost weight.

"You definitely need help taking all this upstairs." He picked up the red vibrator lying on his shoe.

"I can make two trips." She could *not* have this stranger gathering sex toys and carrying them to Gloria's office. No telling how Gloria, she of the supersized libido, would react. She might decide to educate him. Amanda reached out with her free hand. "I'll take that . . . that red doohinkus and get the rest on my second trip."

"I wouldn't advise leaving this stuff lying around." He put the vibrator in his coat pocket and leaned down to snag a couple of videos. "There's a fourth-grade field trip from one of Chicago's magnet schools headed for the offices of Cooper and Scott. I've been asked to give them the grand tour."

"Oh, sh— sugar." Visions of little girls in pigtails getting a glimpse of the X-rated videos lying on the steps turned her blood cold. "Then I accept your help, at least to the door of the office." So he was a stock-broker who worked for Cooper and Scott, the company with offices down the hall.

This close to him, she could smell damp cotton, cold air, and his aftershave. No designer, musk-enhanced fragrance for this guy. Old Spice, if her nostrils weren't mistaken. She'd always liked Old Spice.

"And then we will permanently erase this moment from our memory banks," she said.

"Are you planning to give me a *Men in Black* memory flash?" A smile played over his mouth as he picked up a video and a fingertip vibrator. "This is one of those times that will live in infamy."

"I'm afraid you're right."

He had a nice smile, and she truly appreciated his stab at making this incident funny. Maybe in a while, like ten or fifteen years, it would be funny. On this particular February day she couldn't think of anything more humiliating than spilling a bag full of sex toys in front of a complete stranger.

Scooping up the last of the feathers and handcuffs, she snatched the ripped bag and gave the stairway a quick once-over. "That does it. Let's get out of here before the munchkins show up."

"William Sloan, by the way," he said as they hurried up the steps with the goods.

"Amanda Rykowsky. Thanks for making the stairway safe for nine-year-olds."

"Glad to help out. It must be an unusual kind of job, working for a sex therapist."

Especially this one. "It's temporary. I needed to intern with a local therapist this semester as part of a new course requirement at DePaul, and Dr. Tredway had an opening for a gal Friday."

"You're studying to be a sex therapist?"

"Nope. Just happened to land this internship. I haven't chosen a specialty yet. I'll narrow down my options while I'm in grad school, but I'm leaning toward adolescent psychology."

"You sound very focused, Amanda Rykowsky."

"I am."

"Too focused to have lunch with me tomorrow?"

Oh. She hadn't seen that coming. Usually she was prepared for such invitations, but having a guy help her carry X-rated gizmos up the stairs had thrown off her timing.

"I could give you some hot stock tips," he said.

"I, uh, don't have any money to invest." She hoped that wasn't some sort of double entendre about the hot tips.

"I was kidding. Stockbroker humor. I just thought, since you made your sex-toy run today, you might want to have a more normal lunch hour tomorrow. I know a sandwich place that's not too far from —"

"Thank you, William." She finally had the presence of mind to dial in her standard response. "But I'm determined to become a therapist, and I'm putting myself through school. Between work and studying, I have absolutely no free time."

"None?"

"Not even an hour for lunch." She gave

him a smile to soften the blow. "It's a nice offer, and you've been terrific to help me today, but I'll have to say no."

"It was just a thought." He sounded sad, though, as if he'd really hoped she'd take him up on his invitation.

"I wish I could go." Now she was feeling like an ingrate. He'd come to her rescue and saved her from potentially traumatizing an entire class of Chicago fourth-graders, and yet she'd refused to spend an hour in his company eating lunch. She should probably offer to buy *him* a meal for being so gallant.

No, bad idea. She couldn't take the chance that he'd see the lunch date as the beginning of something. And it couldn't be, not with her schedule. Besides, she'd been doing without a guy for so long, she might be tricked into thinking this guy was sexy. A love affair gone wrong had nearly trashed her GPA a year ago, so no more guys, no more sex, until she'd reached her goal of graduate school at Harvard.

"I wish you could go, too." William walked beside her down the hall toward Gloria's office. "But I don't want to muck up your routine."

And didn't that make her sound prissy? Like one lunch date would destroy her entire program. It probably wouldn't, especially if he wore the hat with the earflaps. But there was that smile to consider . . . nope, lunch was out.

"Here we are." She paused in front of the heavy oak door with its frosted-glass upper panel. *Gloria Tredway, Ph.D.* was lettered in gold on the glass. The door looked so professional and imposing that no one would guess what sort of gonzo activities took place behind it.

Amanda clutched her armload of toys to her chest and wiggled her arm until her sleeve edged up and she could see her watch. Ten minutes past one, which meant the Ordwells would be in Gloria's office for their regular Tuesday appointment. She needed to get William in and out very fast.

As she juggled her purchases, trying to free up a hand to open the door, William stuck two videos under his chin and reached out with one long arm. "Let me." Twisting the brass doorknob, he opened the door and stood back. "After you."

"Just dump everything on my desk," she said. "I'm sure your fourth-graders will be here any —"

"Lookee there!" Elmer Ordwell's voice blasted through Gloria's closed office door. *"Just from watching you do that, Dr. Tredway,*

16

I'm stiff as the tailpipe on my Chevy truck!"

"That's a real breakthrough, Elmer." Gloria was no slouch in the voice-projection department, either. *"Now, Gertrude, I want you to try what I was just doing. Yes, use your hand, and let Elmer watch. I'll be right back. I'm expecting some supplies that we'll need for the last half of our session."*

Amanda avoided looking at William. "You can just drop everything and go." She tried to sound nonchalant. "I appreciate your help in getting it this far. I'll be fine, now."

But William didn't show any signs of leaving. Instead he stared in fascination at Gloria's office door. "I had no idea."

"Dr. Tredway's not the norm." Amanda deposited her loot on the desk and reached for the stuff William was holding. "Most sex therapists don't operate the way she does. Look, I'm sure you need to get back to your office."

"They'll page me."

"I should warn you that Dr. Tredway is a little . . ." Before she could decide whether to use the word *oversexed,* it was too late.

Gloria, her shoulder-length red hair tousled and her brown eyes shining from whatever she'd been doing to get Elmer stiff as a tailpipe, breezed through the door of her office. Immediately she spied William

17

with a fingertip vibrator in one hand, porn in the other, and the long red vibrator sticking out of his trench coat pocket.

Her perfectly plucked bows arched. "My, my. I didn't know the G-Spot had a delivery service."

Amanda closed her eyes. Gloria was perpetually in man-hunting mode, but Amanda had thought the earflaps might dissuade her. Not so.

"Love the hat," Gloria said. "Do you demonstrate G-Spot merchandise, too?"

Amanda decided William was too shell-shocked to speak up for himself. "This is William Sloan. He's a stockbroker with Cooper and Scott. The bag ripped on my way up the stairs and he was kind enough to help me carry everything here."

"A knight in shining armor. How dashing." Gloria held out both hands, flashing her rings and her scarlet nails as she wiggled her fingers. "Let me relieve you of your burdens, William, so you can give me one of your business cards. I could use some advice on stocks and bondage . . . I mean *bonds.*" She laughed. "Pardon my Freudian slip."

A moan filtered through Gloria's office door.

William handed over the vibrator and the videos and edged backward toward the hall door. "I should probably make it another time. When you're not busy with clients."

Amanda could understand his desire to leave, but she had to figure out a way to let him know he was still packing heat. She couldn't let him give a tour to the fourth-graders with a red vibrator sticking out of his coat pocket.

"My clients are fine." Gloria dropped the items on Amanda's desk as the moans coming from her office escalated in volume. "I wouldn't dream of walking in there when they're making such obvious progress." She winked at him. Gloria loved eye makeup, so a wink from her was always dramatic.

"Uh, well, right, but I still —"

"I love it when my clients take the initiative. At this rate they may not need the video I'd planned to show them."

"That's great. But I have to give a tour to a bunch of kids. I need to get back." William eased closer to the door.

Amanda moved in his direction. "Uh, William . . . I think you might have forgotten —"

"Never mind the business card," Gloria said. "I'll just pop down to your office later for a consultation. My current broker is at least a hundred and six and terminally boring. I can safely say he'd never show up with

19

a red vibrator in his pocket."

Glancing down in horror, William yanked the vibrator out of his pocket and shoved it into Gloria's hand.

"You're welcome to keep it if you like." Gloria batted her mascara-coated lashes. "Especially if you'll give me visiting privileges."

He cleared his throat. "Thanks, but it's not my color." And with that he hurried out the door.

Gloria laughed. "Amanda, is he the cutest nerd you've ever seen, or what? I think I'm in love."

William had been worried that the fourth-graders would be bored with a tour of a brokers' office, but they surprised him with savvy questions about insider trading and the current value of the Japanese yen. From the content of the questions, William figured they all expected to be Donald Trump by the time they were thirty.

They kept him so busy that he should have had no chance to think about Amanda Rykowsky, but he thought about her anyway. Images of her were constantly wiggling in through cracks in his concentration.

She was the kind of woman who was more beautiful than she realized, and he was a sucker for that type. Her body had been swallowed by the dark blue parka, but he'd noticed silky blond hair that fell in a soft curve to her shoulders, clear blue eyes, a full mouth rubbed bare of lipstick, and cheeks pink from a brisk February breeze. Her cheeks had become even pinker after the bag had ripped.

He liked to think he would have noticed her even if she hadn't dropped a bag full of sex toys at his feet, but that little scene hadn't hurt. Her fresh-faced wholesomeness and the scattered X-rated items made for an arresting combo. She was such an unlikely person to be toting them around, and that made the prospect all the more interesting.

She'd bought them for someone else, though. Still, she had bought them, had marched into the store and made the selections herself. He wondered why she'd chosen that red model, for example, the one he'd almost taken with him. He tried to picture her going through the merchandise at the adult toy store and choosing one over the other.

"Mr. Sloan? Mr. Sloan!" Someone tugged on his sleeve.

He glanced down into the chocolate-colored eyes of a little girl with her hair in cornrows. Her nametag read *Natalie.*

She peered up at him. "Are you okay, Mr. Sloan? I asked you a question two times."

William looked around and realized the entire class was staring at him, including their teacher, Mrs. Jones, who was a plump African-American woman in her fifties.

Mrs. Jones cleared her throat. "I'm sure Mr. Sloan was just collecting his thoughts."

"Exactly," he said. "Economics is a serious subject, and I didn't want to give you the wrong answer." *Whoa.* He couldn't remember the last time he'd allowed fantasies about a woman to absorb him so completely that he lost track of his surroundings. He had no idea what Natalie had asked him. Twice.

"I'll bet he's having one of those miniseizures," said a tall girl who looked as if basketball might be in her future. "I have a brother who gets those, and he just zones out, like Mr. Sloan did."

"Well, *my* brother gets like that when he's thinking about his *girlfriend*," said an impish boy named Elijah whose curly hair was cut very close to his head. He looked at William and grinned.

"Well, I don't have a girlfriend," William said. "So, did everyone hear Natalie's question?"

They all nodded.

Rats. "Even so, let's have her ask it again, so it's fresh in our minds."

Natalie gave him a look, but she repeated the question, which had to do with commodities. William wondered where in the world these kids got so smart. Maybe from watching *The Apprentice.*

He answered the commodities question, and then it was time for the class to leave. Good thing. He wasn't giving a very good impression of a man focused on economics.

As the class filed out, Elijah inched over toward William. "Are you *sure* you don't have a girlfriend?" His grin widened. "Because you look exactly like my brother does when he's thinking about Angie."

"Elijah," the teacher said. "Tell Mr. Sloan goodbye and thank you."

Elijah held out his hand. "Goodbye and thank you."

"You're welcome." William shook his small, sticky hand. The kid probably had a pocket full of jelly beans.

"And good luck with your girlfriend."

"Mm." William didn't bother contradicting the girlfriend reference again.

In fact, he'd been thinking of the girlfriend issue recently. If he didn't watch out, Helen's accusation might come true. When he'd caught her in bed with someone else, she'd blamed her behavior on his neglect. She'd predicted he'd never be willing to invest time in a relationship because he was obsessed with his career.

But that wasn't true, was it? Asking Amanda to lunch had been more than an idle invitation. He wanted to get back in the game and prove Helen wrong, and he wished Amanda hadn't turned him down. How ironic that she'd said no because she was overcommitted.

Or maybe she'd been turned off by the stupid hat. He usually took it off once he was inside, but today, of all days, he'd forgotten about it, probably because he'd been so intent on Amanda struggling with her bag. His ears were supersensitive to the cold, and the earflaps were the alternative to intense pain.

"William, there you are!" Gloria Tredway appeared in the open door of the office and maneuvered around several nine-year-olds. Her black-and-white checked jacket was unbuttoned to show off a black lace chemise and a generous amount of cleavage. "I see the tour is ending. Do you have some time for little old me, now?"

"Um, sure. See you later, kids. Thanks for coming."

Elijah gazed at Gloria. Then he looked over his shoulder at William. "Uh-*huh.*" Then Mrs. Jones hustled him and the rest of the class out the door.

Gloria approached, a predatory gleam in her eyes. "I'll bet you give great tours."

William swallowed. "The kids seemed to enjoy it."

"Can I have a tour?"

"Sure."

She made a low purring sound deep in her throat. "Excellent. Show me all you've got."

Two

Amanda tried not to think about Gloria sitting in William's office. Without Gloria there, she had a chance to go over her notes for a test she had coming up tomorrow morning in abnormal psych. Hauling her notebook out of the backpack she kept tucked in the kneehole of her desk, she flipped to her most recent notes.

As she reviewed the clinical definition of schizophrenia, she picked up the glass hummingbird she kept on her desk. Usually the smoothness of the glass helped her concentrate, but not today. Instead she pictured Gloria crossing her legs so her skirt inched up. She was extremely proud of her legs.

Come to think of it, she was extremely proud of all her body parts. She bragged about having the tits of a twenty-year-old, and right this minute she was probably leaning forward and allowing her chemise to gape open. William, being a nerd, might not be used to that. He might not have the foggiest idea how to handle a woman like Gloria.

And why should Amanda care? She didn't, really, except that Gloria saw men only as a source of temporary pleasure, a conquest, a way of keeping score. She'd use William for what she wanted and discard him when she got bored. In William's case, that just didn't seem right.

Then again, Amanda didn't really know him. Most red-blooded guys would be happy to jump into bed with a woman as experienced as Gloria. Amanda had no doubt Gloria was great in the sack. She constantly boasted about the number of men who'd told her they'd never had it so good.

But when Gloria walked back into the office, she wasn't smiling. Amanda took an unholy amount of satisfaction in that. Maybe William hadn't been so easy to seduce, after all.

"Come into my office." Gloria sailed past her without waiting for a reply. "I need to discuss something with you."

Amanda put down the hummingbird, got out of her chair, and walked into Gloria's office.

"Close the door. I wouldn't want a client

to hear this."

Amanda turned around and closed the door with a soft click.

"Sit down." Gloria waved Amanda to the red leather love seat that rested against one wall.

Amanda moved aside a stack of videos and various tubes of personal lubricant. Every time she sat on this love seat she had to block out visions of what had probably taken place there. Gloria was both an exhibitionist and a voyeur, so anything was possible.

Gloria began to pace. "This is rather embarrassing, but I need some advice."

"From me?" Amanda wondered what on earth she knew that Gloria didn't. "About what?"

"I'm extremely intrigued with that broker." Gloria paused at her desk, picked up the silver vibrator Amanda had recently bought, and tapped it against her palm.

"Mm."

"I think it's because he's so different from the men I usually meet." Gloria caressed the vibrator.

"Because he's a nerd?"

Gloria pointed the vibrator at her. "That's exactly the problem. He's a nerd, and nerds react logically, not emotionally. I find that challenging."

Amanda fought to keep the smile off her face. It wouldn't do to smile in a situation like this. William hadn't taken Gloria's obvious bait. Good for him.

"He's probably not used to having a voluptuous woman like me go after him. He could be telling himself I'm too hot to handle."

"He might, at that."

Gloria began to pace, her five-inch heels sinking into the deep pile of her carpet. "I need to get around that perception and make him realize that he deserves the sexual attention of someone like me. I'd be doing him a favor by convincing him to aim higher. So I have to ask myself, what mind games would work on a nerd?"

"Why even bother with him?" Amanda wondered if she could possibly derail this effort. "I mean, why work so hard, when there are a dozen other guys who would be happy to —"

"See, I knew it! You think like a nerd. That's logic talking, but the reaction I have to William Sloan is at a gut level." Gloria smiled. "Or, more precisely, a bit lower."

No surprise there. Gloria reacted that way to everyone with a Y chromosome in the mix.

Gloria continued to pace. "It takes a certain disdain for convention to walk down Michigan Avenue wearing a hat with earflaps." She gestured with the vibrator. "A disdain for convention can translate into an appetite for the unusual, and in sexual terms, that's very exciting to me."

"You could be reading too much into the earflaps. He could be simply fashion impaired."

Gloria whirled and pointed the vibrator at her again. "There you go, being logical again. That's why I called you in here. You're a bit of a nerd yourself, Amanda."

"Me? I'm not a nerd."

"Of course you are! Always studying, never dating, a regular loner."

Amanda rushed to defend herself. "Okay, I can see how I might appear that way to you, because you haven't known me that long. But this is my last semester, and I can't take a chance on messing it up and not getting into graduate school."

"Precisely!" Gloria waved the vibrator at her. "You don't want to take chances. You've been here nearly six weeks and you've never once asked to borrow a video or a jar of body paint. I've had interns who went through that stuff like locusts through a wheat field. You'd think I'd handed them the keys to a treasure chest."

"Dr. Tredway, I can't speak for them, but —"

"For the hundredth time, call me Gloria. We're colleagues."

Amanda sighed. "All right. Gloria, I can assure you that I am not always like this. It's just that right now, I have to focus."

"Fine, fine. We won't debate the matter anymore. But I'm positive you will have some ideas about how I can attract William's attention. Let's say you were in my place."

That would be quite the stretch. "Uh-huh."

"Just tell me honestly, Amanda, how would you go about getting into William's pants?"

"I haven't the faintest idea." And even if she did, she wouldn't tell. Now might not be the time to mention that William had asked her to lunch.

"You're sure you don't have any thoughts?" Gloria peered at her. "How long has it been since you've had a date, anyway?"

"I don't know, exactly. A while." Amanda wasn't about to get any more specific than that.

"If you don't even remember, then you're obviously out of practice with these things.

But I want you to think about the subject of William and get back to me. I feel certain you could help me with my campaign. I'm switching my brokerage accounts over to Cooper and Scott, so that will give me an excuse to see him."

"Wouldn't it be unethical for him to get involved with a client?"

Gloria propped her hips against the desk. "If that issue comes up, so to speak, I'll simply switch back to the senile old goat I had before. First I have to get William to the point where he has that moral dilemma. I hate to admit it, but he's not even close yet."

"I just don't understand why you would go to all that trouble. What's so special about William?"

Gloria tapped the vibrator softly against her mouth. "I guess you didn't pay attention to his thumbs."

"His *thumbs?*"

"Oh, yes. Gorgeous thumbs. Nice large ones."

"I don't get it."

"My dear Amanda, take it from a woman who's indulged in sexual adventures with men of all sizes — a man with thumbs like that is quite likely to be magnificently, gloriously hung."

■ ■ ■ ■

Later that afternoon, while Amanda was typing up client evaluations and Gloria was in her office previewing videos, William walked in, a manila envelope in his hand. Naturally she looked at his thumbs, and sure enough, he had big ones.

She refused to think about the implications of that. Gloria could be blowing smoke, and besides, Amanda had always been of the opinion that imagination trumped size any old day. How much imagination could a girl expect from a man who constantly dealt with numbers?

"I have some papers for Dr. Tredway to sign," William said. "Our computer was down when she was in the office earlier, but it's back online, so I was able to print out the forms. I decided to bring them over."

"Thanks. I'll see that she gets them." Amanda had to admit that the lack of a hat improved William considerably. He had a thick head of dark brown hair. He wore it short, but not so short that a woman couldn't run her fingers through it. William wasn't a total loss — just not Amanda's cup of tea.

For one thing, his tie was a boring gray

and blue stripe. Amanda admired men who took a chance in that department, daring to wear a Jerry Garcia number, for example, or one decorated with a Warner Bros. cartoon character. She was partial to the Road Runner. Her last boyfriend had worn outrageous ties. He'd also broken her heart, but that was beside the point.

When William hesitated to put the envelope on her desk, she wondered if he might actually want to see Gloria again. "Or would you like me to find out if Dr. Tredway's available?"

"No, that's okay." He handed her the envelope. "She can sign them anytime. No rush."

"All right, then."

He glanced at the little hummingbird on her desk. "That's cute."

"I like hummingbirds." She picked it up out of habit. "Scientifically they shouldn't be able to fly, but they do. They beat the odds."

"And they work damn hard to stay airborne."

"I know. They're so determined. I admire that." He really was a nice guy, and because she still felt guilty about turning down his lunch date, she asked about the fourth-graders. "How did the tour go?"

He brightened. "Smart kids. They knew more about the stock market than most adults. Their teacher deserves some credit, but they were sharp. One of them asked me about —"

"William!" Gloria burst from her office as if shot from a cannon. She held a video in her hand. A rhythmic beat and muted cries indicated that she'd already popped another one in the player. "I thought I heard your voice, but between the exaggerated grunting and moaning on this lame DVD, I wasn't sure."

He backed up a step. "I was just bringing the papers for you to sign. No hurry, really. I should be going."

"Nonsense. Come on in the office while I sign the papers. That will be more efficient." She handed the video to Amanda. "I'd like you to return that one and get a refund."

"Now?" Amanda tried to tune out the orgasmic sounds coming from Gloria's office.

"Yes, while the transaction is still fresh in the clerk's mind."

"I thought you wanted the client evaluations finished by tomorrow."

"I do. Take a few home if you need to. But I need this video returned."

"All right." There went any hope of extra

sleep tonight.

Gloria was picky about her porn, but as one of the G-Spot's best customers, she was allowed to return almost anything. Holding the video, Amanda stood, walked around her desk and headed toward the coat rack next to the door.

From inside Gloria's office came a woman's voice on the DVD begging, *"Give it to me! Give it to me now!"*

"Bring me a mocha cappuccino on the way back," Gloria said. "The video I'm watching now is more promising than that one, but if it doesn't stimulate me, either, I can always resort to caffeine."

"Whipped cream?"

"Of course. Whipped cream gives me such a sensual buzz. William, can I interest you in a cappuccino?"

"No, no, thanks."

"Deeper, deeper!" cried the woman on the video. The drumbeats grew faster.

William shifted his weight uneasily. "I really need to get back to the office. The papers can be signed anytime in the next couple of days."

Gloria waved a hand in the air. "Don't look so worried. I have clients coming in ten minutes. It's not like I'll throw you on the floor and have my way with you.

Amanda, don't let them give you any guff because that DVD's been opened."

"I won't." She'd become a pro at X-rated movie returns.

A man's voice replaced the woman's on the video, and now a saxophone wailed. *"Take it, baby,"* said the man. *"Take it all. Oh, yeah!"*

"They should cheerfully give you a refund," Gloria said. "That video is a waste. I don't know how they expect to arouse a viewer if they won't show full frontal nudity or zoom in on the genitals. The pumping action was a complete fake, if you ask me. I'll bet Tab A was never inserted in Slot B. What a rip-off."

Amanda resisted the urge to glance at William as she took her coat off the hook. She was used to this kind of behavior in Gloria's office, but he wasn't. She had one arm in her coat sleeve before she felt the weight of the coat lighten and realized that William was holding it for her.

Drums and saxophones combined for what was surely the climactic moment for the couple on the screen in Gloria's office. *"I'm coming!"* groaned the man.

"Thanks, William." Amanda transferred the rejected video to her other hand and slipped her arm into the sleeve. In the

37

process she got another whiff of Old Spice.

"That is *so* precious," Gloria said. "How many men hold a woman's coat these days?"

"Blame it on my upbringing," William said.

"Did you also learn how to help a woman out of her coat? That could be even more valuable."

"I'm coming, too!" screeched the woman in the video.

Amanda turned in time to catch a plea for help in William's green eyes. Well, he'd have to find aid somewhere else or learn to fend for himself. He was the one who'd chosen to make a personal delivery of the papers.

"See you later," she said, and escaped into the hall.

It was true that clients were due in ten minutes, but that gave Gloria a window of opportunity that was more than ample for a quickie. She seemed determined to make a conquest with or without Amanda's advice. And maybe she would succeed, but Amanda figured it wasn't in her job description to hang around and watch.

When the door closed behind Amanda, William wished he'd decided against bringing the papers down. He could have sent Bonnie, the receptionist. But then he would have missed the chance to see Amanda again.

He should abandon the cause, but the more he found out about her, the more intrigued he was. She was as determined to fly as that little hummingbird on her desk. He had no idea why, but maybe she'd had a screwup older brother like he did. Maybe she was carrying the banner for the whole family, the same as he was.

William admired that kind of determination, but, because he was a normal guy, he admired other stuff, too. Her soft blue sweater gave him X-rated ideas of his own, for all the good it did him. Arriving without his hat had seemed to make no difference in her reaction. She didn't even want to be friends.

A potential friend wouldn't have left him to deal with Gloria and her raging hormones. William had never met anyone like Gloria before, and he hoped never to meet anyone like her again. But he needed to build up a client list, which meant he couldn't afford to turn down business, especially from a woman with a portfolio like Gloria's. She might be a sex maniac, but she also had a ton of investments.

"Come on into my office, William." Picking up the envelope from Amanda's desk,

Gloria turned and sashayed through the door.

William didn't want to go in there. The video playing on her TV was bad enough, but he was worried that she might start peeling off clothes, and he wanted to avoid that at all costs. They hadn't covered this situation in his orientation with Cooper and Scott. Vowing not to look at the television screen, he squared his shoulders and walked into Gloria's office.

Holy den of iniquity! The X-rated video playing on the screen was the least of his problems. He'd never been in any therapist's office, let alone one who dealt with sex, but he would have expected framed diplomas and professional citations on the wall. Instead Gloria's walls were decorated with enlarged, framed illustrations of couples in various sexual positions.

William had some knowledge of those positions. He believed in studying any subject in which he had an interest, and he definitely had an interest in sex. Obviously Gloria had more than an interest. He was no psychologist, but he thought it would classify as a fixation.

"How do you like the art I've chosen?" she asked.

He turned, half afraid of what he'd find

when he looked at her. Thankfully she hadn't removed any clothes. "I guess it's appropriate to your job."

"Do you recognize it?"

"Uh . . ." Of course he *recognized* it. Any guy over the age of ten would recognize what those pictures were about.

"I mean the source of the illustrations. I assume you understand the subject matter. It's self-explanatory."

No kidding. Over her red leather love seat hung the male and female versions of something labeled underneath as *Mouth Music.* One of those illustrations was being mimicked on the TV screen. He'd tried not to look, but it was like trying to ignore an elephant in the room.

"So, do the drawings look familiar?" Gloria asked again.

"I don't know the artist, if that's what you mean."

"They're from Alex Comfort's *The New Joy of Sex.* Have you seen that book?"

"No, can't say that I have."

"It's a classic. I could loan you a copy if you —"

"You were going to sign the forms?" Gloria didn't tempt him, not even slightly, but the emphasis on sex in this office was working on him, anyway. No guy could be surrounded by the power of suggestion to this extent and not have a reaction. He was sure Gloria was counting on that.

"Yes, of course." She walked behind her desk and picked up a pen.

Grateful that she was finally about to do what he'd asked, William watched her sign the forms, which meant he noticed the pen in her hand. It was flesh-colored, and thicker than a normal pen. At the top were two round . . . oh, dear God.

She glanced up. "Like my pen?"

"It's unusual."

"I love my job, William." She lifted the pen and licked the tip of it. "And I've learned a great deal."

"I'm sure you have." He sounded as if he had laryngitis. What an impossible situation. "All done?"

"For now." She picked up the forms and tucked them slowly back inside the envelope. "Tell me, have you ever let a woman tie you up?"

"No. Listen, I have to get back. I'm sure I have a stack of messages piled up by now." He wouldn't have a stack of messages. He hadn't reached that level of success yet. But it sounded good and it was all his distracted brain could think of.

"I'm sure you do. I'm sure you have a big,

thick stack of urgent messages by now."

"Right." He grabbed the envelope.

She hung on. "Let me take you to dinner tonight."

He tugged on the envelope. "I have plans." Plans with his television set and the Bulls game. Justin, his roommate from college days, was batching it this week while his fiancée was on a business trip. Justin was coming over for pizza and a couple of beers.

She gripped the envelope tighter. "Cancel them. Better yet, we can have dinner at my place."

"Sorry, can't cancel. Very critical."

"A woman?"

"Uh, yeah." He'd call his mother during the first commercial. He hadn't talked to either of his folks in a while, and he needed to let them know how the job was going. Up until now, it had been going just fine.

"Well, then." Gloria released the envelope. "If she doesn't work out, you know where to find me."

"Absolutely." He left her office so fast he ran straight into Amanda, who had just returned, a mocha cappuccino clutched in one hand. The lid flew off and whipped cream and coffee splashed over both of them.

"Damn it! I'm sorry!" Dropping the

envelope on the floor, he pulled a handkerchief from his hip pocket and began dabbing at the coffee and whipped cream on the front of her nylon jacket.

"Don't worry about me," she said. "It washes. I doubt you can say the same for that suit."

"Doesn't matter."

"What have we here?" Gloria strolled out of her office. "I do believe I'm the one who was supposed to be playing with the whipped cream, not you two."

"Sorry about that." William picked up the envelope from the floor and noticed it had been baptized by the coffee, too. At least there wasn't any on the carpet. "I can get you another cappuccino."

"And bring it personally?"

"I'll probably need to have it delivered. I really am pressed for time."

"In that case, I'll make do with this one." Gloria took the cup from Amanda and licked at the remaining whipped cream. "But I think you may have to redo those forms and bring them back for me to sign."

"I'm sure they'll be fine." William edged toward the door. "Amanda, if that doesn't come out of your coat, let me know."

"It'll come out, but thanks."

"Sure." He took another second to enjoy

the sparkle in her blue eyes and the pink in her cheeks. If he could be alone with Amanda in an office filled with graphic pictures on the wall and an X-rated video running, he wouldn't mind at all. She might, though. They'd shared spilled sex toys and a spilled coffee drink, but they hadn't bonded over either incident.

"See you soon, William," Gloria said. "I need to warn you that I have lots of questions about my portfolio. I'm the kind of client who needs plenty of personal attention."

"Right. I'll be in touch." As he headed out the door, he regretted his choice of words.

"That's exactly what I'm hoping for," Gloria called after him.

THREE

"Well, Amanda, so far, so good." Gloria took a sip of her cappuccino. "I managed to work in a mention of Alex Comfort's work, and he was noticeably rattled by the framed illustrations and the video I had playing."

Amanda didn't want to think about William looking at pictures of people having sex. The concept of sex shouldn't be mixed with William in her mind, ever. Even so, that mixture had a certain appeal, probably because she'd been doing without for so long. The last thing she needed was to have sex with a guy who would probably take it way too seriously.

She unzipped her damp coat and hung it on the coat rack. "I couldn't get a cash refund for the video, but they gave me store credit."

"That's fine. I'll be sending you for more merchandise, I'm sure. I'm running low on edible panties and flavored oils." She gazed at the doorway as if envisioning the man who had just left. "I know what. I'll have William research the companies that make that sort of thing so I can buy stock in them. If I engage his brain, the rest will follow, don't you think?"

Amanda mentally rolled her eyes. "I couldn't say. I've never tried to seduce a nerd."

"Neither have I, but I'm having such fun with this one. He was trying so hard *not* to watch the naked couple in the video, but something like that is virtually impossible to ignore."

"That would be true."

"And his pupils got *huge,* which tells me that if I could have kept him there longer, something else might have started expanding, too. But he left before I could work on his libido some more. I'm dying to find out if my thumbs theory holds up."

Desperate to change the subject, Amanda glanced at her watch. "Shouldn't the Crutchfields be here by now?"

"Yes, they should, now that you mention it. Call them and find out if there's a problem. I'll be in my office."

Amanda sat at her desk and picked up the phone to forestall any more conversation about the sexual responses of William Sloan.

Until now, she'd only dealt with Gloria's unusual therapy techniques, which involved demonstrating how to use the various sex toys and previewing videos with the couples she had as clients.

To be fair, Gloria didn't exactly have sex *with* them. If she'd done that, Amanda's conscience would have made her report her boss, no matter what the personal consequences might be. No, Gloria skirted that, but she certainly had sex in front of them.

Amanda considered that unprofessional, but she wasn't sure if it would be actionable. Still, she had to deal with what was going on in Gloria's office, which was sort of like being in the middle of an X-rated movie. She'd thought that was bad enough.

But watching Gloria go after a sexual partner for herself was turning out to be even more uncomfortable, especially when Amanda kind of knew him. William didn't seem like the sort of guy who deserved to be stalked by the likes of Gloria.

Mimi Crutchfield answered the phone sounding out of breath. "Oh, Amanda! I was just going to call! I don't know if we can make the appointment. We've been in bed all morning and we lost track of the time."

"You're already ten minutes into your hour, I'm afraid," Amanda said. "Would you

48

like to reschedule?"

"Actually, I wonder if I can talk to Dr. Tredway a minute. You see, I have Franklin tied to the bedposts just like she suggested, and he's gone to sleep. I've tried everything — massage, penile stimulation, erotic music. Nothing works."

Alarm shot through Amanda. "Is he breathing?"

"Oh, my, yes. He's snoring, as a matter of fact. Dr. Tredway didn't mention anything about this reaction, so I need to speak with her."

"Sure thing." Amanda buzzed Gloria's office and tried to block the visual of Franklin Crutchfield, bank president and distinguished member of the community, spread-eagled on a four-poster. "Mimi Crutchfield needs to talk to you," she said when Gloria answered.

"What's the problem?"

"I think I'll let her tell you about it."

"Amanda, you are far too squeamish to be a sex therapist. I hope you know that."

"I'll work on it." She'd decided not to tell Gloria that she had no intention of becoming a sex therapist. Better to let Gloria think she was actually training her. Amanda didn't want to be in the position of potential convert. She had no idea what that might look like, and she had no urge to find out.

Two minutes later, she heard a whoop of laughter coming from Gloria's office. Then Gloria sauntered through the door, a cat-who-ate-the-cream smile on her face. "Franklin Crutchfield began therapy complaining that Mimi never took any sexual initiative."

The unwelcome picture of Franklin staked out on the mattress popped into Amanda's head. "So that's fixed, now, I assume?"

"I would say so! She worked him over all morning, making sure they tried each of the fifteen positions I'd taught them, and all the alternate locations, as well. They did it on the dining room table, up against the washing machine, under his desk, on the kitchen —"

"I get the idea." Amanda thought she might have to switch banks. Managing her small amount of money was stressful enough without being reminded of the sexual acrobatics of the bank president every time she walked into her local branch.

"Anyway, by the time she'd tied him to the bedposts for a little friendly bondage game, the guy was exhausted. Mimi thought she'd done something wrong. I told her he'd shown incredible stamina for a man his age and she should be proud. So, yeah, the problem seems to be fixed."

"She didn't reschedule the appointment, then?"

"No need to." Gloria leaned against the doorjamb. "Listen, I've been thinking I'd send William a video as an icebreaker. I mean, Valentine's Day is coming up next week, so I'd like to get something going with him by then."

Interesting. Amanda wouldn't have thought Gloria gave a damn about Valentine's Day. It was all about mushy love, not the kind of hot sex Gloria preferred.

"Don't look so surprised," Gloria said. "I celebrate Valentine's Day. I'm more into crotchless lace panties than little lace hearts, but I don't like the idea of spending that night alone any more than other women do." She paused. "I guess that's your fate, though, isn't it?"

"I won't be alone," Amanda said.

"Oh, that's right. You have that bartending job at Geekland. See, there's another reason you have the background to advise me about William. You serve drinks to nerds five nights a week."

"Six."

"*Six?* Really? When do you study?"

"After work."

"When do you sleep?"

"After I study."

"Amanda, I don't know how you do it, but you're obviously used to that routine, and I suppose it keeps you from feeling quite so frustrated about your lack of a sex life. So, what do you think of me sending William a video?"

"You'd send it to his office?"

"Why not? They're all adults down at Cooper and Scott. And I don't have his home address."

"I think . . . it might be a little bit inappropriate." Amanda wondered if Gloria had any concept of what constituted appropriate behavior.

"Okay, I'll send it to his home, then. You can find out later where he lives. Come in and help me pick one out. We don't have time for me to show you complete videos, so I'll fast-forward to the juicy parts."

No! This is so unfair! "I don't know that I'm the one to suggest —"

"You most certainly are the one. I want your nerd mentality on this project. If we don't find exactly the right one, I may have to send you shopping again. After all, we have store credit."

"But what about the client evaluations? I still have a pile to type up before tomorrow."

"Take them home, for God's sake. You'll be up all night, anyway, so you can do them then. Come on into the office and take a look at these videos."

Short of refusing to do what Gloria asked or faking a sudden case of stomach flu, Amanda couldn't figure out a way not to view a selection of videos with her boss. After about forty minutes of that, she was not in a good mood. A woman who had sworn off sex for the duration should not be forced to watch approximately twenty-six orgasms in a row, not that she'd been counting or anything.

"You don't think any of these are right for William, then?" Gloria hit the pause button at a strategic point, when the well-endowed actor was in mid-thrust.

"I don't know, Gloria." Amanda looked away from the screen and told herself that such activities were highly overrated. A degree and a job, now those were things worth sacrificing for. "If it were me, I wouldn't send him one to begin with."

"What, then?"

"Nothing. I would send him nothing."

Gloria blew out a breath. "That's ridiculous. I can't get anywhere by next week if I don't plant some ideas in his head. I know what. Go back to the G-Spot and browse around. Find something you think he would like that invites sexual feelings. If it has a valentine theme, so much the better."

Amanda felt the trap closing in. "Maybe this is something you need to do yourself."

"No, I'm convinced you'll have a better idea of what a guy like William would get excited about. I don't need you in the office right now, and you'll be typing the evaluations tonight, so take as long as you need."

"But —"

"Go on, now. I have clients due in five minutes and I have to check my inventory of nipple clips. I think I'm low, so pick up a few pairs while you're out."

Someday, Amanda told herself, she'd be a graduate student at Harvard specializing in adolescent psychology. Someday her world would not be dominated by Gloria Tredway and her nipple clips and vibrators and feathers and velvet ropes. In the meantime, she had to find William a sexy present that might have some vague connection to Valentine's Day.

Going to her desk, she pulled out the drawer where she kept her purse. But as she reached for it, she noticed a white square envelope lying on top of it. *Amanda* was printed in block letters on the front. Instinctively she glanced up to see if Gloria was in the doorway watching. She wasn't.

Snatching both her purse and the envelope out of the drawer, she hurried over to grab her coat. The envelope obviously contained some sort of card, and the block letters on the outside looked like a man's handwriting. If Gloria hadn't mentioned Valentine's Day just now, Amanda might have wondered what was in the envelope. But now she thought she knew.

Worse yet, she could guess who'd put that envelope in her desk. He'd had ample time when she wasn't there. If Gloria found out that William had sent Amanda a valentine, the shit would really hit the fan.

She waited until she was outside the building before she opened the card. The rain had stopped, but an icy wind slapped her face and blew off her hood. She turned her back to the wind and pulled out . . . a valentine, sure enough. Two white kittens on the outside were playing with a ball of red yarn, and the unrolled end was looped into a series of little hearts. Above the picture was the inscription, *You're too cute, Valentine.*

Had William actually gone to the drugstore half a block from the office building and picked out this card? She braced herself and opened it. The message inside said *Let's play around.* And it was signed *Your Secret Valentine.*

Amanda groaned. This was even more embarrassing than she'd thought. How was she supposed to react to something like this? Did he think she'd guess and respond in some way? She'd made her position clear, yet here was this cutesy valentine with a vaguely sexual reference inside.

The card was so not her type, just as William was not her type. She didn't care whether he had big thumbs or not. Sneaking into her office and leaving a fairly unimaginative card with kittens on the front was a dumb way to pursue a woman. A single red rose in a crystal vase with elegantly embossed stationery — now that might get her attention.

Or it would have, if she weren't so involved with work and school. At least the kitten card was something she could ignore. That's exactly what she would do. Ignore it. Pretend it had never happened.

Passing a trash can, she tossed the valentine inside. For a brief moment she felt guilty. He'd probably meant well, even if he didn't have good taste in cards or the slightest idea how to be romantic. But he had taken the time to buy her that card, and she'd blithely thrown it away.

Then she told herself not to be stupid. She didn't want William in her life, and keeping the card might backfire in some way, especially if Gloria ever found out. William needed to get the message that she wasn't interested. That would save trouble on her part and humiliation on his.

Maybe she should put some real thought into this gift Gloria had sent her to buy. If Gloria succeeded in snagging William's attention, Amanda wouldn't have to worry about him anymore. He'd be off her conscience.

Harvey Kenton watched from a Starbucks across the street as Amanda walked out of her office building carrying the card. Excitement churned in his stomach, like on his first date with Louise when she'd begged to do it doggie style. Louise had looked decent back then, but marriage had sure changed her. Now she was fat, ugly, and oversexed. Worse than that, she was making him go to stupid therapy, which he certainly didn't need.

Amanda wasn't fat and ugly. Every time he looked at her, he could tell she was thinking about him, probably thinking about him naked. He liked to think about her naked, too. She was so hot.

And now he'd made his first real contact with her, not counting the times he'd said hello on his way into Dr. Tredway's office. Those times he'd been sort of careful how he spoke to her, because of Louise, but he'd managed to get in a wink or two. He liked the idea of putting one over on Louise. She had it coming.

If only he could see the expression on Amanda's face when she opened the card, but he was too far away. Expressions could tell you a lot. He could always tell from Louise's expression when she was getting mad. She could be kind of scary when she got mad, but kind of exciting, too. Usually he hated having sex with Louise, but when she was mad it wasn't quite so yucky.

But he couldn't see Amanda's expression, especially because this late in the afternoon on a cloudy day, there wasn't much light. Bringing a pair of binoculars to Starbucks and using them to spy on somebody across the street would probably get the management on his case. He didn't want to get anybody on his case.

Maybe he could tell something from her body language. She took her time opening the card. He hoped she liked the kitties on the front. She liked little hummingbirds, and kitties were even cuter. He'd seen the card and thought about Amanda, all soft and cuddly. Or she would be, once he got her alone.

He had most of it planned. First he'd send her a bunch of valentines to get her in the mood. Then on Valentine's Night he'd sneak into her apartment and carry her off, just like in the movies. She might scream at first, and he hadn't worked out what to do about that.

The screaming wouldn't go on long, though, because once she recognized that he was her secret valentine, she'd be happy. He'd use the Mercedes as the getaway car. That should impress her, and it had a great back seat.

He gazed at her standing on the sidewalk and thought about how great it would be, undressing her on that back seat. She would love that. She must have liked the kitties he'd sent her, too, because she stared at them for a long time. She looked cold out there in the wind. He could warm her up fast, but it wasn't time for that, yet. First he had to lay the groundwork.

Amanda had stopped looking at the outside of the card and was finally opening it. He had to clap a hand over his mouth to keep from laughing as he thought about what the inside of the card said. *Let's play around.*

The minute he'd read that, he'd known it was the perfect card to start with. He'd bet Amanda would love to play around. She always looked as if she could hardly wait to get free of Dr. Tredway. He wouldn't mind getting free of Dr. Tredway, himself, except Louise had said she'd divorce him if he stopped going to stupid therapy.

A divorce wouldn't be so good. He'd been forced to sign a pre-nup, so he wouldn't get any of Louise's money. That would mean going back to the assembly line at the feminine products factory, and he was never doing that again. He'd put up with Louise forever if it meant he didn't have to go back to work.

At first Harvey had hated the idea of sex therapy, but that was before he'd seen Amanda looking so sexy as she sat at the desk in the front office. She had great hooters. She always smiled at him, and her voice was low and sweet, as if she'd like to tell him how much she craved his body, but she didn't dare.

He loved watching her holding his card, her blond silky hair blowing in the wind. She stared at the inside of the card for a long time, too. She must know who'd sent it, considering they'd been secretly flirting with each other for weeks, now. He wondered if she'd plaster the card against her chest, like he'd seen girls do in the movies.

Instead she put it back in the envelope. Maybe girls didn't clutch messages to their chest anymore. She might take the card home with her, though, and put it up on her refrigerator with a couple of magnets. That way she could look at it all the time and think about him.

She started walking down the street, away from him. He imagined what she'd do if he ran across the street, dodging traffic, and caught up with her. If he did that, he'd glance at the card and go, *Whatcha got there?* And she'd give him a sly smile and go, *Wouldn't you like to know?* Then he'd go, *I already know.*

After that they could leave and have a drink together, and she might invite him to her place. But that would be boring. What he had in mind would be way more dramatic. So he wouldn't run across the street.

On her way past a trash can, she tossed something into it. That something looked an awful lot like the card he'd sent. But she wouldn't do that! The card would mean everything to her!

Finally he figured it out. She wanted this

to be their little secret. If she kept the evidence around, anybody could find out, like Dr. Tredway, for example. Dr. Tredway wouldn't approve of this. Harvey knew that as sure as he knew the exact length of his dick — six and five-eighths inches long.

Just because Amanda had thrown his valentine in the trash didn't mean that she wasn't thinking of him right this minute. She was thinking of him, Harvey Kenton, and how much she wanted to be alone with him. But being a smart girl, she understood that they had to be careful. There was Dr. Tredway, and there was Louise. Louise kept a shotgun in the closet.

Four

Amanda spent far too much time at the G-Spot trying to find a gift that Gloria could give to William. She had to come back with something, or Gloria would probably send her out again tomorrow. Gloria didn't have a lot of time to wage her campaign before Valentine's Day, and she'd obviously decided Amanda would be doing the legwork.

Lack of sleep and decent food must be taking its toll, because Amanda found herself standing in the aisle of the G-Spot mesmerized by a wiggling purple dildo that the proprietor had switched on to grab the customers' attention. With real effort she pulled her gaze from the dancing dildo and continued with her search. Every time she came in here, which seemed to be a lot lately, she got the impression that everyone in the world was having amazing sex. Everyone except her, of course.

She found the nipple clips and put those in the basket dangling from her arm. And finally she decided on the only item she could imagine might fascinate William. Glow-in-the-dark condoms. If he'd ever been a *Star Wars* fan — and what nerd wasn't? — he might get a kick out of creating his own personal light saber. He might also be curious about how the manufacturers had created the effect.

And that was all the attention she planned to give to the subject, because thinking about William putting on a condom was not helping her goal, which was complete detachment from both him and the topic of sex. Had she passed him on the street she would never have thought of him in connection with that topic. But ever since they'd met on the stairs surrounded by adult toys, William and sex had been linked in her mind.

It was similar to the imprinting syndrome she'd learned about in Psych 101. She and William had met in a sexually charged atmosphere, and now she couldn't think of him without remembering that red vibrator lying across the laces of his brown shoe. Like it or not, that was an erotic image that would stay with her for a long time.

At the last minute she remembered that

Gloria wanted William's gift to have something to do with Valentine's Day, and glowing condoms didn't seem to fit that criteria. Fortunately, her store credit allowed her to throw in a box of chocolate truffles she found up near the register. Each one was shaped like a miniature breast.

As the clerk, a young guy named Lester, rang up her purchases, she thought of those breast-shaped truffles riding on the conveyor belt, bouncing and jiggling along, and she began to laugh. Maybe the stress was making her hysterical, too.

"When you get right down to it, sex *is* hilarious," Lester said.

Amanda cleared her throat. "I suppose so."

"Most people take it way too seriously."

"And you don't?" She studied Lester more closely. He was a skinny man in his mid-twenties, and nobody would accuse him of being handsome. His chin receded and his eyes were set too close together.

"Hell, no," Lester said. "I think sex is strictly for fun, and once in a while, you need to do it to keep the human race going. But worrying about how we look naked, or how good we are at the various positions — that's nuts. It's like getting uptight about your score at goofy golf. Sex should be a tension reliever, not a tension creator."

Amanda gazed at him with new respect. "And with that attitude, I'm sure you don't have trouble finding partners."

He smiled, revealing slightly uneven teeth. "Nope."

"I probably should adopt your philosophy."

"Trust me, you'd be a happier person. Pardon my saying, but you don't look all that happy, or you didn't until you started laughing just now."

"Point taken." Amanda picked up the small bag he'd filled with her purchases and started out the door. "Thanks. I'll think about what you said."

"Just being a good salesman. If you follow my advice, you'll need to come back and buy things for yourself instead of always running errands for Dr. Tredway. Then I'll have gained another customer."

"Lester, you're a very together guy." With a wave, she left the warm shop and stepped into the icy blast of a Chicago winter afternoon. Putting up the hood on her parka, she bowed her head and pushed against the wind as she walked back to the office building.

She knew that she took sex too seriously. And even though Gloria put out the same message as Lester, she was so obnoxious that Amanda wasn't ready to hear it coming from her. Lester made the pill more palatable.

Not only was Amanda aware that she took sex too seriously, she'd had enough psych classes to understand why. Her mother, Kathryn, had invested her whole being in her relationship with her husband. She'd abandoned the idea of a job, even a menial one, because that would have drawn her attention away from Timothy.

She'd concentrated so hard on the love of her life that she'd barely had enough time left over for Amanda. When Timothy Rykowsky died at forty of emphysema, Amanda's mother had never recovered, emotionally or financially. After Kathryn's death five years ago, Amanda had vowed that she'd never be that dependent on a man. She'd enrolled in college, determined to have a career.

But last year she'd met Jack Canterbury and let down her guard. After that heartbreaking disaster of a romance, she knew that she was vulnerable to the same dependency issues as her mother, which made her take sex *very* seriously. She wondered if she had the ability to treat it as recreation the way Lester did. That would be nice, but she didn't quite trust herself to pull it off.

Back in the office, she showed her purchases to Gloria, who was in the process of packing up for the day.

"That will do nicely," Gloria said. "I'll write a little note to go in with the package, and then I want you to call William's office and get his home address. Tell him I need it for my files. Then you can wrap everything up and take it to the post office on your way home."

Amanda wondered if there was any way she could get William's home address without talking directly to William. She'd try. "All right. I'll take care of it," she said.

Moments later Gloria dropped a note on her desk. "That's to go in the package. Send it priority." Gloria pulled on a mink coat that was probably the real thing. Then she paused and looked at Amanda. "I was thinking about that incident with the spilled coffee, and it came to me that you might develop a crush on William if you're not careful."

"Me?"

"It could happen out of sexual frustration and envy for my lifestyle."

Amanda almost choked. "I'm not envious."

"Don't be silly. Of course you are. I have

both a career and glamour, while you're little more than a drudge."

Amanda opened her mouth, but nothing came out.

"In any case, I want to make something perfectly clear. You are not to flirt, or whatever passes for flirting in your world, with William. In fact, that goes for any man who walks into this office. Is that understood?"

"Perfectly." If Amanda didn't know better, she'd think Gloria felt a little threatened by her. But that seemed unlikely. And Gloria had nothing to worry about, because there would be no flirting. Flirting wasn't on Amanda's scheduled list of activities.

"Excellent." Gloria wound a colorful scarf around her neck. "I'm off."

Truer words were never said. "I'll see you in the morning, then."

"Don't forget, I won't be in until ten. In fact, I could be a little later than that. Who do I have at ten?"

Amanda glanced at the calendar she kept for Gloria and noticed Gloria's massage at nine. "You have the Kentons at ten." Harvey Kenton seemed like a harmless sort, but Louise gave Amanda the creeps. That was one hard woman.

"Ah, yes. If I'm late, take them into my

office and start up a video. Give them a stack of magazines, too. That should keep them busy."

"I'll do that."

Gloria headed for the door. Then she paused and glanced back. "I just thought of something. Does William ever come into Geekland?"

"I've never seen him there."

"That's a shame. If he did, you could talk me up."

"If he ever does, I will." Amanda had decided that she was most definitely on board for this campaign now that William had sent her the valentine, the valentine Gloria would never, ever find out about.

"Good. In the meantime, I want you to observe and take notes on your customers tonight, and report back with anything that might help me snare William. For one thing, I have no idea what nerds drink. I'm sure you're an expert on that by now."

"They order unusual drinks."

"Like imported brandy, that sort of thing?"

"No, mixed drinks with several ingredients. They're constantly trying to come up with new combinations."

Gloria wrinkled her nose. "Sounds like a high school chemistry lab."

"That's not a bad comparison. Flaming shooters are popular."

"I can't imagine. Flaming shooters. I stay far away from all those weird concoctions. Someone offered me a Buttery Nipple once, which I drank because it sounded sexy. Eeuuww. Much too sweet. Give me a gin martini, extra dry, anytime."

"If you're ever in Geekland, I'll remember that." Actually, Amanda enjoyed making the more complicated drinks. Anybody could serve a beer or a glass of wine. But she might be the only bartender in the world who knew how to make a Chi-Town Lakefront Breeze, because it had been invented by her customers at Geekland.

"I don't ever expect to set foot in Geekland. One geek, in the form of William Sloan, is interesting. An entire bar full of them would be a bit much. See you in the morning." With that she whisked out the door in a swirl of dead animal skins.

Once she was gone, Amanda glanced down at the note Gloria had left on the desk. Gloria hadn't bothered to fold it, as if she didn't care whether Amanda read it or not. So she did.

William — I sense animal magnetism in you, although you may be trying to repress

71

it. Did you know that repressed sexual desire can manifest itself in overwork, which can lead to all sorts of health problems?

Amanda paused. She'd thought it was the other way around, that overwork caused a person to repress sexual desire. At least that was how her situation seemed to shape up. Maybe it was a chicken-and-egg sort of argument and nobody really knew which came first. She continued reading.

You are such a young and vibrant man that I would hate to see that sort of thing happen to you. I'm sending these gifts in the spirit of offering you an alternative, one that could easily lead to more productivity for you in the long run. An active penis stimulates the entire man to greater endeavors. Call me.

Then Gloria had scribbled her home phone number, her cell number, and her name, which she'd underlined with a flourish. The note was pure Gloria, and maybe she would be good for William, just as she'd implied. One thing was certain — after a few rounds with Gloria, William wouldn't be sending people valentines with fluffy kittens on the front.

Turning on her computer, Amanda did a quick search for the Cooper and Scott Web site. Then she picked up the phone and dialed the number. While it was ringing, she clicked on the link for brokers. There was William with all his credentials listed.

He'd been quite the academic whiz kid, not that she was surprised by that. If she ever had any money to invest, William would be the go-to guy, for sure. Except after that valentine, she couldn't risk it.

A receptionist answered. "Cooper and Scott. This is Bonnie. How may I direct your call?"

"I'm calling for Dr. Gloria Tredway, who has recently become Willliam Sloan's client," Amanda said in her most official voice. "Dr. Tredway has a policy of keeping all the pertinent information on anyone with whom she does business. She requires the home address and phone of Mr. Sloan for her records. Can you please give me that information?"

"I'm so sorry, but that can only be given out by the brokers themselves," Bonnie said.

Damn, she'd have to talk to him, after all.

"Would you like to speak with Mr. Sloan?" the receptionist asked. "I can see if he's available."

"That would be fine." Amanda found to

her dismay that her heart was pounding. Did she think that he'd somehow know that she'd thrown away his valentine? If he hadn't sent it in the first place, she wouldn't feel this awkwardness.

Then William came on the line. She was surprised by the rich, deep quality of his voice. It even sent a little tingle up her spine.

Earlier in the afternoon, she'd been so busy thinking about vibrators and earflaps that she hadn't paid much attention to how he sounded. Turned out he sounded . . . sexy-ish. Not that it mattered to her.

"I'm calling for Gloria," she said.

"Hi, Amanda."

She winced at the note of eagerness and prayed he wouldn't allude to the valentine in some veiled way. "Hi, William. Listen, it's Gloria's policy to keep contact information on everyone she does business with, so I need to get your home address and telephone number for our files."

Silence.

"I can assure you the information won't go beyond this office."

William cleared his throat. "I don't know how to say this, but under the circumstances, I would rather not give that information to Gloria."

"She won't like hearing that."

"I don't suppose she will, but as you've probably noticed, she's interested in expanding our relationship beyond that of broker and client."

"I've noticed." And if Gloria succeeded, that would let Amanda off the secret-valentine hook.

"Does she do that often?"

"I don't know, William. I've only been here since the first week in January."

"Is she there? Maybe I need to speak to her directly."

"No, she's gone home." Amanda thought fast. "Let me give you her home number and her cell number."

"I have those on the forms she filled out. Maybe I will call her. But as long as she's not there, would you be violating any special trust by telling me exactly why she wants my home address and phone number? That would help me know how to handle this."

Because she wants to jump your bones. Amanda took a deep breath. "She, uh, wants to send you something."

"She could send it to the office. Or better yet, you could bring it down now, if you have time."

"I don't think this is something you want to open in front of your colleagues."

William groaned. "What is it, porn?"

"No."

"Then what?"

Amanda thought fast. She wasn't about to describe what was in the package, but if she didn't get it to him somehow, there would be hell to pay in the morning. "I don't suppose you have a P.O. box?"

"Nope. But if I get any more clients like Gloria, that might be a viable option."

She laughed. She hadn't meant to, but what he'd said struck her as funny — William Sloan getting a P.O. box so he wouldn't be stalked by his female clients. Only Gloria, the reader of thumbs, would take a look at William and immediately think of mattress games. Well, maybe if a woman who'd never met him heard his voice on the phone, she might get ideas. Amanda found herself enjoying the firm resonance of it.

"I guess you don't think I'm in serious danger of being overrun by women." He seemed amused rather than insulted.

"Oh, no, I didn't mean that at all! It's certainly possible, and maybe a P.O. box would be a wise thing, so long as you're single. Women are getting more aggressive these days, and it might not hurt to take precautions."

"Thanks, but I'll go with your original assessment, that it would be a silly thing to do. In any case, I don't have one, and I really don't want to give Gloria my actual address. What if I just run down there and pick up whatever it is? Would that solve the problem?"

"I . . . well, I suppose it would." And create a host of new problems. But at least he'd have his gifts and she could tell Gloria they'd been delivered. The issue of address and phone could be handled later. Maybe William would be so enchanted by the items Amanda had bought that he'd decide to call Gloria and get chummy. One could always hope.

"Then I'll do that," he said. "I'm finished for the day, anyway. I'll stop by there before I catch my bus home."

"All right." As she said that, she came to a decision. She'd confront him about the valentine and make sure he understood she was not in the market. Maybe if he felt thoroughly rejected, he'd be more eager to take Gloria up on her offer.

Getting William and Gloria together had multiple benefits. He'd no longer be trying to make an impression on Amanda with kitten-themed valentines, and Gloria should be in a perennially good mood if her seduction succeeded and her big-thumbs theory proved correct.

"I'll see you in five minutes, then. Bye."

"Bye." Amanda hung up. Then she had a strong urge to take out a mirror and re-apply her lipstick. Obviously she got some enjoyment out of being the object of William's admiration, even though she was rejecting him. Well, she would stop enjoying it right now and forget about the lipstick. Wrong guy, wrong time.

FIVE

William walked down to Gloria's office carrying his briefcase and trench coat. The earflap hat was in the briefcase, out of sight. This might be his last chance to break through that barrier Amanda had erected around herself, and he didn't want to saddle himself with any handicaps.

That meant he needed to turn on the charm. Being of a practical nature, he wasn't sure if he had a handle on charm, but he might if he could channel the French part of his ancestry. After all, his mother had been born in Paris. That should count for something.

Maybe not much, though. He'd modeled himself after his very strait-laced, very military father, the parent who was so disgusted with Miles Sloan Jr., William's older brother. His brother couldn't seem to hold a job for more than a few months. There was no doubt Miles junior took after

William's free-spirited mother, who loved being spontaneous.

But William had French blood, too, and he needed to capitalize on that part of the gene pool right now. He believed that Amanda had a tight schedule, but most women, even ones with tight schedules, could fit in lunch or a coffee date. Something else was going on.

Unfortunately, first impressions could be lasting impressions. He'd at least learned that much during the Cooper and Scott orientation. Amanda's reluctance could still boil down to the earflaps. He'd have to work extra hard on the charm to overcome her initial mental picture of him.

He walked into the office, ready to make some witty comment. No matter that he wasn't the witty-comment type. For this occasion, he'd think of something. He was half French. It would come.

"Hi." Laying his briefcase and coat on a chair, he looked into Amanda's blue eyes.

"Hi."

The longer he looked at her in her soft blue sweater, the more his brain seemed to be gunked up with some kind of warm honey that jammed the circuits. "How was your afternoon?" he asked. Wow, talk about witty.

"Fine."

God, she was pretty. But he couldn't let that distract him. He needed to pour on the wit and charm. "My mom's French. She was born in Paris." He couldn't believe he'd said that out loud. The plan was to act as if he had some French savoir faire, not baldly announce his one and only French connection.

"That's interesting," Amanda said. "My mother was born in Gary, Indiana. I'm not sure she knew where France was, exactly."

"That's too bad." Belatedly he realized she'd spoken of her mother in the past tense. "Then your mother's . . ."

"Deceased."

"I'm sorry." He'd hoped to talk about something that would make her laugh, but this topic showed no promise whatsoever. Still, they weren't discussing Gloria, which was progress. "And your father?"

"Also deceased."

Boy, he was really ramping up the cheerful factor, here. No wonder she admired the determination of little hummingbirds. "That's tough."

"It has been, yeah." She took a deep breath. "William, the kittens were cute, but I'll have to ask you not to continue with that kind of thing."

"Kittens?" Completely disoriented, he glanced around as if a litter might come scampering out from under her desk. "What kittens?"

She looked at him with what a generous person would call sympathy. Someone less generous might call it pity. "Nice thought, tucking a valentine in my desk drawer, and I'm honored, really. But you have the wrong girl."

He scrambled to get his bearings. The conversation had taken a bizarre turn. "Someone tucked a valentine in your desk drawer?"

"Come on, William. There's no use continuing this charade. I appreciate the effort, but I'm really not the right person for you."

"There's no charade. If someone gave you a valentine, it wasn't me." He'd love to find out who had, though. If competition was in the vicinity, he wanted to know about it.

"Okay, you don't want to admit it. I understand. We can leave it at that." She held out a paper bag. "This is the gift from Gloria. I know she's come on kind of strong, but if you give her a chance, you might find out she's not so bad."

He took the bag gingerly, as if it might explode any minute. "What is it?"

"I, um, think you need to find that out for

yourself." She moved the papers on her desk into a neat stack and pushed back her chair. "My bus is due any minute. I need to be going."

That was certainly a broad hint that she wanted him to leave, but he couldn't make himself do it. He might never be alone with her again. "I'm sure you do, but my curiosity is killing me." Although he had a feeling he'd be sorry, he reached in the bag and pulled out a black box. The label on the front read *lighten up.* In smaller letters underneath, it said *Glow-in-the-dark condoms for that special event. Extra large.*

He glanced at Amanda. She'd taken a backpack out from under her desk and tucked her purse and the papers inside. Now she was headed for the coat tree and focusing on it as if it were the Holy Grail.

He remembered her shopping trip earlier and had to ask. "Did Gloria pick these out?"

She paused and faced him. "Not exactly."

"You did?"

She looked nervous. "She asked me to. I don't want you to read anything into it. I was only doing my job."

"Okay." He swallowed. "But what made you decide on these?"

She blushed. "Well, you're tall, and so I thought you might take . . . that is, reason told me that your size would be . . ."

"Not the size." He could feel his face growing warm. "I meant the glow-in-the-dark part."

"Oh." Her color was still high, but her gaze had softened. "I, um, thought they might intrigue you."

"Well, they do. The concept is fascinating." He looked at the box. "I'm not sure how it works, considering that anything with a phosphorescent compound has to be introduced to strong light first."

"I didn't look to see if there were instructions."

He glanced up to see if she was making fun of him. But she didn't seem to be. He kind of wanted to check for instructions, but he'd be wise not to do that now. They were, after all, talking about condoms.

"Anyway," he said. "Thanks." He pulled out the other box. A window of cellophane gave him a view of a dozen little chocolate tits. Justin would love those, but he'd also want to know where they came from. William wasn't sure he was ready to discuss his oversexed client with Justin. He'd never hear the end of it.

"It's . . . ah . . . candy," Amanda said.

He looked up. "I figured."

"For Valentine's Day."

"Uh-*huh.*"

"Look, there wasn't a lot to choose from that wouldn't be mortally embarrassing."

"This is fine. I like chocolate."

"Good."

"You did well, Amanda. I appreciate the effort. Interesting stuff."

"I'm glad you like it." She paused. "Gloria will be happy about that."

"I'm not interested in Gloria."

"That could change."

"I seriously doubt it."

"Whether it does or not, you should give up on me."

Although the words were discouraging, William couldn't help noticing that something in her manner had undergone a subtle change. The barrier didn't seem quite as impenetrable.

She took a deep breath. "Although I do appreciate that you took the time to buy a valentine and put it in my —"

"No I didn't. The valentine came from someone else. I didn't even remember that Valentine's Day was coming up, if you want to know the truth."

For a moment she looked as if she believed him. Then her expression became more resolute. "William, the condoms and candy are from Gloria, not me. I'm only the messenger. I urge you to call her. You two could have fun together. I really do have to be going. My shift starts in an hour, and I have to change clothes."

"Shift?" Even though her words were unrelenting, her expression a few seconds ago had given him hope. Maybe if he gathered enough information, he'd break the code that would allow him access to Amanda.

"I've told you, I'm very busy. I go to school, I intern with Gloria, and I tend bar six nights a week."

"Where?"

She opened her mouth as if to tell him. Then she seemed to think better of it and looked away. "If you're thinking that you'll come to the bar, then don't."

"All right. You don't want me to come to the bar, I won't come to the bar." He put the condoms and the candy back in the bag. "But we need to get two things straight. I don't plan to become sexually involved with Gloria, and I didn't put a valentine in your desk drawer."

"If you say so."

He blew out a breath. "Sneaking a valentine into your desk drawer is not my style. If I wanted to give you a valentine, I'd give it to you, straight-out. There would be flowers involved, at the very least. I've never seen the point in secret valentine messages. They only waste time."

A smile broke through her obvious effort to stay serious. "Now that's the first argument you've made that rings true. But I have to tell you, I don't have men pining after me. I've shut down any overtures during the past year or so. You asked me to lunch, and we work in the same building. Logic points to you. There's really no one else it could be."

"But it's not me."

"Right." She opened the door and gestured for him to go through it. "I have to lock up and leave or I'll be very late." She glanced at her watch. "In fact I've missed my usual bus. I'll have to take a different one and transfer."

"Which one is that?" He didn't think it was his, or he'd have seen her on it before.

"Fifty-nine."

"Then we're headed in different directions, but we can still walk out together."

"Yes, we can do that."

She turned off the lights and locked the door behind her. Then she slung her backpack over one shoulder and started toward the stairway.

"So you're a bartender."

"It pays well for the hours invested."

"Did you go to bartending school?"

As she walked down the stairs, she shifted the weight of her backpack, which looked heavy. "I did. I'd waitressed ever since high school, didn't know what I wanted to do with my life. Bartending was a skill I could add to my repertoire. When I started school, it made for a good combination, classes during the day, bartending at Geekland by night."

"Sounds like it." He didn't call attention to the fact that she'd just told him where she worked. It was a slip on her part, one he wouldn't take advantage of. She didn't want him in her life, so he wouldn't push.

Interesting spot for her to work, though. The place was a joke with the cool crowd, but according to an article in the *Trib,* Geekland was wildly popular with its target audience. He'd never been there, because a person had to be a confirmed nerd and proud of it in order to set foot inside. William knew he had some of those tendencies, but he rejected the label.

Amanda had some of those tendencies, too, but he didn't think that was why she'd taken the job. She didn't want to date, and a bartender as cute as Amanda would get asked out by the clientele. If she surrounded herself with geeks, she wouldn't be tempted to say yes.

"Have you always wanted to be a stockbroker?" she asked.

"No." They reached the small lobby and headed toward the revolving doors that led out to the street. "I wanted to be a fireman, and then I wanted to be a trucker or a pro football player. Couldn't decide which."

"That's a long way from stockbroker."

"Oh, I don't know. I protect people's future, which is kind of like a fireman, and I'm involved in the economy, which is part of a trucker's job."

"And how about pro football?"

"I'm in there dodging and weaving, hoping to score for my clients. I just don't get to wear the shoulder pads and the tight pants."

She laughed at that, which gratified him. He might have no chance with her, but at least they could be pleasant to each other when they met in the hall. He let her go ahead of him out the door. It looked dark out there, and very cold.

Bracing himself for the pain that would hit his unprotected ears, he pushed through the door and joined her on the sidewalk. Yikes. The wind had a bite like a Doberman.

She pulled up her hood and glanced at him. "You're not wearing your hat."

"Uh, no, I'm not." So she had noticed the hat the first time they'd met.

"Did you forget it?"

"It's in my briefcase."

She gazed at him, as if trying to figure out what was going on. The whoosh of air brakes on the bus half a block away made her turn. "Whoops, there's my bus! See you later!" She turned and ran for the bus, her backpack banging against her shoulder. Her hood fell back and her hair gleamed in the light from the street lamps.

He didn't believe in love at first sight or anything dumb like that, but he couldn't shake the feeling that they could have had something good together. Unfortunately, making that happen would have taken some cooperation on her part. She hadn't been particularly cooperative.

As her bus went by, he glanced up, figuring she'd already put him out of her mind. Instead he saw her face in the window, and she was looking down at him. She gave him a wave.

He waved back. It would be risky to assign any special significance to that gesture of hers. He shouldn't get his hopes up because she'd taken the time and effort to locate him on the sidewalk and wave. But he was a stockbroker, and any stockbroker worth his salt took risks now and then. He let his hopes rise, just a little bit.

Amanda lived on the ground floor of her apartment building, and when she was running late like this, she was grateful that she didn't have stairs to climb. Her only obstacle was Mavis Endicott, the retired school-teacher who lived next door. With thinning red hair she colored herself and a plump figure that showed off her love of bakery items, Mavis was a cheerful person to have around.

Amanda wished she had more time to spend getting to know her neighbors. Under different circumstances, she'd be thrilled to chat with Mavis, who must have been a dynamite teacher in her day. But Amanda had been forced to cut their conversations short. That didn't seem to deter Mavis, who always left her door open a crack at five-thirty so she could hear Amanda coming home.

On her way down the hall tonight, Amanda noticed that everyone on her floor had decorated their apartment door for Valentine's Day with the exception of Amanda and her neighbor on the other side,

Chester Ambrose. Mavis must have been at work organizing the troops. She treated this floor as if they were all back in third grade and holiday decorations were mandatory.

Amanda always tried to participate. Mavis had managed to bring a sense of community to the first floor of the apartment complex, and in an urban setting that was an accomplishment. But Amanda had forgotten all about Valentine's Day, and even if she'd remembered, she didn't have the time to paste doilies on her door.

As for Chester, a balding guy in his sixties who liked to dress in luau shirts, he always resisted on principle. He claimed the decorations were a waste of time and money. Because he was also retired, money might be part of the problem, but it was more likely that Chester didn't appreciate being herded into any group activity. Chester had been a bachelor all his life, and he marched to his own drummer.

Mavis's door opened as Amanda put her key in the lock. "Amanda, there you are!"

"I'm running late, Mavis." The lock was temperamental and she had to wiggle the key to get the door open, which gave Mavis time to bustle over with a plastic bag from Hallmark in one hand.

"I bought you a few Valentine's Day

decorations," she said. "I know you don't have time to shop."

"Thanks, but I don't have time to put them up, either." As Amanda walked into her apartment, she thought she heard Chester's door open. She hoped not. Because she'd taken a later bus than usual, she didn't have time to deal with one of Mavis and Chester's confrontations.

Mavis followed right on her heels. "Then I'll put them up for you. All I need is your permission. I found some adorable cupids, and —"

"Mavis, are you at it again?" Chester walked in behind Mavis. "I thought I heard you over here pestering this poor girl."

"I'm not pestering her. I'm helping her with Valentine's Day decorations."

"Which I appreciate." Amanda put down her backpack and took off her coat. "Except right now, I have to —"

"Amanda, don't let her put a damned thing on your door if you don't want her to. This is a free country."

Mavis spun toward him. "It's a glorious country, Chester, where people are allowed to celebrate all these wonderful holidays! Do you realize how lucky you are that no one is forbidding you to celebrate?"

"No, I don't, because I'm too busy dealing with a meddling woman who is forcing me to celebrate!"

"Would it kill you to put up a couple of construction-paper hearts, Chester?" Mavis glared at him through her trifocals. "Everybody else on this floor thinks it's a great idea, and it makes the place look cheery. You're getting a reputation as a regular Grinch."

"Good! I like that reputation just fine."

"Guys," Amanda said, "I hate to interrupt, but you'll both have to go home. I have to change clothes and leave for work."

"Don't mind us," Mavis said. Then she turned back to Chester. "Tell me this, Mr. Grinch. What are you going to do if you ever need help from one of your neighbors?"

Chester rolled his eyes. "I'll worry about that when the time comes. In the meantime, I don't have to spend my valuable time cutting out paper hearts!"

"Because you spend all your *valuable* time cutting out coupons. Don't think I haven't heard you asking people for their supplements to the *Trib* so you could cut the coupons out. It's a wonder they give them to you, the way you are."

"Uh, guys . . . it probably would be better if you —"

"Go get ready for work," Chester said. "Or

94

you'll be late, and you need that job. As for you, Mavis Endicott, quit buying door decorations for people who don't want them."

"It's not that I don't want them," Amanda said. "It's just —"

"See?" Mavis said. "She wants them. Amanda, go get ready for work. You can't afford to get fired."

Amanda finally realized they weren't leaving, so she went into her bedroom, closed the door, and pulled her uniform out of the closet. The Geekland management had decided on short-sleeved plaid shirts, complete with pocket protector, and khaki pants. To complete the outfit, Amanda always loaded the pocket protector with pens.

Opening her dresser drawer, she took out her flask-shaped Barmaster, a battery-operated gizmo that fit in her hand and had hundreds of drink recipes stored on it, both the ones loaded at the factory and the Geekland creations she'd added to its memory. A lot of her customers owned one, and she'd finally invested in one, too, so she could keep up.

Grabbing a couple of small elastic bands, she put her hair up in two pigtails. Then she tucked the Barmaster and a pair of

Geekland-issue glasses in her purse. The glasses had heavy black frames with clear lenses, and whenever she put them on, she seemed to transform into a nerd. It was the strangest thing. She was even better at operating the Barmaster.

While she was getting ready, she could hear Mavis and Chester bickering like an old married couple. She had to admit that having them around was more of a perk than a liability. Sure, they interfered with her schedule sometimes, but she liked that they both watched out for her and cared whether she kept her job and graduated from college.

And no matter how much they fought, she believed they cared about each other. Maybe her psych classes had made her too analytical, but she'd decided that Mavis and Chester relished their battles. Like tonight, for example. No doubt Chester had been lying in ambush for Mavis, knowing Mavis was lying in ambush for Amanda.

All in all, Amanda liked having Chester and Mavis for neighbors. Sometimes, when she was feeling especially lonely, she pretended they were her folks.

Six

William's cell rang while he was still on the bus heading home to his apartment.

"Yo, it's Justin."

"Hey, Justin." William envied his friend, who'd met the right woman and was up to his neck in June wedding plans. Seven months ago William had expected to be in the same boat, until he found Helen in bed with an old flame that had somehow rekindled when William wasn't looking.

"Listen, Will, can I come on over now?" Justin said. "I need to talk to you about something before the game starts."

"Wedding related?" William was the best man, so he was in on most of the plans.

"Yeah, wedding related."

"Sure. Come on over. I'll be home in ten minutes." Justin had a key to his apartment, and they never stood on ceremony. "If you get there first, order us a pizza. Beer's in the fridge."

"Thanks, buddy. See you soon."

William looked forward to a night of beer, pizza, and basketball, something he and Justin hadn't done in a while, not since Justin's engagement to Cindi. She was a travel agent currently on a junket to Hawaii with a bunch of other travel agents. It was what they called a "familiarization trip" so she could handle her job better when clients asked about hotels over there.

While Cindi was soaking up the tropical sun, Justin had to put up with a drizzly cold day in Chicago. William decided to pull out the chocolate tits, after all. He might even show Justin the condoms and get his advice on dealing with Gloria.

Justin was already at the apartment when William arrived. He'd parked himself in front of the TV with a beer and was watching ESPN. He looked up when William walked in. "Hey."

"Hey." William could see Justin was in a foul mood. Normally the guy was a neat freak, but his blond hair was uncombed, his glasses were smudged, and his beige pullover sweater had a ketchup stain on the front. "So did you order the pizza?"

"Yeah." Justin hit the mute button on the remote.

"Wait'll you see what a client gave me

today." Will set his briefcase by the door and tossed the bag in Justin's direction.

Justin caught it but didn't open it. "Cindi broke our engagement."

"What?" William stopped unbuttoning his coat and stared at Justin.

"You heard me." Justin put the bag next to him on the couch. "She called from Hawaii today. It seems she had some sort of epiphany over there. She wants to live on the beach and take up surfing."

"Cindi? She's uncoordinated as hell."

"She is not! It isn't her fault that nobody in her family played sports. With some training, she could —" Justin paused. "Wait, why am I defending her? She just dumped me! And you're right. She'll be a disaster out on that surfboard. She's a nerd, like me."

"You're not a nerd." William maintained that he and Justin weren't true nerds, and he didn't want Justin backsliding. "You're intelligent and you're good at details, which is why you make a good chemist. But your clothes match . . . usually . . . and your social skills are fine."

"Oh, they're peachy. That's why my fiancée canceled the wedding. I'm not cool enough for her."

"That's not why." William took off his coat and tossed it on a chair. "This is her problem, not yours. And not that I care, but how does she plan to put food on the table and a roof over her head?"

"She said something about making shell necklaces for the tourists." Justin stared morosely at the bottle of beer in his hand. "I think she found a surfer dude over there, somebody with muscles."

"If she's stupid enough to settle for that, angsting over her is pointless. She's not worth it." William took off his tie and tossed it on top of his coat. "I'm getting a beer. Want another one?"

"Yeah. I'm liable to drink all you've got."

"Feel free, but I don't think you should get wasted on Cindi's account. Consider yourself lucky that you didn't marry somebody so unbalanced."

"Oh, yeah, I feel lucky all right." Justin chugged the last of his beer.

In the kitchen, William grabbed two beers from the refrigerator and a bag of pretzels from the cupboard. Considering this turn of events, he wasn't sure whether to show Justin the condoms and chocolate tits or not. Something like that could tip the scales either way — toward crazy laughter or suicidal despair. Better not take the chance.

But when he returned to the living room, the decision had been taken away from him.

Justin was studying the directions for the condoms. "Amazing," he murmured.

"Pretty wild, huh?"

"No kidding." Justin glanced up. "I mean, logically, you'd be in dim light when you use them, so I'm not sure how you'd make them glow. Maybe you have to shine a flashlight on yourself for three seconds."

"Don't know. Haven't tested them."

"And you say you got these from a *client?*"

William nodded. "She's a sex therapist who has an office down the hall from Cooper and Scott."

"You mean Dr. Gloria Tredway?"

"You know her?"

"Nope. It's that photographic memory thing. I saw her name on the door that time I came to see your setup."

"That's her." He sat on the couch and set Justin's beer on the coffee table. "She's . . . different."

Justin rolled his eyes. "Gee, you think? I take it the glowing condoms and candy boobies clued you in."

"That, and the X-rated video she had playing on her office TV when I went in there this afternoon."

"No shit! How long has she been a client?"

William glanced at his watch. "About four

101

and a half hours."

Justin let out a whoop. "Man, you stumbled on a hot one! What does she look like?"

"She's okay. She's a redhead, about five seven. Brown eyes."

"Built?"

"I guess."

"You *guess?* A woman who happens to be a sex therapist is sending you condoms and teasing you with skin flicks, and you aren't sure whether or not she's built? What's wrong with you, buddy?"

William took a swig of his beer. "She's not my type."

"She sounds like she's everybody's type! I mean, you're not getting any these days. I'm not saying you should marry her. Hell, I'm beginning to think nobody should get married. Go for the sex and forget all the hearts-and-flowers crap."

"You may have a point." William had to admit that the hearts-and-flowers routine hadn't worked out that well for him up to now.

"Of course I have a point." Justin grabbed his beer and drank deeply. "Look at me. I'm the poster boy for romantic schmucks who get the shaft. Did you know that next week is Valentine's Day?"

"As it happens, I do know that."

"Well, so do I, as all engaged men are expected to know. I've made reservations at the Pump Room and ordered a dozen roses. The Godiva isn't bought yet, but that's only because I wanted it to be fresh. I was planning to handpick the kind of truffles Cindi likes. Oh, and I nearly forgot the diamond stud earrings I have sitting in a velvet box in my apartment."

"I'm sorry, man." William sighed. "Cindi's an idiot."

"No, I'm the idiot, thinking I had something solid when a trip to Hawaii was all it took to turn her into a beach bunny. And you —" Justin pointed the neck of his bottle at William. "Your deal was almost as bad. You weren't actually engaged, but damned close. Then bam! Helen turns on you. Poor slob, you didn't see it coming."

"No, I didn't." But looking back on that time, William realized he'd missed some important indications that Helen was losing interest. He'd been concentrating on his master's dissertation and interviewing for jobs, so he hadn't noticed that she'd stopped telling him she loved him, stopped writing him cute little notes, stopped initiating sex.

Justin might be guilty of the same complacence. Cindi could have been showing signs of restlessness that Justin chose to ignore. Now wouldn't be the time to bring that up, because the guy already felt bad enough. But William thought it might be a danger in any relationship — thinking that it would rock along in the same rut forever.

"Women," Justin muttered. "You can't count on them."

"Maybe not."

"From now on, I'm in it for the sex, and that's all. Are you with me, Will?"

"Guess so." Now wasn't the time to argue.

"Then let's drink to it." Justin held up his beer bottle. "To mindless sex!"

"To mindless sex." William clinked his bottle against Justin's and took a swallow of his beer.

"I have an awesome idea."

William could tell Justin was getting smashed, because when he was sober he would never use the word *awesome*. "What's that?"

"Let's watch the game and eat our pizza."

"Justin, that was always the plan." Poor guy, he was starting to babble.

"I know, but here's the new wrinkle. *After* the game, let's blow this joint and go some-where."

"Like?"

"That place I keep hearing about. It's supposed to be a riot. What is it, again? Geekland! That's it. Let's go there."

William couldn't believe his bad luck today. It hadn't all been bad, though, because he'd made contact with Amanda. Still, she'd be convinced he was stalking her if he showed up at Geekland. "Are you sure you want to go there? I can think of a ton of other bars that would be way better."

"I can't. Other bars are all the same. This one's different. A guy at work loves the drinks there, and he said they serve great burgers and wings. The waiters and waitresses dress up like geeks, and the customers play trivia and stuff."

"But we're not geeks. We won't fit in."

Justin gazed at him. "Not to be insulting, but you'll fit in just fine. Let's go. It's exactly what I need."

William weighed his loyalties. Sure, he'd promised Amanda he wouldn't come to her place of work, but he'd known her only a few hours. Justin had been his best friend for years. They'd pulled each other through all-nighter study sessions and had pooled their money whenever they both ended up broke. Justin had been there for him when Helen had defected. William had to stand by his friend now.

"Okay," he said. "Geekland it is."

■ ■ ■ ■

"Hey, Amanda, what's the name of that guy who did the experiment with the dogs and ringing bells? It's on the tip of my tongue."

Amanda squirted seltzer water into the blue-green drink in her hand and glanced over at Leonard, a short, stocky nerd who was one of Geekland's regulars. He sat at the clear acrylic bar that created a hundred-and-eighty-degree curve — Amanda's domain. Behind her, arranged in colorful rows, were the bottled items she used to work her magic.

Most of the customers preferred sitting at the bar so they were closer to the trivia monitors. For the overflow, or those few who didn't play trivia, there were clear acrylic tables and chrome chairs scattered throughout the room. Abstract neon sculptures on the walls gave off an otherworldly glow. As usual, the place was packed.

Amanda had to raise her voice to be heard over the sound system, which was belting out "Material Girl." "Pavlov!"

"Right. I knew that." Leonard punched a button on his remote keyboard. "Yes! Five hundred points!" He held both hands in the air and undulated in time to Madonna.

"Leonard, quit bugging Amanda while she's making my drink." Bertrand, a long-haired premed student who always dressed in black, slapped money on the bar before walking over to Leonard and peering up at the television screen flashing the multiple-choice trivia questions. Then he leaned close to Leonard. "Number four. Occipital bone."

"Thanks, man!"

"No fair!" A girl in an oversized *Star Trek* T-shirt glared at Leonard from her position two stools down. "You shouldn't get points for that."

"Hey, it counts for Geekland, too, you know," Leonard said. "And being number three in the country is just not good enough."

"Damn straight!" called a guy on the far side of the wraparound bar. "Number one or bust!"

Several shouts of agreement went up from the customers concentrating intently on the TV screens mounted around the perimeter of the bar's center island.

Tina, a thin waitress wearing the requisite plaid shirt and khakis, came toward Amanda. In Tina's case, the black-framed glasses were prescription. "Can I have a Theory of Evolution?" She set her round tray on the bar. "I have a fan of layered drinks over at table three, so I recommended that."

"Coming up." Amanda pressed the touch screen on her computer before setting Bertrand's drink on a cocktail napkin. Then she reached for the Baileys that formed the bottom level of the Evolution, another drink that had been invented at Geekland. She'd stayed busy all night, which had helped distract her from thoughts about William.

But whenever she did think about him, she pictured him standing in the cold Chicago wind without his hat as he gazed up at her bus. She would bet her night's worth of tips that he'd left off the hat because of her. If he would do that, then surely he'd also sent the valentine.

If not him, then who? It could be somebody at Geekland, except she didn't think anybody here knew about her day job. She supposed they could have taken the trouble to find out, though. And they were geeks, so they knew how to look things up.

Leonard seemed to have a crush on her, although he'd never asked her out. No one did anymore, unless they were new to Geekland. She'd spread the word early that she wasn't dating. Leonard might be capable of sending a secret valentine, though.

Maybe she should test that theory and

find out what he knew about her. After she poured the crème de menthe carefully over the bar spoon to finish off the Evolution, she handed it to Tina and turned back to Leonard. "So here's a trivia question for you, Leonard. Where do I work?"

He laughed. "Here. At Geekland."

"I mean my other job."

Leonard shrugged. "I dunno. Isn't it in some therapist's office? What, are you suggesting I need therapy?"

"No. I just —"

"Because I probably do, now that you mention it. I have an unhealthy fixation on this trivia game and I have no social life other than coming to this bar and hanging out with the likes of Bertrand. All those burgers and wings are putting on the weight, and I should exercise more. But as for knowing exactly where you work, I have to answer in the negative."

"Okay. Thanks." She was satisfied it wasn't Leonard. He wouldn't be able to lie that easily.

"Why did you want to know?"

"It's not important. I —" She stopped speaking as she glanced over Leonard's shoulder and saw a man who looked a lot like William come through the front door. But it couldn't be William, unless this was some weird sort of coincidence. He didn't know where she worked.

The man who looked like William had walked in with another guy who was about William's height and build, only he was blond instead of dark-haired. She was probably seeing things, imagining William around every corner because of what had happened today. The valentine had her freaked out.

No, it *was* him, damn it! He didn't even have the good grace to look surprised to see her as he started toward the bar. Maybe he'd called Gloria and asked where Amanda worked. That explained his being here, except that she'd distinctly told him not to come. Fat lot of good that had done.

"Hi, Amanda." He leaned on the bar.

"Hello, William." She kept her tone neutral and didn't smile, not even a little bit. She wanted him to know he wasn't welcome.

"Cute outfit."

"Thanks."

"Amanda!" called a guy on the far side of the bar. "Can you make me a Monkey Gland?"

Happy for the distraction, she grabbed her Barmaster to double-check the ingredients. Her customers loved to see if they could stump her, but it didn't happen often any-more.

"I'm sure you're not happy to see me here," William said.

"Not particularly." She measured the gin and the orange juice into the cocktail shaker before reaching for the grenadine. Although she concentrated on making the drink, she couldn't eliminate that edgy awareness of William.

He'd changed clothes. Instead of the suit and tie, he was wearing jeans and a gray, crew-necked sweater topped with a brown bomber jacket. The more casual clothes reduced his nerd factor, especially since he'd come in hatless. But his ears were pink, as if the wind had done a number on them.

He looked worried. Obviously he knew he was treading on thin ice. "Amanda, I'd like you to meet my buddy, Justin Haskell. Justin, this is Amanda Rykowsky. We work in the same building."

"Hi, Justin." She paused long enough to glance up at William's friend, but once again she resisted the urge to smile, although Justin seemed like a nice enough guy. Maybe William had brought him along so that she wouldn't land into him about disregarding her wishes.

Justin gave her the sort of loopy grin that

signaled he'd already had a few too many drinks tonight. "Nice to meet you, Amanda. On the way over Will told me you're the bartender here. Must be a fun place to work."

"It is. But I'm curious how he knew that I was here." So William's friend called him Will. The nickname seemed to go with the casual clothes. "I don't recall mentioning it to him."

"Actually, you did," William said. "I don't think you even realized you said the name of the place. And it's pure coincidence we're here."

"I'm sure." She glared at him. "Pure coincidence. But now that you are here, are you planning to order, or are you just hanging out?"

"I want one of the specialty drinks," Justin said. "This guy Tom from work is always talking about something called the Chi-Town thingamajig. He claims to have invented it."

"Tom from Amherst Labs?" Tom was one of Amanda's favorite customers, and a brilliant chemist. She expected big things from him someday. He'd recently started dating a biology professor at Northwestern, and Amanda was happy for both of them.

"He's the one," Justin said. "We work

together. He keeps telling me I should try this place, and especially the drink he invented."

"The Chi-Town Lakefront Breeze."

"That's it! We'll have two of those. Will, I'm buying. Put your money away."

Amanda strained the Monkey Gland into a chilled glass. "Be right back." As she delivered the drink on the other side of the bar, she realized that her breathing was different, as if William's presence were exciting her, somehow. Surely not.

By the time she returned, Leonard had sidled up to Justin. "You're a chemist, huh? I'll bet you're pretty smart."

"On good days. This isn't what you'd call a good day."

"I'll bet even on a bad day you'd know the answer to some of these science questions." Leonard gestured toward the TV screen. "Like, for instance, how about that one?"

"Trivia!" Justin's face lit up. "That's the other thing Tom was telling me about. I love trivia. Yeah! Punch number two. Better yet, let me see that thing." He appropriated the keypad from Leonard.

William leaned closer to Amanda, bringing the scent of his Old Spice with him. "It wasn't my idea to come here."

"Sure." She started making their drinks, keeping her eyes on her work.

"Seriously. You heard Justin. He's wanted to come to Geekland for months."

"Strange that after months of yearning for the place, he picked this very night to do it." She threw the twist of lemon in each martini glass with enough force to slop the vodka and curaçao mixture over the edge. Stupid, stupid. She was only making more work for herself.

"It was important for Justin to come tonight."

"Oh, I see." She wiped off each glass, flipped two cocktail napkins on the bar and set the drinks squarely in the middle of each one. "And you simply had to tag along, is that it?"

"I'm afraid so."

"Of course you did, because you refuse to accept what I've told you. For all I know, this is your typical mode of behavior — wear a woman down until she finally agrees to go on a date with you."

Justin turned. "Will, do you want a date with this gorgeous woman? You didn't tell me that."

"No, I don't want a date with her," William said. "I mean, I would, but she's made it clear that she doesn't have time, so I'll respect that."

"Hang on." Justin peered at Amanda. "You don't have time to date my good buddy Will?"

"That's correct. And if you could convince him to stop pursuing me by sending secret valentines and showing up at my place of work, I'd be grateful."

"Wow." Justin spun on his bar stool and eventually managed to end up facing William. "You've sent this woman secret valentines? I have to say, you didn't succeed in keeping them a secret." He leaned closer and spoke in a stage whisper. *"She knows."*

"There was only one," William said. "And I didn't send it."

"Oh." Justin winked at Amanda. "He didn't send it."

"I didn't, damn it!"

"There, there." Justin patted William on the shoulder. "No need to get upset because the lady's smart and guessed right away."

William blew out a breath and picked up his drink. "I see a vacant table over in the corner."

"We need to stay at the bar if we're going to play trivia, buddy."

William looked trapped. "In that case, there are a couple of stools over there." He headed to the other side of the wraparound bar, as if he wanted to get as far away from Amanda as possible.

"Okay." Justin picked up his drink. "I think I'm beginning to get the picture."

"Hey, Amanda!" A girl playing trivia glanced up from her keypad. "Can you make a Harvard Cooler?"

"Sure!" Amanda consulted her Barmaster.

"That's a nifty gadget," Justin said.

"Comes in handy." She started on the cooler.

"I'm sure you're a very busy lady."

"That's right. I am."

"But if you're letting that stand in the way of getting to know my best friend, Will, you're making the biggest mistake of your life. Take it from me, they don't come any better than William David Sloan."

She stirred the powdered sugar into the apple brandy. "I'm sure he's a good friend." *And you're prejudiced.*

"He's the best. He didn't want to come here tonight, and now I see why. Coming here makes it look like he's chasing you."

She stopped stirring and glanced up. "Yes, it does."

Justin nodded. "Then I need to 'splain. You may have noticed that I'm a wee bit wiped."

"I did notice."

116

"The thing is, my fiancée broke up with me today. The wedding's off. So good ol' Will indulged me in my wish to party at Geekland. He knew it would tick you off, a woman he has high regard for, but he did it, anyway."

"Oh. That's too bad. About the wedding, I mean." Great. She'd been a bitch when it hadn't been called for.

"I'll get over it. But I might not if I didn't have Will around to prop me up. That's the kind of guy he is, sacrificing his own welfare for a bud." Justin lifted his glass. "Top drawer, that Will." And then he walked over to the far side of the bar where William had already started punching in numbers on a keypad.

Amanda sighed. So she owed William an apology. But if she made one, wouldn't that lead to a conversation, and more match-making on the part of Justin? Better to leave things as they were. At least this way she wouldn't be getting any more secret valentines.

SEVEN

But the next day, when Amanda came back from a quick lunch at Starbucks and opened her bottom drawer to put away her purse, there lay another envelope, this time in red. Her name was printed in block letters across the back of it, exactly like the first one.

"Amanda, finally, a moment alone!" Gloria came barreling out of her office.

Amanda slammed her drawer shut. "It has been kind of crazy today."

"You're telling me. I love the money, but I could do with a less packed schedule, not to mention being behind because my massage ran overtime." Today Gloria wore a leopard-skin jumpsuit, but at least it didn't look as if it had come from an actual leopard.

"This afternoon should be quieter," Amanda said. The red envelope waited in her drawer. In her mind's eye it had started to glow. She couldn't imagine how William had the nerve to send her another valentine after last night. He and Justin had relayed their drink orders through Tina and so Amanda hadn't spoken to either of them again. She had figured that was the end of that.

"I shouldn't really complain." Gloria gave a wiggle that made the leopard spots dance. "My massage was primo. Thor is *excellent.*"

"Your masseur is named Thor?"

"Mm. Very blond and very Swedish. He's a closely guarded secret among a few select woman, and for a little extra, he'll massage whatever you want massaged." Gloria ran her tongue over her lips. "Fortunately his facility is soundproof."

"Sounds . . . interesting." Every time Amanda thought she'd heard it all, Gloria came up with some new and surprising revelation.

"Maybe that's what I should give you as a graduation present, a session with Thor."

That might be the most shocking revelation of all, that Gloria was planning to give her a graduation present. "You don't have to do that."

"I know I don't, but the idea intrigues me. You're so uptight that even Thor might not be able to loosen you up, but at least I'd know the gift was unique. You won't get a duplicate."

"I suppose not." Duplicates weren't a big concern of hers, anyway. Mavis would throw her a little party because Mavis loved any excuse to celebrate, and some of her working buddies at Geekland might buy her a drink or two, but Amanda wasn't expecting a mountain of gifts. As for relatives, she was down to a couple of cousins out in Oregon, and they didn't even have her current address, let alone know that she was in school.

"That's settled then. I assume you finished the client evaluations?"

"Yes." And because of that she was working on about three hours' sleep.

"And you printed hard copies for the files?"

"First thing this morning."

"And how about that package to William? You mailed it, right?"

"As it turned out, when I called to get his address, he offered to come down to the office and pick up the package."

"He did? In that case, maybe I should have hung around. Oh, wait. That means he could have called me last night and didn't. Hmm." Gloria tapped her finger against her lips. "Maybe you bought the wrong presents."

Amanda had no interest in making another trip to the G-Spot. "Or maybe he needs a little time to digest the significance of them." *And maybe he's too busy giving me valentines to think about anything else.*

"Oh, well. Did you get his home address and phone number?"

"Not exactly."

Gloria's gaze sharpened. "He was reluctant?"

"A little." Amanda tried for diplomacy. "After all, he only met you yesterday." He'd only met Amanda yesterday, too, and he was already tucking valentines in her desk. That boggled her mind. No man had ever been that persistent.

"I'll give him a little time," Gloria said. "But not much. I'll start planning my next strategy. I'll need some nerdy ideas from you."

Considering the valentine that had once again appeared in her bottom drawer, Amanda was more than willing to be helpful. She needed Gloria to distract this guy. "Guys like William usually like trivia."

Gloria made a face. "Are you suggesting I get him Trivial Pursuit?"

"I suppose not. He probably has all the versions, anyway."

"I never could see the point. All those arcane little factoids about dry subjects nobody cares about. Now if they had trivia about sex . . ."

"Who knows? They might. Not necessarily a trivia game, but there might be books out there."

Gloria's eyes lit up. "There might be! Go online and see what you can find and get back to me. If it looks promising enough, have them do a rush delivery."

"I'll let you know."

"Money is no object. I want to find the perfect thing to get his juices flowing, preferably before Valentine's Day. I —"

She was interrupted as the door opened and Mimi Crutchfield walked in.

"Dr. Tredway!" she wailed. "The most awful thing has happened!"

"What's that?"

"I . . . broke it."

"Broke what, Mimi?"

"Franklin's . . . Franklin's schwanz!"

"Really." The unflappable Gloria looked taken aback. "How did that happen?"

"We were role-playing, like you said we should. He was the captive and I was the captor. So there he was lying on his back, with his schwanz sticking straight up, and I was under the bed, pretending to hide, but he knew I was there."

"You were *under* the bed?" Gloria asked.

"We have a really high bed."

Amanda desperately wanted an errand so she wouldn't have to hear the rest of this bizarre story. "Sorry to interrupt, but I'm sure we're running low on stamps. I should head on over to the post office."

Gloria waved her back down to her seat. "Not now. I think we're fine on stamps. Go on, Mimi."

"So I crawled out from under the bed, creeping, creeping, slithering up onto the mattress on my belly. Oh, I had war paint on, by the way, and . . . this next part is so hard to tell."

"Tell it, Mimi. You need to purge yourself of the memory."

Amanda would have to purge herself of this memory, and the sooner, the better. If only she could stick her fingers in her ears and hum. She was so changing banks.

"Once I was up on the mattress, I yelled *Geronimo!* and leaped on him, planning to impale myself, you see, but I . . . missed the mark."

"Oh, my." Gloria winced and covered her mouth.

Amanda wanted to crawl under her desk.

"There was this loud cracking sound and Franklin yelled. He kept on yelling, so I called an ambulance. To cut to the chase, his schwanz is wrapped like a mummy, and he says he never wants to have sex again!"

"It's because of the initial trauma," Gloria said. "Come into the office and we'll talk about this. I'll give you some ideas to soothe him. He'll get over this, but it will take some intensive therapy." She took Mimi's arm and guided her into the office.

"I'll do anything, Dr. Tredway. Anything at all."

"We'll start by finding you a short, tight nurse's uniform," Gloria said. Then she closed the door.

Amanda sank back against her chair in relief. She had no desire to know what came after the uniform suggestion. Besides, with Gloria safely closed in her office with Mimi, Amanda could find out what was in the red envelope.

Opening her bottom drawer, she took it out and held it to her nose to see if it smelled like Old Spice. Not really. But a valentine William had handled for only a few minutes might not pick up his scent. The lack of Old Spice aroma meant nothing one way or the other.

Slowly she pulled out the card. On the front was a cartoon guy with a smirk on his face. The message said, *Hey, Valentine, we need to talk.* Holding her breath, she opened the card. The inside showed the same guy in bed. Above him was the question *Your pillow or mine?* The card was signed as before, *Your Secret Valentine.*

The first valentine had been vaguely sexual, but this one was more explicit. Looking at it, she felt warm and disoriented, as if she'd had two shots of brandy on an empty stomach. Maybe William had a split personality that allowed him to seem like a slightly boring nerd on the outside, but inside he was a mass of raging hormones.

The image of William's raging hormones wasn't entirely unpleasant, and that scared her. She'd told him that his campaign wouldn't work, and she intended to keep that promise. If this valentine had her thinking of William lounging against the bar looking semisexy, instead of William coming up the stairs wearing a hat with earflaps and looking totally nerdy, then she was in trouble.

The phone rang, and she picked it up while still staring at the valentine. "Dr. Tredway's office. How can I help you?"

"Amanda, it's William."

The sound of his voice made her tummy quiver. Uh-oh. "William, I want you to stop this, and I want you to stop it right now!" She slammed down the phone and started ripping the valentine to shreds.

As the remains fell to her desk in a flurry of torn card stock and red envelope pieces, the phone rang again. She grabbed the receiver. "Dr. Tredway's office. Can I help you now?" She groaned. "I mean, how can I help you?" She must be really rattled if she couldn't even manage her standard phone greeting.

"It's William, and don't hang up on me. I have a stock recommendation for Gloria."

"Oh." Her face grew hot. "Is that why you called just now?"

"Yes."

"Oh. Sorry about that. I was . . . upset."

"You sound upset. Is this still about last night?"

"Of course not." She took a deep breath and tried to compose herself. "It's about your latest valentine. William, you have to stop sending them."

"You got another one?"

"Don't toy with me, William, or *Will,* as your friend Justin calls you. We both know what's going on here, and it's not funny."

"How can I convince you that I'm not the one sending those? And speaking of likely suspects, after spending a couple of hours at Geekland, I don't know why I'm even in the running. There are at least three guys there who have a major crush on you. I think you need to start reading them the riot act instead of picking on me."

"They don't know where I work. You do."

William sighed. "If you won't believe me, then we need to run a test. Is the signature in cursive or printed?"

"You should know, since you wrote it."

"Amanda, for God's sake, give me the benefit of the doubt!"

For the first time, a crack appeared in her certainty. She'd been so convinced that he was the sneaky valentine sender, but what if she was wrong? How embarrassing. "The signature was printed," she said.

"And what, exactly, does it say?"

" 'Your secret valentine.' "

"Then here's what I'll do. I'll print that same thing on a sheet of paper and you can compare my writing to what you have on the card. To save time, I'll fax it over."

Amanda surveyed the confetti on her desk and doubted she could reconstruct it into anything recognizable. "I threw away the first card, and I just finished destroying the new one."

"I see. You *really* don't like getting these valentines, do you?"

"No. Keep that in mind."

"Trust me, I have no intention of sending

you anything resembling a valentine. Tell you what. I'm going to fax over a sample of my printing, anyway, in case you get another one of these things. Do me a favor and compare before you shred, okay?"

"Okay." His willingness to test the situation widened the crack in her certainty.

"I'm writing it out now. Expect the fax in about thirty seconds. And would you give Gloria the message that I need to talk with her about that stock recommendation?"

"I will. She's with a client at the moment." *A client who broke her husband's schwanz, but we won't go into that.* "I'll give her the message when she's finished."

"Make sure she understands it's a business call."

"You haven't dealt with the issue of the condoms and the candy?"

"Not yet. I will. Bye."

"Bye." Amanda stood and walked over to the fax so she could grab the paper immediately when it came out. Belatedly she'd realized that misunderstandings could arise if Gloria should happen to see a fax come through on Cooper and Scott stationery that had *Your Secret Valentine* written on it.

Thirty seconds came and went. Thirty more passed without a peep from the fax machine. Amanda paced in front of it, but the damned thing sat there doing nothing. She checked to make sure the phone line was plugged in, which it was. Something must have delayed William.

She started back to her desk so she could call and tell him to forget it, but Gloria and Mimi came out of Gloria's office before she could pick up the phone.

"I feel so much better," Mimi said.

"You need to give him some time." Gloria handed Mimi a sheet of paper. "I made notes while we talked, so here's a list of all the things we mentioned."

Amanda edged back over to the fax machine and stood with her back to it, shielding it from Gloria's view.

"Thanks." Mimi scanned the paper. "Sexy nurse's outfit, scented massage oils, mood music, medical-themed adult videos, fingertip vibrator, wand vibrator. Yep, that sounds like all of it."

"The key is not to rush things." Gloria walked Mimi to the door. "Tease him with the nurse's outfit for a while. If you need orgasms, and I'm sure you will, do it in another room."

"Can I make noise?"

"Absolutely! Let him hear you, but don't let him see you masturbate until he's been released from the doctor's care. He might still be reluctant to get back on the horse, so to speak, but a few sessions of watching you with the wand vibrator should do the trick."

In spite of the ick factor she had to deal with, Amanda was impressed. If anything would get a guy interested after a trauma like that, Gloria's program would. She crossed her fingers that the fax wouldn't come until Gloria was safely back in her office.

"Best of luck, Mimi," Gloria said.

"Thank you." Mimi sighed. "I'll let you know how it goes."

"Please do." Gloria showed her out the door, closed it, and turned back to Amanda. "Can you freaking believe that? She broke his penis! If I were Franklin, I wouldn't go near her again!"

"You don't think your recommendations will work?"

Gloria threw her hands in the air. "How should I know? I've never dealt with a broken penis. I had to think fast, and that's what I came up with."

"It sounded like a good plan to me."

"I hope so. But I'll bet Franklin regrets the day he woke that sleeping tiger of a wife. He deserves a purple heart. Wait, make that a purple penis. I should have one made up for him, as a joke. Except I don't know how long it'll be before he can laugh about this." She glanced at Amanda. "What do you think? Would a medal in the shape of a penis be in poor taste?"

If Amanda had a dollar for every time Gloria left her speechless, she could quit her bartending job. But right now she needed Gloria back in her office before the fax came through. "William called," she said, hoping to speed up that process. "He has a stock recommendation for you."

"Really?" Gloria brightened. "Now that's encouraging!" She rubbed her hands together. "He called. I like that. How did he sound?"

"Businesslike. Very businesslike. But I think you need to call him. Stock prices can rise and fall quickly."

"Oh, I'll call. But I don't think this is about a stock." Gloria winked. "I think this is about something else that's rising. And I plan to ride that upward trend. I'll go call him."

The fax hummed right as Gloria started into her office. She paused. "We're getting a fax."

"Go make your call. I'll take care of this. It's probably fax spam."

"Probably." But Gloria hung back as the

fax began sliding into view.

"Sure enough. Spam." Amanda tried to pull the sheet of paper from the fax, but the machine gripped the bottom edge, not quite ready to relinquish the incriminating message. She wanted to get a good look at the writing, but it wasn't easy doing that when she was also hiding it from Gloria.

"It's from the offices of Cooper and Scott!" Gloria pounced, and right as Amanda gained control of the fax, Gloria jerked it away from her. "Excellent! The condoms and the chocolates are working!"

"Um, I don't think . . ."

"You don't think what, Amanda? Could this be from anybody but William?"

"No, I guess not." Unless she was ready to spill the whole story, she had to let Gloria believe the fax was intended for her.

"It's from him, all right. He's so cute. Signing Cooper and Scott stationery with *Your Secret Valentine.* What a droll sense of humor."

"Extremely droll."

"I was going to call him, but now I think I'll simply waltz on down there." Gloria waved the fax. "This is practically an engraved invitation, wouldn't you say?"

"Looks like it."

"Have you gone online yet to find a book

on sex trivia?"

"Not yet." She'd been too busy dealing with a second valentine from someone who might not even be William. But she hadn't been able to evaluate his writing on the fax, so she still didn't know what to think.

"You can do that while I'm gone." Gloria glanced at Amanda's desk. "What's that mess? Your desk looks like the bottom of a hamster cage."

"I tore up some notes from school."

Gloria gazed at her. "You're wound way too tight, Amanda. Go into my office and pick out a vibrator to take home with you tonight. I don't want stressed-out people working in my office. You'll give off stressed-out vibes and make the clients nervous."

Put that way, she couldn't very well refuse. "Thank you," she said. "I'll take a look at the vibrators."

"I insist. Oh, and while you're online, jump on over to some of the other sites I've given you and see what sort of thing you might be able to order for William that's different from what the G-Spot carries. If you find some juicy stuff, get them to overnight it."

"All right."

"I don't know how long I'll be in William's office."

"You have the Burnsides in twenty minutes." It was the only roadblock Amanda could think of to throw in front of this runaway train.

"I would cancel it, but I've seen the setup at Cooper and Scott." She folded the fax and tucked it in her cleavage. "They have those movable partitions that don't go all the way to the ceiling. Sound carries in a place like that, so my options are limited. I'll probably be back in twenty minutes."

"See you then." Amanda could think of no way to save William at this point. For whatever reason, he'd delayed sending the fax, and now he'd have to deal with the fallout.

But she could warn him. Maybe she shouldn't bother, but it seemed like the fair thing to do. Once the door closed behind Gloria, Amanda picked up the phone and punched in the number for Cooper and Scott.

EIGHT

William hadn't counted on a lineup at the fax machine and he'd had to wait until everyone cleared out before he sent the fax to Amanda. He knew it was risky to send it ten minutes after he'd told her it would be there, but she'd said Gloria was with a client. Sessions usually took an hour, so he figured the coast was clear for at least another twenty-five minutes.

When his phone rang, he picked up hoping it was Amanda telling him he was cleared of all charges. This valentine thing was getting ridiculous. He might not be the smoothest character in the universe, but he wouldn't continue lobbing valentines at a woman who didn't want them. He resented being labeled that kind of a schmuck.

Sure enough, Amanda was on the line. "Am I exonerated?" he asked.

"No, you're in deep shit. Gloria got the fax before I could. She thinks you sent it to her, and she's on her way down there, prepared to seal the deal between you two."

Dread washed over him. "How could she get it? You said she was with a client! Sessions take an hour!" This couldn't be happening. His luck had never been this bad.

"It wasn't a regular session. A client came in with an emergency, and she left a little while ago. Gloria was right there when the fax came in."

"And you just stood there and let her see it?"

"No, I didn't just stand there! I tried to keep it away from her, but you know how she is."

William sighed. "Yeah, I do." The clicking of a pair of high heels grew louder. He had a feeling those high heels belonged to his newest client. "Listen, I have to go."

"Good luck."

"Right. Bye." He hung up the phone and took a deep breath.

Gloria came strolling into his cubicle, all smiles. "I got your message, William. Loud and clear."

"Amanda just called to tell me about the fax."

"Yes, the fax." Gloria sat in the chair in front of his desk and pulled the folded paper from between her generous breasts. "What do you say we eliminate the secret part of this message and go public?"

William had never thought so fast in his life. "Gloria, this is very embarrassing, but . . . that message wasn't meant for you."

She laughed and tossed back her red curls. "You're not going to convince me it was meant for Amanda. That girl is such a sexless nerd it's pathetic."

"No, it wasn't meant for Amanda, either. It was meant for . . ." *Oh, God, what story can I make up that she'd buy?* "My mother."

"Your *mother?*"

"Yes. She works at a real estate office in Springfield, and we fax each other things all the time." That was partly true. His mother was a realtor in Springfield.

The rest was a big fat lie, and he wasn't proud of himself, but he was a desperate man. His mother wouldn't approve of this lie on many levels. For one thing, he and his mother didn't have a faxing kind of relationship. They didn't e-mail, either. She preferred the sound of his voice, so he called, and he owed her a phone call, one he'd meant to make last night. But he'd been a bit distracted.

In point of fact, he hadn't been operating at an optimum level ever since meeting Amanda and her bag of sex toys on the stairs yesterday. He should have dealt with the issue of Gloria's libido right away, when it first presented itself. By the time he'd received the condoms and the candy tits, he'd already waited too long.

But he could have taken the time to react to those with a phone call last night. Sure, Justin had his problems and William was concerned. And yes, he'd spent a good part of his evening fuming about Amanda and the stupid valentine fiasco.

None of that excused him. He could have headed off this current excruciating moment with a call to Gloria, and he hadn't done it. Because of that, he was reduced to lying through his teeth.

Gloria gazed at him for several long seconds. "I don't believe you."

So much for his ability to lie effectively. Apparently he couldn't do anything very well these days.

"But if you want to play the secret valentine game, I can do that." Gloria began unzipping her leopard-print jumpsuit.

William froze. "What are you doing?"

"Amanda said you had a stock recommendation for me." She drew the zipper down to her waist, revealing a black lace bra.

For the life of him, William couldn't

remember what the hell it was. He glanced at the doorway to his cubicle. There was no actual door there. Anyone walking by could see right in.

He lowered his voice. "Please zip your outfit."

"Silly boy. People have better things to do than worry about what's going on in here."

"Gloria, I'm not interested in that kind of relationship with you. I appreciate your business, but —"

"I don't have much time. My clients will arrive at two. Just tell me about the stock you want me to buy." She fingered the clasp of her bra.

"Do *not* unfasten that."

"Just tell me the company. Then I'll give the okay and be on my way."

"Software." He swallowed and glanced at the door again. "I'm going to have to ask you to zip up."

"I will in a minute. What do you like about this *software* company?"

"I was impressed with their assets."

"I love it when you talk dirty."

He groaned. "Gloria, please . . ."

"That's all I needed to hear." She flipped open the catch on her bra and her breasts spilled out. "Allow me to introduce *my* assets."

He tried to keep the panic from his voice. If a senior member of the firm saw this, William would be history. "Please cover up. You're endangering my position."

She smiled, pulled the bra back together and fastened it with a click. "Speaking of positions, what's your favorite?"

Under the circumstances, silence seemed the only way to go.

"Your face is red, William, which I find endearing. It's fine to be shy in the beginning, but when I'm finished with you, all that shyness will be gone. For the time being, I'll let you be my secret valentine. Just so that doesn't go on too long." She zipped her jumpsuit and stood.

He let out his breath. For all his bad luck recently, at least no one had wandered by his doorway while Gloria was showing off her knockers. He might as well be thankful for small favors.

"Go ahead and buy that stock," she said. "Use the money market funds. I've been asking my very old broker to invest those and he never got around to it. I'm glad to have a young and virile man handling my . . . assets."

William kept his voice as low as possible. He didn't want anyone in the office overhearing this volatile conversation. "I think

140

we need to rethink doing business together, Gloria. I'm not comfortable with how you see our relationship developing."

"Oh?" She lifted her eyebrows. "I wondered if we'd get to this point, and here we are already. I can understand if you don't feel right having sex with a client."

William winced. That statement had been way too loud. But what could he do, run around the desk and clap a hand over her mouth? She'd probably interpret that as foreplay.

"If that's the case," she continued, "then I'll be happy to transfer my accounts back to my old and creaky broker. I'd rather have sex with you than increase the value of my portfolio. I have my priorities."

He lowered his voice another notch. "You won't be having sex with me."

"Oh, yes I will." She gave him a long, appreciative look. "But unfortunately I have to leave, now. I'll talk with you later, my secret valentine."

He decided getting her out of the office was priority number one. Getting rid of her as a client would be priority number two, except that she'd think he was only doing it to clear the way for sex. Maybe keeping her as a client while maintaining a moral stance was the safest way to go.

Then again, when it came to Gloria, he wasn't convinced anything was safe.

Although Amanda tried to tell herself she wasn't interested in what had happened in William's office, she was on the edge of her seat waiting for Gloria's return.

Gloria arrived sporting a tiny smile. She looked smug, in fact. And she headed directly for her office. How could she do that? She was always giving Amanda way too much information, but the one time Amanda wanted it, Gloria was withholding.

"I found a book on sex trivia," Amanda called after her. "It's titled *Titillating Trivia.* I put a rush on the order."

"Good." Gloria kept walking.

"Do you still want me to look for other toys? I didn't have a chance to do that yet."

"Yes, please." Gloria started to close her door.

Amanda couldn't stand it. "Did he admit to sending the fax?"

Pausing with one hand on the door, Gloria glanced back at her. "Yes, but his story was totally lame. He claimed the fax was meant for his mother. I don't *think* so."

Amanda bit her lip to keep from laughing. His *mother?* Nobody would believe a goofy story like that. Of course, he hadn't had much time to come up with one, and at least he hadn't spilled the beans about the valentine situation. She was grateful for that, because no telling what would happen if Gloria flew into a jealous rage.

"He sent it to me, all right," Gloria said. "But he wants to play games for a while, so I'll humor him, although he's leaving me really hot and bothered. When the Burnsides arrive, delay them five minutes. I need some time alone." Then she closed her office door with a firm click.

Amanda stared at the door for a moment before turning back to her computer to look up some sex toy sites. If there were such a thing as sexual Olympics, Gloria would take home the gold. William had won Amanda's grudging respect for not taking advantage of all that throbbing sexuality.

When the outer door opened, she expected to see the Burnsides, but instead Justin, William's friend, walked in. Yikes. She wasn't supposed to recognize him. So far as Gloria could know, last night had never happened.

Poor Justin looked the worse for wear. His eyes were bloodshot and he kept sniffing, as if he'd come down with the flu. She couldn't shoo him out when he looked so pathetic.

"Hey, Amanda."

"Hey, Justin." She left her chair and

walked over to him. "Listen, my boss isn't supposed to know that I have a relationship with William. Well, it's not a *relationship*, because there is nothing between us, but my boss sort of has the hots for William, and —"

"No *sort of* about it. Any woman that sends condoms and X-rated chocolate has major designs."

"So you know about that, too."

"Yeah." Justin sniffed again.

"Well, she'd have a coronary if she thought he was the least bit interested in me."

"I get that. Listen, if she comes out and finds me here, tell her I'm a customer from Geekland, which is true. She doesn't have to know I'm Will's best friend or that he was with me last night."

"So you're not here to see him?" She'd assumed he'd stopped by on his way to William's office.

"Nope. I'm here to see you." Unzipping his coat, he pulled out a box about the size that tissues came in. But this was no tissue box.

Amanda recognized it immediately — the deluxe version of Barmaster.

"I feel terrible that I made things worse between you and Will," Justin said. "So this is a peace offering." He grinned sheepishly.

"I bought one for myself, too."

She resisted the urge to grab the box. "You didn't have to do that. You didn't know that I'd told William . . . Will . . . not to come to my workplace."

"No, but he tried to steer me to a different bar, and I kept insisting it had to be Geekland. So take this. It talks."

"I know." One of her customers had the deluxe version. She'd coveted it for months but hadn't been able to justify the expense.

"I took the day off. I've been playing with the silly thing since I bought it this morning. After I leave here, I'm heading over to Geekland so I can order something outrageous. I'm in the mood to try new things, do new people."

She gazed at him. His eyes were bright in his flushed face, as if he had a fever. "Don't take this wrong. I don't really know you. But you look as if you need to go home and go to bed."

"Nope. 'Fraid not. That would be the sensible thing to do, and I'm finished with being sensible."

"You could end up really sick." Behind her, she heard Gloria's door open.

"Don't care." His gaze flicked over her shoulder and he raised his voice. "Well, Amanda, like I said, I thought you could use this new and improved version of Barmaster. You do a great job at Geekland, and you deserve a top-of-the-line model."

"Amanda, who's our visitor?" Gloria asked.

"A customer from Geekland," Amanda said. "Justin Haskell. Justin, this is my boss, Dr. Gloria Tredway."

"Nice to meet you, Justin." Gloria came forward, hand outstretched. "If you're hoping to date Amanda, you're out of luck. She seems to have confused a degree from DePaul University with entering the nunnery."

"Nope, nope, wasn't looking for a date. Dating's too tame for this boy these days. I'm just looking for cheap, tawdry sex."

Gloria laughed. "I like that attitude. Good luck with that goal, Justin."

"Thanks. Well, I need to be going. See you at Geekland, Amanda."

"Sure." Amanda held up the box. "And thank you for this."

"No problem." With a wave and a sniff, Justin left the office.

"What did he give you?" Gloria continued to gaze at the door after Justin had closed it behind him.

"This."

Gloria refocused her attention. "What is it?"

"A deluxe version of Barmaster. It's a little flask-shaped computer that gives you the ingredients and mixing instructions for most of the drinks ever invented. And you can record any new drinks in there, too."

"A geek gift!" Gloria studied Amanda with narrowed eyes. "Don't tell me he's hot for you."

"God, no."

"Because you know the rule. Any man who walks in this office is off limits."

"Gloria, I'm not dating, period. Besides, I wouldn't date a guy who's still reeling from having his fiancée dump him." Then Amanda wondered if she should have mentioned that. Probably not.

"Really?" A speculative gleam lit Gloria's eyes. "Too bad I already have my Geek of the Week, because a man who's been dumped is ripe for experimental sex. He even admitted as much." Then she waved a hand dismissively. "But I can't do them all, now, can I?"

"Guess not." *But I'll bet you'd love to try.*

Harvey thought foreplay was highly overrated, but Dr. Tredway had spent today's entire session on the topic. Now Louise expected Harvey to waste the rest of the effing afternoon demonstrating how much he'd learned. He'd planned to spend the afternoon at Starbucks, hoping Amanda would come out of the building across the street.

Louise obviously didn't care that he had other things to do. She wanted orgasms, and she refused to do anything except lie there like a lump while Harvey, his head wedged between her thunder thighs, did all the work. What kind of fun was that?

Even worse, Louise had taped a picture of some guy named Heath Ledger on the ceiling of their bedroom. Whenever Harvey accidentally did something she liked, she'd cry out *Oh, Heath, do that again!* It was bad enough that Harvey was the work horse without some movie star getting the credit.

Then he had an idea. If she could call out somebody else's name, so could he. "Mm, *Amanda,* you taste like . . ." He searched for a good comparison. "Like draft beer!"

Louise sat bolt upright. "Who the hell is Amanda?"

"My fantasy lover." Harvey lifted his head and gazed up at Louise. He had a funny angle from here. Her boobs looked gigantic and her head was small. It was kind of like watching a balloon in the Macy's Thanksgiving Day parade on TV. Louise had recently gone blond, so now she was two-toned — frizzy blond on her head and beer-bottle brown on the part Harvey was currently stuck with.

"Your fantasy *what?*"

"You have a fantasy lover, this Heath guy, so I decided I'd have one, too, honey cakes." He used pet names to soften her up. Sometimes it worked and sometimes it didn't.

"Huh. I didn't think you had enough imagination to have fantasies."

"Well, I do, lambkins." Louise would be amazed at what kind of an imagination he had, especially where Amanda was concerned.

"And her name is Amanda?"

"Yes." Harvey felt the thrill of danger. Louise was a jealous woman, and whenever she got jealous, anything could happen. Being married to Louise was so boring that sometimes he made her mad on purpose, to relieve the boredom.

"You mean that actress from *Boys and Girls?* Amanda Detmer?"

Harvey thought about telling her it wasn't Amanda Detmer, that it was Amanda Rykowsky, the receptionist in Dr. Tredway's office. But he didn't want her to find that out until after he'd carried Amanda off, like a pirate. In the meantime, he was having fun with the valentines.

He had the best one yet to deliver tomorrow, and if he told Louise about it, she'd get really, really mad. As exciting as that might be, he wanted to put it off until he'd completed his plan. "Yeah, Amanda Detmer," he said.

"I guess that's all right." She flopped back onto the pillow. "But Amanda Detmer would never go with a guy who looks like you."

"What do you mean, candy lips? I look good."

"Your nose is too big and your chin is too small. Plus you should color that mousy brown hair, and you're on the scrawny side. You have no muscle definition whatsoever."

He considered telling her that she was a big pile of blubber who had no room to talk, except that wouldn't get him anywhere except in divorce court. But once she found out that another woman thought he was very handsome and smart, Louise would have a whole different opinion of Harvey Kenton.

"Harvey?"

"What?"

"What are you doing down there?"

"Nothing."

"My point, exactly. Nothing. And on top of that, you'll have to start all over. I was

150

working up to a climax, but then you said that thing about Amanda, and I lost momentum."

That was discouraging. "Can I still say her name, though? I mean, in between using my tongue the way Dr. Tredway taught me."

"Yeah, yeah. Just get on with it."

"Okay, sugar tits." He settled into position again. "Amanda, you are so hot." This fantasy lover thing rocked. Now that he could pretend that he was doing Amanda instead of Louise, he didn't mind the work nearly as much. On Valentine's night, he really would be doing Amanda, so this was a way of getting used to the concept.

NINE

By the time Amanda arrived for her shift at Geekland, Justin was still planted on a bar stool, and from the looks of him, he was feeling no pain.

"Hey, 'Manda." He gave her a lopsided grin.

"Hey, Justin."

Ethan, the bartender she was relieving, looked exactly like the Verizon guy, especially when he wore the Geekland glasses. As a result he had to put up with a lot of "Can you hear me, now?" jokes.

When he spied Amanda, he came over, put an arm around her shoulders, and led her a little distance down the bar, out of earshot from Justin. "That guy's been picking drinks at random from his Barmaster. So far he's had six different combinations. The last thing I fixed him was a Bahama Mama."

Amanda winced. "Almost all booze."

"Yep."

"Well, he's drowning his sorrows. His fiancée canceled the wedding yesterday."

"So he said, but it's time to cut him off."

Amanda made a face. "Thanks for leaving me with that job."

"You're tougher than me, Rykowsky." Ethan gave her shoulder a squeeze, pocketed his tips and left.

Cutting off the liquor supply was Amanda's least favorite thing to do, but Justin looked in need of that particular service. He'd positioned himself at the bar with a trivia keyboard and he punched buttons at random. When he missed a question, which was most of the time, he laughed hysterically. Not a good sign.

Leonard hopped up on a stool in front of Amanda. "Finally! I want a Hot Apple Pie, and I didn't trust Ethan to make it right."

"A Hot Apple Pie? Are you sure? Last time —"

"My mouth's all healed. See?" Leonard puckered up. Then he crossed his eyes and imitated fish lips.

She couldn't help laughing, although that would only encourage him, which wasn't good because he seemed to have a crush on her. "Leonard, what's coming up next week?"

"The finals in a Magic tournament. Want to come and watch me win?"

"Sorry, no time. So you don't know that Valentine's Day is next week?"

"It is?"

"Yeah." She grabbed the Baileys bottle so she could start making the Hot Apple Pie.

"Is that a hint? You want a box of candy or something?"

"No! I just —"

"See, Amanda?" Justin called out. Then he laughed his crazy laugh. "I missed 'nother one! See how stupid I am? No wonder she dumped me."

"You're not stupid." She layered Goldschläger over the Baileys. "But it might be time to retire that Barmaster for the night and tuck into a hamburger and fries, maybe a hot cup of coffee." She wondered if that would be enough of a hint for him.

"Not hungry." Justin went back to stabbing at the trivia keyboard.

With a sigh, Amanda took out the 151-proof rum and poured it on top of the Goldschläger.

Leonard lowered his voice. "You're trying to cut him off, aren't you?"

She nodded.

"I don't think it'll be all that easy."

"Unfortunately, you could be right."

Reaching into her pocket, she took out a lighter and set the top layer of 151-proof rum on fire.

Leonard stared at it in obvious delight. "Now that is totally cool."

"No, it's hot, Leonard." She handed him an empty rocks glass. "You'd better snuff it out before you end up burning your mouth on the glass."

"Hey, gimme one of those!" As Justin leaned in their direction, he almost fell off his bar stool.

"I think that's a bad idea, Justin."

"Aw, c'mon." Using the bar as support, he climbed down from his stool and worked his way around to Amanda and Leonard. "You made him one. My turn!"

"No. It could be dangerous." She watched Leonard out of the corner of her eye. He was slowly extinguishing the flame, but the glass would still be hot. "Let it cool some," she warned him.

Justin edged closer. "Lemme taste."

"No." Amanda put her arm out to stop him. "It's too —"

"Lemme *taste*." Justin lunged over her arm and grabbed the glass away from Leonard.

Amanda knocked it out of his hand before he could take a drink and scald himself on the hot rim. Baileys, Goldschläger, and rum went everywhere as the glass tumbled to the bar, where it shattered.

Justin surveyed the damage through bleary eyes. "Whoopsie-daisy."

"Hey, Amanda," Leonard said. "Take a look at the spray pattern on my shirt! The three kinds of booze didn't completely mingle, and I actually have different-colored dots. Awesome."

Amanda took off her liquor-spattered glasses. "That's not exactly the word I'd use, but I'm glad you're not upset."

"Heck, no. You can just make me another Hot Apple Pie. Half the fun is watching you make it and light that puppy."

Tina came by with an empty drinks tray. "Hey, Amanda, I need — Whoa, what happened here?"

"A whoopsie-daisy." Justin leaned on the bar. His arm was a quarter inch from a jagged piece of glass.

Amanda panicked. "Don't lean on the bar! There's broken glass everywhere."

"There is?"

"Look, both of you back up a little and then stay put. Tina, can you get somebody from the kitchen to help me clean up? And stall anyone who wants a drink until I get resituated."

"Will do." Tina hurried away.

Amanda wiped her hands on a bar rag. Then she carefully picked up the biggest pieces of glass and dropped them in the trash.

"I need 'nother drink."

She paused to look at Justin. "No you don't. You need food."

"Don't want food." His expression turned belligerent. "Want 'nother drink."

"I could get security if you want," Leonard said.

"That's okay." She didn't want Justin thrown out of here, not after he'd been nice enough to buy her a deluxe Barmaster. Besides, he was William's best friend, and . . . that was her answer. "Justin, what kind of cell phone do you have?"

He brightened. "The best."

She'd figured that. A nerd would be proud of his technology. "Can I see it? I'm thinking of getting one."

Instead, Leonard took the bait. He leaned forward. "Then you should see mine!" Wiping his hands on his shirt, he unclipped his phone from his belt and handed it over. "The screen's incredible, and I have a list of features as long as this bar."

"Thanks." She took the phone, flipped it open and pretended to care what she was looking at. "Justin? Can I look at yours, now?" She handed Leonard's back to him.

Justin shrugged. "Guess so." He unclipped his without wiping his hands. "Catch."

She caught it one-handed and wiped the stickiness off with her bar towel. Luck was with her, because Ed from the kitchen arrived right then with a bucket of soapy water and several rags. She stepped out of his way, putting him between her and Justin.

Opening the phone, she quickly clicked on his list of contacts. Sure enough, William was right there. In no time at all she had him on the line. "William, this is Amanda."

"What's wrong?" He sounded scared. "Why do you have Justin's phone? Has there been an accident? Is he okay? What —"

"He's fine, but he's really drunk. Can you come and get him?"

"I'll be right there. Thanks for calling me." He disconnected the line.

Amanda closed the phone, stepped around Ed, and handed the phone to Justin. "Looks like a good model."

"Can I get 'nother drink, now?" Justin wobbled a little, as if he might not be able to stand much longer.

"We'll see." She took a rag and walked around the end of the bar so she could wipe off the stools. "First I need to take care of the backed-up orders. But you can sit down, if you want."

"Okay." Justin climbed unsteadily onto a stool and watched as she made another Hot Apple Pie for Leonard. Then she took care of several orders for Tina. About the time she'd run out of things to do, William came through the door.

She couldn't remember the last time she'd been so glad to see someone. That was only because he was here to save his buddy from humiliation, of course. It wasn't William she was glad to see, but the prospect of solving a big problem.

At least that's what she was trying to tell herself. But she couldn't ignore the appealing picture William made as he walked up to the bar. His dark hair was windblown, his cheeks ruddy, his coat unzipped. Under his coat he wore an old Northwestern sweatshirt and jeans that had been lovingly broken in.

In short, William didn't look at all like a nerd tonight.

William had thrown on a coat, raced out of his apartment, and hailed a cab in order to get to Geekland as soon as possible. He cringed at the idea of showing up in front of Amanda in his oldest clothes, but he couldn't take time to change. If she'd thought Justin was in bad enough shape that she'd wangled his cell phone to call a guy she was trying to avoid, then she must have been desperate.

As he drew closer, he noticed that both Amanda and Justin were covered with coffee-colored spots. Justin hadn't even bothered to clean his glasses after whatever disaster had taken place here. William decided there was no point in asking. Suffice it to say, Amanda wanted Justin out of her hair. She must be heartily sick of dealing with both of them.

"Will!" Justin frowned. "Whatcha doin' here?"

"Trying to get you to buy me a burger. Pizza last night was on me, so tonight it's your turn."

"But you're not s'posed to be here, ya know." Justin tilted his head in Amanda's direction and wiggled his eyebrows.

"I know. But I hear they have good burgers." He took the stool next to Justin. He'd never seen his buddy so trashed.

Amanda moved in his direction, her expression hopeful. "Would you like to order, then?"

"I would love to order." He was trying to

concentrate on Justin and his problems, but here was Amanda, looking gorgeous, even though spattered by some unknown substance. Whatever the liquid was, a blob of it had landed on each breast right about where the nipple was. The color of the liquid made it seem as if someone had painted two nipples on the plaid material of her shirt, almost like a pair of bull's-eyes.

"Could we have a drink, instead?" Justin weaved back and forth on the bar stool. "I'm getting way too sober."

"Getting sober's not a bad idea."

"Easy for you to say. You're not trying to block out memories of Cindi Finkelstein the Defector."

"No, I'm trying to get something to eat. How about two burgers, medium?"

"Got it." Amanda turned away and entered the order on her computer screen. "Skinny fries or wedge-cut?"

"I like wedgies," Justin said. "Wait. That didn't come out right."

"I know what you meant." Amanda sounded like she wanted to laugh but was holding back. "William? Which do you want?"

"Just call him Will," Justin said. "William makes him sound like a dork with a stick up his butt. I keep telling him that, but he says William sounds more stockbrokerish, whatever that means."

She glanced over at William, laughter dancing in her eyes. "How would you like your fries, *Will?*"

"Wedge-cut." He didn't even care that Justin had made that crack about his name. Seeing Amanda lighten up was worth the humiliation. He wondered if she had the slightest clue how beautiful she looked, and how much he wanted to vault the bar, kiss her, and see if he could bring that laughter out in the open.

"Coming up." She turned away when a waitress named Tina arrived and ordered some drinks.

Justin leaned toward him. "I think she likes you more tonight than last night." He smelled like a brewery.

"I think you'd better not lean like that or you're going to fall over."

He straightened, gripping the bar for balance. "How did you know I was here?"

"Good guess." Apparently Justin had been so out of it he hadn't realized Amanda had purloined his cell phone. "Listen, buddy, don't do this to yourself. Cindi's not worth the damage to your liver."

"I know, but what if she's the only woman who ever wants to marry me and have sex

162

and stuff?"

"She's not."

"I asked a couple of women in this bar if they wanted to have sex, and they turned me down flatsky."

William choked back a laugh. "We might have to work on your approach."

"I'm smoother when I'm not drunk."

"I certainly hope so."

Justin's mouth tilted in a sloppy grin. "I know one woman who might have sex with me."

William sincerely hoped Justin wasn't going to name Amanda. That would put a big old crimp in their friendship. "And who would that be?"

"You won't get mad?"

"That depends."

"On what?"

William was getting nervous about this conversation. If Amanda had turned him down and accepted Justin instead, life was going to generally suck. "Just tell me, okay?"

"Gloria Tredway."

William stared at him. "What makes you think that?"

"I was in her office today, and she gave me the *look,* if you know what I mean."

"I know what you mean." He'd been getting that look from the moment he'd met dear Dr. Tredway. "What were you doing in her office?"

Justin waggled a finger in the air. "Well you might ask. Making amends. I was making amends."

"With Gloria Tredway?" William struggled to follow the conversation.

"No, with *her.*" Justin pointed to Amanda. "To make up for dragging you here last night. Gave her a deluxe Barmaster."

"A *what?*"

"Barmaster. I got one for me, too." Justin patted his shirt pockets. "Had it right here. Oh, there it is." He started unsteadily to his feet.

"Sit, sit." William put a hand on Justin's shoulder, which was all the pressure needed to coax Justin back onto the bar stool. "That gray thing over there?"

"Yeah."

William retrieved the flask-shaped object lying on the bar several feet away. From the buttons and screen on the front, he figured out that it was an electronic drink reference tool. Too bad he hadn't thought of buying something like that for Amanda. Justin had outclassed him on that one.

Justin took the small flask. "This is great. Let me show you."

"In a minute. Listen, about Gloria Tredway, I don't think you want to go there."

"You jealous?" Justin peered at him through his speckled lenses.

"God, no. Concerned. Now might not be the right time for you to hook up with somebody so . . . so . . . ."

"Totally hot?"

"Predatory. She strikes me as a man-eater."

Justin nodded. "Perfect. Stringless sex."

"No strings, maybe, but I'm guessing there would be ropes involved." William shuddered to think of Justin in Gloria's clutches.

Justin's eyes widened. "Ropes? Like in bondage?"

"Yep. And you're not up to it."

"How the hell do you know?"

"It's obvious. You're used to sweet little Cindi, who never had an S and M thought in her life."

"And look where I am now. Dump City." He grinned at William. "You convinced me. I'm asking Tredway out."

Willliam groaned. "Don't do that."

"I'm doing it." He punched a button on the front of the flask and a recorded voice welcomed them to the Barmaster. "See? It talks!"

"Wonderful. Listen, aren't there some

165

women at Amherst Labs you'd like to take out? Personally, I'd hold off on dating for a while, but if you really feel the need, you should pick somebody more normal."

"Been there, done that. Name a drink, any drink."

"Manhattan."

"*Bor*-ing. Something else."

William searched his memory. He wasn't a hang-out-in-the-bar kind of guy. "Gin gimlet."

"Oh, come on. Give me something cool."

"For crying out loud. Sex on the Beach!"

Of course Amanda was walking by at the very moment he belted out his response. She turned. "Was that a drink order?"

"No, not exactly." He didn't even know what was in one. He'd heard a client mention it, somebody who took Caribbean vacations and was much cooler than he was.

"My mistake." She turned away.

"Wait a sec."

She turned back, and he looked into those incredible blue eyes that reminded him of a clear day on Lake Michigan. He'd never had Sex on the Beach, the drink, and he'd never had sex on the beach, the experience. He longed to share both with this woman.

Because that was a hopeless cause, he had to settle for having her make him a cocktail with a suggestive name. He decided to go for it. "It is a drink order," he said. "Sex on the Beach. That's what I have a taste for."

The guy was getting to her. Amanda tried to tell herself it wasn't so, but her pulse rate picked up every time she glanced over at the table where William and Justin sat eating their burgers and fries. William looked way too good in his old clothes and his windblown hair. When he ordered another Sex on the Beach, she got honest-to-God goose bumps.

She loved the way he took care of Justin, too. She was a sucker for that kind of loyalty. If he'd come charging to the rescue when Justin was in trouble, then he was a person who could be counted on in a crisis. Amanda had known precious few people like that, so she relied primarily on herself. Justin had William to rely on, and she envied Justin that.

Good thing her job involved standing behind the clear acrylic bar. If she'd had Tina's job, she would have spent far too much time over by Will and Justin's table. When she needed a bathroom break, she forced herself to go the long way so she wouldn't be tempted to stop and chat.

But when she came out into the narrow

corridor, there was William, leaning against the wall, smiling at her. Her heart thumped wildly at the look in his green eyes.

"I wanted to thank you," he said. "You could have had Justin thrown out of here."

"I wouldn't have done that."

A female customer came down the hallway. Amanda had to move closer to William in order to let her by, and she caught a whiff of Old Spice. Yum.

"You're a good person," William said.

She glanced up at him. Big mistake. He looked like he wanted to kiss her, and with two Sex on the Beach drinks under his belt, he might have the Dutch courage to do it. Worse yet, she wanted him to.

"I should get back."

"Yes." He hesitated. "Aw, what the hell. You only live once." Pulling her into his arms, he kissed her. Their glasses got in the way, but still he managed to make full contact with her mouth.

A video of this kiss would probably be hysterical, but she wasn't laughing. Far from it. The sensual jolt from that lip-to-lip contact traveled all the way to her toes and significant points in between. He had a great mouth, and without their glasses interfering, she'd be happy to stay plastered against it for some time. She wanted to suggest they take off their glasses and start over.

" 'Scuse me." The customer came out of the ladies' room. "Sorry to interrupt."

William let Amanda go instantly. They stared at each other as the customer edged past them and returned to the bar.

Amanda struggled to breathe. "Um . . ."

William gulped for air. "Yeah, I know. That was probably the dorkiest kiss in history."

"No, no, it wasn't."

"I can do better."

Dear God, if he could do better, she was in big trouble. "I . . . I have to get back."

"Right."

She fled before she did something really stupid like whipping off her glasses and his so she could find out what he meant by *better*. She wished he hadn't said that, because now that would be all she'd think about every time she saw him.

TEN

Usually Amanda's heavy schedule meant that she slept like a dead person, but that night after work she fought for every moment of blissful unconsciousness. That stupid, awkward kiss kept repeating itself in her head. When William and Justin had left the bar around ten, she'd felt as if the warmth had been sucked out of the room.

She'd now made the unfortunate discovery that William knew how to kiss. Even with two sets of glasses in the way, he'd made a substantial impact on her libido. She could imagine the effect with no glasses.

Once she had that concept firmly planted in her brain, it was a short leap to imagining a kiss with no glasses and no clothes, either. Then she began thinking of Gloria's big-thumbs theory, which resulted in urges that caused her to remember the vibrator Gloria had wanted her to bring home. She'd forgotten.

Maybe the vibrator wasn't such a bad idea. It wouldn't be nearly as much trouble as sex with an actual boyfriend. But the thought of a vibrator didn't turn her on at all. She wanted William.

Too bad. She wouldn't, *couldn't* scratch that particular itch. She had to be strong. But self-sacrifice could distract a person. On her way out the door to her morning class, she'd grabbed what she thought was a packet of trail mix, only to discover on the bus that she was holding a package of uncooked rainbow noodles.

After class she forgot to zip her backpack completely, and when she hoisted it over her shoulders, half the contents fell out. That little stunt caused her to miss her bus to work. On top of that her jacket was still stained from the coffee accident because she hadn't had time to wash it.

Arriving late, hungry, unkempt, and frustrated to the sex-drenched offices of Dr. Gloria Tredway was not a pleasant prospect. As she hung her jacket on the coat tree next to the door, Gloria walked out of her office, and Amanda figured the day was about to get worse. The always voluptuous, often shocking Gloria had gone nerdy.

"What do you think?" She pirouetted in front of Amanda's desk in the ugliest plaid shirtwaist Amanda had ever seen. Her wild red hair was pulled into a tight bun with a pencil stuck through it. To complete the look, she wore glasses on a beaded chain and flat-heeled shoes.

"Depends on what you're going for." But Amanda had a pretty good idea.

"Last night I decided I was conducting my William campaign all wrong, so I borrowed this dress from one of my neighbors and picked up the glasses and chain at the drugstore on the way to work this morning. I'm embarrassed to admit I own the shoes, but I had them in a bag of things going to Goodwill."

"Did William tell you he was partial to plaid?" She couldn't imagine anyone being partial to this particular plaid, which included alternating shades of poop and barf.

"Of course not! But he was clearly intimidated by my leopard-print jumpsuit. I really shouldn't have unzipped it and flashed my tits at him, either, I suppose. But I do have such great tits that I like to show them off."

Amanda blinked. "Excuse me?" Maybe she'd misheard.

"When I went down to his office yesterday, after he sent the fax he pretended was for his mother, I was teasing him by unzipping my jumpsuit. Then I thought I'd see his reaction if I unsnapped my bra and gave him a glimpse of the goodies."

"Wow."

Gloria cupped her breasts. "You have to admit that I have bragging rights when it comes to my girls."

"Uh, sure." Amanda couldn't remember ever being asked to comment on another woman's boobs, but life with Gloria was a constant adventure.

"However, I'm worried that I might have scared the poor boy."

"That's possible." Poor William, just a decent guy with a talent for kissing, a guy who took care of his friends and tried to make a living in the stock market. He hadn't asked to have his newest client flashing him at his place of business, but he'd been the flashee, anyway. Amanda's sympathy knew no bounds.

"So today I'll stroll down there on some pretext or other, and let him see the other side of Gloria Tredway. I can play the nerd game. Did you know I could get into Mensa if I wanted to?"

"Didn't know that."

"It's true. There was a sample test in one of the psychology journals I subscribe to, and I knew all the answers. When I was in school, I could have graduated with honors, but I was too involved in extracurricular activities."

Amanda would bet that Gloria wasn't talking about the chess club, either.

"Help me think of a reason to go to his office," Gloria said. "A nerdy reason."

"Gloria, I'm really not a nerd. I know you think so, but —"

"Don't be silly. Of course you are. Just put your mind to it."

"I thought you needed the billing to go out this morning."

"Use your lunch hour for that. This is more important. I need the equivalent of borrowing a cup of sugar — some semilegitimate excuse to go down there, which also demonstrates that I have a brain and I know how to use it."

Amanda could tell Gloria wouldn't rest until she suggested something, so she tried to come up with an idea. "How about showing him an article you read in the *Wall Street Journal*?"

"That's not bad, except I don't want to read an article in the *Wall Street Journal.* I hate a newspaper with no pictures."

"Then I don't —"

"But *you* could read an article in the *Wall Street Journal,* give me the Cliffs Notes version, and I'd be all set. Go on down to the drugstore, buy one of those boring papers, and find an article you think William would like, or might have already read."

Amanda reached for her coat. Going out for a newspaper wasn't the worst assignment she could have right now. The drugstore would have some sort of junk food on the rack.

"And pick up a latte at Starbucks while you're out."

"Will do." So maybe she could get a muffin for herself and stave off her hunger pangs. Once she wasn't so hungry, she might not feel quite as sex-starved, either.

She left the office and automatically glanced down the hall toward Cooper and Scott. If she wanted to do William a favor, she could stop by there and warn him of Gloria's latest scheme.

No, too risky. After that kiss, she had to avoid seeing him whenever possible. He might pick up on her new fixation, and she couldn't allow that.

Harvey sat by the window drinking his hot mocha cappuccino. Being in Starbucks was a lot like being in church, except better, because of the coffee and muffins. Everybody was glad to see him, the music was good, and he could stay as long as he wanted. Louise didn't like Starbucks all that much because they didn't sell doughnuts. She came with him on Saturdays, though, mostly to complain about the lack of doughnuts.

So guess what? No Louise today. That was a plus, because the best thing about this particular Starbucks was its location right across from Dr. Tredway's office. From this spot he could see when Amanda came out and then he could grab the chance to deliver another valentine.

Today he'd bought her a frosted heart cookie Starbucks was selling for Valentine's Day, and he'd put that in her desk, too, along with the card. He'd been thinking more about how he could tranquilize Amanda in case she put up a struggle when he went to get her on Valentine's night, and putting something in a cookie would be one way. But he couldn't be sure she'd eat the cookie.

He had to be sure she'd be nice and quiet when he took her out of her apartment. Hitting her over the head would work, but that might give her a headache and she wouldn't be so ready for sex when she came to. He wanted her to be really ready for sex, once she realized he was the one who'd carried her off.

So far he hadn't seen her this morning. He might have to wait until lunchtime, but that was okay. Starbucks was warm and it smelled good in there, lots better than his house.

His house smelled bad because Louise smoked. Well, so did he sometimes, but not like Louise. Whenever he wanted excitement, he'd hide her cigarettes and watch her go crazy. That was Louise — either completely boring or foaming at the mouth.

Maybe this afternoon he'd take her carton of cigarettes out of the refrigerator and put them in the freezer. Then he'd act like she'd done it, like she was losing her marbles so much that she'd put her cigarettes in the freezer. Even better, they'd be frozen, and she'd have to thaw one to smoke it. He wondered what would happen if you put a cigarette in the microwave. Maybe —

Oh, cool! There was Amanda, heading for the drugstore. He left his coffee right where it was, along with the *Enquirer* he'd bought to read, and his scarf over the back of the chair. You could do that in Starbucks, leave your stuff to save your seat. And they had the greatest gum at Starbucks.

On Valentine's night, before he went to Amanda's apartment, he'd chew some of that gum so she'd have extra fun kissing him after she came to. He knew exactly where she lived. The Internet was good for stuff like that. Maybe he'd look up ways to make a person temporarily unconscious. You could find anything on the Internet.

A copy of the *Wall Street Journal* tucked under her arm, Amanda walked into Starbucks and inhaled the scent of roasted coffee beans and sugary baked goods. Then she had an idea. Why go back right away? Why not scan the newspaper here while she drank her coffee and devoured carbs?

Gloria was in a session right now and wouldn't care. Amanda couldn't deliver Gloria's latte until the session was over, anyway, and the answering machine would pick up any calls. Yes, the work was stacking up on her desk, but when a girl gave up the prospect of more kisses from a guy like William, she deserved a treat.

She couldn't remember the last time she'd allowed herself the luxury of sitting in a coffee shop with the newspaper, a steaming hot cappuccino, and a banana-nut muffin. She would have preferred the *Sun-Times*. In point of fact, she really would have preferred a roll in the hay with William. But she'd take coffee, a muffin, and the *Wall Street Journal.*

By the time she had her order, all the tables were filled except one. A coffee mug and a copy of the *Enquirer* sat on the table, and a red wool scarf was draped over the back of the chair. The cup was still half full, so the person could be in the bathroom. Or they might have absentmindedly left all this here.

She glanced at a college-girl type sitting at the next table. "Do you think this person left?"

The girl stuck a finger in the crease of her book to mark her page. "You know, I thought I saw him go out the door. I'd take the table if I were you."

"Thanks. I think I will." Moving the cup and tabloid to the side, Amanda sat down with a sigh of pleasure. Someday she'd be financially secure, with a career she could be proud of, time to relax, and maybe even a man in her bed once in a while.

For a moment she imagined coming in here with William and the thought was definitely appealing. Too appealing. With a different sort of sigh, she opened the newspaper and began looking for an article that Gloria could use to shore up her nerd status.

This had to be Harvey's lucky day. He'd managed to go into the office and leave his valentine without anybody knowing. Dr. Tredway's door had been closed, and Harvey had stood outside it for a little while listening to the therapy session.

That had been kind of fun. He couldn't be sure without opening the door to look, but from the wheezing sounds he thought Dr. Tredway's clients were doing it right there in the office, maybe on the love seat or on the floor, or even propped up against the wall. Dr. Tredway had told him and Louise they could do that whenever the urge came upon them, and she'd be available to coach.

Harvey might have done it, except he hardly ever got the urge anymore with Louise. He had to really work up to it. If Dr. Tredway had said he could do Amanda in the office, that would be a whole different story. Maybe once he and Amanda got together, she'd have a key to Dr. Tredway's office and they could sneak in there at night to watch videos and play with the toys.

But now he had to get out of the office and out of the building before anybody saw him. If anybody did see him, he had an excuse. He'd say Louise asked him to stop by for a tube of flavored lubricant. But that would only work once, and he had more valentines to deliver.

Once he was on the street again, he breathed easier. The wind had picked up, though, and cold, wet snow flew into his face. Checking for traffic, he jaywalked over to Starbucks. Fortunately he looked in the window before walking in, or he could have been in deep shit. There was Amanda *sitting at his table.* What were the odds?

He couldn't go in there until she left. Zipping his jacket up to his neck, he shoved both hands into his jacket pockets. He could sure use the scarf right now, but he'd left it to hold his place. If anybody besides Amanda had taken his table, he'd march in there and tell them off. But Amanda could have his seat, no problem. He just hoped she wouldn't be in there too long.

To get out of the wind and avoid having her see him, he ducked into a recessed doorway. Standing still like this, he could feel his feet starting to get cold, so he stomped them to keep the heat going. He didn't know how the street people made it, living outside with nothing but cardboard and newspapers.

Some of them didn't. Without Louise's money, he could be looking at being a street person. Harvey reminded himself of that all the time.

After what seemed like three hours but

was only fifteen minutes according to his watch, Amanda stepped out on the sidewalk and jaywalked across the street just like he had. Two peas in a pod. He wished he had a camera hidden in her office that would take a picture of her face when she opened his card. He'd had to go to a special store to find it.

Once she'd crossed the street, he left the doorway where he'd been huddled and walked quickly into the warmth of Starbucks. His nose tingled from the change in temperature. His coffee was cold, but his seat was warm. As he sat there thinking about Amanda's ass planted right on the very same wooden chair where his was now, he got an erection.

Maybe she'd known he liked to sit there. Maybe she'd picked up his vibes, like they talked about in those woo-woo movies, and she'd been drawn to this chair by his sexual potency. He could believe that.

The person sitting at the next table spoke up. "I wasn't sure if you were coming back or not. I told someone she could sit there."

Harvey smiled at her. "That's fine. She's my girlfriend." He liked saying that. Amanda was the kind you could be proud of, not like Louise.

"Oh?" She looked as if she didn't believe it.

"I mean, she will be by next week. Right now I'm her secret valentine."

"Oh." She stared at him a moment longer. Then she picked up her stuff like she was in a big hurry, put on her coat and left Starbucks.

Amanda walked into the office as Gloria was bidding the Driscolls goodbye. The couple, both in their fifties and slightly overweight, looked flushed, but they were smiling. Amanda couldn't very well disapprove of a method that seemed to make people so happy. She set Gloria's latte and the newspaper on the desk and walked back to the coat rack to take off her jacket.

Once the Driscolls were gone, Gloria came over to pick up the latte. "You can cancel the Driscolls' appointment for next week." She popped the lid off the coffee. "I talked them into spending time at a Jamaican resort I like that has a nude beach."

That statement coming from Gloria was typical, but she'd never delivered a line like that while wearing a nerd costume. Amanda struggled not to laugh. "I hope you told them to wear lots of sunscreen."

"You know, I didn't mention that, but they

should be able to figure it out, don't you think?" She blew across the surface of the drink before taking a sip. "Although now that you mention it, I remember one guy down there who put it everywhere except on his tallywhacker. For the next three days he looked like an X-rated version of Rudolph. The peeling stage was pretty strange-looking, too, like a snake shedding its skin."

"Now there's a visual."

"Supposedly he was ready for sex by then, but his wife couldn't stop laughing long enough to participate." Gloria picked up the *Wall Street Journal.* "So are these the articles you think I should use for nerd bait?"

Amanda had circled two. "Take your pick. The problems inherent in leveraged buyouts or how natural disasters affect the prime interest rate."

"They sound so utterly fascinating that I'll never be able to choose." Gloria rolled her eyes.

"Believe it or not, they're both pretty interesting." Amanda had learned quite a bit during her Starbucks break, and if she ever had coffee with William, which she wouldn't, she'd ask him about both subjects.

"I'm not surprised they're interesting to you." Gloria handed her the paper. "Pick one and write me a short report. I have a free hour this afternoon and I'll drop by William's office then. I'll transition from discussing the article to us having dinner together tonight."

And if she succeeded in her goal, William wouldn't be quite so available to haul Justin out of Geekland, should another rescue be needed. The prudent side of Amanda hoped Justin had recovered from his grief, but the reckless side wanted William to show up at the bar looking the way he'd looked last night.

Gloria glanced at her watch. "Send the Irvings in when they arrive. I'll be in my office straightening up the furniture and wiping down the surfaces."

Amanda gulped. "All right." She should keep a journal about this internship and get it published as a memoir. Assuming anyone believed it, the thing could end up selling millions of copies.

"The Driscolls got a little wild, apparently due to my prim little nerd outfit. I never dreamed dressing against type would inspire my clients to be even naughtier than normal." Carrying her latte, Gloria walked into her office and closed the door.

Time to get some work done. Amanda settled into her desk chair and opened her bottom drawer to put away her purse. That was when she discovered a large heart-shaped sugar cookie frosted with cherry-colored frosting lying on a Starbucks napkin.

Had Will done this? She found it hard to believe. The guy she was coming to know wouldn't keep tucking things in her desk drawer and denying he was doing it, would he? She picked it up, napkin and all.

Good thing she'd had the muffin or she'd be tempted to eat the cookie, and no telling what was in it. About that time she noticed the pink envelope that had been lying under the napkin.

Checking to make sure Gloria's door was still closed, she took the envelope out. For a long time she gazed at her name printed in block letters on the back and tried to remember what William's printing had looked like on the fax. Without having it to compare, she couldn't tell if the two matched or not. Gloria had kept the fax.

Slowly she pulled the card out of the envelope. The front was a cartoon of a guy with his arms outstretched. The message below said, *Valentine, I have something special for you.*

She opened the card, which turned out to be the pop-up variety. But instead of roses or a heart, this one featured something different. What flipped up as the card unfolded was a pink, anatomically correct paper penis.

Eleven

When William picked up the phone, Amanda was the last person he expected to find on the other end of the line. He thought he'd permanently blown his chances by kissing her the night before.

He hated that, because awkward as the kiss had been, he'd loved every second. She might not have felt the chemistry, but he'd been bowled over by it. He'd thought of little else since then, and his mind was filled with schemes for making another kiss happen, a smoother, more seductive kiss.

If she was calling him, all might not be lost. "It's great to hear from you," he said. "I —"

"You asked me to lunch a couple of days ago." She sounded agitated.

"Yes, I did. But you said you didn't have time, and I respect that."

"I'm going to make the time. Can you meet me at noon?"

"Today?"

"Today."

"Sure!" He had no idea what had made her change her mind and if the kiss had something to do with it. Maybe it wasn't important why she had decided to go to lunch. "Is the Loaf and Leaves okay with you? It's across the street, about a block down on the right."

"I've seen it. I'll be there at noon."

"I'll go ten minutes earlier. That way Gloria won't be as likely to see us together."

"Oh. I hadn't thought of that. Okay."

Something was wrong. Otherwise she wouldn't have forgotten to be careful. "Anyway, I'm glad that you —" A click told him she'd hung up. "I'm glad you think this is a good idea," he said into dead air. "Your enthusiasm overwhelms me."

He replaced the receiver and stared into space for a good two minutes while he tried to figure out what this was all about. Only one thing made sense. The valentine jerk had struck again.

On impulse he dialed her number. When she answered, all he said was "Did you tear it up?"

"Not this time."

So it *was* the valentine. "Save it."

"Don't worry. I'm not only saving it, I'm

189

bringing it." Then she hung up again.

He took a deep breath. It must be some valentine.

To say the morning dragged after that would have been a gross understatement. He printed out a sample of his handwriting again on Cooper and Scott letterhead, folded the sheet of paper and tucked it in his suit jacket pocket. Then he made calls to clients, calls to prospective clients, more calls to prospective clients, and obsessively followed the stock market trends.

None of it took his mind off Amanda. Did she still believe he was sending those valentines? Because he knew he wasn't, he was getting worried about her. Maybe the sender was a clueless guy from Geekland or somebody she had a class with at DePaul.

William wanted to believe that the person was harmless, but his instincts told him otherwise. One secret valentine was harmless. Three secret valentines were more likely the sign of an unbalanced person who wasn't harmless at all.

At twenty minutes before noon, William left the office. He wanted to be at Loaf and Leaves ahead of the crowd so he could stake out a table in the back. No point in taking a chance that Gloria would walk by and see them through the front windows.

Loaf and Leaves was a trendy little place with small oak tables and chairs, lots of hanging plants, and a menu of salads, soups, and sandwiches served cafeteria-style. Most of the customers arrived after noon, so he had no trouble getting a table in the far corner away from the bank of windows along the front of the restaurant.

As he waited for Amanda, he became aware that he was breathing too fast. Sinking back in the chair, he drew in several deep breaths. Anyone would think he'd never had a lunch date before.

Well, he wouldn't have one now if Amanda hadn't received another valentine. He wondered what she'd do once he'd convinced her he wasn't the culprit. He'd love to help her find out who it was, but she might not let him do that. If he had even the slightest chance of helping her, he'd have to forget about that kiss and concentrate on the problem at hand. That wouldn't be easy.

The minute she pushed open the front door, he could feel the anxiety radiating from her. Her quilted jacket, which still had a coffee stain down the front, couldn't hide the rigid set of her body. Her full mouth, the one he longed to kiss all over again, was a slash of repressed emotion, and a deep frown had settled into the space between her eyebrows.

She marched over to him, pulled an envelope out of her purse and put it on the table. "If this is you, you are one sick puppy," she said. Then she pulled something else from her purse and put it down next to the envelope. "This came with the valentine."

It was a heart-shaped cookie from Starbucks. "Was it cracked when you got it?"

"No, I broke it when I dumped it back in my desk so Gloria wouldn't see it."

"Good thing you didn't eat it," he said. "It could be laced with something."

"I know. And as much as I hope it *is* you so I don't have to be scared, I'm even more afraid it isn't you."

"Maybe we should eat lunch while we talk about this."

"I'm not here to eat. I just want to know whether or not you sent this valentine, and then I'll be on my way. I have work to do. And if you didn't send this, then I probably should contact the cops."

He decided against mentioning how ineffective that would be. She wasn't even being threatened by this person, so it would be difficult to work up any interest among Chicago's finest.

"You don't think they'll care, do you?"

So she was able to read him. "No, I don't

think so. They have murders and drug lords to worry about."

"Then I'll . . . I'll think of something."

And he wanted desperately to help with that. "Let me take a look at what you got." He picked up the envelope. "And by the way, I brought a sample of my printing to compare with this." He opened the flap.

"Take it out under the table." She glanced around the restaurant as if making sure they hadn't been recognized.

Because they'd attracted a few curious stares, he did as she asked, although he thought that would only make them more conspicuous. He put the envelope in his lap, pulled the card out and read the greeting on the front. Then he opened it. And closed it very fast.

"Amanda, I'm sorry." Shoving the card into the envelope, he laid it on the table.

"Not as sorry as I am."

"I'm sure. I hate that you were subjected to that." He pulled the stationery out of his jacket pocket and spread it out on the table next to the card. "Please sit down. Let me prove once and for all that it isn't me."

Her gaze focused on the page where he'd printed her name, then swung to the envelope. Turning both the envelope and the Cooper and Scott stationery to face the chair opposite him, she sat down, but she didn't take off her coat.

"Those two things weren't written by the same person," he said.

"I'm not so sure." She leaned her arms on the table and scrutinized his sample and her name on the envelope.

"Yes you are. Mine is in black ink, which is the only color I like to use. That other one's in blue. I write in caps. I've done that ever since I escaped from the handwriting Nazis in elementary school. This guy, and I'm assuming it's a guy, writes in both upper and lower case."

She continued to stare at the two versions of her name. "The ink color and the upper and lower case could be on purpose, to fool me."

Although he admired her dogged determination to prove that she didn't have a stalker, clinging to that hope was getting in her way. "Then I'll demonstrate how I have to force myself to print in upper and lower case. You'll see how awkward it is for me." Reaching inside his jacket, he took out a pen.

"You could fake that, too."

He sighed. "Amanda, I think you're perceptive enough to be able to tell the difference if I'm doing it right in front of you."

194

She shoved the stationery across the table with some reluctance. "I guess it can't hurt anything."

"Thanks for giving me the chance to convince you." He leaned over the paper and concentrated on an unfamiliar way of writing. Twice he made a capital letter when he'd meant to write in lower case. He wrote both her name and the *Your Secret Valentine* signature that he thought was inside, although he wasn't about to open the card and double-check the wording.

When he was finished, he glanced up. "Did that look natural to you?"

She looked uncertain. "Not exactly, no."

"Are you willing to believe maybe I'm *not* the one sending these?"

"I'd like to compare your writing with the inside of the card."

He should have known it wouldn't be that easy. She could imagine herself dealing with him, but being forced to believe she was being stalked was a whole other thing. "How are you going to do that?" he asked.

"Not right here, obviously. Let me take them both into a bathroom stall." She pushed back her chair and stood. "If you're hungry, please go ahead and get something while I'm gone."

"I'll wait. Listen, why not leave your coat

and purse here?"

She shook her head. "If I decide you didn't send this after all, I won't be staying."

"That's when you *should* stay, so I can help you come up with a strategy."

She hesitated. "I'll be back soon." Then she turned and walked toward the hallway that led to the restrooms.

Frustrated with all this wasted time, he watched her go. But her stubbornness was an important part of her makeup and probably what had taken her this far. Without that stubborn streak, she wouldn't be the person who fascinated him so much.

Settling back in his chair, he prepared to wait. The food smelled good, and if she'd just hurry up and agree that he was innocent, they could enjoy a decent meal together. They could spend it strategizing a way for her to uncloak this weirdo. After seeing the pop-out penis, William was convinced they were dealing with a nutcase.

"I thought that was you sitting over here all by yourself! I have this fascinating article from the *Wall Street Journal* that I'm dying to discuss with you."

With a sense of impending doom, he glanced up to see Gloria heading in his direction. Except she looked very different.

She'd done something strange to her hair, and she was wearing glasses. Sure enough, a copy of the *Wall Street Journal* was tucked under her arm.

For one wild moment he wondered if she was wacko enough to send these valentines to her assistant as a joke. The way things were going, anything was possible.

Amanda sat on the toilet seat with the stall door closed and opened the pop-up card. Although it wasn't easy to ignore the wiggling penis, she did her best so that she could study the writing underneath it. Then she held up William's version of the same words.

Deep down, she'd known what she'd find. William had not been sending the valentines. In a way she was relieved to discover she hadn't been such a terrible judge of character. She was embarrassed that she'd falsely accused him, though. He deserved a huge apology. First she'd refused to go to lunch with him and now this.

Embarrassment wasn't the only emotion she was dealing with, either. Uneasiness, even a touch of fear, was edging out embarrassment. If William hadn't sent the valentines, then someone else had. Whoever would leave a pop-up penis card in her desk drawer was not the sort of person she cared to meet . . . ever.

Tucking both the card and the folded stationery in her purse, she left the bathroom. She was so busy preparing her words of apology that she almost missed seeing Gloria sitting in her seat at the table. She and William both had food in front of them and the *Wall Street Journal* on the table between them. Fortunately, Gloria had her back to the hallway leading to the restrooms.

William saw Amanda, though. He'd probably been watching for her. His gaze flicked up and flashed a warning before he returned to his conversation with Gloria. Her stomach rumbling with hunger, Amanda edged toward the front of the restaurant while keeping her attention on the table in the back.

When she'd reached the door, she decided that she wasn't leaving without food. All she had to do was pretend to be coming in instead of going out and she could join William and Gloria for lunch. Yes, it would be a nauseating experience, but as famished as she was, she could handle it.

At least she hoped so. Gloria was working her nerd schtick to the max. She kept adjusting her glasses and fooling with the pencil stuck in her bun. Every once in a while, she'd reach over and touch William's arm as if to help make a point.

That touching ploy irritated Amanda more than a little. If anybody should be touching William, it was her, not Gloria. No, that was wrong. Amanda had no business touching him, either. She just didn't want Gloria doing it.

Smiling broadly, she approached the table. "Hi, there, you two! May I join you for lunch?"

William blinked, but to his credit he handled her move with admirable grace. "Sure thing. I'll get you a chair."

Gloria wasn't quite so welcoming. "Considering your schedule, do you really have the time? I believe you have some client billing to take care of." Her tone clearly said *Don't butt in.*

"I need to take the time. I didn't get breakfast and I've been surviving the day on a Starbucks muffin."

"Well, in that case." Gloria didn't look very happy, but she wasn't enough of a witch to deny Amanda food if she was hungry. "William and I were just discussing an amazing article on the prime interest rate. I don't suppose you get a chance to read the *Wall Street Journal*." Her glance told Amanda she'd better pretend ignorance.

"I don't read it much. Just happened to see it today, though, and I'd love to talk about the prime interest rate." Maybe she imagined it, but she could have sworn Gloria made a little snarling sound. Amanda sat in the chair William brought over and smiled at him. "Thanks."

The smile seemed to take him by surprise, and he flushed just the slightest bit. "Anytime."

That flush was very endearing. Now that she knew he wasn't her valentine stalker and he'd abandoned the hat with the earflaps, she was running out of reasons not to like him. And then there was the kiss, too brief yet full of potential.

On top of that, her list of reasons to like him was growing exponentially. He'd handled her suspicions about him with good cheer. He was loyal to his friend. He was discriminating enough not to fall for Gloria's obvious come-ons.

And then there was the matter of his thumbs, which were large and capable looking. Amanda wasn't the kind of shallow woman who insisted a man be huge in that department, but then again, all other factors being equal, it didn't hurt, either. And with Gloria constantly turning her thoughts to libido issues, Amanda admitted to being highly curious about the thumbs theory, especially after the previous night's liplock in the hallway.

Or maybe this sudden obsession was only a function of being hungry. Food might satisfy the sexual curiosity she felt every time she looked at William. She hoped so, because food was a lot less trouble.

"If you'll excuse me, I'll get something to eat," she said.

"Yes, do that," Gloria said. "And let the waitress know I need another cup of coffee."

"I will." Amanda thought the order had been given to remind her of her place. Gloria was the one in charge here.

Amanda couldn't deny it. She needed Gloria's blessing and good intern evaluation in order to graduate, and if that meant standing by while Gloria put the moves on William, she'd have to do exactly that. In the meantime, she'd love to hear William's opinion about the rise and fall of the prime rate. Someday she intended to have money to invest, and she'd worked too hard to fritter it away out of ignorance.

But when she returned to the table with a turkey sandwich and a Caesar salad, she could see that rational discussion of the prime rate might not be possible. You could put nerd clothes on Gloria all day long, and she'd still be focused on her topic of choice.

"So, in essence," Gloria said, "the prime rate *expands* due to external *stimulation.*"

Amanda glanced at William and choked back a laugh. He had a trapped-animal look.

"I suppose that's accurate." He took a huge bite of his sandwich, as if eager to finish it and leave.

"So then, as the prime thrusts upward, the economy experiences friction." Gloria toyed with a button on the bodice of her shirtwaist, slipping it back and forth through the buttonhole.

Amanda didn't dare meet William's gaze or she'd lose it. "Interesting way of describing financial change," she said.

"Yes, well, I'm trying to put the concepts into terms that I understand. So continuing along those lines, I'd guess the friction caused by the rising prime could be pleasurable for those who know how to respond." She pinned William with a hot stare. "Would you agree?"

He nodded and took another big bite, chewing vigorously.

Gloria leaned forward. "I never realized that economics could be so exciting." Her voice lowered to a soft purr. "Do you find it exciting, too?"

William swallowed, coughed, and adjusted his tie. "I, uh, suppose I do." He glanced at Amanda as if looking for a lifeline. "By the way, I've had that turkey sandwich you ordered. It's really good. The Reuben is good, too, if you ever —"

"William." Gloria drew out his name, accenting the *yum* at the end.

With obvious reluctance, he brought his attention back to his client. "Yes, Gloria?"

"I'm so open to an investment right now. Right this very minute. Can you manipulate my portfolio and make it happen?"

"Uh, sure." He grabbed his coffee and drained the cup. "I need to get back to the office. Once I'm there, I'll take a look at your holdings and see what sort of liquidity you have and what sort of assets you have available." Then he squeezed his eyes shut. "What I meant to say is —"

"I know exactly what you meant to say. And let me assure you that when I focus on that rising prime, I perceive my assets as extremely liquid and exceedingly available."

"Right." He pushed back his chair and stood. Then he put some bills on the table for the tip. "I do have to leave. Enjoy the rest of your lunch."

"Actually, I'm finished." Gloria stood and grabbed her mink coat off the back of her chair. "I'll walk back with you."

Amanda hated to leave William to joust with Gloria by himself. "I should probably leave, too," she said.

"Sit, sit," Gloria said. "Enjoy your salad and sandwich. You work too hard." She turned to William. "Shall we?"

He hesitated as if he didn't dare answer such an open-ended invitation.

Seeing how nervous he was about walking back to the office with Gloria, Amanda made up her mind. William had been a friend to her, and he deserved a friendly gesture in return.

She quickly folded the remains of her sandwich into her napkin and got up. "I have tons to do at the office," she said. "I'm coming back with you."

Gloria rolled her eyes. "I shouldn't be surprised. You're such a workaholic. Let's go, then."

As Gloria headed out of the restaurant, William hung back. "Thanks," he murmured. "I owe you one."

"Nah. We're even. And for the record, I know you're not the valentine guy."

His shoulders dropped in obvious relief. "That's good, but we need to talk about who is."

She shook her head. "Not your problem."

"But —"

"No, seriously. Now get moving, before she thinks something's going on between us."

He looked her straight in the eye. "You know what? Something is." Then he turned and followed Gloria out of the restaurant.

TWELVE

Maybe he shouldn't have said that. William worried about his impulsive comment all the way back to the office. He walked along between the two women, with Gloria on one side chattering about dinner plans, which he deflected as best he could, and Amanda on the other side being very, very quiet.

She'd looked shocked when he'd made that statement to her, but it was true, damn it. She might not want a boyfriend, and he wasn't elevating himself to that position, but she needed someone to help her figure this thing out with the valentine stalker. He was prepared to be that someone, and that fit, because he was the only person who had all the background, being the first suspect in the case.

As he left both women at the door of Gloria's office, Gloria continued to badger him about going to dinner with her while Amanda unlocked the door and went inside.

Any hope he'd had for another moment alone with Amanda was crushed as she walked into the office with a little wave of goodbye.

"If you're not available for dinner tonight," Gloria said, "then I claim tomorrow night. I know this cozy little French bistro not far from my apartment. That way, after dinner we can go back to my place and relax."

He didn't think any male could ever relax in Gloria's presence. "Gloria, I have to level with you."

"By all means!"

"I don't believe in dating clients, but —"

"Then I'll go back to the old fart I was with before. See, problem solved." She beamed at him.

"I was going to say, I can't afford to lose any clients at this stage in my career." Warmed by the heat in the hallway, he unbuttoned his overcoat.

"And I enjoy giving you my business." She moistened her lips. "Couldn't you make an exception in my case?"

"I'm afraid not."

"I'm not asking you for a lifetime commitment. Strictly fun and games." She reached over and fingered the lapel of his coat. "You do know how to have fun, don't you, William?"

Shit. If he gave her up as a client, she'd think he was doing it so he could go to bed with her. "You're putting me in an awkward position."

"I'd love to put you in a comfortable position. A stimulating and enjoyable position. I know several."

He sighed. There was no way he could win this one.

"Oh, dear. I can see you have strong moral issues. I think we can get around those, eventually, but I'll have to give you a little more time. I'll stop pushing." She winked at him. "For now."

"I appreciate that. I'll let you know later this afternoon what investments I recommend."

"Will you be delivering those recommendations personally?"

"I think a phone call is wiser."

"But sometimes a person needs to be foolish. I could give you a really, really good time." Without warning she reached between the lapels of his coat and palmed his crotch.

Muttering a curse, he leaped back.

"It's such a shame to let that wonderful equipment go to waste, William." Smiling, she turned and walked through her office door.

As he walked quickly to his own office, sweat trickled past the earpiece of his glasses. If he'd been more of a ladies' man in school, he might have the skills to handle this. Other guys, the more popular ones, had talked about aggressive women, but he'd never experienced one firsthand.

He hadn't been the type that attracted them, apparently. Until now. To think he used to envy those Romeos who had girls swarming all over them. If this is how they'd felt, harassed and valued only for their penises, then he didn't envy them anymore.

Amanda talked Gloria into letting her go home early, but only after agreeing to finish the billing at home. But although Gloria saddled her with more work, she also made Amanda promise to take a vibrator with her and use it to relax. Perversely, she picked the red one, tucked it in her backpack and headed off to the bus stop. Whenever someone looked at her on the way home, she imagined they'd noticed the telltale outline of the vibrator inside her nylon backpack.

But carrying home extra work and a vibrator so that she could duck out early was better than leaving on time and running the risk of meeting William on the way out. She couldn't forget the spark in his green eyes when he'd told her something was going on between them. The look he'd given her had made her knees wobble.

Wobbly knees meant that he was right, and she needed to nip this attraction in the bud right now. The easiest tactic was avoiding any situation where she might run into him. Then, if she did encounter him, she would be polite but distant.

Too bad Chicago seemed to be going bonkers over Valentine's Day, with every bit of lace and sentiment reminding her of William. No place was more bonkers than her floor of the apartment building. She ran the gauntlet of decorated doors and arrived at her own, which was now decorated with lace hearts and two almost-naked cupids, arrows at the ready.

Before this year, Valentine's Day hadn't held any special significance other than the obvious emphasis on love. Her unwise yearning for William, added to the threat of a stalker who was sending her objectionable cards, made her wish all the hearts and cupids would disappear. She thought of taking down the ones on her door, but couldn't bring herself to do it. That would break Mavis's heart.

And speaking of Mavis, here she came, right on schedule. She was wearing oven mitts and holding something with a foil top.

"I saw you coming from the bus stop, but you're an hour early! Is everything okay?"

"Just fine." Amanda unlocked her door and walked in. "Dr. Tredway let me leave at four today."

Mavis followed her in and closed the door behind her, as if they were roomies. "Good. You need a break. And now you have time to eat the chicken alfredo I made for you."

"Mavis, you really don't have to feed me." And because Mavis wasn't much of a cook, Amanda would rather grab something at Geekland.

"I enjoy it. Besides, I'm practicing with my new microwave. I think this is a little overdone, so if it is, just say so and I'll nuke you another one. Say, what's that red pointy thing sticking out of your backpack?"

Damn. Amanda took off her backpack, and sure enough, all the jostling on the bus had caused the vibrator to shift and poke through the zippered opening. No wonder people had been staring.

She shoved it back inside and cast around madly for an explanation. She felt like she was trapped in the Steve Martin movie *Parenthood.* "It's . . . a battery-operated curling iron."

"Can I see? I've been thinking I needed to

211

do something different with my hair."

"The batteries are dead."

"Then let me get you some! I have a whole drawerful of batteries. What size does it take?"

The doorbell rang, and Amanda would love to think she'd been saved by the bell, but somehow she doubted it. "Let me get that."

"Go ahead, but be sure to check the peephole. There are some wackos out there."

Didn't she know it. At least her particular wacko hadn't contacted her here, so she felt reasonably safe in the apartment building.

"I'll get you a napkin and fork so you can start eating this before it gets cold," Mavis said.

"Thanks, Mavis." Amanda checked the peephole and wasn't surprised to see Chester standing there. He was holding something in a cellophane package. She opened the door.

"I saw you come home early, and I decided you need to put some meat on your bones." Chester shoved a package at her. "Here's Ding-Dongs."

"Why, thanks. You didn't have to do that."

"No problem. With my coupon, these were practically free. Don't pay any attention to that expiration date. They only put that on there to make people think you have to buy right away. Those Ding-Dongs will be good until next Christmas." As he talked he kept glancing over her shoulder.

"Thanks for the Ding-Dongs, Chester." Amanda suspected she'd turned into an unknowing matchmaker. By befriending Amanda, Chester could have contact with Mavis and not seem to be seeking her out. Amanda took pity on him. "Would you like to come in for a minute?"

"Don't mind if I do. I half expected that Mavis woman to be over here, pestering you."

"She brought me a chicken alfredo."

"In that case, I should make myself scarce. She'll only start in about the door decorations if I give her the chance." But instead of leaving, Chester remained where he was. He was obviously dying to spar with Mavis again.

Amanda thought it was funny, but sweet, too. She was happy to help out. "Why don't you come in, anyway? I don't get home early very often. It gives us all a chance to talk."

"Maybe for a minute. But if she starts in on me, I'm outta here."

"I understand completely." As she stepped

back to let Chester in, she heard a buzzing sound.

"These batteries are fine," Mavis said, "but I can't figure out how you curl your hair with this contraption."

Turning, Amanda discovered Mavis trying to wrap a section of her red hair around the humming red vibrator.

Chester made a weird choking sound, and when she glanced at him, his face was the color of the vibrator and his shoulders were quivering.

Laying the Ding-Dongs on the table next to the chicken alfredo, Amanda turned to Chester. She had to clear her throat a couple of times before she could speak. "Could you excuse Mavis and me for a minute?"

Eyes brimming, he nodded.

"I just don't get it," Mavis said. "Must be a new salon technique, and I never bother with salons."

"Come on in my bedroom," Amanda said. "I'll explain how it works." She wondered if this was how parents felt when they had to discuss the facts of life with a kid. She didn't feel at all prepared to educate a seventy-two-year-old woman about sex toys, but it looked as if the job had fallen to her.

"That's okay." Mavis shut off the vibrator

and laid it on the table. "You can show me later. Eat your food before it's stone-cold."

"But —" She peeked at Chester to see how he was holding up. He seemed to have gained some control of himself. She lifted her eyebrows, and he shrugged in response. With a little sigh of resignation, she sat down at the table and tried to avoid looking at the vibrator.

Chester sat across from her, and Mavis sat to her left. "Wait," Mavis said. "You don't have anything to drink."

"That's okay." Amanda peeled back the foil and stabbed at the crusty food with her fork. No doubt it would taste like packing peanuts, but she wanted to make the chicken alfredo all gone as quickly as possible. She'd never eaten a meal with a vibrator lying six inches from her plate, and she found it disconcerting.

"No, you need something. Milk." Mavis got up and hurried into the kitchen.

Chester gazed after her and shook his head. "Clueless," he murmured.

"It's cute, in a way."

For a change, Chester didn't leap in with some disparaging remark. "She could get herself in trouble someday."

Amanda recognized an opening when she heard it. "Maybe she needs someone around to keep that from happening."

Chester reared back in his seat. "Don't look at me."

"Oh, I didn't mean you." They both knew she meant exactly him, but he couldn't admit that yet.

"Here you go, a nice big glass of milk." Mavis reappeared and set the glass next to Amanda's dried-out microwave meal. Then she picked up the package of Ding-Dongs. "Chester Ambrose, you should be ashamed of yourself. These Ding-Dongs expired on October tenth."

"They're perfectly good."

"Not for Amanda, they're not." Mavis shoved the package across the table at him. "You eat 'em if you want. I doubt you have taste buds, anyway."

"At least I know what a hair curler is supposed to look like."

Amanda ate faster.

"How would you know?" Mavis gave him a scornful glance. "You don't have any hair."

"I don't have hair because I'm highly sexed."

"You? Ha!"

Shoveling the last of the petrified meal down her throat, Amanda washed it down with milk. She hadn't realized matchmaking could be so perilous.

"It's a fact," Chester said. "Men with higher levels of testosterone lose their hair faster."

"And what's that good for? You can't even be bothered to decorate your front door."

"Oh, it's good for something." Chester waggled his eyebrows.

Amanda decided that was about all the geriatric flirting she could handle at the moment. She slid her chair back. "That was great! Now I really need to change clothes."

"You need a Ding-Dong." Chester pushed the package toward her.

"Don't eat those." Mavis grabbed the package. "You could get ptomaine poisoning."

"It's a good thing you taught third grade and not high school science," Chester said. "Those there are carbs. You get ptomaine from putrefied protein."

"Well, la-de-da." Mavis fluffed her hair. "Maybe a person would get some other kind of poisoning, then. They put those dates on things for a reason, you know."

Chester looked wounded. "She won't get poisoned. I wouldn't give her something that would make her sick."

Amanda ripped open the package. "I'm sure they're fine." She took a bite of a very stale Ding-Dong and smiled. "Delicious."

"If you feel sick later, it's all his fault."

Chester leaned toward Mavis. "Listen, woman, I'm not taking any more from you." He picked up the vibrator and waved it in her direction. "And this is *not* a curling iron."

"Is so. Amanda said it was."

"She was trying to protect you."

"From what?"

Amanda swallowed the last of the Ding-Dong. "Mavis, I'm sorry. It isn't a curling iron. It's a vibrator."

Mavis's eyes widened and her cheeks turned pink. "You mean one of those gizmos you use for sex?" Her voice rose to a squeak.

"Yes, and before you start thinking I'm the kind of girl who carries vibrators around all the time, let me explain why I have it." And she proceeded to fill them in on the secret valentine deliveries, William, and her reasons for coming home early today.

"But this William sounds so nice!" Mavis looked upset. "If he's a nice man, you should spend some time with him. You could use a nice man."

"Someday. Not now. I can't afford to get sidetracked."

Chester waved a hand. "You do what you have to in that regard. What concerns me is this valentine nut. I don't like the sound of it."

"I'm not crazy about the situation, myself."

"But he only leaves these things at your office?" Chester gazed at her intently.

"So far."

"Then maybe he doesn't know where you live."

Mavis shuddered. "I hope he doesn't know that. What you need is a dog. Except we're not allowed to have pets. I always thought we should be able to have pets, and I would have moved to a place that allows pets, but I've made so many friends here that I hate to leave. I think a dog would —"

"Mavis, you're drifting from the point," Chester said. "And that point is that we need to keep a closer eye on Amanda from now on."

Amanda couldn't imagine either of them keeping a closer eye than they were already doing. She could barely make a move without one or both noticing. From that standpoint, they were probably better protection than a dog.

"I understand we need to keep a closer eye on her, Chester. I just wish we could have pets. Maybe I'll get up a petition."

"That's a fine idea," Chester said.

Mavis and Amanda both stared at him. He'd never approved of anything Mavis proposed.

"Don't look so amazed," he said. "If you get on a kick about allowing pets in the building, you won't have time to hassle me about my blessed door."

"I don't hassle you! I've merely suggested that —"

"I'm going to change clothes," Amanda said. "And I'll get this thing out of sight." She reached for the vibrator.

"Wait." Mavis glanced at it with poorly disguised curiosity. "I've never seen one up close."

"You have so," Chester said. "You just tried to use it to curl your hair."

"That wasn't my fault."

"No, it was mine," Amanda said. "I should have told you the truth right away, but I was afraid I'd shock you."

"I have an open mind." Mavis gazed at the vibrator. "I'd like to look at it again."

"That's my exit cue," Chester said. "When women start playing with vibrators, it's time for me to vamoose."

"I didn't say I would play with it, Chester Ambrose! I just want to look. There's no crime in looking, is there?"

"Looking can lead to other things, and

220

I'm not sticking around to find out if it does or not. For the record, I believe in old-fashioned sex." With that, he left in a swirl of male indignation.

Mavis watched the door close behind him. "You wouldn't think a man like Chester would be spooked by a little old vibrator."

Feeling a little Gloria-esque, Amanda gestured toward the red wand in Mavis's hand. "Would you . . . uh . . . like to borrow it?"

Mavis smiled at her. "I thought you'd never ask."

THIRTEEN

William decided he wouldn't sleep tonight if he didn't go to Geekland and talk to Amanda about her problem. He knew so little about her — whether she had a roommate, a Doberman, or a triple lock on her door. Maybe the valentine guy wouldn't track her down to where she lived, but that wasn't at all certain.

She'd made it clear that she didn't want his help. He could accept that more easily if he knew she had some protective measures already in place. For all he knew she was a martial arts expert who could take him down in three seconds flat. If she could reassure him that she wasn't as vulnerable as she seemed, he'd back off.

Then he walked into Geekland and saw her behind the counter consulting her Barmaster, her fake glasses sliding down her nose and her hair in those two adorable pigtails, and he didn't want to back off. She was so . . . plucky.

Take for example the way she'd handled lunch. Instead of slinking out the door when she'd spotted Gloria at the table, she'd pretended to be arriving and eager to share a table. She'd tried to help him out with his overenthusiastic client, and he was grateful.

But his feelings were going far beyond gratitude lately. Why couldn't Amanda be hot for his body? Why did her boss have to be the one angling to get him naked? Sometimes he caught hints that Amanda wasn't completely indifferent to him. She'd responded to that kiss they'd shared. And now, when she glanced up from the drink she was concocting, her first unguarded response was to smile.

She quickly changed her expression, though, masking any apparent pleasure with a blank stare. He took heart from her first reaction and ignored her second one as he walked over and took a stool right in front of her.

"Be with you in a minute." She didn't look up from the layered drink she was concocting.

"What is that?" Her technique with the bar spoon fascinated him. Oh, hell, it wasn't only that, it was every little move she made. She radiated competence, and he found that extremely sexy.

"It's called a Raging Bull."

That sounded like a macho drink to him, and he could probably do with some macho. A man who ordered something called a Raging Bull would drink hard and love hard. That should counterbalance his image as a boring stockbroker.

"I'll take one." He should probably find out what was in it first, but if he asked that, it would destroy the bar-savvy image he was going for.

She glanced up, then back down again. "Okay."

He'd caught the beginnings of another smile. "What? You don't think I'm the Raging Bull type?"

"I didn't say that."

"Good, because I'm all about Raging Bulls."

"Uh-huh." She finished fixing the drink and took it down to a customer on the end, a burly guy who was deep into the trivia game on the television screen above his head.

He looked like a truck driver, but here he was at Geekland playing trivia with a vengeance. As he picked up his drink in one beefy hand, William decided maybe geeks came in all shapes and sizes. He still wouldn't classify himself as one, but the category was broader than he'd thought.

Amanda returned to stand in front of him. "Do you know what's in a Raging Bull?"

"All the good stuff."

She arched her eyebrows.

Well, if she wasn't buying the hard-drinking, hard-loving image, he'd try a different approach. "If you let me borrow your Barmaster I'll tell you."

That little smile flashed again, but then she turned serious on him. "I'll just tell you. Kahlúa, sambuca, and tequila."

"What's a sambuca?"

"Licorice-flavored liqueur. In other words, this drink is all booze, sort of like the Bahama Mama Justin had last night, the one that made him drunk enough that I had to call you."

"Yes, but that was on top of a truckload of other drinks. This is my first of the night. I think I can handle it."

She gazed at him. "Did you come here to drink?"

"No, I came here to talk to you. But it wouldn't be fair to you or Geekland for me to sit here with nothing but a glass of water. A Raging Bull sounds about right."

She held his gaze a little longer. Then she concentrated on making his drink. "Since you want to talk, let me tell you a story."

"I'm listening."

"Once upon a time there was a smart girl who fell head over heels for a guy and focused entirely on him. When he died at a fairly young age, she had no money, no career, nothing to live for. Not long afterward, she died, too."

His chest tightened. "Sad story."

"My mother's story."

"I'm sorry."

She glanced up. "I just want you to know that nothing, and I mean *nothing,* is coming between me and my goal. I intend to graduate with honors and a glowing recommendation from Gloria. Then I'll head to Harvard for my postgrad work. Someday I'll have an office and clients, just like she does."

"You will?" He had a tough time picturing her in leopard-print jumpsuits and a cabinet full of sex toys.

"Okay, not *just* like she does. She's nuts."

"Justin's ready to take her on."

"Uh-oh. Is that what you wanted to talk about?"

"Not really. But I thought I'd warn you, in case he shows up there. Maybe you could talk him out of pursuing that course of action."

She layered what looked like the licorice stuff on top of the Kahlúa. "Are you sure that's such a bad idea?"

"It's a terrible idea. He's not that sexually experienced. He'd be in way over his head with a woman like Gloria. You just said yourself that she's nuts."

"She is, but she's a therapist, too, and believe it or not, she has some very satisfied clients." She topped off his drink with tequila. "She might take Justin's mind off his problems."

"That's assuming she'd be interested. If she rejected him, I don't think he could take it right now."

"She wouldn't reject him. After he left the office the other day, she said if she didn't already have her . . . um . . . that is, if you weren't in the picture, she'd consider —"

"Back up a minute. Exactly how did she refer to me?" He imagined all sorts of labels a woman like Gloria would use. *Boy toy. Studmuffin. Love slave.*

"Never mind."

"Come on, Amanda. I deserve to know how she talks about me behind my back."

"Promise you won't get mad?"

"I promise."

"Geek of the Week." She set his drink quickly on a cocktail napkin. "Excuse me.

227

Tina needs an order filled."

Geek of the Week. That hat with the earflaps had done more damage than he'd thought. If Gloria knew him better, then she'd . . . wait a minute. Justin thought William was a geek, too. He'd said that William would fit into the Geekland atmosphere just fine.

And, damn it, he did like it here, but that was only because Amanda was the bartender. Without her he wouldn't be attracted to the place at all. Or maybe a little bit. Playing trivia was kind of cool because the people who came here presented a competitive challenge. He also got a kick out of the inventive drinks, and the clear acrylic bar and the neon sculptures on the wall.

But that didn't make him a geek. Grabbing the glass in front of him, he took a big gulp and got a mouthful of straight tequila. His eyes watered, but he swallowed it, by God. He didn't cough and choke, either.

Sneaking a glance down the bar, he tried to tell if the truck-driver type had taken his Raging Bull as it was served or if he'd mixed it before drinking. Just his luck, the glass was already empty, giving him no clue as to the manly way to approach this drink. Fortunately the very act of tipping it had stirred up the contents some, so his next sip, and he did take only a sip this time, went down easier.

He should have ordered a beer. A beer was uncomplicated, but it had a solid, non-nerd sound to it, especially if you stuck to the domestic brands that used promotion images like rearing stallions and men in hard hats. William had never worried about things like that before, but no one had ever called him their "Geek of the Week" before, either. Time for an image makeover. He took another sip of his Raging Bull.

Amanda seemed to be avoiding him, probably because she didn't want to discuss his Geek of the Week status. So he grabbed a keyboard so he could play trivia. The first step was choosing a screen name.

The liquor hadn't made him drunk by any means, but it had made him loose. The last time he'd played here with Justin he'd used his initials. This time he typed in DOW DUDE. He liked it. A screen name with attitude.

Because he soon was kicking serious butt at trivia, he attracted a small crowd. Some wanted to compete, although he annihilated all comers. Some wanted to cheer. A skinny woman in a *Star Trek* T-shirt bought him another Raging Bull.

Every once in a while he'd scan the bar area for Amanda. A couple of times he caught her looking back at him. He still needed to talk to her and tell her his big idea about foiling the valentine stalker, but it could wait. At the moment he was busy showing off. If he was a Geek of the Week, he would be the best damned Geek of the Week she'd ever seen.

"Hey, Dow Dude," said the woman in the *Star Trek* shirt. "What's your real name?"

William didn't have to think very hard. "It's Will," he said. "Will Sloan."

Normally, Amanda was extremely efficient at her job. Not tonight. She confused drink orders and spilled things, all because she couldn't concentrate on what she was doing. Bartending wasn't nearly as interesting as watching William draw in the crowd.

He was easily the best trivia player Geekland had ever seen, and in this bar, that counted for a bunch. William happily rode the wave of popularity, laughing in triumph as he racked up an unbelievable number of points.

The category didn't seem to matter. He knew everything. Sometime around eleven-thirty, Geekland moved into first place in the country on the master trivia board, mostly thanks to William. The crowd went wild.

Amanda didn't want to be impressed, but brains had always had a seductive power over her. Add to that the animation in William's expression and the flash of white teeth every time he smiled, and she couldn't seem to look anywhere but at him. He was having the time of his life and she felt . . . left out.

The man who had been interested in her was suddenly the object of interest from several other women. One had even bought him a drink. The attention William was getting now was different from Gloria's all-out assault. William hadn't wanted Gloria's brand of aggressive sexuality, but he might be delighted to go home with one of the nerds hanging around his neck watching him ace each trivia question.

That shouldn't matter a flying fig to Amanda. It did, though. No matter how she talked to herself, she hated that William was enjoying himself with other people, specifically other *women,* and seemed to have forgotten that she existed.

Maybe he'd accept another Raging Bull from the woman in the *Star Trek* T-shirt. That could easily put him in the mood to go home with her after the bar closed. Amanda braced herself for another order to come through and was surprised when it didn't.

As the hands on the bar clock edged toward closing time, she tried not to think about what would happen after that. She would go home alone, as usual, and William would most likely not. He had at least three choices, and why wouldn't he pick one? A good trivia player was catnip to the women who gathered at Geekland. Like Amanda, they were turned on by brains.

She raised her voice, as she did every night at this time. "Last call!" That would probably bring the drink-buying woman over for one more Raging Bull to clinch the deal with William. Amanda had a last-minute flurry of orders, but none of them involved Kahlúa, sambuco, and tequila.

Then she happened to notice William's hand in the air, motioning her over.

She kept her tone businesslike. "What can I get you?"

"A glass of water, please."

"Aw, Will!" said the *Star Trek* woman. "One more for the road, baby!"

"Thanks, but I'm switching to water."

"Bummer." The woman's shoulders slumped, as if she knew the switch to water meant the evening might not end as she'd hoped.

Amanda added a wedge of lemon to the water before bringing it to him. She told herself she'd do that for any customer, but it wasn't true. She saved those touches for the people she liked. And she very much liked William. Or was it Will, now?

She set the water on a cocktail napkin.

"Thanks." He shoved a tip across the bar.

"Not necessary." She shoved it back. Tips helped her survive financially, but sometimes it felt good to pretend she didn't need to take the money. Tonight with William was one of those times.

"I still need to talk with you," he said. "It's important."

She tried not to feel gratified by that and failed. The other women hadn't won him over, after all. "We're getting ready to close."

"Then I'll walk you out."

"Okay." Then as she totaled her receipts, she eavesdropped shamelessly as each of the women who'd clustered around him during the evening made a bid for spending more time with him, extending invitations for coffee, hot chocolate, a nightcap at their place.

William was gentle, but he turned each one down. Gradually the crowd thinned. By the time the cleanup crew started stacking chairs on tables, Will was the only customer left.

Amanda grabbed her coat and purse from behind the bar. "Ready? My bus will be here in ten minutes."

"Then let's go." William walked over to the coat rack on the wall beside the front door. After helping her with her coat, he held the door for her as they stepped into the night. The breeze came from the land tonight instead of blowing in from the lake, so the temperature wasn't nearly as breath-stealing as it had been the past few evenings.

"Nice night," William said.

"Not bad." Amanda decided William was in tune with Chicago weather if he thought a temperature hovering around freezing was *nice.* Or maybe he wasn't talking about the weather. Maybe he was referring to his trivia-playing triumph.

"You really knocked 'em dead at Geek-land." She started walking toward the bus stop.

He fell into step beside her. "My mind is crammed with useless facts. I can't seem to help myself. I read or hear some silly bit of information and it sticks."

"You should go on a TV quiz show."

"Nah. That would freak me out. Listen, I've been thinking about your valentine guy.

What kind of personal safety measures do you have in place?"

It was an unsettling question, one that made her think of things she'd rather not. "Like what?"

"Do you know any self-defense tactics?"

"Not exactly. A kick to the groin is about all I know to do."

"That's something." He paused as they reached the corner where the bus stop shelter stood. "How about security where you live?"

"The person's never contacted me there. I'm not worried about it." The street was deserted, as it often was when she waited for the bus after work. Usually she didn't think about it, but tonight she was glad to have William there, even if he was scaring her a little with the direction of the conversation.

"But you have dead bolts?"

She turned to face him. "Sure." And now she was ready to change the topic.

"A roommate?"

"No." She thought of Mavis and Chester. "But I have a couple of nosy neighbors. One's a retired schoolteacher and the other is retired from the railroad, I think. They don't miss a trick."

"Too bad one's not a retired cop."

A car cruised by and she shivered. But it was just a car, not somebody trying to abduct her. She needed to get a grip. "It's probably not as big a problem as I've made of it. I may have overreacted. I'm sure it's someone I know playing a practical joke."

"Maybe."

"You're not helping calm me down, William. Or is it Will, now?"

"Will is fine. And I'm not trying to calm you down." His breath frosted in the cold air. "I don't think you should treat this lightly."

"Why not? It's only cards and a cookie. It's not like anybody's threatened me or anything." That was true. If she concentrated on that fact, maybe she could convince herself that whoever was delivering the valentines was some practical jokester.

"You could be right. I'd like to agree with you, which would make us both feel comfy about it."

"Then agree with me, and we can talk about something else. Whatever happened to your hat with the earflaps?"

"I retired it."

She studied him in the light from a nearby street lamp. "Your ears look a little red. Are they sensitive to the cold?"

"A little. I'm used to it."

She didn't think so. She thought he'd abandoned the hat because he didn't want to wear it in front of her. "You should take care of your ears."

"No big deal."

So that topic was closed. She grabbed another. "What did you think of those Raging Bulls?"

"Not too bad, once you mix everything together. Amanda, please don't ignore this valentine stuff. Speaking from a guy's perspective, I'm sure it isn't normal, not even as a joke." The streetlight brought out the angles in his face, making him look rugged and intense. Sexy.

She resisted the urge to move closer to him. "What if it's not a guy? What if it's Gloria?"

"I thought of that, too. I can't believe it's her. She's too self-absorbed to go to all that trouble."

Amanda had to agree. "Okay, so it's not Gloria."

"I think the problem is that you seem available."

"Me?" She laughed. "I'm the least available person in the world. I'm either working or going to school. I never stand still."

"I mean that you don't have a guy around. You're unattached." He coughed into his fist. "That kind of available."

"Oh." She had an uneasy feeling where this conversation was headed. It wouldn't be so bad, except that the longer she stood here, the more inclined she was to weave sexual fantasies about William. Or rather, *Will.*

The puffs of condensed air when he spoke made her aware of his mouth, and what it would be like if she kissed him, if she took the initiative this time. She'd already put her glasses away. She had the urge to see if she could fog his.

His lips would be chilled at first, as would hers. But she didn't think they'd stay that way. She thought he'd kiss her back. No, after last night, she *knew* he would kiss her back.

"I could pretend to be your boyfriend, just until this guy realizes I'm around and gives up."

She was tempted more than she could ever let him know. If she said yes, how long would the pretending last? Not long, in her estimation. Soon they would be playing for keeps.

"It wouldn't work," she said. "For a million reasons, but the most obvious one is Gloria. She'd get rid of me immediately if I horned in on what she perceives as her territory. She's warned me not to flirt with any guys who come through the office door, and I need this internship."

"I think we could work around Gloria."

"Ha. Gloria isn't the type to be worked around. Although she's self-absorbed, she has instincts like you wouldn't believe. But aside from her, there's me. I've explained that I have no time for a relationship. And that includes a pretend relationship."

With every passing second, she wanted his kiss even more. Staying put took all her concentration. She wondered if he was fighting the same battle, knowing that if he reached for her the way he had the night before, he'd ruin any chance of having her agree to his plan.

"I'd stay out of your way." He shoved his hands in his coat pockets. "Or I could help you study. Whatever, I think you need someone around who —"

"Whoops, there's my bus." She touched his cheek, the only thing she'd allow herself to do. His cheek was surprisingly warm, and she let her hand linger there a fraction longer than she should. "Thank you for the thought. It wouldn't work."

His gaze had softened from the moment she'd touched him. His voice took on a rougher texture, as if he had been holding himself in check. "I don't like the chance you're taking, being on your own so much."

"I've been on my own for years. This is no different." She hurried toward the bus. "Thanks for walking me here," she called softly over her shoulder.

"Be careful, Amanda."

"Of course!" She climbed onto the bus. Then she deliberately took a seat on the far side, where she wouldn't be able to see him as the bus pulled away. She was afraid that if she looked down and saw him standing there, she'd pull the emergency cord, get off the bus, and run into his arms.

FOURTEEN

Will was fourteen blocks from home, but he walked it rather than taking a bus. He needed the exercise to work out his frustration. Apparently he'd invested a lot of himself into that plan to protect Amanda. When she'd refused to go along, he'd suffered more disappointment than he'd expected.

If he were totally honest with himself, his motives hadn't been pure. Yes, he thought Amanda needed someone around to scare off the creepy guy. But any fool could see that landing that job would give him the inside track. He'd been trying to help, but he'd also had his eye on that inside track.

She didn't want anyone on the inside track, or even the outside track. She wanted the track perfectly clear. Now that he'd heard that message several times, he needed to pay attention and let her the hell alone. If the valentine guy turned out to be dangerous, then . . . she'd have to figure that out for herself.

The idea made his chest hurt, so he walked faster, then broke into a jog. About five blocks from his apartment, his cell sounded a familiar tune. Justin. Will unzipped his jacket and dug out his cell phone.

"Hey, buddy," Justin said. "Hope I didn't wake you."

"Nope."

"You at home?"

"Nope." He struggled to catch his breath.

There was a brief pause. "Yikes. Bad timing. I didn't think you had anything going right now, but I —"

"I don't have anything going. I decided to walk home."

"Walk? Since when do you like to walk?"

"Exercise is good for you, Justin. It floods the system with endorphins and elevates your mood."

"Then why do you sound so pissed off?"

"I'm not pissed off."

"Oh. My mistake. Where are you walking home from?"

Will sighed. He felt like such a schmuck. "Geekland."

Another pause. "I thought you were avoiding Geekland."

"I will be from now on."

"Shot down, huh? The secret valentines might work for some women, but obviously Amanda's not one of them."

"I didn't send the valentines, damn it."

"I'd stick to that story, too, since they didn't work."

"Justin, I really didn't send —"

"Okay, okay. But if you need a new tactic, she was excited about the Barmaster. You might go online and see what kind of bartending gear you could find. I'm pretty sure I saw a singing swizzle stick on some site or other. Maybe you could find one that plays 'I'm in the Mood for Love' or something along those lines."

"Thanks, but I'm abandoning the cause." And Justin was right about him still being pissed. The endorphins that were supposed to be elevating his mood had achieved squat. He still felt as crappy as he had when he'd left the bus stop. This particular mood might require hydraulics to jack it up to the cheerfulness level.

"I'm sorry it didn't work out, buddy. She seems like your type."

"Apparently I'm not her type."

"Her loss. Want me to come over? We could have a few beers, diss a few women, play some gin rummy."

"Don't you have to get up and go to work

at eight?" Justin had always been an early-to-bed, early-to-rise kind of guy. Will had hoped that two nights of drinking would have been enough to settle him back into his old pattern.

"I'm not sleeping worth shit, Will. I deliberately laid off the booze tonight, to see if that would help, but I just lie there staring at the ceiling."

When Will compared his situation to Justin's, he couldn't feel very sorry for himself. He'd never had a chance with Amanda, but Justin had been engaged to be married. "Then come on over," he said. "We can be pathetic together."

Amanda's answering machine light was flashing when she walked in the door of her apartment. She was probably the last person of her generation to have a regular phone instead of a cell, but for her it was the cheaper alternative. She never made long-distance calls, so basic service worked fine.

Assuming it was a recorded telemarketing call, she punched the button to make sure before she erased it. Instead of a voice, the message was music, an old Duran Duran tune called "Hungry Like the Wolf." She paused in the process of taking off her coat to listen for a message of some kind. None came.

The quality of the sound wasn't that great. She heard coughs and clunking noises in the background, as if someone had dialed her number and then held a phone up to a stereo. As that possibility took shape in her mind, she began to shiver.

Walking to her door, she threw the dead bolt into place. It wasn't a habit, and she needed to make it one. Then she prowled through the apartment checking window locks, closing her drapes tight, and peeking into her bedroom closet. She even moved the clothes aside to make sure no one was hiding behind them.

For the first time she wished she hadn't rented on the first floor. Nothing had been available on the other levels, and she'd liked the apartment's location near a bus line. The price had been decent. Being on the first floor meant no stairs, and she'd convinced herself that was a good thing. It was the reason Mavis and Chester had taken their apartments.

But living at ground level meant that an intruder would have an easier time of it. A person needed a key to get in the main door of the building, but windows, especially old single-paned ones like this, could be jimmied, broken, even scored with a glass cutter. Amanda had downplayed that by telling herself that she didn't want to live scared.

Some people focused on all the bad news out there and were convinced that rapists and muggers lurked everywhere. Amanda had rejected that view of the world, which allowed her to move around the city without fear. Nothing had interfered with her belief system. Until now.

Her apartment was its usual temperature of seventy-four degrees, but she couldn't make herself take off her coat. A quilted jacket was no protection against anything, but she felt better with it on. Walking over to her dinette set, she sat down at the table and took a deep breath.

So the valentine guy knew her phone number. That didn't mean he knew where she lived. She'd opted out of having her address in the phone book to cut down on junk mail. Yet she knew that these days a determined person could get almost any information they wanted online. She was surprised Gloria hadn't asked her to snoop around the Internet to find Will's address and phone number.

But there was a reason for that. If a person voluntarily gave the information, then using it didn't seem like harassment. Gloria might be obsessed with sex, but she understood that much about social interactions. The valentine guy did not, which meant he had at least a borderline personality disorder.

Carefully she reviewed her options. As Mavis had pointed out, dogs weren't allowed in this apartment complex, and even if they were, a dog didn't usually become protective of a person or place overnight. It was also a little late for her to take up one of the martial arts.

She could install an alarm system, but that would be permanent and cost money she didn't have. An alarm seemed like overkill, anyway. The guy could lose interest and she'd have a system that would be a pain in the butt to operate and cause Mavis and Chester all kinds of problems. Mavis had a key as backup, and she'd learned to jiggle the lock just fine. But she'd never figure out how to deactivate an alarm.

There was a solution, of course. It would cost her nothing financially, but she wasn't sure if she could keep the psychological cost down, as well. There would have to be a ton of ground rules. Then there was the issue of Gloria. Amanda didn't have a plan for how to deal with Gloria, but Will had sounded as if he did.

Before she even considered going to bed,

she scoured the apartment for a weapon, should she need one. She was ludicrously low on weapon material. A pointy umbrella would be worth something, but she owned the compact kind that folded in on itself. She didn't cook, so she didn't own a rolling pin.

She had one large carving knife, but she couldn't imagine stabbing someone with it. If she had to fight, she'd rather have a club than a knife. Finally she settled on the wand attachment to her vacuum cleaner, plus the collected works of Sigmund Freud. She laid them both on the floor by her bed.

Leaving all the lights on, she lay down fully clothed and pulled the quilt over her. She couldn't begin to sleep as she strained to hear every little noise outside the window. Her muscles ached from keeping them contracted.

She couldn't last through another night like this. Only one thing made sense under the circumstances. If Will could figure out a way to get around the problem of Gloria, she'd ask him to be her pretend boyfriend. It was risky, but she had no choice.

Justin laid down his hand. "Gin."

"That does it. You win." Will gathered up the cards and began to shuffle. He should be exhausted, but instead he felt wired. "Another round?"

"Why not? But first I have to ask you something."

"Shoot." Will kept shuffling as he glanced up at Justin.

"Now that Amanda's out of the picture, are you going to consider Gloria?"

"No." Will couldn't imagine substituting Gloria for Amanda. It would be like choosing moonshine over fine blended whiskey.

"You're sure?"

"Absolutely sure." He had an inkling what this was about and hoped he was wrong.

"So if I try to get something going with her, you wouldn't care?"

Will groaned. "Look, I know you're upset about Cindi, but Gloria Tredway is not the answer." Amanda might not think it was a bad idea, but she didn't love Justin like a brother. Will did.

"I'm not looking to marry her, buddy. I just want to buy a little of what she's selling. Once I get my groove back, I'll call it off. From what you've said about her, she's interested in a temporary good time. So am I."

"You only think that. I know you, Justin. You've never had a temporary good time in your life. It might start out as sex, but before long you'd be daydreaming about getting her to mend her ways and settle down."

Justin polished off his beer. "Would not."

"Would, too."

"I'm telling you, I'm a changed man. That phone call from Cindi created a whole new me."

Will remembered the feeling of belligerent rebellion. If someone like Gloria had been around six months ago, he might have been tempted, too. He was lucky there had been no Gloria type, because he was past that stage. "Your feelings are still raw from the shock, but that will pass if you give yourself some time. You don't have to climb that mountain tomorrow."

"I was thinking about climbing Mount Gloria."

"Listen, she'd be the one doing the climbing. I don't think you have any idea what —"

"You're right, I don't, but I sure as hell want to find out."

"Don't do something rash. This is a knee-jerk reaction. Eventually someone else will come along, someone you could have a future with."

"You mean like a nice girl?"

"Yeah, I do."

"I'm finished with nice girls, Will. I've

hung out with them my whole life, and what do I have to show for it?" He pointed the empty beer bottle at Will. "What do *you* have to show for it, speaking of success stories with nice girls?"

Will gazed at him. "I can't argue that one."

"So I'm saying, if you want a fling with Gloria, tell me now. Otherwise, I'm going to find out if that look she gave me the other day could lead to something."

"I don't want a fling with Gloria." He didn't want a fling at all. He wanted something solid and lasting. Helen had not been right about him. He was sure of that now. Amanda wasn't in the market, so he'd have to keep looking.

Amanda was in no danger of oversleeping. She'd been awake all night. She didn't have class that morning, and she was almost sorry about that. Someone in her class might be the valentine guy, and she wanted a chance to scrutinize everyone and look for a guilty face. She'd have to do that tomorrow.

In the meantime, she'd study every man she came across in her daily life. Gloria only counseled couples, but that meant at least one man per visit. They were all suspects, except for Franklin, who was still recuperating at home after his unfortunate penis accident.

Amanda hated to think one of her customers at Geekland was responsible when the atmosphere of the bar had always been fun and friendly. But one of the regulars might not be so fun, after all. She intended to watch them all more carefully from now on.

Her first order of business once she got to the office was talking to Will. Even so, she put it off all morning, always finding an excuse for not calling him. Finally she faced the reason for the delay. She wasn't used to asking anyone for help.

Late in the morning FedEx delivered *Titillating Trivia,* the book she'd ordered for Gloria to give Will. She signed for it, but now that it was here, she had to let Gloria know. Picking up the FedEx package, she walked into Gloria's office. "The sex trivia book arrived."

"Perfect!" Gloria had given up her nerd disguise and was back to vintage Gloria. Her red hair billowed around her shoulders and her V-necked black sweater and black leather skirt revealed plenty of skin accented with gold jewelry at her neck and wrists. "I want you to take it to him."

"Me?" She wanted to talk to him, but handing him a copy of *Titillating Trivia* might set the wrong tone for their discussion.

"Yes. My new technique is to withdraw and be mysteriously absent. He'll have long-range contact with me through you, and that will intrigue him and ultimately make him curious enough to come around."

"O-*kay.*" Amanda wondered how Gloria managed to live her life. She was so divorced from reality it was frightening.

"I can see you're skeptical, but it'll work. Besides, the Silversmiths are due any minute, and they're in desperate need of guidance in oral sex. Edna keeps leaving teeth marks. So while I'm dealing with the Silversmiths, you can run that book down to William's office and let him know I sent it."

"I'll definitely let him know you sent it."

"As if he'd think it was you! But you might as well state the obvious and avoid any confusion. Oh, and before you go, I have to ask because you seem even more uptight today than usual. Did you use that red vibrator?"

"Not yet."

"Use it, Amanda! You look like a zombie. There's nothing like a few orgasms to put the spring back in your step and erase those dark smudges from under your eyes. You probably stayed up all night studying."

"Sort of." She'd stayed up all night paralyzed with fear.

"That's pathetic. Use that vibrator and you'll sleep like a baby afterward." At the sound of the outer office door opening, she glanced over Amanda's shoulder. "The Silversmiths are here," she said in a low voice. "Be sure to tell me how William reacts to the book. Now, take off."

Amanda smiled at the Silversmiths as Gloria ushered them into her office. Was Jacob Silversmith a suspect? He didn't look suspicious, but maybe there was a reason Edna was leaving tooth marks. Maybe Jacob wasn't a nice man. He looked sweet, with his ruddy complexion, thinning hair, and the beginnings of a paunch, but maybe he was her stalker.

She hated the idea of looking at every male client as if he might be the one harassing her. It threatened to suck any remaining joy out of her life. But unless the boyfriend ruse worked or she figured out who was doing this, she'd have to stay alert.

On her way down the hall to the offices of Cooper and Scott, she made a detour into the women's bathroom. Gloria's comments about the dark smudges under her eyes had made her wonder if she was in any shape to ask Will to be her pretend boyfriend. A couple of days ago she wouldn't have worried about it, and it was a sign of her new interest in him that she cared now.

The bathroom mirror didn't give her a lot of comfort. There *were* dark smudges under her eyes, and she hadn't brought any concealer to work. She never brought makeup, other than lipstick. That was pretty much gone, too.

Detouring back to the office, she opened her desk drawer to take out her purse. As she reached for it, she paused. Was there another valentine underneath? Her heart rate picked up. Slowly she removed her purse from the drawer. It was empty.

With a sigh, she took her lipstick and a small mirror out of an inside compartment. Lipstick helped, but she still looked as if she hadn't slept. Not much to do about it, now. Fluffing her hair with her fingers, she put her lipstick and mirror away and replaced her purse in the drawer.

In the hall she glanced both ways. Whoever was planting the valentines used the time she was out of the office to do it. If there was somewhere she could hide and watch the outer office door . . . but there was no place, and besides, she couldn't stake out Gloria's office. Her job was to be in there working, not hanging around outside trying to catch the valentine guy.

FedEx box in hand, she walked down to the door marked COOPER AND SCOTT, INVESTMENT BROKERS. A brunette receptionist, who looked much more pulled together than Amanda felt, greeted her with a smile and a cheery welcome.

"I'm here to see Will Sloan," Amanda said.

"William? Let me see if he's in. Who shall I say is here?"

Amanda gave her name and waited while the receptionist did her thing. So Will was still called William at Cooper and Scott. Amanda liked the idea that she, Justin, and the customers at Geekland knew him as Will. She felt as if she had access to another side of him. It wasn't quite the Clark Kent/ Superman transformation, but it leaned in that direction.

He came to the front of the office looking more William than Will. In his gray suit and conservative blue tie, dark hair neatly combed, he gave no indication that he'd been at the bar last night slamming down Raging Bulls and kicking trivia butt. Then again, that image might not work so well with potential investors.

The surroundings ratcheted up the nerd factor, too. It was *Dilbert* personified, a gray-partitioned cube farm with computer keys clicking and phones buzzing. The fluorescent lights overhead made everyone look a little gray. Amanda had never thought about the lighting in Gloria's office, but now she appreciated the discreet wall sconces and table lamps.

"Hi, Amanda." Will looked pleasant, but his gaze created a distance between them.

This would be tougher than she'd thought. He'd obviously decided to write her off after last night's conversation at the bus stop, and he might not be willing to reverse that decision. If he took the package without inviting her back to his office, she wouldn't have the chance to ask him about the boyfriend thing.

No, not *boyfriend*. That term belonged in high school. The word that applied in this situation was *lover*. As she stood there looking at him, she had a decidedly sexual reaction to the idea of Will as a faux lover.

She easily could be tempted to get rid of the *faux* part, despite, or maybe because of, his buttoned-down exterior. She wanted to muss him up and bring out the person who'd had such a high old time last night. Whoops. She was in major attraction mode.

That meant that asking him to help her was a really bad idea. Okay, she'd go into debt and get that alarm system. Setting up a pretend relationship was too risky for her, and unfair to him. She'd been right to reject the idea last night.

"Gloria asked me to give you this." She held out the FedEx box.

He glanced at the package and then looked into her eyes. The distance he'd created before had somehow evaporated. "Come on back."

His eyes really were gorgeous. She'd never made love to a man with green eyes. She wouldn't be making love to this man, either, no matter how much electricity was shooting back and forth between them.

She needed to blow this cube farm before something happened that she'd regret. "I need to go." She extended the box in his direction, wiggling it slightly to indicate he should take it off her hands.

"Let me talk to you for a minute." As if assuming her consent, he started down the hallway created by the partitions.

She'd been outmaneuvered. She could set the box on the receptionist's desk and leave, but that would be awkward and impolite. She followed him into his cubicle.

Once there, he turned to her and lowered his voice. "Okay, what's going on?"

Her heart was beating a mile a minute. "I brought you something from Gloria."

"I don't mean that. I mean the way you were looking at me just now."

She had no choice but to lie. "I don't know what you mean."

"The hell you don't." He took off his glasses and kissed her.

FIFTEEN

Kissing Amanda today was the best decision Will had made in ages. He should have done this last night, too, when they'd been standing all alone at the bus stop. But he'd been worried about ruining his plan, so he'd let her call the shots.

At the moment, she wasn't calling any shots. She was going along with this kiss in a most gratifying way. The package she'd been holding dropped to the commercial-grade carpet with a muffled thud as she wrapped both arms around his waist.

She felt so good, so perfect in his arms that he almost forgot she'd never been there before. They'd spent too much time talking. Kissing was more straightforward, and he sent his message with all the clarity he could muster. She seemed to read that message perfectly.

When she opened her mouth a little bit, his brain cells began to disintegrate in the heat. If he didn't call a halt now, he'd have his tongue in her mouth and his fingers at the buttons of her blouse. The kiss was a great idea on a personal level, but not so smart on a professional one. He was still a very junior member of this firm.

But he didn't want to stop. This mouth-to-mouth communication with Amanda seemed like the most natural thing in the world. Ending the kiss when she was so eager seemed totally unnatural. He did it anyway.

The moment he lifted his head, the spell was broken. With a gasp, she backed away as if he had cooties. She was trembling, though, and he took some comfort in that. So was he.

Her eyes were wide with shock. "What was that all about?"

He put his glasses back on. He could think better wearing his glasses. "I should ask you the same thing. Last night you told me to get lost, and this morning you were looking at me with bedroom eyes."

She had the good grace to blush. "I . . . have to admit that I . . . find you attractive."

"That's nice."

"No, it's inconvenient."

"Not for me. I'm enjoying it." He crossed his arms over his chest so he wouldn't reach for her again. The next kiss would undoubtedly pick up where the first one left off, and that could mean violating Cooper and Scott's company standards of office behavior.

She took a deep breath. "I can't allow myself to do that. I've explained my reasons."

"Something tells me you're nothing like your mother."

"I'm more like her than I thought. Two semesters ago I fell for a guy and in no time my grades were in the dumper. It was hell salvaging that semester, but I poured on the extra credit and saved myself."

His telephone rang. "Excuse me a minute. Don't go anywhere." He picked up the phone, and just his luck, it was Gloria.

"I'm taking a break while my clients complete a little oral exam in my office," she said. "I noticed Amanda's not back yet. How did you like the book?"

"It looks very interesting." He glanced at Amanda and mouthed Gloria's name.

She rolled her eyes, reached for the FedEx carton, and pulled the book out. Turning it face out, she held it so he could see the cover. *Titillating Trivia* was written in gold script against a whorehouse-red background. Cartoon characters in various

262

bawdy positions and states of undress surrounded the title.

He grimaced.

"I thought it was right up your alley," Gloria said. "Good for cocktail chatter. Speaking of that, I would invite you for a drink tonight, but I'm swamped with work. Glad you like the book. Bye."

After she hung up, he stared at the phone for a minute. "Something's wrong. She didn't push for a date."

"She's going for mysterious and unavailable, to see how that works."

"Oh." He replaced the receiver on the phone. "Well, it won't. Now where were we?"

"I think we were at the part where I leave and go back to Gloria's office, a sadder but wiser woman."

"Please don't go yet. You were telling me about some guy who turned into a roadblock. Whatever happened to him?" After that kiss, Will was in deep enough that he needed to know if some ex was lurking around.

"He told me I was stupid to worry so much about grades. When I wouldn't abandon my studies for him, he took off. I have no idea where he is."

"I don't mean to malign your ex, but . . .

Cancel that, I do mean to malign him. He sounds like an idiot."

She shook her head. "I was the idiot, thinking I could maintain a love affair, a job, and my studies all at the same time. Something had to give."

"Not if he'd had a better sense of time management."

That made her smile. "There was no time to manage. If I want to follow my dream, I need to make the tough choices." She gazed at him. "Thanks for the kiss." Then she started out of the cubicle. "It was lots of fun."

"Wait."

She glanced over her shoulder. "You don't understand. I really can't take a chance that I'll sabotage myself."

"What if I commit to making sure that doesn't happen?"

"You can. Keep your distance."

"Ouch."

"I don't mean that to be as negative as it sounded." She paused. "The problem is that I like you too much."

"Damn it, that shouldn't be a problem."

"At this point in my life, it's a big problem. See you later, Will."

He searched for something, anything to make her stay a little longer. "Have you found any more valentines in your desk drawer?"

She paused again, but this time she didn't look at him. "No."

Good thing he'd put his glasses on, because otherwise he might have missed her slight shiver and the way her body went rigid afterward, as if she were bracing herself against another involuntary, telltale movement.

"You must be relieved," he said. She didn't look at all relieved.

She glanced at him. "I am."

Something else was going on. That heated look she'd given him in the outer office had created a bond between them. Sharing an enthusiastic kiss had strengthened the bond, and now his radar was locked in and picking up every nuance. "What's happened, Amanda?"

Fear flashed in her eyes and she hesitated.

"Tell me, please." His gut tightened. He couldn't let her handle this by herself.

She swallowed. "It's probably nothing, but it freaked me out. When I came home last night, there was a message on my answering machine."

He took a breath and tried to stay calm. Getting agitated wouldn't help her. "So he knows your phone number. That's not good, but if you've saved it, we could try and identify the voice."

"There was no voice, only a song, 'Hungry Like the Wolf.'"

All the hairs on the back of his neck stood up. "That's creepy."

"I know." She held his gaze. "I live in a first-floor apartment, and I didn't sleep very well after that."

He blew out a breath. "I wouldn't imagine you did. Knowing the phone number is one step from knowing where you live." Although he was dying to ride to the rescue, he held himself in check. "What are you going to do?"

"Well, this morning I'd planned to ask if your boyfriend offer was still open . . ."

Yes.

"But obviously we can't consider the idea, now."

"Why not?"

She stared at him as if he weren't right in the head.

He shrugged. "Okay, so we kissed."

"Twice."

"That first one barely counts as a whole kiss."

"And this one?"

"No big deal." It was a huge deal, but he was ready to minimize it if necessary. She

266

needed someone to hang around and keep her safe, and he was the man for the job.

"No big deal?" She looked crushed.

"Bad choice of words. I meant that we could get beyond our one-point-five kisses if that's what it takes for you to feel comfortable with me. You need me around, Amanda."

She smiled gently. "That's what I'm afraid of."

"I didn't mean it like that. You need a guy to make it look as if you're spoken for. I'm the logical choice."

"Maybe so, but after this morning, I don't think we can pull off a pretend relationship."

"And I say we can. This weirdo seems to be focused on Valentine's Day, so once that's over, he might fade into the woodwork or crawl back under a rock. Then we can end the charade, and each go back to our regularly scheduled programs."

She still seemed skeptical. "I'm not saying that we could pull it off, but just supposing we tried it. How would we handle Gloria?"

He'd thought about that last night before he'd proposed the idea to her. "You tell her about the stalker and explain that you need me to step in for a few days. She's so convinced of her own sexual attractiveness that I'll bet she won't see you as a threat."

"That might be true. She thinks I'm pretty dorky."

He laughed. "Gloria's perceptions of reality are so skewed that I wonder how she functions."

"Thanks for the vote of confidence."

It was more than a vote. It was a freaking landslide. But he had to play this close to the vest.

Amanda studied him. "How do you see this working, you being my boyfriend?"

"For one thing, I'd drop by the office from time to time, in case the guy is one of Gloria's clients. And I'd hang out at Geekland, where we could advertise our status to all your regular customers."

"That sounds logical. Anything else?"

He paused. He doubted that she'd go for his other thought, but he'd suggest it, anyway. "Considering that first-floor apartment of yours, I should probably move in." He waited for her to blow a gasket.

She took a shaky breath. "I think so, too."

You could have knocked him over with a paper clip.

All morning Amanda had blocked the terror that she'd felt while lying in her apartment last night, wide awake and listening for every scrape and rustle outside her windows. In the light of day, she'd felt silly being so afraid of a dumb song on her answering machine. But when Will had asked about any new valentine deliveries, all the fear had come rushing back.

Yes, she could install an alarm system, but an alarm system was a cold piece of technology. She needed to hear another human voice, preferably the voice of a man with broad shoulders and more upper body strength than she had, in case someone needed to wield the vacuum cleaner wand or the collected works of Sigmund Freud.

"I didn't think you'd agree with me," Will said.

"I didn't know I was going to, either. But the truth is, I'm afraid to stay alone, and Mavis Endicott sleeping on the couch isn't going to make me feel any safer." She felt a stab of guilt. He was at least six inches longer than her couch. "That's all I have to offer you, unfortunately. Or maybe I should take the couch, and you can have my —"

"No way. The couch will work fine. We're only talking about a few nights. I'll head back to my apartment during lunch and pack a few things so I can go home with you tonight."

"Maybe we shouldn't tell Gloria about this part."

"We don't have to tell anyone about this part. Well, that's not quite true. I should tell Justin."

"I would expect that. And I'll need to tell Mavis and Chester."

He nodded. "Right. But don't worry, Amanda. I won't take advantage of the situation."

"I believe you." She thought he might have greater control over his emotions than she did. Maybe his dedication to the cause would inspire her to squelch her lusty urges.

"It'll be fine. I'll bet having me on the scene will discourage this guy really fast. He might give up before Valentine's Day."

She hoped so. Will looked better and better with every passing moment, and she didn't know how well she'd be able to resist the temptation of having him in residence. "Bring pajamas, okay?"

He looked startled. "Uh . . . okay."

"You don't own any, do you?"

"I'll get some on my way back from lunch."

She was glad she'd mentioned it. She couldn't have a naked Will sleeping on her couch. A pajama-clad Will would be difficult enough to ignore. "Oh, and another thing. I don't have much to eat in the house. If you're used to breakfast, you're out of luck."

"I usually grab an energy bar."

"I'm relieved to hear it. Some guys think the ability to fix breakfast is a gender-based skill."

"I won't expect you to wait on me, Amanda."

"Well, I can brew coffee." Waiting on him didn't sound like such a chore, the more she thought about it. "I'm pretty sure Mavis has instant pancake mix, and she'd loan me butter and syrup, if you'd like to have —"

"Not necessary." He stepped closer. "You don't have to do anything to please me, or make me feel more at home. Just go about your regular routine, and I'll fit myself into that."

There shouldn't have been anything sexual about that statement. The fact that she took it that way didn't bode well for this sleepover routine they were contemplating. What had she let herself in for?

"Look, I can see this plan makes you uneasy, but I promise to be as unobtrusive as possible. You'll hardly know I'm there."

She didn't believe that for a minute. But it would only be for a few days, as he'd said. The days weren't the problem, though. The nights were her chief concern. She took a steadying breath. "Well, I'd better get back."

"So you'll tell Gloria ASAP? I should start this hanging-around stuff soon, so anyone who knows you gets the idea."

"I'll tell her."

Will smiled. "You look as if you're going to the gallows. Hold on a sec." He walked over to his desk and consulted his day planner. "I have some free time. I'll go with you. We'll face her together."

"I'd appreciate that. I have my doubts that she'll love this plan."

"Then we need to soften her up." Will picked up the *Titillating Trivia* book and flipped it open. "I'll take this with me and let her know how much I like it."

"You can do that with a straight face?"

"Sure." He scanned a page. "Might as well have a few examples to trot out so she'll know I at least glanced at it. Did you know that if you took the total number of condoms used in New York City in a month and laid them end to end, they'd reach to the moon and back?"

"Can't say that I did. Would that be still in the package or unrolled?" Amanda swallowed a laugh. Will might actually like the book.

"Doesn't say. I'll bet unrolled." He flipped the page. "Here's another interesting factoid. An independent study found that the average number of orgasms experienced in a week by the women living in one square block of Pittsburgh was two point four."

"That's assuming everyone told the truth."

"Granted. But assuming they did, in a similar socioeconomic neighborhood in San Diego it was two point nine. I wonder why that is? Sunshine, maybe. Or salt air. The surf produces negative ions, which are mood elevators. That might account for the half percent difference."

"I wonder where they get the decimal points?"

"That happens all the time in statistics." He was already skimming another page in the book.

"But not in reality. You either have an orgasm or you don't." And for her, it was mostly the second option. If they polled her square block, she'd really bring those numbers down.

"Mm." He gave no indication he'd actually registered her comment.

That was a good thing. She had no business discussing orgasms with him, now or in the future.

"Hey, did you know that pigs are extremely orgasmic? And their orgasms last for —"

"I hate to interrupt, but we really have to

leave." All this talk of orgasms was not helping her eliminate thoughts of sex, specifically sex with Will. But now she knew why he was so outrageously good at trivia in the bar. No matter whether the subject was baseball or sex, he soaked up facts like a sponge.

"We can leave in a second." He kept reading. "Did you know there's a native custom in the Brazilian rain forest where the women rub —"

"Unless you want me to go alone."

He glanced up. "Of course not." He closed the book. "Let's go."

She eyed the cover. "You might want to stick that back in the box before you parade through the outer office."

"Good thought." He dropped the book neatly into the FedEx box. "Where did she find this thing, anyway?"

"She didn't. I ordered it online."

His gaze was openly curious. "So you buy Gloria sex toys at the shop down the street and order up racy books online. That's some job description you have."

"I may have to package my résumé in a plain brown wrapper."

"Do you ever find yourself wanting to try out —"

"No."

274

He nodded. "Right. You're avoiding all that for the time being."

"Yep."

"Consider the subject closed."

"Good."

Sixteen

Will had no idea how he'd spend his nights in Amanda's apartment and keep his hands to himself, especially considering the role he'd be playing during the day. When they were in public, touching her once in a while would help make the boyfriend ploy look real. Like now, as they walked down the hall together, he should be holding her hand.

At least that was how *he* perceived a committed relationship. He should probably find out her preferences. "Since we're planning to advertise ourselves as a couple, how do you stand on the issue of public displays of affection?"

"That depends. The category stretches from fond looks to doing the wild thing on a park bench."

"I was thinking of a middle ground, like holding hands."

"That's fine, I guess."

"Then we might as well get started." He

reached for her hand and laced his fingers through hers. "How's that?"

"That'll work."

Her hand was soft, but her fingers felt strong and capable — capable of turning him on if she decided to adopt that native rubbing technique practiced by the women in the Brazilian rain forest. He was still thinking about that custom. They used an ointment made out of indigenous plants, but he hadn't recognized the names.

Her hand became warmer the longer he held it. He could feel the heat traveling up his arm and moving through his body. Maybe she wouldn't need any special ointment, after all. He couldn't remember ever getting turned on simply by holding hands with a woman, but it was happening.

He needed to make conversation. "Going beyond hand-holding, how do you feel about a guy putting his arm around you in public?"

"I don't have a problem with that."

"Kissing?"

She hesitated. "I don't object on general principle, but in this case . . . maybe we'd better not risk it."

"You could have a point." Too much yearning was going on, and what might start out as a simple peck on the lips could turn

French in no time.

Even the hand-holding had escalated without his realizing it. He caught himself stroking her wrist gently with his thumb. It was involuntary, as if contact with her skin threw him into automatic stroking mode. He stopped.

"This could get a little tricky," she said.

"We'll handle it." He couldn't let her back out of the deal, not with some sicko leaving eighties tunes on her answering machine. "We know the dangers, so we're prepared to —"

Gloria walked out of her office, caught sight of them, and gasped. "What's *this?*"

They let go of each other like a couple of school kids caught making out beside the lockers. Will hated that knee-jerk reaction and wished they'd braved it through, but they hadn't, and it couldn't be helped.

"Hey, Gloria, I really appreciate the book." He held up the FedEx box.

"So I see." Fury glinted in her eyes. "You have the book in one hand and Amanda in the other. How cozy."

"We need to talk to you," Amanda said. "This isn't what it looks like."

"No? Then what is it? Did the building suddenly adopt the buddy system so no one would get lost in the halls?"

278

"Let's go back into your office," Will said. "We shouldn't be discussing this out here. And we do have an explanation."

"I certainly hope so." Gloria tossed her hair over her shoulders. "Because what I just saw makes no sense whatsoever." She stalked back through the office door.

"As Amanda said, it's not what it seems." William didn't think he sounded very convincing, but he was counting on Gloria's high opinion of her own desirability.

"Come on into my office and close the door," she said. "I prefer not to discuss personal matters in front of my clients, and my next appointment will be here in ten minutes. They had a sexual emergency, so I'm giving up my lunch hour to them."

Amanda went over to her desk. "Before we get started, I want to check this drawer." She opened it and lifted up her purse.

"Anything in there?" Will asked.

She pulled out a red envelope.

"Damn!" He was beyond frustrated. "The guy was right *here* in the last half hour! We need a hidden camera or something."

Gloria looked bewildered. "Who was here? What's going on?"

Amanda walked toward her and held out the envelope. "Someone's been leaving valentines in my desk drawer."

"You're kidding." Gloria took the envelope. "Why would someone do that?"

Will swallowed his indignation. Gloria didn't mean to be insulting. She just didn't understand subtle sexuality, and Amanda was all about that. "It seems that some guy has become obsessed with her," he said.

Gloria shook her head in disbelief. "There must be some mistake." She opened the envelope, pulled out the card, and read the front. " 'I take the position that you are the perfect valentine.' " Then she opened the card and her eyebrows rose. " 'You can take any position you want. Your Secret Valentine.' "

After gazing at the card for several seconds, Gloria turned it so they could both see the inside.

It reminded Will of Gloria's *Joy of Sex* illustrations. He glanced at Amanda. Her breathing was shallow and her face pale. He could imagine her thoughts as she looked at that damned card. How he'd love to have that creep in front of him right now.

He'd had only one fight in his life, when he was eleven and someone had started picking on a smaller kid. Despite that lack of experience, he was certain that given the chance, he would cheerfully knock this guy from here to next week.

Gloria looked at the card again. "Are you sure this wasn't meant for me?"

"It has my name on the envelope," Amanda said.

Turning the envelope over, Gloria glanced at the writing on the front. "So it does. Amazing. I . . . wait a minute." She gave Will a sharp glance. "That fax. You signed it *Your Secret Valentine.* Are you somehow involved in this?"

"Not like you're thinking," Will said. "Maybe we should go in your office, like you suggested. This is complicated."

"After you." Gloria gestured toward the open door and they all trooped in. "Don't sit on the love seat," she said as she closed the door. "I haven't wiped off the flavored oil yet." She picked up a chair that was lying on its side and placed it next to another one in front of her desk. "Here you go."

As Will sat down, he noticed that one of her framed pictures was hanging crooked, and magazines had been knocked off the coffee table.

Gloria followed the direction of his gaze. "Clients do get wild. I'm thinking of partitioning off an area and covering it floor to ceiling with padded vinyl. Then I'd throw in padded hassocks of various sizes, any sex toys they wanted, and let them go to it.

Cleanup would be a cinch."

Will told himself not to think about that scenario. It would do him no good whatsoever to picture himself with Amanda in the equivalent of an adult playpen. Sex wasn't an option with them, and the sooner he accepted that, the happier he'd be. Well, not happy, but stable. Resigned. Frustrated as hell.

Amanda sat in the chair next to him. He breathed in her scent, a gentle floral fragrance, and was immediately transported back to the moment when he'd kissed her. He couldn't think about that, either. His best bet was concentrating on the violence he'd like to visit on the valentine guy.

Leaning forward, Amanda cleared her throat. "Here's the situation." She quickly outlined what had happened, including the song someone had left on her answering machine at home. "At first I thought it was Will . . . uh, William, but I was wrong."

"Of course you were." Gloria glanced at Will. "You couldn't possibly be interested in her."

He lied. "Right."

"I'm distressed to know the fax wasn't for me, however."

Will shrugged. "You're a client. Ethically, I can't —"

"Yes, yes. So you've said." Gloria adjusted the *V* of her sweater to show off a little more cleavage. "I'm sure I can loosen up your morals eventually. But considering that you're not interested in Amanda, what was with the hand-holding business?"

"A pretense," Amanda said. "I asked William if he'd pretend to be my boyfriend for a few days. Maybe if I'm seen as unavailable, the guy will back off."

"A pretend boyfriend? How would that work?"

"It's all fake, of course." Will was impressed with his ability to stretch the truth. "Nothing will be going on between us, but to the general public, we'll look like a couple. We'll hold hands and stuff."

Gloria stiffened, and her eyebrows drew together in obvious disapproval. "What other *stuff* are we talking about?"

"Not much else, really."

Gloria relaxed a little and leaned back in her office chair. "Okay, then."

"I might put my arm around her once in a while."

"But not often," Amanda added quickly. "And only in public, when we want to make a statement, especially if there's a chance the guy might be there, watching."

"Who do you think he is?"

Amanda shifted in her seat. "I hate to throw out accusations, but . . . Jacob Silversmith was just here, so he had the opportunity to leave the valentine."

"No, he didn't." Gloria looked at Will. "I'm in a dicey situation, here, William. As my assistant, Amanda has access to client information, but you . . ."

"He's trying to help me figure out who's sending the valentines," Amanda said. "I completely understand client confidentiality, but in this case, I think Will needs to know as much as possible. I'm sure he can be trusted."

"Did you just call him *Will?*"

Amanda's cheeks turned pink. "His friend Justin calls him that, and I got in the habit of using that name, too."

"Either way is fine." Will squirmed under Gloria's sudden scrutiny.

"Will," she said again as she continued to study him. "I like it. There's a little harder edge to Will. It has a sexy ring to it. I'm going to call you that from now on, myself."

Now he was completely embarrassed, but he tried to toss it off with a shrug. "Whatever."

"In any case," Gloria said, "I think Amanda's right. As part of this investigation you need information, and I'm sure I can trust you. But let's stop using names, unless there's reason to think the person is sending the valentines."

"That's fine," Will said.

"Concerning the last male client who was in the office, I can guarantee he was kept quite busy with his wife and the flavored oils."

"But what about at the end of the session?" Amanda asked. "Was he ever alone in the outer office before they left?"

"Never. I taught her some licking techniques and the man was wrung out by the end of the hour. He had to lean on her for support as they walked out the door. Trust me, there was no valentine drop involving that man."

Licking techniques. Will hadn't imagined the investigation would create such vivid pictures in his brain. To think there were techniques that would bring a man to near exhaustion. Had Amanda picked up any of that knowledge by hanging around Gloria's office?

It doesn't matter. His conscience shook an accusing finger at him. Amanda could be educated in all sorts of sexual techniques and it mattered not one bit, because they weren't going to become involved that way. He'd given her his word that he wouldn't take advantage of the situation. He always kept his word.

"So we can eliminate him as a suspect," Amanda said. "And . . . the man who broke his —"

Gloria nodded. "Yes, we can. Poor guy. His noodle is still firmly bandaged and he refuses to go anywhere because it sticks out like the flagpole on a government building."

Will grew uneasy. Licking techniques sounded great. Injuries, not so much.

Gloria glanced at him and laughed. "You should see your face. You're whiter than a New Hampshire nudist. Accidents like that couple had are extremely rare. I've never encountered one, and I've been in practice for fifteen years."

"Exactly what did happen?" Now that he was privy to this insider info, he decided knowing was better than letting his imagination fill in the blanks.

"He was very erect," Gloria said. "She leaped on him and missed. Broke the damn thing."

Will winced. "I didn't know . . . you could."

"It takes a great deal of enthusiasm, believe me. I don't recommend leaping, in any event. I've always counseled my clients to move with fluid grace." Gloria surveyed her office. "Some are more successful at that than others."

A knock sounded on the closed office door. *"Anybody here?"*

"Be right out!" Gloria rolled her chair away from her desk and stood. "That's probably my next appointment."

Will hoped he was wrong, but the voice sounded a lot like Justin's.

"We can continue this conversation later." Gloria lowered her voice and glanced at the closed door. "This couple is a priority. He's developed such an uncontrollable foot fetish that his wife has to wear running shoes to bed. Unfortunately she has a tendency to kick in her sleep. I'm going to try hypno-therapy."

Will kept his voice low, too. "What about this guy, then? He sounds strange enough to leave secret valentines."

Amanda shook her head. "I've never met him. They're new clients. He'd have no reason to know who I am."

Will wasn't giving up that easily. A man with that kind of weird obsession could have others. "Unless he's also a customer at Geekland and faked this fetish thing to get closer to you. Take a good look at him as we go out. See if you recognize him from anywhere, even school."

Her hand on the doorknob, Gloria gave him a glance filled with admiration. "For a number cruncher, you're not bad at this investigative business."

Will wasn't a number cruncher. That label applied to accountants. Will wooed numbers instead of crunching them, but he decided not to say that. "I'd like to find out who's doing this. But barring that, maybe I can help run him off."

"I hope you do. He's interfering with the efficiency of this office." Gloria opened the door.

Sure enough, Justin stood on the other side. He'd cleaned up his act. A shave and fresh clothes made him look like the old Justin except for the dark circles under his eyes. "Hey! Looks like the gang's all here."

"Well, if it isn't Will's friend." Gloria sounded pleased.

"Justin, were you looking for me?" Will sincerely hoped so. He'd left word with Bonnie that he'd be down here if anyone wanted him.

"Not exactly. But we can grab lunch if you want."

"I have some errands to do during lunch."

"I'll help."

"Uh, okay." He glanced quickly at Amanda, who gave him a little shrug, as if acknowledging the inevitable. Justin might as well find out about the new arrangement now and save confusion later.

"Then let's go," Will said. "I have a book I want to show you. There's some great stuff in it." He said that partly to butter up Gloria, but in reality he loved the book. He was a trivia nut, and sexy trivia was even more fun. The book was more from Amanda than Gloria, anyway, so he felt good about enjoying it.

"That's fine," Justin said, "but first I want to see if Dr. Tredway has an opening in her schedule."

Will stifled a groan. His buddy was going for it, despite all Will's best efforts.

"For you and a partner?" Gloria asked.

"No partner. My fiancée called off the wedding. Needless to say, I could use some counseling." He adopted his most pitiful expression.

Will had seen him use that expression with deadly accuracy in the past. Women always wanted to take care of him when he made that face.

Gloria gazed at him with obvious sympathy. "I appreciate your position, but I restrict myself to couples."

"Could you make an exception? After this trauma, I don't know if I could ever have sex again." Justin looked even more pathetic.

Will didn't want Gloria making any exceptions. Putting these two together was a train wreck. "Tough luck, buddy." He clapped Justin on the shoulder. "Chicago is full of therapists. I'm sure you can find one by letting your fingers do the walking through the Yellow Pages."

Gloria smiled. "Why, Will, is that jealousy talking? I'm very flattered!"

Shit. "I wasn't . . . I mean, that wasn't —"

"He just wants Justin to have someone who specializes in his particular problem," Amanda said. "Right, Will?"

"Right." He sent her a look of gratitude. "I'm sure couples therapy must be totally different from individual therapy."

"It is, of course." Gloria glanced at each of the two men as if sizing up her best prospect. "And I find that by sticking to couples, I eliminate the temptation to become involved with clients, which could get messy."

"So you have that rule, too?" Will was astonished.

"I do. But somehow it seems more necessary in my case than in yours. Besides, I'd become your ex-client in a heartbeat, but then I'd deprive you of income. I think you deserve both me and the money."

Will had painted himself into such a corner he couldn't imagine how he'd ever get out.

"And now the poor guy's speechless," Amanda said.

Gloria preened. "I have that effect on men. But then, talk is highly overrated."

Will thought he'd better get out of there before Gloria grabbed him by the tie and reeled him in. He came up with a tired cliché and used it without remorse. "Hey, I'm out of time. Justin, are you coming with me?"

"Guess so." Justin looked deflated. "Dr. Tredway, are you absolutely sure you can't fit me in?"

"Tell you what. Let's have a drink tonight and talk about it."

"He can't," Will said. "We have that thing after work today. Remember?"

"What thing?"

"You know." Will tried to think of what would capture Justin's attention. "At Geekland. There's that trivia tournament. You don't want to miss it."

Amanda stared at him. "What trivia tournament?"

"Leonard and some of the guys set it up. You might have been too busy to notice."

"I don't remember it, either," Justin said.

Then he brightened. "I know what! Dr. Tredway and I can have a drink together at Geekland." He turned to Gloria. "How's that?"

This wasn't turning out at all the way Will had hoped. "Gloria would hate Geekland."

"Probably." She smiled. "But if both of you cute nerds will be there, how can I resist?"

Will ignored the nerd remark. After all, he had been spending much of his free time at Geekland recently, so being labeled a nerd was partly his own fault. He appealed to Amanda. "Tell Gloria that Geekland is not her style."

Amanda looked amused. "It's not, but sometimes a person needs to explore new options."

That's when he remembered that Amanda had thought maybe Gloria would be good for Justin. With no allies left, he might as well wave the white flag and get off the field.

"Then Geekland it is," Gloria said. "See you boys at six."

SEVENTEEN

Harvey rode the bus home, which gave him a chance to think. He could be driving the Mercedes or the BMW, but on the bus you could watch people and imagine them naked. Sometimes he'd think of someone naked like the girl across the aisle and get worked up. Other times he'd think of someone naked like the bus driver guy, and start laughing. The world would be a lot more fun if people weren't allowed to wear clothes.

Or maybe he'd get bored if everyone ran around naked all the time. He was bored thinking about it now. Besides, he had Amanda to figure out. He wondered if she had seen him hiding in the stairwell when she'd come walking back to the office with that guy from the investment company. She must have. That would explain why she'd suddenly started holding that nerd's hand.

Women were like that — making you think

they liked you one minute, trying to get you jealous the next. Good thing he'd given her that supersexy valentine this time. That should make her forget the nerd. Once he got her alone, she'd probably want to try all those positions shown in the card.

He'd do it, too, as long as he got to be in charge. One thing he hated about sex with Louise was that she never let him be in charge. Amanda wouldn't be like that, though. She would recognize that Harvey was the sort of man who should be in charge of sexual doings.

Tonight he'd call her answering machine and play her another song. He'd just thought of that idea yesterday, and it was a good one. He'd play her some of his favorite songs, which would help her get to know him better. One of them could become *their* song.

He and Louise had a song, "Girls Just Want to Have Fun," but Louise liked it better than he did. She was the one who'd said it should be their song, and he'd had to go along. He always had to go along with whatever Louise said. It wasn't fair.

But then he remembered that he'd put her cigarettes in the freezer right before he'd left for Starbucks. She slept later than he did. She'd be getting up about now, and she'd go for the cigarettes.

He hopped off the bus and hurried toward the two-story brick house Louise had inherited when her folks died. It was so big it had maid's quarters, except they had trouble keeping a maid. Louise would be mean to them and they'd leave, so the house was always a mess.

By the time Harvey put the key in the lock, he could hear her raving. He was just in time for the show. Walking into the huge kitchen, he ducked just as the frozen carton sailed past his head. It hit the paneled wall with a thud, which showed how hard it was.

Louise stood in the middle of the kitchen panting hard, her bathrobe untied, and she wasn't wearing anything else, so he could see her boobies wiggling with every breath. Her frizzy hair sat on her head like a yellow scouring pad, and her eyes reminded him of the cartoon ones that looked like whirligigs going round and round.

He smiled like nothing was wrong. "What's the matter, honey pot?"

"You know damn well!" She gasped for breath. All that smoking was starting to have an effect on her lung power. "You put my cigarettes in the freezer, you mealybug."

"No, I would never do that, sugar bum." He gave her his sincere look. "But now that you mention it, when you came home from the store yesterday, you must have been a little distracted."

"I was *not* distracted." Her nostrils flared like a horse after it had been running a lot.

"I think you were, sweet bunions. I wondered why you'd put the ice cream in the refrigerator, but I thought maybe it was too hard and you wanted it softened up. I guess you put the cigarettes in the freezer instead of the ice cream."

"I did not." She looked as if she could take him apart with her bare hands.

He shrugged. "Go look." He'd enjoyed reversing the two items, which made it look logical that she'd done it.

Turning, she stomped toward the double doors of the refrigerator. Louise was a woman who knew how to stomp. This episode was proceeding nicely.

Harvey took off his coat and watched Louise open the refrigerator. There sat the carton of rocky road, and Louise stared at it like it was possessed. Then she began to swear, and she used all the words Harvey knew and a few that he thought she'd made up. They sounded great.

Taking the ice cream out of the refrigerator, she threw that at him, too. She missed, of course, and the ice cream splatted all over the kitchen floor. "You're making me *crazy!*" She looked crazy, too, with her face all red.

Then she advanced on him, her fingers flexing. He knew what was coming next, and it was the price he'd have to pay for yanking her chain. At least she wasn't boring right now.

She made a sound low in her throat. "Take your pants off, maggot mouth."

He only got them partway down before she was on him, shoving him down onto the slippery ice cream. Dropping to her knees, she rode him hard. His butt kept sliding around on the gooey floor, which shifted the angle each time. Right before he came, he congratulated himself for dreaming up the cigarette and ice cream switch. He hadn't been bored since he walked in the door.

After they finished, she tried to unfreeze a pack of cigarettes in the microwave and started a fire. He'd always wanted to try this trick, so he stood on a chair and peed on the fire. It went out, but the microwave was history.

Harvey didn't care. They could always buy a new one, and if he could create this kind of excitement all the time, life would be worth living. As Louise sat at the kitchen table trying to light a frozen cigarette, he sat down, too.

Time to start teasing the lion again. "Have you ever noticed how pretty the girl is who works for Dr. Tredway?"

Louise put down the lighter and the cigarette and gave him the kind of stare he imagined a cobra gave its victim. "If I ever find you fooling around with that girl, I'll personally feed your privates to the nearest junkyard dog."

Harvey shivered with pleasure. Dr. Tredway thought she knew how to put zing into this marriage, but she didn't know anything compared to Harvey. Even Louise didn't get it. Only Harvey knew how to torpedo them both out of the same ol', same ol' rut. When Louise saw that he could get a woman as hot as Amanda to have sex with him, Louise would have to treat him with more respect. Then it would be time for Harvey to be in charge.

Toward the end of the afternoon, Amanda wondered what she'd been thinking to agree that Will could spend the next few nights sleeping in her apartment. He'd dropped by the office a couple of times already to play his role as boyfriend, and each time she'd felt like a fool carrying on this charade.

Now she was actually inviting him into

her home. There must have been better alternatives, if she'd only stopped long enough to think of them. For example, she could have bought barbed wire and strung it in a crisscross pattern over her windows.

She didn't know where a person found barbed wire in the heart of a big city like Chicago, but if not barbed wire, then something else to discourage a person trying to come in. She could have brought beer bottles home from Geekland, broken them, and placed the jagged edges along her windowsills. Except an intruder would probably be wearing gloves, and he'd be able to sweep that broken glass to the floor with no trouble.

Maybe she didn't have as many alternatives as she thought. But Will in residence seemed like a very rash idea. If she could come up with another plan before he arrived to ride home with her on the bus, then she could tell him she'd changed her mind.

Bells. She could string little bells across her window, and if someone tried to come through, the bells would ring and alert her. And then what? She didn't have a lot of confidence in her vacuum cleaner wand and collected works of Sigmund Freud. She could buy a gun, but she knew so little about them that she'd probably end up doing damage to herself instead of the stalker.

As Amanda racked her brain for other ideas, Gloria escorted out the couple who had been her last appointment of the day. "If the feathers make you sneeze, try the velvet gloves," she said. "And beforehand, use plenty of lotion. You want your skin to be supple and sensitized. Go easy on the pinching. That's something to be used sparingly, right before climaxing."

This was exactly the sort of thing Amanda didn't need to hear before taking a man home for the first time in a solid year. Fortunately she had no supply of feathers and velvet gloves. Or condoms. That should keep her honest.

Gloria waved goodbye to her clients and walked back to Amanda's desk. "What's the dress code at Geekland? Bowling shirts?"

"What you have on is fine." Amanda thought Gloria would cause quite a stir in her shape-hugging sweater and short leather skirt.

"But I won't fit in. Maybe I should go back to that shirtwaist, the glasses, and the sensible shoes."

Amanda shook her head. "The essence of nerdiness is to be exactly who you are. Nerds don't try to be anyone else. I'd say fitting in means following that rule."

"You're the expert."

Amanda opened her mouth to refute that, but then she closed it again. She might not have started out to be a nerd, but she could be turning into one thanks to her job at Geekland, her long hours of studying, and her lack of a social life. She wondered if entertaining a pretend boyfriend in her apartment for several days counted as a social life. Probably not.

Speaking of that, Will walked through the door carrying a small gym bag. He'd already told Amanda that a new membership in a health club would be his cover story.

"Will!" Gloria looked him up and down with obvious pleasure. "Headed for a workout?"

"Right. I spend way too much time riding a desk."

Amanda gave him a wide-eyed stare of disbelief. Surely he hadn't just given Gloria an opening you could drive a truck through.

He closed his eyes briefly. Apparently he had.

Gloria laughed in delight. "You are too cute. I could have *so* much fun with that remark, but may I simply suggest that you try riding girls, instead?"

"Good one, Gloria." He shifted the gym bag from one hand to the other.

"You make it too easy, Will. So, are you going from the gym to Geekland for the tournament?"

"I checked that out, and I was confused. It's not tonight. But, yeah, Justin and I will see you there about six."

Nice save, Amanda thought. She'd been reasonably sure there was no trivia tournament tonight. Will had been trying to keep Gloria and Justin apart, but that was a lost cause.

"I guess you'll be looking for suspects," Gloria said.

"Definitely. Any more ideas on that?"

She shook her head. "Amanda and I went through my list of clients and eliminated all the ones she's never met, plus the two we mentioned today and Franklin. As for the rest . . ."

"We did some random checking," Amanda said. "There wasn't enough time to go through all the files, but it could be anyone in them. There are guys with performance issues, some with S and M tendencies, a few Oedipus complexes, and a bunch who display a mixed bag of neuroses."

Will scrubbed a hand over his face and sighed. "In other words, a fertile field of potential stalkers."

"Instead of calling this person a stalker,"

Gloria said, "I prefer to describe the phenomenon as transference. The client imagines himself in love with the person who's helping him and is convinced that his love is returned. Normally that transference target would be me, but in this case, someone seems to have settled on Amanda, instead."

"And they're scaring the stuffing out of her," Will said. "That falls into the realm of stalking, in my book."

"Then again, we don't know that it's one of my clients. A customer at Geekland could have developed an inappropriate crush. At least my clients are in treatment. Any kind of borderline personality type could walk into that bar and fixate on Amanda."

"I know that's possible," Amanda said. "But I've been paying more attention to my customers since this started, and I'm having a hard time believing any of them are sending the valentines. They're goofy, not aggressive."

"I agree with that," Will said. "Not saying it's impossible, but I'm more willing to believe the guy's a client. He would have contact with Amanda and a plausible reason to be in the office."

Gloria clearly didn't like the idea of suspecting someone she was counseling.

"We have a third group, don't forget. Amanda has constant contact with psychology students. Believe it or not, some people are drawn to this field because they're screwed up."

"You're kidding." Somehow Will managed to look shocked.

"No, it's true. I've met my share of strange people since getting into this business."

Amanda kept a straight face, but only because she didn't meet Will's gaze. "Speaking of my bartending job, I need to cut out of here. Gloria, I've finished all the filing, and the reports I typed this afternoon are all right here." She laid her hand on a stack of folders on her desk.

"I'm surprised you don't have everything on disk," Will said.

"We do." Amanda patted the CD file box on her desk. "But you never know when technology will change, and good-quality paper in a fireproof filing cabinet is a safe storage method."

"Besides, playing with computers doesn't appeal to me," Gloria said. "I'd rather play with less complicated toys." She settled her attention on Will. "Like vibrators, for instance. Amanda, on the other hand, can't be bothered with them."

"I really have to go." Amanda rolled back

her desk chair.

"Amanda's the exact opposite of girls I've had in here before," Gloria continued. "They can hardly wait to get their hands on my vibrators. I had to insist that Amanda take one home. And then, does she use it? No. She —"

"Geez, the bus will be here any minute." Grabbing her backpack and shoving her purse inside, Amanda made a beeline for the coat rack. Gloria should come with a warning label attached, CAUTION: DANGEROUS WHEN MOUTH IS OPEN. "Move it, Will."

"I'm right behind you."

"You're leaving with her?" Gloria sounded bereft.

"Doing the boyfriend thing," Will called over his shoulder as he followed Amanda's flight out the door and down the steps. "She can't help herself," he murmured as he hurried along beside her. "I'm convinced she has no idea how she affects people."

"Maybe not, but *God.*" Amanda's cheeks felt hotter than a Starbucks latte.

"She forced a vibrator on you, huh?"

"I'd rather not talk about it."

"I understand."

But when they reached the bus stop, they were early and had to stand there waiting. A couple of people sat on the bench, but Amanda and Will stood off to the side. She struggled to come up with a conversational topic, but it wasn't easy moving from the subject of vibrators to . . . anything.

"I think it's a little colder today than yesterday," she said.

"Some." He put his arm around her shoulders. "Does this help?"

"Uh, sure. Thanks." Now that they were even cozier, the silence between them seemed ten times more awkward. Finally she couldn't stand it. "Here's what happened."

"You don't have to tell me."

"Yes I do, because I want you to know the thing isn't even in my possession anymore."

"Don't tell me you threw it away."

"No. And it was the red one, so you get the complete visual. I stuck it in my backpack, and on the way home it worked its way up through the zipper, so it was sticking out. Of course I had no clue."

His body began to shake.

She glanced up at him. "You're laughing, aren't you?"

"Yeah." He grinned at her. "Is that not allowed?"

"You might want to pace yourself. It gets better. Mavis always pounces whenever I come home, so naturally she saw this red thing before I realized it was showing and wanted to know what it was. I told her it was a battery-operated hair curler and the batteries were dead."

Will snorted.

"So then my other neighbor, Chester, comes to the door, and as I'm talking to him, I turn around, and Mavis is testing the curler on her hair. She says the batteries are fine, but she can't figure out how it curls your hair."

By now Will was laughing so hard he had to let go of her so he could take off his glasses and mop the tears streaming down his face.

Watching him, she couldn't help smiling, herself. She was smiling on the inside, too, where all kinds of good feelings blossomed in ways she'd been missing for a long time. She couldn't remember the last time she'd shared a funny story with a guy.

Finally Will replaced his glasses and shoved his handkerchief in the pocket of his coat. He took a shaky breath, but he still couldn't get rid of the grin. "So did you ever tell her what it was for?"

"Well, I had to, and she was fascinated. So Chester got uncomfortable and left, but Mavis was so intrigued that I let her take it back to her apartment."

"Oh . . . my . . . God."

"I know. Don't think about it."

"How can I help it?"

"You have to. In about twenty minutes you'll be meeting her."

Will groaned. "This won't be easy."

"But necessary. You'll need to meet both of them. I can't bring a man into my apartment without letting them know. They'd hurt themselves trying to find out what was going on, so I might as well explain you right in the beginning."

"How are you planning to explain me? Am I supposed to be the real boyfriend as far as they're concerned, or the decoy?"

"You pretty much have to be the decoy." She wondered if she'd imagined the sudden flash of disappointment in his eyes. "Yesterday I told them the whole story, including your part in it."

"You emphasized that I'm not the valentine guy, I hope."

"Absolutely. I think they'll be happy that I have someone staying in the apartment with me. Mavis thought I needed protection, and the complex doesn't allow dogs, so she'll heartily approve of . . ." She paused as she realized how tacky that sounded. "I'm sorry. That didn't come out right. I don't think of you as a substitute for a dog."

"I know."

"I mean, really, I don't. I'm deeply appreciative that you've interrupted your routine to help me out. Considering we've only known each other a short time, you're making quite a sacrifice, and I —"

"It's not a sacrifice." His green gaze softened.

That kind of look could be her undoing. It could put her in the mood for all sorts of activities that she couldn't afford to indulge in. Time to change the mood.

"That's what you think," she said. "You haven't spent a night on my lumpy couch or been forced to eat one of Mavis's nuked meals. You'll have to share a small bathroom and keep weird hours."

The warmth in his eyes didn't go away as she'd hoped.

"Seriously, Will. The next few days could be pure torture."

He smiled. "You could be right about that."

EIGHTEEN

As they approached Amanda's three-story apartment building, Will looked it over from the standpoint of security and wasn't cheered. Evergreen bushes shielded the view of many of the first-floor windows. Unless the windows were newer than they seemed from the outside, someone would have no trouble getting in that way.

He put his arm around Amanda's shoulders, in case the nutcase happened to be watching. "Which windows are yours?" Every time he touched her, he fought the surge of desire that threatened to turn this entire charade into chaos.

She pointed them out. "Right there. Fifth and sixth from the front."

"Think you could get anybody to trim those bushes?" His hip brushed hers as they walked. When she'd said the next few days could be pure torture, she'd nailed it.

"I could ask, but I doubt it. They have a

schedule of trimming in the spring and in the fall. We're between trimming times."

"Would they care if I did it?"

She glanced up at him with a little smile. "You keep hedge clippers in your pocket?"

"Well, no. But I could buy some. I —" Then he noticed something glinting in one of her windows. He stopped in the middle of the sidewalk to identify it for sure. Damned if she didn't have a stained-glass hummingbird dangling from a suction cup.

Because he was hanging on to her, Amanda had to stop, too. "What's the matter?"

"That's your hummingbird in the window, right?"

"Uh-huh. That's the living room window. I found that sun-catcher at an art festival and I . . . Oh, God." She began to tremble. "I'll take it down right now."

"Okay."

"But it could be too late, couldn't it?"

He hated for her to be so frightened. Instinctively he tightened his grip on her shoulder and tried for a reassuring smile. "Maybe not. We don't even know for sure the valentine guy left the song on your answering machine. Someone could have dialed by mistake and the radio was on.

Could be a little kid playing with the phone."

She took a shaky breath. "Right. But let's get inside and take down that sun-catcher. I didn't even think about it, but if he has any idea I'm in this apartment building, then he could make the connection of the sun-catcher and the hummingbird on my desk. What an idiot I am."

"Lots of people like hummingbirds." He wanted to hold her and rock her and tell her everything would be fine. But first he'd have to convince himself of that, and he wasn't particularly convinced.

Amanda found her key and unlocked the entrance to the building. "Prepare yourself for a valentine blitz."

Will surveyed the hallway with amazement. "Wow. This takes me back to my days at Taft Elementary."

"Which is no coincidence. My neighbor Mavis Endicott used to teach third grade. She lives for holiday decorations."

"She did all this?" Will had a mental image of his third-grade teacher, Mrs. Nadworthy, running up and down this hall slapping hearts and doilies on everyone's door. He could picture it.

"She cons everyone into decorating. Or shames them, depending. Her methods work for everyone except Chester and me. I don't have time, so I let Mavis do my door, but Chester objects on principle. He . . . I'll be damned."

"What?"

"There's a big red heart in the middle of Chester's door. I wonder if he knows?"

Will felt as if he'd fallen down *Alice in Wonderland*'s rabbit hole. "She would tape a heart to his door without his permission?"

"I didn't think so, but it looks as if she did. The war must be escalating." Sticking her key in the door, Amanda turned it. Then she wiggled it. Still nothing happened. "Darn thing sticks."

"Let me."

"Be my guest." She handed over her set of keys.

Will worked with the key and finally felt it turn in the lock. "You need some graphite. I can pick some up tomorrow."

A portly woman with bottle-red hair opened the apartment door on his right. "That sounds promising." She walked toward them carrying several brownish lumps on a flowered plate. "Do we have a handyman among us?"

This had to be the woman who'd snagged the red vibrator. Will prayed for self-control, but he could already feel himself wanting to laugh.

Amanda turned, completely deadpan. "Hi, Mavis. This is Will Sloan, the man who —"

"The man who did *not* send the secret valentines!" Mavis shifted the plate to her left hand and reached out with her right. "I'm so pleased to meet you. I've heard wonderful things."

"Is that so?" Will's eyes widened as he glanced at Amanda.

"I told her you were nice. Which you are. This is Mavis Endicott, my neighbor." Amanda was one cool customer. Only a glimmer in her blue eyes gave any indication that she was thinking about that red vibrator.

Will, meanwhile, had to clear his throat before he responded. "Glad to meet you, too, Mavis. Amanda has . . . excuse me." He cleared his throat again. "Mentioned you."

The apartment door on Will's left swung open and a short bald man came out. "Has she mentioned that Mavis is crazy as a bedbug?"

"Will," Amanda said, "this is Chester Ambrose. Chester, this is Will Sloan, the man who —"

"Who didn't send the valentines!" Ches-

314

ter stepped into the hall and stuck out his hand. "Glad to meet you!"

"Same here." Will had never in his life been so glorified for not doing something.

Chester finished shaking hands and swung his arm to encompass the hall full of red, white, and pink decorations. "Will, would you look at this frippery? I'm the only sane one left on the floor. *My* door is bare, the way nature intended it." Reaching back, he closed his door with a flourish. "See?"

There was a moment of complete silence as the eye of the storm passed over. Then Chester exploded. "What the hell is this?" He ripped the heart off his door, marched over to Mavis and waved it in her face. "You know what this is?"

Mavis stood her ground. "I most certainly do. Do you?"

"It's trespassing! You trespassed on my door!"

"Fiddlesticks." Mavis stuck out both chins. "That door belongs to the apartment complex, not to you. And the manager thinks my decorations are festive. I had to do something about your door. It didn't fit in."

Chester's whole body quivered with rage. *"I don't want to fit in."*

"Oh, cool your jets, you old windbag."

With a wave of her hand, Mavis strolled into Amanda's apartment as if she owned it. "I brought over a treat, but with the way you're behaving, I don't think I'll offer you any."

Chester stood there blinking. "Didn't want any in the first place," he muttered. "Probably tastes like rabbit droppings." Then he followed Mavis into Amanda's apartment.

Will turned to her. "Is it always like this?"

"Pretty much. My apartment is the DMZ." She smiled at him. "Come on in and have some rabbit droppings. Then we can tell them why you're here."

"Don't forget about the hummingbird."

Her smile vanished. "I haven't forgotten. But I'm going to do that quietly. I don't want to scare Mavis and Chester."

Will nodded. If he'd had no other reason to become entranced by this woman, and he had several, her compassion for these two eccentric neighbors would be enough. She might not want him, but at the moment there was no one else he wanted more.

While Mavis was setting out plates, napkins, and whatever soft drinks she could find in Amanda's refrigerator to go with her micro-wave cheese balls, Amanda edged over to the living room window. She made sure Mavis and Chester weren't looking before pulling the suction cup from the window, along with the stained-glass hummingbird. She felt like an idiot for not realizing that this could lead someone to her, but until last night she hadn't thought the valentine guy knew where she lived.

She should cut herself some slack, because stress and lack of sleep were affecting her brain, but she'd always been proud of her ability to think through her problems. She hoped her love of the miraculous little hummingbirds wouldn't turn out to be her undoing.

Tucking the sun-catcher and suction cup between a couple of books in her bookcase, she glanced at the answering machine on her desk in the living room. One message. She tried to tell her rolling tummy that the message was a recorded sales call for satellite TV or a political message of some kind. Her tummy didn't believe that.

But she wasn't about to play the message, whatever it was, while Mavis and Chester were still here. As she walked back to the dining nook where Chester and Will had already taken a seat, Will glanced up. He must have seen something in her expression, because he frowned.

"So I tried commodities a while back,"

Chester said. "Lost money. Then I bought Enron stock. You know how that went. Finally I decided to buy stock in this feminine products company that's based right here in Chicago. Purely Hers. I figure women always need that stuff. That stock's doing okay."

"Playing the market's always a gamble." Will loosened his tie. "I could steer you toward a couple of mutual funds I like, if you want something that's a little less volatile."

Amanda paused, struck by how manly Will looked sitting there with his suit coat off, his sleeves rolled back and his tie at half mast. She envisioned coming home to a guy like Will every night, and the thought heated her up more than a little. She was capable of postponing that kind of reward, though.

"But you can't make as much money in those mutual funds." Chester had leaned the red cardboard heart against the rungs of his chair. Although he'd ripped the heart from the door with seeming force, he must have used a certain amount of finesse, because the heart remained intact.

Amanda had the urge to kiss his bald head. His bluster hid a very soft center.

"Over the long haul you might make even more, but the choice is yours," Will said.

"Ultimately, you're the investor."

"Chester the Investor. It rhymes!" Mavis came in with a liter bottle of ginger ale and added it to the half-full liter of cola already on the table.

"Isn't that hysterical," Chester said. "Next thing I know you'll make up a song about it."

"I might, at that. Or a picture book. I've always wanted to write one."

"And you could dedicate it to Chester." Amanda was grateful for this wacky pair. They were taking her mind off valentines and songs on answering machines.

"I don't want a dumb dedication," Chester said. "I want a cut."

"Why am I not surprised?" Mavis gestured toward the two bottles. "This is all I could find. There's wine, but I didn't think Amanda would want that before she goes to work."

Chester glanced at her. "Good thinking for a change. Are you two women going to sit down or what?"

"Sure." Before Amanda reached the chair, Will leaped up and pulled it out for her. As he helped her scoot in, she breathed in Old Spice. Lust could be another distraction from terror. So could her battle with lust. She'd take all the distractions she could get.

Mavis sighed. "Isn't that adorable?"

"I suppose you'd like similar treatment?" Chester scowled at Mavis.

"I wouldn't dream of expecting it."

"Oh, for crying out loud." With a groan, Chester left his chair and yanked out the vacant chair for Mavis.

She sat down and gave him a prim smile. "Thank you, sir. That was most kind."

"Yeah, yeah, yeah. Don't get used to it." Chester flopped into his chair. "What do you think the market's gonna do, Will? If you have any hot tips, I'm listening."

Mavis glared at him. "Don't you know that's rude? It's like asking a doctor during a cocktail party whether he'll take a look at the mole on your backside to see if it's skin cancer."

"In the first place, this isn't a cocktail party." Chester glared right back. "In the second place, I don't take off my pants for just anybody. I have to have a real special reason. Just so you know."

"I'm sure our guest is delighted to hear such intimate details about you, Chester." Mavis smiled at Will. "I didn't think I'd ever get to meet you, because Amanda seems so determined not to date anyone, but here you are."

"I need to explain that." Amanda picked

up a cheese ball. It felt like a lump of Silly Putty. "Will has agreed to pose as my boyfriend, in hopes that will discourage the guy sending me valentines." She bravely popped the cheese ball into her mouth, but when she tried to crunch down on it, the cheese ball didn't give.

"Brilliant." Mavis took a cheese ball and rolled it between her thumb and forefinger. "Whose idea was it?"

Amanda gave up trying to chew the cheese ball to death and swallowed it whole, pretending it was an oyster. Except oysters slid down, and this cheese ball was stubbornly clinging to her esophagus. Finally she washed it down with ginger ale.

After some delicate coughing, she was able to speak again. "It was Will's idea."

Speaking of Will, he'd also taken the cheese ball plunge, and judging from the way his jaw muscles were working, he wasn't making much progress with it, either.

"Having a little problem with the cheese balls, are you?" Chester gave them each a sly grin.

"Not at all." Amanda grabbed another one. "These are great."

"Mm!" Will nodded enthusiastically.

"So anyway, Will and I decided he should sleep here overnight — on the couch, of course. That way he'll look like a serious boyfriend."

"Forced together by circumstances." Mavis got all dreamy-eyed. "Just like Clark Gable and Claudette Colbert in *It Happened One Night*."

"But this is different. Will and I are just friends." Amanda tried to pull the cheese ball apart. It seemed like half a cheese ball should go down easier than a whole. "This is only to get rid of the valentine guy. Nothing permanent." No matter which way she tried to rip the rubbery little bastard, it refused to split.

"Makes no never mind how you arrange it." Chester took a cheese ball from the plate. "I think it's a good idea for two people to live together, try out the deal."

Amanda's cheeks warmed. "But that's not what this is. It's not an arrangement. We're not moving in together because we're involved. It's all pretend." She looked to Will for backup, but he was still busy trying to chew his cheese ball.

"It's pretend for now," Mavis said. "But you never know. Being in the same apartment all night could lead to things you can't predict in advance."

"It won't lead to anything." Amanda resorted to squeezing the cheese ball to try and make it thinner. "This is my senior year. I'm not taking any chances."

"I wouldn't, either, if I was you." Chester continued to study his cheese ball. "Use protection."

Will grabbed a napkin and coughed into it.

"Chester Ambrose!" Mavis shook her cheese ball at him. "You're embarrassing them. Now stop it."

"I am?" Chester's eyes widened. "I thought this was the modern age. Listen, I'm not the one who came home with a red vibrator in my knapsack."

Amanda didn't dare look at Will. Finally she thought she'd be able to reply, but she still had to clear her throat before she could do it. "Will and I are not going to become involved. That's all I wanted you both to know."

Chester shrugged. "If you say so. In my view, there's nothing wrong with a little fooling around. It's a whole lot better than resorting to artificial methods, which may or may not be red, if you get my drift." He put his cheese ball on his plate. "I think I'll run next door and get my hacksaw."

"Very funny," Mavis said. "Innovative cooking is obviously wasted on you." She glanced at her watch and pushed back her chair. "This has been fun, but I have to go. *Wheel of Fortune* comes on in two minutes."

Chester looked up. "You watch that?"

"Yes, I do, and don't you dare make fun of me for it."

"Wasn't going to." Chester stood. "I tune in once in a while, myself."

Mavis headed for the door. "Well, if you think I'm going to invite you to watch it with me, you're sadly mistaken."

Chester picked up his cardboard heart and followed her. "Why would I want to watch it with you? I'll bet you shout out the answers and don't give anyone else a chance to guess."

"You'll never know, though, will you?" Mavis opened the door. "Nice to meet you, Will."

"Same here, Mavis," Will said.

"Ditto for me," Chester said as he followed Mavis out the door and closed it behind him.

Will glanced over at Amanda. "They're crazy about each other, aren't they?"

"I think so. But they haven't figured it out yet."

Will nodded. "That happens."

Amanda looked into his eyes as silence settled around them. So this was what being alone with Will was like. The air seemed to quiver and pulse as they gazed at each other. She'd made a slight tactical error. In evaluating how easily she'd be able to resist him, she'd based her conclusions on the evidence presented in more crowded conditions.

Even when he'd kissed her, they'd been in an office where anyone could walk in. The rest of the time, they'd had people around to dilute this magnetic pull. Deprived of that diluting influence, they could be in some serious trouble.

"Amanda?"

Holding his gaze, she leaned closer. Her breathing changed, and her body seemed to melt into the contours of the chair. "What?"

"Was there a message on the answering machine?"

That was the end of that. She sat upright, all the warm yummies chased away. "Yes, there was."

"Then we'd better listen."

"Right." As she left the table, she told herself to be grateful that he'd remembered why he was here. Eventually she would be able to dig down and find that gratitude. For now, she hated, positively hated, that he'd ruined the mood.

That wasn't particularly fair, considering that she was the one who kept announcing she didn't want to become involved. But she couldn't remember the last time she'd felt that liquid sensation as her body prepared for sex. She'd forgotten how wonderful the sensation could be. Unfortunately, now she remembered only too well, and that would make the next few days . . . hell.

NINETEEN

Close call. Will took a deep breath before following Amanda over to the answering machine. Sitting at the table looking into each other's eyes had been a very bad idea. He needed to keep them both moving, both thinking about the valentine guy and his shenanigans. Otherwise they'd let nature take its course, and although Amanda might want that at first, she'd hate him later.

Besides that, he'd made her a promise that he wouldn't take advantage of this situation. No matter how she behaved or what her smoldering eyes said, he had to remember that promise. He didn't want to be a guy who threw roadblocks in her path. She already had one of those, and he'd probably left another damn song on her answering machine.

"Here goes." Amanda punched play.

At first there was nothing but a few little knocks and shuffling sounds. Will allowed himself to hope that it was a wrong number and soon he'd hear the click of a disconnect. But the intro to Power Station's "Some Like It Hot" destroyed that fantasy.

The reproduction was bad, which confirmed what she'd thought, that the guy was holding the phone up to a stereo. This particular number was far more suggestive than "Hungry Like the Wolf." The valentines had escalated in bawdiness, and now it seemed the songs would become progressively more explicit, too. Great.

"That's enough." Amanda pushed delete and a robotic female voice with a British accent announced that the message had been erased.

"I wonder if you should be saving those."

Amanda turned to him. "Why? We both know the police aren't going to want to investigate penny-ante things like this. I don't know what they could figure out from this kind of message, anyway."

Will took off his glasses and massaged the bridge of his nose. "I suppose you're right."

"It's close to Valentine's Day. I'll bet all kinds of people end up with secret admirers right about this time. I think the cops would laugh in my face if I complained about mine."

"I don't think the guy's into hearts and

flowers."

"No." Lines of tension showed around her mouth and eyes.

Will longed to suggest buying two tickets to Tahiti. She needed a break from all this. The jerk wouldn't follow them there, and by the time they came back, he might have lost interest. Of course, Amanda's semester would be ruined along with her career plans, but a tropical vacation with her would be so incredible.

Neither of them could afford incredible right now. Someday she might be able to lounge on the beach with an umbrella drink, but not this week. "I noticed you took down the hummingbird," he said.

She nodded. Then she sighed. "This sucks."

"Yep. But we might as well get on with the routine. What's next on the schedule?"

They looked at each other for a little longer than was wise, judging by the reaction in his groin. He'd have to work up an immunity to those big blue eyes.

"Work," she said. "I need to change."

"Then go ahead. I can change out here." He noticed her hesitation. Her apartment furniture was basic and a little worn, but the place was neat, without things scattered everywhere. He liked that. "I'll fold my clothes so I won't make a mess."

"You need to hang up that suit." She glanced at the duffel bag he'd brought. "Did you bring another one in there?"

"No. I took a garment bag to the office with enough stuff to last me for a few days. All I have in the duffel are casual clothes. And pajamas."

Her cheeks turned a sweet shade of pink. "This feels very weird. We don't know each other all that well."

"Is there another guy friend you'd rather have do this?" He didn't like the idea, but he wasn't going to force the issue.

She shook her head. "I hate to admit it, but my current friendships are on the superficial side. Work and school have made a social life damned near impossible. I don't know anyone well enough to make this kind of request. You offered, and after that first song on the answering machine . . ."

"Then we'll just go with it."

"Yeah." She took a deep breath. "Thanks."

"No problem." She looked so vulnerable, so in need of having someone hold her. But they were alone, and that was against the rules. He could only touch her when it would make an impression on someone else, and that way he wouldn't be tempted to take that next step and start removing clothes.

"Once you change out of the suit, I'll hang it in my closet so you won't have to cram it into the duffel bag." She gave him a quick smile. "See you in five minutes. Eat all the cheese balls you want while I'm gone."

He laughed, glad she hadn't lost her sense of humor. Once she'd walked into her bedroom and closed the door, he pulled off his tie and started unbuttoning his shirt. From inside the bedroom came the sound of Madonna, turned up to blast level. He didn't blame her. He wondered if she was in there dancing away her angst, and he hoped so.

As he was zipping his jeans, the phone rang. She wouldn't be able to hear it with the music playing so loud, and maybe that was just as well. He should answer it, anyway, and establish his presence here.

Crossing to the phone wearing only a T-shirt, jeans, and socks, he picked up the receiver before the machine clicked on. "Hello?"

Silence.

The skin on the back of his neck prickled. "Hello?" He thought he heard someone breathing, but he couldn't be sure. "Listen, whoever the hell you are —"

A soft click told him the caller was gone. Anger boiled in his chest, and he fought the urge to fling the phone across the room. No one had the right to harass another person like this. No one.

The music stopped and Amanda came out of the bedroom dressed for work and holding her geek glasses in her hand. "Did I hear the phone?"

He wanted to lie in the worst way. He seemed to be able to pull it off with someone like Gloria, but with Amanda, no such luck. "Hang-up."

"You mean they hung up when they got the machine?"

"They hung up when they got me."

A slight shiver passed through her. Then she pressed her lips together and fooled with the earpieces on her glasses. "I guess that's good."

He hated the fear that she was trying so valiantly not to show. "Especially if the valentines and song messages stop." He prayed it would be that easy.

Harvey slammed his fist into the wall beside the stereo, because that seemed like the right thing to do under the circumstances. What was a guy doing in Amanda's cute little apartment? Harvey was the only guy who was supposed to be in there, not counting the old fart who visited her sometimes. This hadn't sounded like the old fart.

His hand hurt like hell, though, and now his knuckles were bleeding. Not only that, there was a hole in the wall the size of a Big Mac. Louise would kill him when she came home from her nail appointment and saw that.

Sucking his bleeding knuckles, he looked around for a way to disguise the damage. Then he spotted his and Louise's framed wedding invitation hanging over by the front door. Perfect.

But the picture hanger holding it up wouldn't come out of the wall, so he had to get the hammer and pry it out. When he finally got it loose, a chunk of plaster came with it. Hell. Now he had two holes. The one by the stereo was bigger, so he hammered the picture holder above that one. In the process he hit his thumb.

Just great. Now his knuckles were bleeding on one hand and his thumb was swelling on the other. He hoped it went down by Valentine's night, or he'd have trouble carrying Amanda out of her apartment.

But a swollen thumb wouldn't keep him from following Amanda tonight to find out what was up with this guy answering her telephone. If she wanted to make Harvey really jealous, she was doing a fine job of it. Or maybe this was a pushy guy, and she needed someone to move in and rescue her.

If he watched them, he'd figure out what was going on. He needed more information. But first he had to cover up the holes he'd made. The wedding invitation worked on hole number one, but now he needed something smaller to put over hole number two.

Scouring the house, he found the little plaque in the master bathroom that said LOVING YOU COMPLETES ME. Louise had bought that for him, and then he hadn't known what to do with it. She'd finally suggested hanging it in the bathroom over the toilet, which he took to mean that loving him made her regular.

The plaque was exactly the right size to cover up the hole by the front door. But he wasn't moving the hook it was on and risking another hole. He'd learned his lesson about that. The plaque could hang on a pushpin.

And on the hook could go . . . the spare roll of TP! It even had a yellow crocheted cover, so it didn't look that bad hanging there. As an added bonus, it freed up the back of the tank for other stuff, like Louise's gun magazines.

Harvey would have rather had some copies of *Hustler* in the bathroom, but Louise wouldn't let him keep those around. So if he took a break, he had to read her gun magazines, which he found mostly boring. Louise loved them, though.

Some gun dealer had convinced her the sawed-off shotgun she'd bought was an antique once owned by Al Capone, himself. Harvey thought the gun dealer was a rip-off artist who figured out Louise had money to burn, but Louise was so stuck on that gun that there was no talking sense to her about it.

Ten minutes later, Harvey was bundled up for his trip to Geekland, where Amanda worked at night. Harvey had been in there once since he'd started keeping track of Amanda. He'd worn a Cubs cap pulled down low, and he'd chosen a table far away from the bar. Tonight being Friday, he could take cover in the crowd with no problemo.

If that stockbroker was in the bar tonight bothering Amanda, Harvey would do something about it. Amanda was his, and no geek was going to horn in on his territory. Halfway out the door, he turned and went back in. He needed to send another song to Amanda, and the nerd had distracted him from doing that. But he'd send a different tune than the one he'd planned on. This one would leave no doubt in her mind that he meant business.

Dealing with a stalker was the only thing keeping Amanda from jumping Will's bones. If not for that anonymous phone call, she and Will might be rolling in the sheets instead of riding a bus to Geekland. When she'd walked into her living room and found him in jeans and a T-shirt, all rational thought had disappeared.

Some men wore padded jackets to broaden their shoulders, and she'd wondered if that could be Will's story. But the T-shirt didn't lie. Will had the wide shoulders and narrow hips of a running back.

He wasn't all muscled up, though. He had the lean thing going on, but there wasn't an ounce of mean in the guy, which was all to the good in Amanda's opinion. Those glasses and soft green eyes only added to the hottie factor. She was getting X-rated bedroom ideas.

Looking at Will standing there in all his nerd glory had inspired her to call in sick. But then he'd told her about the phone hang-up, and fear had sapped all the lust right out of her body. That was a good thing, but she wouldn't go so far as to say the valentine stalker was doing her a favor.

Given a choice, she'd take her old life back in a heartbeat. With a dose of luck, she'd have that life again in a few days. In the meantime, she stood next to Will on the bus, both of them clutching the same pole and Will's arm wrapped protectively around her shoulders.

The bus was packed with commuters going home or to the nearest bar so they could celebrate the end of the work week. As the bus lurched from one stop to another, Amanda was thrown against Will. She was aware of every point of contact.

She glanced up to find him staring over her head, as if he were immune to the sparks created each time they bumped bodies. Then she noticed how the muscles in his jaw tightened each time they were jostled.

"I have to study all weekend," she said.

"Hm?" He leaned down toward her.

Standing on tiptoe, she spoke directly into his ear. "I have to study all weekend."

"Oh." He looked into her eyes. "I figured."

She'd been spending too much time listening to Gloria, because she noticed that his pupils were larger than normal. Maybe whispering in his ear had been a bad move.

Focus, Amanda. "I'm not sure what you're going to do with your time," she said.

"Please don't think you have to babysit me all day. You probably have things you like to do on the weekends, maybe stuff with Justin, or —"

"Don't worry about it."

She tried to picture the two of them cooped up in the apartment all day. She'd be studying, and he'd be lounging around, maybe in his sexy T-shirt and jeans outfit. He might be reading, thumbing through a magazine . . . with those big thumbs . . .

She shouldn't have loaned the vibrator to Mavis. She should have kept it and used it, just as Gloria had suggested. Then she wouldn't be a mass of hormonal frustration ready to explode.

He smiled down at her. "You are worried about it, aren't you?"

"It would be so boring for you."

"No it wouldn't. I'm amazingly self-sufficient, and I brought reading material."

Do you thumb through your reading material? "I'm sure you are self-sufficient, but —"

"You're nervous about spending the day together."

Damn straight. I'm even more nervous about the nights. "Not at all. We're two responsible adults." And two *consenting* adults. The bus lurched again, heaving them together. She enjoyed it entirely too much.

Will steadied her before shifting his weight so they weren't plastered quite so tightly against each other. He'd gone back to staring over her head, and his jaw worked. "Maybe hanging out with you and reading is a little too passive."

"You should have brought your free weights." It was a joke. She didn't picture him as owning free weights.

"I should have."

So, another surprise. The stockbroker nerd worked out with free weights. He was becoming sexier at every turn. Not good. "There's always housework."

He laughed. "Then I could go for a jog. If things are too tense, then I can go for another jog. And so on, ad infinitum. Eventually I'll be so exhausted, you'll have no worries."

She didn't think watching him getting hot and sweaty would be much help, but telling him that would only put a finer point on her case of lust. "We'll manage," she said.

"Yeah, we will." He leaned down and glanced out the window. "We're almost there. Before we go in, you need to know I'm going to do everything I can to keep Gloria and Justin from hooking up. You might think there's no harm in it, but —"

"Gloria would be easier on his liver."

"But hard on his heart."

"You think?"

"You don't know Justin. He'll get attached, and from what I've seen, Gloria doesn't do attachments." As the bus slowed, Will relaxed his grip on her shoulder and slid his hand down to twine his fingers through hers.

The move was so natural, as if they really were a couple. Amanda allowed herself a moment of regret. "You're right that Gloria doesn't do attachments, but if Justin wants her . . ."

Will shook his head. "I can't let him do that to himself. He was there for me in a similar situation and kept me from doing something stupid."

"A woman?" Amanda was intrigued.

"A woman. I caught her —" He gave Amanda a quick glance. "Never mind."

"Hey, come on."

He gazed at her, his expression neutral. "I caught her with another guy."

"Caught her where?"

"In bed. Our bed."

"Yikes."

"At the time I was too stunned to do anything, but later I decided to fight him. Justin pointed out that he was a jock, which meant I'd be beaten to a pulp and Helen wasn't worth it."

Amanda's heart ached for him. "I'm sure she wasn't worth it. That's a low move."

"To be fair, I wasn't paying enough attention to her. She flat-out told me I mostly cared about my thesis and looking for a job."

"But those goals are important."

He shrugged. "So was she."

The direction of the conversation made her uncomfortable. She wasn't going to ask Will if he regretted how his life had turned out. She didn't want to hear the answer.

Air brakes sighed as the bus came to a stop. Will took her hand and helped her down the steps. "So anyway, where Gloria's concerned, I —"

"Watch yourself," Amanda said. "There she is." A Checker Cab had pulled to the curb behind the bus and Gloria was climbing out, her fur coat billowing around her.

She spotted them immediately. "Thank God you're here." She hurried over, her five-inch heels cracking the thin layer of ice on the sidewalk. "I need a geek guide to escort me in there. If anybody asks, I'm doing psychological research."

"Listen, you don't have to do this," Will said quickly. "I'll be glad to tell Justin you changed your mind."

"Not on your life." Gloria took Will's free arm and faced the entrance. "I'm going in."

Amanda decided to support Will's efforts to derail Gloria. Maybe the nerd stereotype would do the trick. "You'll hate it. Lots of technical conversation, nasal laughter, mismatched clothes, and glasses held together with tape. Not your scene at all."

"That may be true of the other men in there," Gloria said. "But it doesn't apply to either Will or Justin, who are nerdy in a sexy way. I've decided to widen my net and see which one I can coax in first. Or maybe I'll get them both." She glanced up at Will. "Ever considered a threesome?"

TWENTY

The evening proved to be the suckiest Will had ever slogged his way through. Everyone else seemed to be enjoying the festivities, but he was miserable. He was supposed to be the boyfriend, but he couldn't hang around Amanda that much and put her job at risk.

That left him to pursue his other assignment — trying to identify her stalker in the crowd. As the night wore on, any guy who ordered a drink from Amanda became a suspect. Finally Will was ready to clear the bar of everyone with the ability to pee standing up.

Meanwhile Gloria threw herself into trivia and was too damned good at it to suit Will. But he couldn't defend his title tonight, not when he needed to watch Amanda's back. Even more galling, Gloria's consumption of martinis had no noticeable effect on her mental ability, but they obviously eliminated her inhibitions, and Gloria didn't have many to start with.

Each time she won a round, she hopped on the bar and did a victory dance, giving the guys below an eyeful. Of course they loved it, but Will had expected the women in the bar to resent Gloria and make life unpleasant for her. No such luck. Gloria had come with a purse full of fingertip vibrators, and in between trivia rounds she gave out sexual advice.

Everyone was enthralled, and the most enthralled in the batch was the one person Will had hoped to protect. If Gloria asked Justin to go home with her, he'd jump at the chance. Short of locking Justin in the Geekland men's room, Will couldn't think of a way to stop the inevitable.

He had only one ally. Several times Will had watched as Amanda drew Justin aside and talked earnestly with him. Judging from the way she kept glancing at Gloria during those conversations, she had to be filling Justin full of reasons to steer clear of the wild sex therapist.

Will was grateful. He was also in serious lust. All night he'd been aware of her working behind the bar, her blond hair shimmering in the light, her funky Geekland glasses making her look like a cross between a prom queen and a spelling bee champ.

From the evidence, he was becoming obsessed, and that wasn't the best mental state when he was heading into a one-on-one weekend with the lovely Ms. Rykowsky. Closing time drew near, and then true torture would begin.

He stuck to virgin drinks all night. Staying sober was the only way to watch out for Amanda now and keep himself from jumping her later. Sobriety also gave him a fighting chance to block Gloria if she tried to whisk Justin away to her lair. He was expecting that move any time, now.

As he was nursing his last virgin Chi-Town Lakefront Breeze of the night, Gloria approached, martini glass in hand. Her smile was seductive and her hips undulated with each step. Appropriately, the sound system was belting out Hall & Oates' "Maneater." Will would have to duct-tape Justin to a bar stool to keep him from falling for temptation this hot.

She slid onto a stool beside Will. "Where've you been keeping yourself, cutie pie?"

"I like to stay in the background."

"You shouldn't hide your talents like that." She took a sip of her martini and left a lipstick print on the rim. "I have a proposition for you."

Now there was a shocker. "Gloria, it wouldn't work, especially not now, when I'm committed to helping Amanda get rid of her stalker guy."

"I have a solution for everything." She held up a finger with a perfectly manicured nail. "Number one, you have scruples about dating a client, but it's the weekend. You're not at work and neither am I."

"That's splitting hairs, but it's irrelevant because of this deal with Amanda." And thank God for that, even if it promised to be the biggest challenge of his life. At least it kept him at a safe distance from Gloria.

Apparently unfazed by his argument, she held up a second finger. "Number two, I agree that someone needs to pose as Amanda's boyfriend, but it doesn't have to be you."

"What?" He had the feeling he was losing control of the discussion.

"All she needs is a place holder, and how silly to waste your talents in that kind of generic position. Let Justin do it. I've already discussed it with him, and he —"

"Hold it." Panic took Will by the throat. He was worried about his sexual restraint if he spent the weekend with Amanda, but at least he *had* some sexual restraint. Currently

Justin was one big throbbing impulse.

Justin couldn't be trusted to stay alone with a woman who looked like Amanda. Come to think of it, Justin couldn't be trusted to stay alone with any woman, not even a complete dog. Any person who marked an *F* in the gender column on a driver's license application was off-limits to Justin for the foreseeable future.

"Wait here," Gloria said. "I'll go get him. He'll convince you that I have the perfect plan."

"No. I'm not —" But Will was talking to an empty stool. For someone who had consumed enough martinis to put a major dent in the bar's gin supply, Gloria possessed surprising speed. He turned on the stool, looking for Amanda. He needed backup, and he needed it now.

She caught his glance. Bar rag in one hand, she came toward him. "What's up?"

"Gloria."

"Don't worry. I worked on Justin all night. I think I've convinced him to take a pass on what Gloria's offering."

He noticed that her nose was adorably shiny. She'd been working hard tonight, and her makeup was fading. He wanted to kiss the tip of that shiny nose and then move on down to her mouth, which had lost all traces of lipstick. She'd be great to wake up to.

"I appreciate what you've been trying to do," he said. "But Gloria is nothing if not resourceful. Her new plan involves —"

"Here's Justin!"

Will turned on the revolving stool as Gloria appeared, one hand on Justin's shoulder as she propelled him forward. Justin looked mildly potted.

"Boyfriends 'R' Us," Gloria said. "He's ready for his assignment, aren't you, Justin?"

"Yeah." Justin nodded. "You were Gloria's first choice, buddy, and I've decided I'm not ready for the big time yet. You go for it. I'll fill in as Amanda's boyfriend this weekend, okay?"

"No, not okay." Will wondered if this could get any more complicated. "We're not playing musical boyfriends."

"That's for damned sure," Amanda said from her position behind the bar. "Thanks, anyway, Justin, but I'm sticking with Will."

Gloria blew out a breath. "That's not very accommodating, Amanda. You only need a token nerd, so what difference does it make whether you have Justin or Will?"

"It matters," Amanda said.

Will felt a warm glow in the pit of his stomach. She'd chosen him. That counted for something.

"I know what," Gloria said. "We'll toss a coin. Whoever wins the coin toss gets her choice of nerds."

"Nope, sorry." Will eased off the stool. "Thanks for the thought, Justin, but Amanda and I have a plan, and that's what we're going with."

Gloria tossed back the rest of her martini. "Well, *fine.* I can be flexible. As a point of fact, I'm *extremely* flexible. Justin, are you coming home with me, then?"

Justin hesitated. "You know, Gloria, I think we need to get to know each other better before I have sex with you."

"If that isn't the most provincial attitude I've ever heard." Gloria rolled her eyes. "I should have known better than to get myself mixed up with a couple of nerds."

Justin cleared his throat. "We could have lunch tomorrow."

Will started to interrupt and remind Justin of some imaginary racquetball game they had scheduled. He caught himself before he did that. Justin was acting with amazing self-control, and there was such a thing as being too protective.

"I'll think about lunch." Gloria folded her arms, tapped her toe on the wooden floor, and gazed at the ceiling. Then she looked at Justin. "I can't decide right now. Call me."

"I don't have your number."

"Got a pen?"

"Got a BlackBerry." He reached into his pocket and pulled out the palm-sized database.

Gloria waved it away. "BlackBerrys aren't sexy. I want a pen."

"Okay." Justin took one out of the breast pocket of his shirt. "But I don't have any paper."

"I didn't expect you to." Gloria clicked the ballpoint. "Hold out your hand."

Justin obliged, and Gloria wrote her number on his palm.

"That feels . . . good."

Gloria handed him the pen. "That's only a small sampling of the delights I can offer you."

As Justin stared at her with complete devotion, Will knew it was no longer *if* but *when.* Will couldn't save his buddy from this disaster.

Gloria walked to a nearby table and grabbed her fur coat from the back of a chair. Will wished he could avoid his early training, but it ran too deep. He stepped toward Gloria and helped her into her coat.

"You are a treasure," she said in a low voice. "Once this business with Amanda's stalker is over, we'll get together, you and I."

"Don't count on it."

"Oh, I'll count on it, all right. But in the meantime, I'll amuse myself with your friend." She raised her voice. "Justin, the ball's in your court. Be sure you copy that number before you give yourself a hand job tonight, or you'll smear the ink." With that, she swept out the front entrance of Geekland.

All the way home on the bus, Amanda babbled about the customers at Geekland, identifying potential suspects in descending order. She didn't really believe any of them were guilty of sending her valentines and playing songs on her answering machine, but going through the exercise distracted her. Sitting next to Will on the mostly deserted bus, she was all about distractions.

With his arm wrapped around her and his thigh brushing hers, he was way too potent. She should be exhausted after one sleepless night, but she had a feeling that she was in for another one. There was a remedy for her insomnia, of course. Certain activities were guaranteed to relax her and ease her into slumber.

The bus arrived at her stop long before

she was prepared. Will helped her down and kept her hand in his as they walked through the biting cold toward her apartment building.

"Do you plan to study tonight?" he asked.

"I should, but I'm beat."

"I'm sure you are." He squeezed her hand. "You work very hard."

That little squeeze started her heart pumping faster. A squeeze wasn't a requirement of the charade. Anyone watching them wouldn't notice something that subtle, which meant Will had done it for her, not for show.

But she pretended not to notice the extra helping of tenderness. "Thanks for not saying I work *too* hard."

"That's a judgment call, and I'm not qualified to judge."

They reached the entrance door and she dug out her key. He was quite a guy, this Will. She thought about the girlfriend who'd cheated on him and wondered if he still loved her. If he did, that would help keep the lid on any emotional involvement.

Yeah, right. She was already in this emotional swamp up to her chin, and the alligators of lust were circling, waiting to make mincemeat of her. Funny how pretending someone was your boyfriend and having him hold your hand a few times could trick a girl into thinking she was really part of a couple. That extra squeeze he'd given her had been the cherry on top of her fantasy sundae.

She'd told herself earlier that she didn't want to know about his ex, but that was a lie. Hell, yes, she wanted to know. He might not want to tell her, though, so she'd have to approach the subject indirectly.

"I probably do work too hard." She unlocked the door. "But sometimes a person has no choice."

"True." He made sure the door was shut and locked behind them.

"I'll bet you had to work pretty darned hard to get where you are today."

"Uh-huh."

Amanda started down the Hall o' Valentines. Now that they were inside the building, he didn't have a reason to hold her hand, but he was doing it, anyway. She decided not to remind him that it was unnecessary.

He wasn't taking the bait regarding hard work and sacrifice, though. Maybe he was so wounded by his ex that he couldn't bear to talk about her anymore. Or maybe he was just tired. But the more she thought about it, the more she itched to know if the flame still burned.

So she tried again. "Sometimes people in our lives don't appreciate how hard we have to work to get ahead."

"Sometimes."

Well, this line of attack wasn't getting her anywhere. As they approached her door, she checked to see if either Mavis or Chester were peeking out. Both apartments appeared to be locked, which was normal for this time of night. Both Mavis and Chester lost power after nine in the evening.

She shoved her key in the lock of her apartment door and wiggled it. "But then you have to wonder if those people who object to your dedication really want the best for you."

"Right."

As she opened the door into the dimly lit apartment, she gave her investigation one last shot. "If they looked at it from your perspective, they would see you were sacrificing short-term pleasure for long-term gain."

He closed the door and twisted the dead bolt into place. "Okay." He turned to face her. The living room lamp didn't shed much light in the entry hall, so his face was in shadow. "I get it, Amanda."

"Get what?" Confused, she paused in the

middle of unzipping her quilted jacket.

"You don't have to belabor the point. Go ahead and work as hard as you want." He took off his jacket and laid it over the arm of the couch. "I won't interfere with that."

She stared at him. "I wasn't talking about *you* not understanding that."

"Sure you were. You were reminding me not to get in the way of your program. And I won't."

"I was talking about your ex-girlfriend."

"Helen? What does she have to do with you and me?"

Caught. "Nothing." She jerked the tab on her zipper and got the damned thing stuck on the placket. "I was just making conversation." She tried to pull the zipper up the other way, but she'd wedged a piece of nylon in there good and tight.

"You were making conversation about Helen?" He sounded bewildered.

"I was making the point that she probably didn't understand your dedication to your goals." She struggled with the zipper, which now seemed welded in place. "So you can't blame yourself. It wasn't your responsibility that she ended up in bed with someone else."

"Interesting theory."

The stupid zipper refused to budge, so

she kept talking. "The way it looks to me, there was a lack of empathy on her part, maybe even a lack of self-confidence and maturity."

"Hm." His voice softened. "Need some help with that?"

"Thanks. I've got it." Nothing budged, and her fingers hurt from tugging on the metal tab, but she'd put herself in this fix, and she'd get herself out of it.

"That's what you said right before the bag ripped the other day."

"That was an embarrassing moment." She glanced up. Now that her eyes had adjusted to the dim light, she could see his face better.

His gaze had become as soft as his voice. "You handled that bag-ripping incident with style."

"So did you." Turning away would be smart, but she couldn't make herself do it.

"Thanks." His expression went from tender to something more potent.

Unless her coat was causing her to overheat, she was responding to that potency. She was afraid the coat had nothing to do with it. "I think you'd better stop looking at me like that."

"Sorry. Can't help it. You're something else, Amanda Rykowsky. So damned independent, so determined to do everything by yourself."

Her throat muscles weren't operating any better than her zipper, and she still couldn't seem to break eye contact. "That . . . that works for me."

"Does it?"

Her heartbeat thundered in her ears. "M-mostly."

"Let me fix that zipper." Without waiting for a reply, he dropped to his knees in front of her and began gently wiggling the metal tab.

She wondered if any of Gloria's sex manuals would consider this move foreplay. Highly unlikely, and yet . . . the longer Will fiddled with the zipper, the more she imagined him paying that kind of attention to parts of her that had become incredibly moist and warm all of a sudden.

A woman had to be seriously deprived if a guy could make her dream of orgasms as he fooled with the zipper of her coat. Or maybe his kneeling position had something to do with her fantasies. She longed to comb her fingers through his hair, cup the back of his head, and guide him to the X-rated spot where her sexual frustration lived.

If a man could manage to unstick one zipper, he could certainly get past a second one, one that had no known problems. Her damp cotton panties would be no challenge at all, and then . . .

"Nearly there."

The small whimper was out before she could swallow it.

"Amanda?"

Flooded with embarrassment, she manufactured a cough. "Sorry. Got something in my throat." When he didn't respond, she had the distinct impression he hadn't bought that line.

The zipper came free, and he slowly drew it down. "Fixed." The word came out rough around the edges, and he hadn't quite let go of her jacket.

"Th-thanks."

Still on his knees, he drew in a deep breath. "God. You smell . . . amazing."

She would walk away. Any second now. All she needed were two functioning legs to replace these wobbly rubber ones.

He took another breath and groaned. "You'd . . . you'd better go to . . . bed."

"Uh-huh."

"Unless . . ."

She felt dizzy. "Unless?"

His low chuckle was filled with regret. "Never mind." He pushed himself to his feet and turned away. "You probably want to handle this by yourself, too."

She began to quiver. He was being strong, being good, being noble. And she was none of those. Not anymore. She'd been worn down to the point of surrender. "No, I don't." Her blood raced through her veins at breakneck speed. "I — I need your help."

TWENTY-ONE

Will's mouth went dry. Slowly he turned back to her. He could blame powerful pheromones, that arousing scent that had reached out and captured him on a basic, irrefutable level as he'd knelt in front of her. But there was more going on here.

She'd portrayed herself as an impenetrable fortress, a bastion of self-sufficiency that would never be breached, especially by the likes of him. And for this sliver of time, she'd let down the drawbridge. He couldn't walk away from that, no matter how he might regret the decision later.

For once in his life, he knew exactly what to do, and exactly what not to do. This moment called for action. If he voiced any doubts, if he asked even one question, she might change her mind. She'd asked for help, and he had no trouble guessing what kind of help she wanted.

After tonight, she might never let him

touch her again. When she'd had some sleep, when she'd had time to collect herself and gather her resources, she might pull that drawbridge back up and lock it in place. He wouldn't worry about that now.

His next move wouldn't be elaborate. She needed direct intervention, and he was happy to provide that. He wouldn't pretend it was the beginning of anything, because it wouldn't be. It was what it was — a woman craving an orgasm, one she didn't want to give herself. He could live with that.

Looking into her eyes, he peeled off her jacket and let it fall to the floor. "Just relax."

She took a shaky breath but didn't respond.

He undressed her quickly, but with care. The softness of her skin, the sweet curve of her breasts, the aroma of her lust all tested his control, but he couldn't lose himself in this experience. He would give her what she needed — nothing more and nothing less.

Once she was standing naked and flushed before him, he allowed himself one sweeping look at paradise. Then he took off his glasses and propped them on top of the coat he'd laid on the arm of the couch. Scooping her up in his arms, he carried her into her darkened bedroom.

Holding her this way and cradling her

warmth almost destroyed his resolve to make this fast, memorable, and all about her. But it couldn't be about him. He hadn't come prepared for that, and she had to know he hadn't. When she'd asked for his help, she hadn't been suggesting they take silly chances. She was too smart.

He could see well enough to find the bed and ease her down onto it, but not well enough to decipher color and patterns. The quilt was cool and satiny against the backs of his hands as he bracketed her hips and pulled her to the edge of the mattress. Then he dropped to his knees for the second time that night.

Had this position planted the idea in her mind? Her little whimper had made him think so, but he'd never know for sure. He only knew that kneeling before her to unzip her jacket, he'd been hit with the possibilities. Fixing the zipper had taken much longer as he'd fought his urges.

Now he could satisfy at least one. When he kissed her inner thigh, she moaned. That single sound told him all he needed to know. She welcomed what he had in store for her, and that knowledge sent a powerful surge of desire straight to his groin.

He'd ignore that for now. Treasures beckoned him, and he began to explore the riches she had to offer. He began slowly, using his tongue gently and feeling the shivers of reaction as he drew closer to his ultimate destination. She tasted like honey laced with lemon and he feasted on her slick heat.

He could abandon himself so easily. Skating along the edge of oblivion, always pulling himself back from total immersion, he touched the tip of his tongue to her clit and held it there as she gasped in response. Gradually he increased the pressure until she began to pant and writhe on the bed.

As he replaced the steady pressure with slow sucking and firm swipes with his tongue, her hips rose to meet his caress. Her eagerness inspired him to use his tongue in ever more creative ways until she cried out and squirmed under him. Then she tensed, reaching for her reward.

When she came, fierce pride rushed through him. She was a woman who wasn't used to asking for what she needed. But she'd asked him, and he'd been able to give it to her.

He held her as the spasms ran their course. Finally she lay limp in his arms and gulped in air. Her whisper was so faint he almost missed it.

"Thank you."

"You're welcome." Standing with some

difficulty, considering his erection, he lifted her again and positioned her more fully on the bed. Then he took the edges of the quilt and wrapped them around her, creating a cocoon. By the time he left, her steady, shallow breathing told him that she was already asleep.

He closed her bedroom door and leaned against the doorjamb while he reviewed his options. He was, as Gloria's client had said, stiff as a tailpipe. He had the kind of erection that wouldn't subside any time soon unless he did something about it.

If he expected to get any sleep at all, he'd need to finish this session in the bathroom. Maybe that would be his salvation this weekend. With a sigh of resignation, he hobbled into the small room, turned on the light and closed the door.

Some time later, he came out, task accomplished. Although he felt obvious relief, it was mixed with dissatisfaction, as if this sexual reaction had required a specific remedy rather than a general one. Specific to Amanda, to be more exact, and that meant that only she could provide the sense of completion he craved. Under the circumstances, that could present a problem.

As he crossed to the couch, he noticed that a pillow and blanket had mysteriously appeared. He glanced at her bedroom door, which was closed. Apparently she'd come out while he was in the bathroom and left these for him. He wondered if she'd had any clue what he'd been doing behind the closed bathroom door. Maybe.

In any case, she wanted to keep the status quo. Could be that the drawbridge was already going up and would soon be bolted against any repeat of their recent activities. He'd thought he was prepared for that, but staring at the blanket and pillow, he discovered he wasn't.

A part of him had hoped that in the morning she'd have rethought her position. What a romantic sap he was to imagine that. He'd provided a much needed service tonight, but that was the end of that.

As he changed into the pajamas he'd bought, pajamas that felt stiff, new, and ridiculous, he decided that the pajamas should help keep him in line. No guy could think about sex while wearing this scratchy stuff. Feeling like a martyr, he plumped the pillow, lay on the couch and pulled the blanket over him. Then he reached behind his head and turned off the table lamp.

The room was dark except for the red light on her answering machine. *Answering machine.* He couldn't believe they'd forgotten about the answering machine. Well, yes, he could. The prospect of oral sex trumped checking messages on an answering machine every time.

With a sigh, he threw back the blanket and climbed off the couch. Might as well find out if the creep had struck again. Putting on his glasses so he wouldn't stumble over the furniture, he walked over to the desk, and discovered that one message had been left. He punched the button on the machine and waited.

Just as he was beginning to think there would be no message at all, he heard the opening bars of the Police and "Every Breath You Take." Shuddering, Will listened to Sting describe in detail the surveillance of some poor ex-girlfriend. If this wasn't a stalker theme song, he'd never heard one.

He hit the delete button and the cultured female voice informed him that the creepy message had been erased.

"Were you going to tell me about it?"

He glanced toward Amanda's bedroom door. She stood there, a shadowy figure wrapped up like a mummy in her quilt. He wondered if she was still naked under it. Probably not. She'd come out earlier to bring his pillow and blanket, and he doubted she'd streaked through the apartment to do that.

That meant she was using the added bulk of the quilt as a suit of armor. Yep, the drawbridge was definitely closed and barricaded.

"Would you want me to tell you?" he asked.

"Yes. I can't assess the danger unless I know everything." She hesitated. "That song . . . it sounds as if he's upset that you're in the picture."

Will's muscles tightened. "Let him be upset."

"I didn't consider all the implications of having you do this. What if he's crazy enough to retaliate against you?"

"I'd love to see him try. Then I'd have him out in the open, where we could identify him."

She met that remark with silence. Finally she spoke again. "I've thought about all the guys that come to Geekland, and I don't think he's one of the regulars. I think it's more likely he's one of Gloria's clients."

"So do I." But he thought they might do better discussing this in the daylight. Standing in a dark apartment with a bed not far away wasn't the wisest venue. The memory of her cries at the moment of orgasm came back to him in vivid detail.

She seemed to be ready to ignore that episode. He needed to take his cue from her and pretend it never happened. That wouldn't be easy. He could still taste her. His fingers remembered the texture of her skin.

"I have a key to Gloria's office."

At first he thought she was suggesting they go there and play with the toys. And damn it, he was ready and able to do that. Then reason prevailed. She had that quilt clutched tightly in both hands. She didn't want to invade Gloria's office to play games.

As his eyes adjusted to the dark, he could make out that her hair was tousled the way it would be after sex. He did his level best to talk like a man who wasn't focused on that subject. "Did you want to take a better look at Gloria's files?"

"I do. It could wait until Monday, but I feel a sense of urgency."

Earlier she'd felt a sense of urgency, too, for an entirely different goal. She'd wanted him to make her come. She couldn't have forgotten what that felt like. If she could, he hadn't done nearly the job he'd imagined.

"Are you suggesting we go now?" He would do it, but he thought she needed sleep. He wasn't going to say that, though, and risk coming off as a patronizing gatekeeper. That would be hypocritical, given that not long ago he'd had his head between her thighs, and that he wanted to do it all over again.

"Not now." Her voice gentled. "We both need sleep."

"Right." He hoped sleep was a possibility, but he doubted it.

"Tomorrow."

"I thought you had to study."

"I do, but if some maniac is out there waiting for me with God knows what on his mind, then my degree becomes a little less important, doesn't it?"

He couldn't argue with her logic. "And if I help you go through the files, we can be done sooner."

"Exactly. Good night, Will."

"Good night, Amanda."

"By the way, cute pajamas." Then she walked into her bedroom and closed the door.

Amanda slept better than she had in months, but she woke up with a huge case of the guilties. What kind of woman would reject the idea of a boyfriend and then invite a man to give her oral sex? Amanda knew exactly what kind — the Gloria Tredway variety.

Now that was humbling. Amanda couldn't condemn Gloria for taking her sexual pleasure where she could find it when Amanda had done the selfsame thing last night. At the time she'd loved every second of the pleasure Will had served up. That man could do amazing things with his tongue.

Lying in bed thinking about Will's tongue was liable to land her in the same fix this morning, and that would be selfish and unwise. She had no intention of taking what had happened last night and expanding on the theme. She had enough problems without adding full-blown sex with a man who had big thumbs.

Dim light seeped around the edges of her bedroom curtains. She glanced at the clock and discovered it was almost eight. Even disregarding a trip to Gloria's office to check through the files, she had a ton of things to accomplish this weekend. A paper on antidepressants was due Monday and a test was scheduled for Wednesday.

She needed to get up, but that meant facing Will. She wasn't sure how to do that in the light of day. Darkness had protected her last night when they'd talked about the song on the answering machine and the trip to Gloria's office. This morning there would be no hiding.

As she procrastinated, the aroma of coffee drifted under her closed door. Damn. First he gave her a stupendous climax and now he was making coffee. He had no mercy.

She didn't crave the coffee quite as much as she'd craved the orgasm, but it was a close call. Weekday mornings she didn't allow herself the luxury of making a pot, but she treated herself on weekends. Having coffee made *for* her was wonderful beyond belief. Having it made by the same man who'd given her the orgasm bordered on embarrassing.

How would she balance the scales? The obvious wasn't a possibility. That moment of indiscretion last night had to stand as her only lapse where William was concerned. She'd put it in the same category as the filet mignon she'd ordered when she'd aced her finals last semester — tender and juicy, but not something she could afford again anytime soon.

So if she couldn't offer Will sex, what could she do for him? Anything other than a good roll in the hay seemed piddly by comparison. In her current state of mind, sex presented itself as the perfect one-size-fits-all gift. No doubt Will would love it. Unfortunately, she might, too.

Maybe coffee would help her think better.

But in order to score some coffee she had to deal with Will. Guaranteed that he would look at her and remember last night's event. Then he'd get that certain look in his eyes, and she would go all squishy and warm, and they'd be in a mess.

Time to deploy the Bathrobe. She pulled it out of the closet and put it on over her flannel pajamas. She'd bought this blue terry robe on sale at Kmart ten years ago, and it hadn't been very attractive then.

Many washings and long study sessions later, it had morphed into the ugliest bathrobe in the universe. Blue had faded to gray, both pockets were ripped, and there were holes at the elbows. Cal, her ex, had called it the best birth control device he'd ever seen.

For the clincher, she rummaged through her closet for her fuzzy white slippers, which were no longer white or fuzzy. Some might say they were gray and balding. She'd bet that if all women wore a bathrobe this disgusting and slippers this moth-eaten and dingy, overpopulation would cease to be a problem.

Armed with the bathrobe and slippers, she opened her bedroom door and peeked out. Will had opened the living room drapes and the apartment was filled with the soft light of a cloudy Chicago day. Coffee dripped into the carafe as she'd expected. But she hadn't anticipated the way her heart would swell with happiness when she saw Will sitting at her little wooden table.

Dressed in black sweats and a black sweatshirt, he was reading the *Tribune.* She recognized the box in the middle of the table, too. He'd not only made coffee, he'd gone to the German bakery down the street and then to the newsstand on the opposite corner.

Now she felt really guilty. But even more than that, she felt hot and achy, just the reaction she'd been hoping to avoid. He hadn't even looked at her yet, and she was in trouble.

Then he glanced up and smiled.

Heaven help her, she wished that she hadn't resorted to the Bathrobe. Gazing into his green eyes made her long for silk negligees and high-heeled mules decorated with rhinestones. She wanted him to want her. Desperately. She was hopeless, not to mention mean and cruel.

He took in the bathrobe and the slippers without comment, but his smile widened. "Good morning."

"Good morning." No man should look this good at eight o'clock and be able to make coffee, besides. "You've been out."

"Borrowed your keys. I hope you don't mind."

"No, of course not." She glanced at the box. "But you shouldn't be buying food. Let me pay you for —"

"I don't think streusel counts as food. I'm sure it's bad for us, but I can't pass a German bakery without buying streusel."

"I love streusel." This wasn't fair. She was so close to her goal, and the perfect man had dropped out of the sky. What were the chances that she'd ever find someone who would provide her three favorite C-words — climaxes, coffee, and cake — without any prompting from her?

"Then have a seat and we'll load up on caffeine and carbs. It's the American way."

"I'll get the coffee." She started toward the small kitchen.

"Nope." He pushed back his seat and stood. "I'll get it."

"That's silly." She kept going. "While I slept in like a princess, you went out and picked up the paper and the streusel. Then you made the coffee. The least I can do is serve it."

He caught her by the arm. "Sit down. Really. I need something to do, and the more stationary you are, the better." He let go of her immediately.

"Why?" She glanced at the open drapes and her lust disappeared as she remembered why this cute nerd was in her apartment in the first place. "You haven't seen anyone prowling around, have you? Maybe we should close the curtains."

"No, no, I haven't seen anybody. I didn't mean to scare you. I opened the curtains on purpose, though."

She looked at him in confusion. "I don't understand."

"To keep me honest." His gaze, flickering with heat, probed hers. "Do you need me to explain that?"

Her nerve endings sizzled. They had no condoms. She recited that as a mantra. No condoms, no condoms, no condoms. *Unless he'd bought some along with the newspaper.*

"In case you need any more clarification, I came dangerously close to buying condoms when I picked up the paper."

She gulped. "That's why I wore my ugly bathrobe and my bald slippers."

"And you thought that would make a difference?"

Her heart thumped faster. "It always worked with my ex."

"I can't speak for him. As far as I'm concerned, the bathrobe and slippers have zero effect on my problem. They might make it worse, because I'm dying to pry you out of that hideous thing."

"I'll get dressed."

"Hey, you don't have to do that. Just sit down and let me run around serving coffee and streusel. I'm sure I'll be able to control myself if I stay busy."

He might be able to, but now that she knew what he was thinking, she couldn't trust herself. "We need to get out of here."

"There's an idea. But do we just leave the coffee and streusel?"

"There are two travel mugs in my cupboard. We can eat streusel and drink coffee on the bus. I'll be out in ten minutes."

"And where would we be going?"

Crazy. "Gloria's office. Maybe looking through her client files will help us remember why we're in this ridiculous situation to begin with."

TWENTY-TWO

Managing the coffee and streusel on the bus gave Will something to deal with besides his libido, so from that standpoint leaving the apartment had been a great idea. But when Amanda locked them inside the office and took off her coat, he began to wonder if they'd made the right move.

The way he figured it, they'd be fine if they stayed out here in Amanda's area. After all, that's where the file cabinets were located, so logically they had no reason to go into Gloria's office. Her door stood open, though, and he could see the red leather love seat from here.

If that love seat could talk, the conversation would be X-rated. Will felt the pull of that office with its framed prints from *The Joy of Sex.* Gloria kept her supplies in there — vibrators and flavored oils and videos and, probably, *condoms.*

"I'll take the As and you can take the Bs."

Amanda turned from the lateral file drawer she'd opened, a stack of hanging files balanced in both hands. "Will? Is something wrong? You're still wearing your jacket."

He shook himself out of his sensual daze. "Sorry." Taking off his jacket, he hung it on the coat tree next to Amanda's. "Daydreaming."

"You're worried about Justin, aren't you?"

He hadn't given a thought to Justin since they'd left him at Geekland. But it was as good an excuse as any. "Yeah, a little bit."

"I don't think you have to be. Gloria's not really evil, and she might be therapeutic for him."

Will hoped that he'd served a therapeutic purpose for Amanda last night. They still hadn't talked about it, and he would guess she didn't want to talk about it, ever. That was beginning to bother him. He didn't like the idea that she could ignore what had happened when it was all he could think about.

"Sexual release can be therapeutic, I guess." He said it on purpose, to see how she'd react.

She flushed, which made her blue eyes even more blue. "Yes, it can." She cleared her throat. "Listen, I'm not proud of taking advantage last night."

Finally. "I don't look at it that way. Nobody

had a gun to my head." He wanted her to know that he'd enjoyed himself, despite the frustration involved.

Her face was so red she looked sunburned. "It wasn't exactly a fair exchange, Will."

"I didn't expect that. You're the one with the extra dose of stress." He'd wanted her to acknowledge what had happened, not heap blame on herself. "If I was of some help, then —"

"You *were,* but I — oh, God, this is so embarrassing. I just took what I wanted with no thought to mutual satisfaction. That was a Gloria move, and I like to think of myself as being more . . . more . . ."

"Hey, you are more. More of everything." He longed to hold her close, but that would lead them to places she didn't want to go. "You've been pushing yourself for months, and now this stalker comes along to add to your troubles. You needed to get rid of all that tension."

She swallowed. "I should have kept the red vibrator. Then I wouldn't have had to bother you."

"It was no bother, and I'm glad you did."

She gazed at him for several seconds. "That has to be the one and only."

"I know." Intellectually he knew that. Convincing his body was another matter.

"Now let's put all that behind us and get some work done."

"Right. Now remember that we're breaking the client confidentiality rule by doing this." She handed him the files. "But I can't wait for Monday, and Gloria might want to help, but she'd be bored in the first five minutes and give up."

As he took the files, he was careful not to touch her. "I promise to forget everything I find out. Now, where should I go with these?"

"You'd be better off with a desk. Do you want to use Gloria's or mine?"

No contest. He had to stay out of that steamy den of Gloria's at all costs. "Yours." And he wouldn't think about Amanda sitting in there surrounded by all those sexual aids and sexy pictures. He'd concentrate on the task at hand. "What am I looking for?"

"Any notations that indicate deviant behavior. Sadism or masochism, fetishes, especially if they seem especially weird, anything that seems sexually aggressive, I guess. Unusual autoerotic methods."

"Say, what?"

"Masturbation."

"Oh." He prayed that his expression didn't give away that he'd engaged in some auto-eroticism last night. So far as he knew, it wasn't the least bit unusual in nature, though. Same technique he'd used since puberty.

"Make a note of any suspicious ones, and when you're done, put those back and start on the Cs." She picked up her stack and walked into Gloria's office.

He took up his position at her desk, and there was the little hummingbird staring him in the face. He picked it up and cradled it in the palm of his hand. The hummingbird image got to him. He wanted to do something to make Amanda's life easier so she didn't have to flap her wings so damned hard.

Years ago he'd seen a hummingbird's nest — this tight little golf-ball-sized cup, extremely neat, barely large enough to hold the tiny bird hunkered down in it. No birdhouse. No protection from the wind or the rain. Will had wanted to build a tiny roof over the nest, and he felt the same urge now with Amanda.

Finding her stalker would help, and he could start with that. He put down the hummingbird and flipped open the top file.

Twenty minutes later, he looked at his list of suspects. Every damned person in the As sounded like a deviant to him. He found guys who liked to do it in a vat of noodles, guys who couldn't get it up unless they were watching CNN, guys who admitted to owning more than one anatomically correct blowup doll.

Gloria must draw nothing but wackos, which meant that almost anyone in these files could be the stalker. Even when he separated out the ones Amanda and Gloria had already identified as having no contact with Amanda, that eliminated only five. Twenty-two potential valentine crazies were left, and he was only in the As.

Maybe Amanda was better at weeding out the superweird from the marginally weird. If not, they were wasting their time.

"How're you doing in there?" he called out.

"I already have fifteen names."

"That's less than me. I have twenty-two in the A section alone." Rolling back the desk chair, he got up and went to lean in the doorway of Gloria's office.

She glanced up from her stack of files. "I was so sure I'd recognize something that would give me a clue. But most of these people are seriously strange."

"Think about it. Gloria's their therapist of choice. That should tell you something."

She nodded. "It does, indeed. Going through these files, I began to wonder why I don't have a dozen stalkers. This office is a hotbed of sexual deviance." She tapped a folder with her pen. "Like this guy. His favorite thing used to be climbing up on his roof, naked, and dancing to the YMCA song. That's how he became aroused."

"Hey, that's a music nut. Could it mean anything?"

"Nah. I read it before I realized Gloria and I had already eliminated him because he hasn't been in since last year."

"So he quit singing naked on the roof?" Will felt like a Peeping Tom, but he couldn't help being curious. He'd never known there were so many strange people out there.

"He quit after he slipped on a loose shingle and cracked his tailbone. Now he and his wife have sex while incorporating the hand movements of the YMCA song."

"Sounds complicated." Will took a closer look at the pen Amanda was using. Sure enough, it was the penis pen. "Couldn't find anything else to write with, huh?"

Amanda looked at it. "Not in her office. She loves these pens. She had me order a case of them."

"And I thought it was one of a kind."

"No way." She opened a desk drawer full of at least thirty of the flesh-colored pens. "She wanted to have them imprinted with her name and number to give out to clients, but I convinced her that might not be such a good idea."

"Sounds like truth in advertising to me." Will glanced around at the framed prints on the wall. He shouldn't look at them, shouldn't even be standing in the doorway.

Two vibrators, a green one and a blue one, lay on the coffee table in front of the love seat, along with a few sexually explicit magazines. The covers of the magazines showed women in various stages of undress. He thought of Amanda and wished there had been more light last night, especially if that would be his one and only, as she'd said.

"Believe it or not, Gloria helps people."

He turned back to Amanda, a little surprised that she'd be defending her boss.

She gestured to the stack of files. "I mean, where else would a guy who dances naked on his roof go for help? One thing about Gloria, she's very accepting of odd behavior."

"I guess that explains why she went after me." Will gave in to the urge to step into the office and explore without having Gloria there ready to pounce. The place fascinated him, especially when he wasn't in danger of being seduced by a wild sex therapist.

"You're not odd."

He picked up a vibrator and set it down again. Then he walked over to the desk and leaned both hands on it. She was still holding the penis pen and seeing her with it drove him crazy.

So he tried not to look at it. "I'll bet you thought I was odd when you first saw me."

"No I didn't." But her expression gave her away.

He thought it was time for them to be truthful with each other. "What about the hat?"

"Different."

"Nerdy."

She blinked, but she held his gaze. "Okay, maybe somewhat. But since then I've come to know you."

"Have you?" He might know her in ways neither of them had planned, but he questioned how well she knew him.

"Well, maybe not . . . completely." The telltale flicker in her blue eyes indicated she might be thinking about what had happened last night. "But I don't consider you a nerd."

The pen, the vibrators, the magazines, the framed *Joy of Sex* prints — he was drowning in sex and the words tumbled out uncensored. "Because you've let me strip you naked and make you come?"

Her eyes darkened and her grip tightened on the pen. "I don't understand what that has to do with anything."

"You don't want to admit that a nerd did that to you, and that you liked it."

She began to tremble. "That was a mistake, letting that happen."

He held her gaze. "Maybe. But it did happen."

"Yes." Her breathing quickened.

"And I didn't think I was a nerd, either. But I've changed my mind. Who else but a nerd would surround himself with this" — he gestured around Gloria's office — "and nobly take the high road?"

"I guess . . . that makes me a nerd, too."

"I'm beginning to feel like an idiot, Amanda." He blew out a breath. "And I want you so much I can't see straight."

Heat simmered in her eyes. "Same here."

The pictures on the wall taunted him, branding him a wimp if he didn't close the deal. "What else is in those desk drawers?"

Without breaking eye contact, she opened the center drawer, reached inside and pulled out a handful of foil packages. "Is this what you're looking for?" She scattered them over the top of the desk.

Amanda wondered if some subliminal impulse had made her suggest coming to Gloria's office. Searching the files had seemed so logical, but subconscious urges might have brought her here, to the place where so many others had abandoned all their sexual inhibitions.

Standing, she moved around the desk and stopped a short distance away from Will. She'd sacrificed so much to get what she wanted, and forces beyond her control seemed bent on sabotaging all she'd worked for. She wanted this man with a desperation that drove everything else from her mind, and denying herself, denying both of them, suddenly seemed pointless.

She began to unbutton her blouse. "Maybe it's time to stop being so noble."

He took off his glasses and laid them on the desk. His chest heaved as he met her gaze. "Nobility is highly overrated." He fumbled with the buttons of his shirt.

"Who wants to be a martyr?" She took off her blouse and reached behind her back to unhook her bra.

"Not me." He unbuttoned his cuffs and started to pull off his shirt. He stopped in mid-motion as she let her bra fall to the hardwood floor. Reaching for his glasses, he put them on and gulped.

She would cherish the look of admiration

in his eyes for a very long time.

"I didn't realize . . . you were so . . ."

"Stacked? I dress to play that down."

He nodded. "And last night was . . . kind of . . . dark."

"I know." She cupped her girls and offered them a silent apology. They hadn't been let out to play in forever, so maybe Cal had been right. "My ex said a rack like this was wasted on a chick like me."

He shook his head as if to clear it. "Wasted?"

"Because I'm so career oriented. I suppose he had a point, because I haven't —"

"No." Taking off his glasses again, he stepped forward and cradled her face in both hands. He kissed her gently. "They were wasted on *him*," he murmured.

Very shortly, he made a believer of her. Lifting her to the desk, he paid so much attention to her unappreciated breasts that he easily compensated for all the months they'd stayed cooped up and unloved.

No doubt about it, Will knew his foreplay. She squirmed on the wooden surface of the desk as her body woke up and began demanding satisfaction. She was about to suggest moving to the next stage, had her mouth open to ask for more clothing removal, when Will seemed to read her mind.

Lifting her down from the desk, he reached for the fastener at the waist of her jeans. "I want —"

"Me, too." Urgency drove her to take over the pants detail. "I'll do mine and you do yours. Faster that way."

"Okay." He wrenched off his shirt with such eagerness that a shoulder seam ripped. He didn't seem to notice as he pulled his T-shirt over his head.

How she loved that kind of eagerness. She nudged off her shoes and unfastened her jeans at the same time.

Then she was distracted by the sizable bulge revealed when Will shoved down his jeans. She remembered Gloria's thumbs theory, and her tummy danced a little jig of joy. Running her tongue over her lips, she waited for the final confirmation of Gloria's theory.

By the time Will had dispensed with his briefs, the theory was proven beyond a doubt, at least in Will's case. Amanda couldn't remember ever seeing a more magnificent example of male equipment, and she was a girl who'd had to watch porn stars in action, so she knew her penises.

"Hey, you're falling behind."

She forced her gaze upward. "Sorry. But you're . . . impressive."

"Funny thing, but Helen used to say a dick like mine was wasted on a guy like me."

"Too career oriented?"

"Something like that."

She wiggled out of her jeans and slipped off her panties. Then she stepped closer to Will and took his face in both hands. "It was wasted on *her.*" She kissed him hard. Then she nibbled and nipped her way down his neck, his chest, his taut belly. Dropping to her knees, she proceeded to demonstrate her appreciation of his considerable endowments.

She had a great time making him groan and gulp for air. And although she hated to admit it, she might have picked up a few tips from Gloria's videos. Nothing wrong with finding out the techniques worked. Apparently they worked too well, because soon Will took her by the shoulders and dragged her back up to his mouth for a searing kiss.

Picking up a condom, he started maneuvering her toward the love seat. But that would be a cliché, and nothing about this encounter was routine. Besides, no telling how many of Gloria's clients had made use of that love seat.

She broke away from his kiss. "Coffee table."

"Coffee table?"

"Coffee table."

"Okay." With one sweep of his hand, he sent the magazines and vibrators crashing to the floor.

Amanda positioned herself on the smooth wood surface and watched Will open the packet and take out the condom. It was purple.

He paused halfway through, as if debating whether he could live with wearing purple. Then he shrugged and rolled it the rest of the way. "Guess we don't have to look at it."

"I don't mind. Purple is for royalty."

"Yeah, well, I'm not a colored-condom kind of guy."

She spread her thighs and put both feet on the floor as her body hummed in moist anticipation. "Then how about we get it out of sight right now?"

"Sounds good to me." He knelt at the end of the coffee table, his eyes hot as they traveled over her body. "You're beautiful, Amanda."

"I'm frustrated, Will."

"Maybe I can help." Cradling her thighs in both arms, he leaned forward and probed her gently.

Her pulse raced. "That feels . . . promising."

"Maybe you're partial to purple." He eased in halfway.

The fit was deliciously tight, all the right places getting contact. "I'm partial to you, whatever you're wearing."

"Good." He moved in a little more.

Oh. This was . . . fantastic. Maybe size really did matter. A wave of reaction surged through her. Surely she wasn't that close. Not yet.

"Almost there," he murmured. "Ready?"

"I'm beyond ready."

He pushed in all the way.

Just like that, she came. With a surprised cry, she arched her back and gripped the sides of the table as the world began to spin.

And that was only the beginning. He began to stroke, and she came again. He shifted his angle slightly and changed his rhythm, and she came a third time. Gasping and speechless, she looked up at him in amazement.

His gaze was hot, but his smile . . . his smile held all the tenderness of a lover. If she'd ever thought they could have sex without getting involved, she'd miscalculated.

She drew in a shaky breath. "Oh, Will. I didn't know it would be so . . ."

"I did." He grasped her thighs more

tightly and began to thrust with more purpose. His breathing grew rough, his expression more fierce.

Incredibly, she felt another orgasm building. As the piston-like motion of his hips took her to the top of the roller coaster once more, she moaned with pleasure. As the spasms shook her, he shoved deep as if to absorb every ripple of sensation.

Then at last, with a bellow of satisfaction, he closed his eyes and shuddered against her. She drifted in the aftermath, more sated than she'd ever been in her life. But she wasn't naïve enough to think this sense of utter completion would last.

Before long she'd want him again. And again. When a man was this good, a girl could never get enough. Her goals might be shifting.

Twenty-Three

Harvey didn't like the looks of this. As usual, Louise had made him bring her to his favorite Starbucks on account of it being Saturday. If she'd changed her mind and insisted on doughnuts, he might have missed seeing this. Instead he'd been sitting there drinking his mocha cappuccino with extra cinnamon sprinkles while trying to tune out Louise, and he'd happened to glance out the window.

And what had hit him in the face? Amanda going into the office, on a Saturday, with the stockbroker. Forty-five minutes later, they were still in there. Harvey didn't like it, not one bit. He'd been in Dr. Tredway's office enough times to know how it could affect a person.

That's why he and Amanda would be so perfect together. She'd spent so many hours in Dr. Tredway's office that she probably had sex on her mind all the time. But he was the guy she needed to give her relief. For some Wall Street type to swoop in and take advantage of Amanda's sex thoughts was just wrong.

Last night at Geekland they hadn't seemed so cozy, so he'd decided nothing was happening. He'd left before anyone could recognize him, especially Dr. Tredway. But if Amanda was hanging out with the stockbroker today, that wasn't good.

"Harvey? Harvey!"

So now he was forced to look at Louise, which he didn't want to do. He needed to keep an eye on the building across the street to see how Amanda acted when she came back out. "What, Louise?"

"I want to leave." Her face was all scrunched up, and she'd made a mess with her bran muffin. Crumbs everywhere.

"Not yet, sugar tits." He'd been drinking his coffee real slow. It was completely cold, but he wanted to make it last so he had an excuse to stay. "I'm not finished."

"I don't care. I'm finished."

That was just like Louise. This morning he'd had a woody, and she'd been the only woman around, so he'd decided to give her a poke. But she'd come real quick, and then she'd pushed him off, before he was done. He hated when she did that. It served her right to sit here while he took his time with his coffee.

But if she got too irritated, she might start yelling, and he didn't want the people at Starbucks to get mad. They might refuse him service next time. He'd seen that sign by the cash register — WE RESERVE THE RIGHT TO REFUSE SERVICE TO ANYONE.

He positioned himself so it would look like he was paying attention to Louise, but he could still see across the street out of the corner of his eye. "I'm gonna rent an Amanda Detmer movie today," he said. "She's so hot."

"She's anemic."

"I might jerk off to it."

Louise's eyes narrowed. "You do and I'll break your fingers."

"Why can't I? You have that Heath guy you think about all the time."

"I need to. It's homework."

"Is not." Harvey was proud of himself. Louise had forgotten all about leaving. But he wished he knew what was going on in Dr. Tredway's office that took so long.

"Is too. I'm supposed to develop my fantasy life. Dr. Tredway said."

"Then I should develop mine, too. I'm renting that movie."

"You don't have to develop anything. Dr.

Tredway said men's lives are one big fantasy, already. They all think they're great lovers with huge dicks."

"Except with me, marshmallow lips, that's no fantasy. It's the God's truth."

When Louise laughed, her boobs jiggled. Right now they were jiggling like mad as Louise knocked herself out.

"I don't get what's so funny." Harvey didn't feel much like laughing, especially when he thought about what might be happening across the street.

"You wouldn't. That reminds me, we have to stop by the store. I need a cucumber."

"Are you going to cook?" He hoped not. She was terrible at it.

"It's not to eat. It's homework."

"I don't remember anything about cucumbers."

"That's because you never listen, Harvey."

True. He spent the sessions with Dr. Tredway thinking about Amanda sitting at her desk while she fought the urge to grab him the minute he came through the door. Except now she was over there with the stockbroker. Harvey hoped she wasn't grabbing parts of the stockbroker.

"If I don't like the looks of the cucumbers, I'll see if they have any zucchinis."

"While you're doing that, I'll get my

video." Harvey caught a movement at the revolving door leading into the building.

"You are *not* getting a video. And you can't call out Amanda's name anymore when we're having sex."

"Amanda's my fantasy girlfriend." It was them, all right. Damn it! They were all lovey-dovey, kissy-kissy. They'd been doing it in there, maybe on the love seat. How could she open her legs for a guy like that when she loved Harvey? Bitch.

"She's not your fantasy girlfriend. Not anymore."

"Yes she is." Harvey wasn't putting up with this. Amanda belonged to him. Had she lost track of that? Maybe she was a little confused. He'd send her a warning and see if that straightened her out.

Whap! Louise slapped him upside the head so hard he saw stars.

"Hey!" He held his head. "Stop that."

She glared at him. "I'll stop it when you stop yapping about Amanda. Got that?"

Cool beans, Louise was jealous. If she got really jealous, she might not be so sure of herself, even if she did have all the money. She would give Harvey more respect. Maybe that's what Amanda was trying to do, too, make him so jealous that he realized what she was worth.

"So no more Amanda for you, Harvey."

"Okay, no more Amanda Detmer." Which was fine with him. He'd never had a thing about her, anyway. He wanted Amanda Rykowsky. And he would have her, too. He wasn't about to let the nerd beat him out.

"I'm going to help you with that paper." Will sat across from Amanda at the Loaf and Leaves where they'd decided to have lunch.

"I can imagine how that would turn out." She smiled at him, but her eyes glowed with the same kind of hunger he felt, one that had nothing to do with the soup and sandwiches they'd ordered and eaten.

He couldn't speak for her, but he'd barely tasted the food. Nothing held his interest except having more sex with Amanda. Even the torn seam of his shirt reminded him of their rush to get naked in Gloria's office.

Focusing on her paper would change that dynamic. "We'll work on it together. I'll look up info on the Internet while you —"

"While I do what? I only have one computer."

"We'll stop by my apartment and pick up my laptop. Do you have wireless?"

She shook her head. "Dial-up, one line."

"Doesn't matter. At least while I'm on the

Internet, our creepo friend won't be able to leave any tunes on your answering machine." He would love to spend the rest of the weekend in bed with her, but he wouldn't be able to live with himself if he did that.

She seemed happy enough with the way things had gone in Gloria's office that she might give up her schoolwork, and he couldn't let that happen. Maybe they had some sort of perfect sexual bond, because he'd never made Helen that happy.

He finished his coffee. "So what do you say? We'll go from here to my place, then back to yours and get busy."

"Yeah." She leaned her chin on her hand and gazed at him with lust in her baby blues. "Let's get busy. That's what I'm talking about."

If she was trying to seduce him, she was doing a damned good job of it. And he couldn't allow it. "Amanda, concentrate."

"I am concentrating. You're good, Will. Incredibly good."

He groaned. "Ordinarily a guy loves hearing that, but I promised you I wouldn't sabotage your schedule. I shouldn't have come on to you in Gloria's office. I shouldn't have lost it the way I did, because now —"

"Now I have a new standard." She rubbed her foot along the side of his calf.

It took him a moment to realize she'd taken off her loafer to give her foot more flexibility as she stroked his leg. He'd never imagined she'd be so uninhibited. "You have to write this paper, and you know it."

"I'll write it. But I've kept my nose to the grindstone for months, and where did it get me? Sexually frustrated beyond all belief. I had no idea how uptight I was. That can't be good for a person, right?"

"Maybe not, but —"

"Look, we have a stalker we can't identify, so I need you to hang around for a while. After what just happened, I know it will happen again. Don't you?"

"If you don't stop stroking my leg, it's liable to happen sooner than you think."

"Good." She ran her foot along his thigh. "I want to find out if all those fireworks were a fluke. Maybe next time won't be anything like that."

He lowered his voice. "Stop it. You're giving me an erection."

"Really?" She wiggled her toes against his crotch. "Mm. I can tell. You may be ready to write a paper, but that bad boy of yours wants to play."

"Let's go get that laptop." He wadded up

his napkin and threw it on his plate.

"Wouldn't you rather have a lap dance?"

He gave her what he hoped was a stern look, and she laughed. Blowing out a breath, he got to his feet while standing was still a possibility. He was beginning to understand the problem.

Amanda was an all-or-nothing person, a woman with a one-track mind. Without fully realizing the danger, he'd thrown the switch and sent her barreling onto a different track. He had to admit she seemed much happier on this track. Her skin glowed and her eyes sparkled. The tenseness had disappeared from her expression and she laughed more.

But was he aiding and abetting as she sacrificed long-term gain for short-term satisfaction? His conscience said yes. His libido told his conscience to shut up and enjoy the most amazing sex in the world while he had the chance.

Amanda preceded him out of the restaurant, and as he followed her, he could swear that even her walk was different. Thanks to his sexual intervention, she'd loosened up, and the effect was spectacular. Too bad he still felt guilty as hell for making it happen.

Amanda wanted to see Will's apartment because she suddenly craved information about this man who had given her the sexual time of her life. She also remembered that Will possessed some glow-in-the-dark condoms. Swiping more than one of Gloria's purple ones hadn't seemed right, but the question of buying a supply hadn't been discussed, either.

When Amanda walked into Will's living room, the drapes were drawn, but there was enough light filtering around the edges that she could see that the furniture was a little more upscale than hers. It probably belonged to him, whereas she'd rented her place furnished.

The neutral colors he'd chosen told her that he was a typical guy — uninterested in decorating and happy so long as the chairs and couch were comfortable. The fabric covering the furniture — one of the new microfibers — told her that he didn't want to worry about upkeep.

"I'll get the laptop." He left his jacket on and headed down a hallway. "I'll only be a minute."

"Take your time." Before they left she planned to bring up the subject of condoms, but she didn't have to hit him with it right away. She could tell he was conflicted about their new direction.

Logically, she should be conflicted, too.

But she'd had no clue that she was multiorgasmic. That kind of information made a girl sit up and pay attention, especially after months of abstinence.

Three framed pictures sat on top of his TV cabinet. Unzipping her parka, she wandered over and looked at them. A family of four, including Will a few years younger, stood in front of the Eiffel Tower. A more recent photo showed the same family, aged a few years, surrounding Will in his cap and gown. The third picture showed Will and Justin, arms slung over each other's shoulders, at the same graduation ceremony.

So Will had both parents, at least as of the last picture, plus a brother. The whole family had been to Paris, unless it was a faked picture. Knowing Will, she didn't think the picture was a fake.

She was acutely aware that she didn't have any pictures like this because she hadn't had a life like this. Someday she'd love to have that kind of life for her children, but that was years away. Because she hadn't been motivated to make something of herself until after her mother died, she was a late bloomer.

But that wasn't necessarily true of Will. Those parents of his probably expected him to get married soon and give them grand-children. Will might expect the same thing. She was so not ready for that routine.

But she could still have some fun for the time being. She'd been a martyr long enough. Fate had dropped a gifted lover at her doorstep and ignoring that opportunity seemed like a crime against nature.

"My family," Will said as he came back carrying a computer case over his shoulder.

"Nice." She couldn't get over the difference in her reaction to him post–coffee-table sex. Last night had been great, but the activity on that coffee table had changed her forever. Now one glance at Will and her engine was lubed and racing. "Paris, huh?"

He walked over toward the TV cabinet, bringing the scent of Old Spice with him. He glanced at the pictures with a smile. "My mother's French. We went to visit my *grandmère.*"

Hearing him speak that one word with the correct accent ramped up her response, for some crazy reason. "Do you speak French?"

"Un petit peu."

She'd never known a man who spoke French. "That's kind of sexy. What else do you know?" Apparently she had a fantasy of some guy whispering *je t'adore* in her ear.

"Not as much as I should. Mom's fluent. She can swear like a French sailor and nobody knows what she's saying. But she wouldn't teach me those words." He shifted the strap of the carrying case. "Ready to go?"

"What's the French word for condom?" Not as subtle as she might have liked, but she wasn't leaving here without those glow-in-the-dark jobs or something equivalent. He was a guy. He should have little raincoats on hand.

He gazed at her. "Amanda, I feel like such a traitor to the cause. If I had any decency, I wouldn't touch you again. You had a program going, and I've screwed with that, literally."

A horrible thought struck her. She'd been so busy telling him how wonderful the sex had been for her, but had he said the same? *No.* The possibility of humiliation clogged her throat so that she could barely speak. "You didn't like it."

His jaw dropped. "Are you kidding?"

"No." She shoved her hands in the pockets of her jacket. "You're a kind person confronted with a sex-starved woman who's been raving about the experience. You don't have the heart to tell me it was only so-so, that you've had a lot better."

406

He put down the laptop. "That's ridiculous."

"It's not ridiculous. You wanted to do it on the love seat, but I made you go for the coffee table, instead. The position was probably hard on your knees, and then you had to wear that purple thing. For all I know, it was the worst sex you've ever had in your —"

"The best." He grabbed her by the shoulders. "The best sex I've ever had in my life."

She searched his expression and tried to tell if he was putting her on out of sympathy. "You wouldn't lie to me, would you?"

With a groan, he tossed his glasses on the TV cabinet, pulled her close and planted one on her. He certainly kissed like a sincere person. Before long he kissed like an aroused person, too. French kissing took on a whole new meaning when administered by a guy who could actually speak the language.

They managed to get out of most of their clothes without breaking the lip lock, which involved some Houdini-like gyrations. It was fun, like a game of Twister, only with a bigger prize. Oh, yes, she remembered the size of the prize very well.

Covering the prize was an issue, though. She hated the thought of maneuvering all the way back to his bedroom, especially when his couch was within arm's reach and she was so turned on. The trip to the bedroom could be a real buzz kill.

Yet the clothes were coming off really fast, and they were both breathing like freight trains. When they had everything removed except their socks, she decided the time had arrived for Will to produce the requisite condom.

She pulled her mouth free. After all that kissing, she only had breath for two words. "Get condom." She sounded like Tonto in a Lone Ranger flick, but at least she'd delivered the message.

"Right." He groped for the computer case strap. Dragging the case along the floor by the strap, he pushed her toward the couch. She hoped he didn't plan to start on her paper now. That would be taking multitasking too far.

After guiding her onto the couch, which turned out to be even more soft and yielding than it looked, he crouched by the computer case and unzipped it.

She gulped for air. "Tell me you're not going to type."

"No." He reached into the case and came up with a foil packet.

"You packed condoms in with the laptop?" Knowing he'd planned ahead made her grin like an idiot.

"Yeah." He grinned back at her. "But I felt *really* guilty about it."

Twenty-Four

Will had enjoyed three sexual episodes with Amanda, and they had yet to do it on a bed. But he wasn't complaining. Once he was buried deep inside her, he hardly cared that he didn't fit and his legs hung over the rolled arm of the couch. But he vowed that the next couch he bought would be two feet longer.

With the drapes drawn, the colors mostly disappeared, even from Amanda, who looked like one of those old-time sepia photographs in this muted light. Even in sepia, she was the most beautiful woman he'd ever seen. She was still wearing her socks, and he felt them rub against his thighs as she entwined her legs with his.

His back had a little crick in it, but he wouldn't think about that. He'd think about how happy his cock was right now, snug inside her hot little vagina. What was a little back pain for a reward like that?

She gazed up at him, lips parted, eyes enormous, breasts quivering with her rapid breathing. "I guess there's not enough light to make it glow."

Glowing condoms no longer interested him. "Who cares?"

"Not me. This feels so good."

"Uh-huh." And he'd thought the wildfire between them could be controlled. What a dope.

"But it's wrong."

He drew in a sharp breath. He should have expected second thoughts. "You're right. But please don't ask me to stop now." He doubted he could, not when lust pumped through him with such demanding force. One more orgasm, just one. Then he'd take the pledge.

"Not stop. Just change positions."

What?" He was so relieved he almost came right then.

"Yes. Get up a minute."

"I don't want to leave." He was still a little shaken, still worried that she'd change her mind and reach for her clothes.

"Two seconds. Then it'll be so much better."

To say that he eased out reluctantly would be the understatement of the century. He'd achieved full contact, and he didn't want to give that up for anything. He couldn't imagine what she could do that would improve on the heavenly sensation he'd just lost.

Once he was clear, she turned over and got to her hands and knees. "See?"

He saw, and his heart rate spiked. He hadn't been able to imagine an improvement, which demonstrated his complete lack of imagination. This new wrinkle promised to be an improvement, all right. Maybe this was what happened when you exposed a woman like Amanda to the pictures and videos in Gloria's office. Amanda might have become an endless source of ideas.

Oh, Lord. If that was the case, he was a goner. Knowing she was highly responsive was thrill enough, but add in a treasure trove of innovation, and he would gladly become her slave. Starting now.

Joining her on the couch, he grasped her hips. Each of them had to put one foot on the floor before they accomplished what they were after, but once they did . . . he nearly passed out from the pleasure. She seemed to be liking it, too, judging from the happy noises she was making.

What a rush. From this angle he could see the sway of one breast as it reacted to each stroke. That alone would have been enough to send him into the red zone, but the friction from this position was unbelievable. He clenched his jaw and slowed down so he wouldn't come yet.

He'd impressed her before, and he had enough ego to want to do it again. When she cried out softly and tightened around him, he bore down while holding back his own climax. The ripples of her orgasm rolled over his penis and he held on while she rocked against him. Moaning, she let her head hang while she caught her breath. Her hair fell forward, curtaining her face.

Not wanting her to wind down, he reached around her trembling thigh and found the trigger that would set off at least one more explosion. Continuing with firm thrusts, he manipulated that sweet spot until she began to pant. Then she threw her head back and he listened to her come again. He paused a few seconds, and took her up again.

By the third time she was tossing her hair around and yelling loud enough to bring the neighbors to his door. He hoped they were all out shopping, because now it was his turn, and he figured on making some noise, too. Oh . . . *yeah.* His thighs slapped against hers, faster, even faster. Now . . . almost there . . . *yes.*

413

Squeezing his eyes shut, he opened his mouth and let go. She might have climaxed again. He might have shouted her name. He was so blown away by his orgasm that he had no idea exactly what happened, except that he was coming, coming, and coming some more. The pulsing seemed to go on forever as he remained firmly anchored to her, holding tight as the world spun around him.

As the haze slowly cleared, he leaned down and pressed his lips against the small of her back. "The best," he murmured, in case she had any doubts left.

Her voice was thick with spent passion. "Yes."

They managed to get Amanda's paper written by forbidding any physical contact whatsoever. Eye contact was potent enough. Amanda told herself that she'd had enough orgasms to last her a month, but that didn't mean she wasn't ready to fool around every time she looked at Will, especially when he looked back.

Those green eyes packed a punch, reminding her of every touch, every kiss, every climax. The paper was done, but the studying would have to wait until she came home from Geekland. She was behind in her work, but she couldn't bring herself to care. Good sex could do that for a girl.

She and Will took turns showering for obvious reasons. Showering together might mean they'd never get to Geekland. As they were about to head out the door, someone knocked.

"That sounds like Mavis's knock." Amanda was grateful neither of her neighbors had shown up this afternoon to further mess up her schedule.

Will pulled on his coat. "You recognize her knock?"

"Two raps, pause, two more raps. And her timing's off. Usually she shows up an hour before I'm ready to leave."

"We have five minutes to catch the bus."

"I know. I won't let her keep us."

Will glanced at her, a gleam in his eye. "Maybe she wants to return the vibrator."

"Too late." She paused before opening the door. "You might have permanently ruined me for vibrators." At his very male look of satisfaction, she laughed.

She was still laughing when she opened the door. Both Mavis and Chester stood there wearing their coats. Mavis had her pocketbook tucked under one arm.

"What's so funny?" Chester said.

"Nothing." Amanda stopped laughing immediately. She'd rather not advertise her current multiorgasmic state. "Are you two going somewhere?" *Together?* Strange as it seemed, that was the definite impression she got.

"Yes." Mavis threw back her shoulders as if marching into battle. "We're going with you to Geekland."

Amanda had trouble processing the information. "Uh . . . why?"

"While we were watching *Wheel of Fortune,* we had a talk about your situation," Chester said. "And we decided you needed more eyes and ears."

"Oh." She was touched, but she couldn't imagine the two of them in the atmosphere of Geekland. She couldn't imagine them staying up past nine o'clock, either. "You realize I have to work until one in the morning. I'm sure you wouldn't want to —"

"We took a nap," Mavis said. "Didn't we, Chester?"

Chester blushed. Because Chester had no hair on his head, the blush was visible over a much wider area. "Yeah. A nap."

You could have knocked Amanda over with a red vibrator. Were Chester and Mavis . . . ? No, impossible. They were bitter enemies. They weren't taking naps in the same vicinity, let alone in the same *bed.*

But Gloria had told her that when an older couple took a "nap" it usually wasn't for sleeping. *They like midday sex, when they're still energetic enough to do it,* Gloria had explained. Amanda decided she'd be better off not thinking about that at all.

Mavis shoved back her coat sleeve and looked at her watch. "Are you ready? If we don't shake a leg, we'll miss your bus." She stood on tiptoe and peered over Amanda's shoulder. "Will, are you ready?"

"Sure thing." He came to the door and handed Amanda her purse. "Let's move out."

The bus ride to Geekland was surreal. Mavis and Chester shared a seat and kept sneaking glances at each other and blushing. Once in a while Mavis would giggle. Then Chester would nudge her shoulder with his, and she'd giggle again.

Amanda and Will stood nearby holding on to a pole. Amanda tried not to stare, but she couldn't believe these were the same two people who had been feuding ever since she'd moved in last year. Sure, she'd thought they were sweet on each other, but they weren't supposed to *do* anything about it. Sniping at each other like a couple of preteens was fine with her. This new development was unsettling.

Will leaned close and murmured in Amanda's ear. "I think they're doing it."

"I don't want to talk about that."

"Why not? They're consenting adults."

"I know that, but it feels very weird." She was too embarrassed to explain that she thought of Mavis and Chester as substitute parents, and a girl wanted people in those roles to be completely asexual. Yes, she'd studied her psychology texts and knew that was unrealistic, but she couldn't help the way she felt.

"Want me to watch out for them tonight?"

"Oh, yes, *please*. They'll be lost at Geekland. Everyone's so much younger than they are, and I doubt they'll know what to make of the trivia and all the crazy drinks."

"I'll help out."

"Thanks, Will. And make sure they don't overdo the liquor, okay? I mean, one of them could be diabetic or something. I'll try to keep track, but Saturday night is always busy."

"It's sweet that they want to come and protect you."

"I know." She glanced over at Chester and Mavis, who looked so vulnerable and clueless. "But it's not like they're experts on deviant behavior. I think they'll be more of a liability than an asset."

Will gave her shoulder a squeeze. "Don't worry. I'll make sure nothing happens to them."

It had seemed like a reasonable promise when he'd made it, but two hours into the evening, Will wondered what he'd been thinking, trying to keep track of a couple of golden-agers at a bar. Mavis had plunged into the trivia and organized teams, whether people wanted teams or not. In between rounds of trivia, she divided the customers into three groups, and made them sing rounds.

Meanwhile Chester sat at the bar with a fistful of Geekland coupons he'd clipped from somewhere, and he insisted on using them for drinks, even though half of them had expired. Besides that, the coupons were for ordinary well drinks. Chester had borrowed Leonard's Barmaster and was ordering up all kinds of strange drinks and asking Amanda to apply the coupon to them.

Will offered to buy him a couple of rounds to get him off the coupon kick, but he said that spoiled the fun. "I'm giving Amanda a challenge," he said. "Expanding her repertoire. When she makes me something, she has to think, and that's good for her."

"What she's thinking is that you're an

impossible old goat," Mavis said. "I don't know what I ever saw in you, Chester Ambrose."

"You know good and well what you saw in me," Chester said. Then he pinched Mavis on the butt.

Amanda grabbed Will by the arm. "Did you see that? Please tell him to stop pinching her. I caught him doing it before, and he thinks it's funny."

"But Mavis seems to like it. She giggles."

"It's embarrassing. And customers are complaining that they don't want to sing rounds anymore." Amanda poured rum over a bar spoon to top off the drink she was making. "Can you talk her out of that?"

Will sighed. "I can try. But she reminds me of my third-grade teacher, Mrs. Nadworthy, and I was always scared of Mrs. Nadworthy."

Amanda rolled her eyes. "Fine time to tell me. I thought you were going to watch over them."

"I am watching over them. They're both in fine shape. They haven't had too much to drink, and they don't seem the least bit lost. I would say they're thriving in this atmosphere."

"That may well be, but they're also driving me and the other customers insane."

Will took note of the couple who had just walked in the front door. "You're in luck, because a distraction is on the way."

"Mavis has total control of that karaoke microphone. Short of a major power outage, I don't know what sort of distraction would help."

"Try Gloria and Justin. And if I'm any judge of these things, and I think I am, they're doing it, too."

Amanda watched Gloria and Justin approach. "At least that doesn't make me flinch like it does with Mavis and Chester."

"It makes me flinch. Justin looks way too happy. He's heading for a fall." Will thought that described his own situation, too. Things were going well with Amanda, too damn well. He was getting used to being with her.

But logic told him that eventually this stalker thing would resolve itself, and she wouldn't need him anymore. She'd realize that her studies had suffered while she was playing patty-cake with him, and she'd tell him goodbye. He couldn't even hold out hope for them at the end of the semester, because she was going on to graduate school, and after that she'd want to establish a practice.

All that took concentration, and he was afraid she'd see him as a distraction. She'd ask him — nicely, of course — to vamoose. If and when that happened, he didn't know if there was enough booze behind the bar at Geekland to make him forget her.

"Will, my boy!" Justin clapped him on the back. "How's life treating you?"

"Not bad." He looked around for Justin's date for the evening. "Where's Gloria?"

"She went to the ladies' room to freshen up. We took a cab over, and we enjoyed a little action on the way, if you know what I mean."

So Will had been right. It hadn't been so hard to guess. The big grin on Justin's face had been enough to clue him in. "Justin, you know how I feel about this. You're going to get yourself attached, and she's only in it for the cheap thrills."

"These thrills aren't cheap, buddy. She has an arsenal of goodies at her place. I'd hate to estimate the total value, but it's high. She introduced me to a few of her top-of-the-line toys. Did you know there's such a thing as a vibrating cock ring?"

"No, but I don't think you're the vibrating cock ring type, if you don't mind me saying so."

"That's how much you know. Gloria says I am, and that's what I choose to believe. Hey, why is everybody singing rounds?"

"You don't want to know."

"How's everything going with Amanda?"

"Good." He glanced toward the ladies' room to make sure Gloria wasn't on her way. "Very good."

"Yeah?" Justin smiled. "That's awesome, buddy. I wondered if staying in her apartment would be the icebreaker. Sounds like it —"

"Cut. Here comes Gloria. She can't know."

"Right. Although she might not care so much anymore."

"There you are, my two nerdlings." Gloria stepped between them and linked her arms through theirs. "Want to hear my fantasy?"

"No." Will extracted himself from her grip.

"I'm not too keen on that one, either, Gloria," Justin said.

She chucked him under the chin. "My provincial little geek, afraid to try a threesome. Or maybe you'd be fine with it if we made it two women, instead?"

Will gave Justin a look that said plainly, *See what you're in for?*

Justin shrugged. "Two women might be cool."

"There you go. Maybe I could talk Amanda into —"

"Don't even think about it," Will said.

"My, my, so protective." Gloria smiled at him. "But you're right. Amanda's too up-tight for that."

Justin smiled at Will but said nothing.

Will should have kept his mouth shut, too, but he hated hearing Amanda described that way. "She's not —" He stopped himself just in time. "She's not cut out for that kind of thing."

"Definitely not." Gloria looked at Will more closely. "I do believe there's a tiny hickey on your neck, William."

Will adjusted his collar and hoped he wasn't blushing. Damn it, his cheeks felt warm. "I pinched myself in the . . ." *Shit. What explained a hickey other than the obvious?* "In the hose from the hand-held shower head," he finished, hoping she'd buy it.

She laughed. "Creative. I have to say, you're quite the guy, pretending to be Amanda's boyfriend by day and schtupping someone else by night. You realize I'm insanely jealous. After all, I asked first."

Justin edged his way into the conversation. "But it doesn't matter now, right? I mean, you have me, now."

Will had his hands full deflecting Gloria's curiosity, but he took a moment to feel sorry for Justin. The poor jerk was already wearing his heart on his sleeve.

"Well, of course I have you, my galloping geek. But that doesn't mean I've forgotten all about Will. My attention span is not that short. So tell me, Will, who's the lucky girl? Anybody I know?"

"No." Will made sure he didn't glance in Amanda's direction. He couldn't look at Justin, either. He should elaborate, make up some imaginary girlfriend, but he was coming up empty.

"If it's that receptionist at Cooper and Scott, I'll be insulted. She's not nearly as stacked as I am."

"It's not her. It's . . . someone in my apartment building."

"Will's notorious about keeping his affairs to himself," Justin said. "He doesn't even tell me half the time."

Gloria turned to him. "Yes, but did he tell you this time? Because if you know, I'll bet I can coax it out of you. I want to know who my competition is."

Will kicked himself for confiding in Justin. Gloria probably could coax it out of him using her arsenal of sex toys. Damn it. As he was reviewing his options, one of which involved kidnapping Justin and keeping him locked in a closet for the next couple of days, he saw Tina bring Amanda a package about the size of a toaster.

It was probably only bar supplies. He was getting paranoid if he thought everything that came to Amanda had something to do with her stalker. Then again, it seemed illogical for bar supplies to be delivered at night.

"What is everybody drinking?" he asked. "I'll buy the first round."

"Gin martini, dry," Gloria said. "And don't think buying me a drink is going to make up for you taking some other woman to bed. I will find out, so I can see what I'm up against."

"But Gloria," Justin said. "You can't have Will and me at the same time."

"Maybe not at precisely the same time, since you won't consider a threesome, but we're not exclusive, Justin. I thought you understood that."

Justin looked crestfallen. "I know you said that before, but after what happened today with the flavored oils and stuff, I thought things might have changed."

Will shook his head in despair. Train wreck. But he had no time to think about Justin's problems. Amanda had started opening the box, and he wanted to be there when she found out what was inside. "Justin, what can I get you?"

"A Bahama Mama."

"Are you sure?" All-booze drinks hadn't been a good idea a few days ago, and they were an even worse idea, now. Between liquor and sex toys, Gloria would have the truth about Amanda in no time.

"Yeah, I'm sure."

Will couldn't very well refuse to buy Justin's drink of choice. "Be right back." He headed over toward the bar and arrived as Amanda reached into the box and pulled out something wedged by sections of molded Styrofoam.

He slid onto a bar stool. "What is it?"

"I'm not sure." She pulled off a section of Styrofoam. "Looks like it's ceramic, maybe a vase."

Not bar equipment. "It was delivered specifically to you?"

She glanced at him. "Yes."

"By who?"

"I don't know. Tina came over and said some guy brought it and left."

Will stifled the impulse to race out the door in pursuit. He had no idea what the guy looked like. The street would be full of people on a Saturday night, and whoever it was would have melted into the crowd by now.

Amanda pulled off the rest of the Styrofoam. "Oh, my God."

Will stared at the ceramic planter in the shape of a pair of jeans. The fly on the jeans was open to allow a penis-shaped cactus to protrude upward. In a different context, especially after a few drinks, it could be sort of funny. Will wasn't laughing.

Neither was Amanda. Her face grew pale. "Not much question what he's after, is there?"

"Just remember that he won't succeed." Will began to think in terms of available weapons. His mere presence in her apartment might not be deterrent enough. "Was there a card this time?"

"I didn't look." She peered into the box. "Yeah, there's a card." She drew in a breath and took it out. The front was a picture of a guy leering at a curvaceous blonde. Across the top of the card was lettered *Valentine, you could use some bed rest.*

Trembling, Amanda put her hand over the card. "I don't want to look inside. You read it."

"Okay." He slid it out from under her hand, opened it, and read silently. *You provide the bed and I'll do the rest.* Underneath was a printed message. *Get rid of the nerd or I'll do it for you. What you need is a real man. Your Secret Valentine.*

He closed the card, folded it, and shoved it in his pocket.

Amanda gazed at him and swallowed. "Anything new?"

"Same old shit. Don't worry about it. We'll take some extra precautions when we get back to the apartment."

"Like what? I don't have a gun or anything."

Neither did Will. And he was beginning to wonder if that was a serious omission on his part. But buying a gun wouldn't help if he'd never shot one in his life. "We'll figure out a strategy. We're both smart. And I can guarantee we're a hell of a lot smarter than this bastard."

There was a problem with that logic, but the color was returning to her cheeks so he didn't mention it. He had no doubt that he was smarter than the valentine stalker. But the stalker was obviously a little crazy. Crazy people were unpredictable, and unpredictability could make hash out of any strategy, no matter how smart it might be.

"I'm glad about one thing," Amanda said.

"What's that?"

"That we'll be sleeping in the same bed tonight."

TWENTY-FIVE

Although Amanda shivered every time she looked at the planter, she managed to pass the thing off as a joke. Not surprisingly, Gloria loved it. She was the first one with the nerve to touch the cactus. It turned out to be artificial, with soft needles.

That didn't soothe Amanda, but it made other people far braver. Justin, who seemed determined to impress Gloria with his worldliness, disappeared into the men's room and came out with a condom. Accompanied by enthusiastic encouragement from those at the bar, he opened the packet and rolled the condom onto the cactus.

Several customers wanted to know where they could get a planter exactly like it, and one woman remembered seeing them on sale at a drugstore chain. Someone else used his cell phone to go online to find a source there. Soon everyone was ordering a cactus planter like Amanda's, which broke up the singing of rounds.

Other than coming over while she opened the box, Will had made himself scarce during the night. He wasn't acting much like her pretend boyfriend, but maybe that wasn't important anymore. Having a boyfriend hadn't discouraged the valentine stalker.

Instead the stalker was becoming more aggressive. Now he'd contacted her at Gloria's office, at home, and here at Geekland. He'd covered every place except the university, and she was only there a couple of hours each morning, so he might not think it was worth pursuing her at that location.

To keep herself from freaking out, she drew on her training in psychology. If the stalker was a bully, he would be intimidated by anyone with the courage to stand up to him. Thinking of him as a bully who would fade away when confronted helped.

But there was also a chance he suffered from a personality disorder. He could be delusional. In that case, standing up to him would do no good. He would only reframe her response to fit into his current fantasy.

One thing she knew without a doubt. He wasn't giving up. He had a plan, and he would follow it through to whatever conclusion he envisioned. She hoped that sex was the only thing on his mind. That was bad enough, but not quite as scary as the alternative.

As closing time drew near, the planter was used as a prize for the last trivia contest of the night, which relieved Amanda of having to toss it in the Dumpster outside Geekland's back door. Gloria was overjoyed to win it, but Amanda groaned at the outcome. The planter could easily become a permanent office decoration that she'd have to live with until May.

Eventually Amanda, Will, Mavis, and Chester boarded the bus and headed back toward the apartment building. Far from looking exhausted, Mavis and Chester seemed ready to party for several more hours. The bus wasn't crowded at this hour, so Amanda and Will took a seat opposite them for the ride home.

Mavis glanced across the aisle and beamed at Amanda. "That was more fun than an end-of-the-year school picnic. I want to go back tomorrow night."

"Me, too," Chester said. "I have coupons left and I know where I can get more."

"You're welcome to go if you want." Amanda hoped she hadn't turned them both into barflies. "But tomorrow's Sunday.

I don't work Sunday nights."

Mavis snapped her fingers. "That's right! I knew that, but when you're retired you lose track of days of the week. I forgot it was Saturday already. You didn't go to work at the sex therapist's office today, did you?"

"No."

Mavis brightened. "And you had a friend around for a change. What did you two kids do with yourselves all day?"

Will cleared his throat. "Amanda had a paper due. I helped her with it."

"Was it a paper about sex?" Chester asked.

Amanda shook her head. "Antidepressants."

"Oh. I was asking because both of you are blushing, and so I figured the paper might have been about weirdo sex."

Mavis swatted him on the arm. "Honestly, Chester. Their cheeks are pink from the cold air. You have sex on the brain." She leaned toward Amanda. "He cornered your boss tonight and grilled her. It was embarrassing."

"Nothing embarrasses Gloria," Amanda said.

"I meant that *I* was embarrassed. He told her that I had her red vibrator on loan."

Will went into a coughing fit.

"Whoops." Mavis clapped her hand over

her mouth and giggled. "I forgot that Will wasn't around when all that happened. He doesn't know about my hair-curling attempt."

Will coughed harder.

"Goodness, is he all right?" Mavis peered at Will. "Pound him on the back, Amanda."

Amanda complied, although she knew that if Will stopped coughing, he'd start laughing. Coughing was better.

This conversation was a good thing, though. It took her mind off the stalker. She'd scanned the smattering of other passengers for anyone who was faintly familiar. She'd recognized no one, but she supposed the person could be wearing a disguise.

Now *there* was an unnerving thought. If a guy went so far as to disguise himself, then he might be heading into Ted Bundy territory. Damn it, she wanted to know who it was! The waiting and wondering was wearing her down.

When the red vibrator wasn't mentioned again, Will eventually stopped coughing. "Excuse me," he said. "Got something caught in my throat."

"Happens to me all the time," Mavis said. "You should carry lemon drops. I usually do, but I switched purses to something fancier when I got ready to leave tonight, and I forgot the lemon drops."

Chester shook his head and gazed at Will. "Do you understand this business about fancy purses and plain ones?"

"Probably not," Will said.

"I have one wallet," Chester said. "How many you got?"

"One."

"Exactly." Chester gave Will a man-to-man look.

"So even if you're not working tomorrow night, Amanda," Mavis said, "do you want to go to Geekland with Chester and me, anyway? As a customer?"

"No offense, Mavis, but I'd rather not. I'm there enough as it is."

"Oh, I understand completely. Just thought I'd check. I guess we won't go to Geekland tomorrow night, either, then." Mavis patted Chester's knee. "We'll have to find something else to do."

Chester gave her a teasing glance. "Now that I've talked to Amanda's boss, I have some ideas."

"Oh, *you.*" Mavis turned red and gave him a shove that almost toppled him from the seat. "You're impossible."

Amanda was dying to ask Mavis what had happened to turn the tables on this relationship, but that would have to wait until they could have a girls-only chat. In the mean-time, they'd arrived at their stop. She could finally be alone with Will and read what had been inside the valentine she hadn't wanted to see while she was working and had to keep her cool.

She could find out if there were any more songs on her answering machine. And she'd experience something entirely new — having sex with Will in an actual bed.

All the way home, except when he was laughing about Mavis and the red vibrator, Will second-guessed his decision not to destroy the valentine in his pocket. He'd had plenty of opportunity during the evening to get rid of it, and he'd come close several times. The threat directed at him might upset Amanda . . . a lot.

But in the end he remembered that she wanted to know everything, scary or not. Part of respecting someone was making sure you didn't overprotect them. And he respected the hell out of Amanda.

Nevertheless, he wasn't looking forward to showing it to her. They also had the answering machine to deal with. And he'd decided they needed to talk about defense tactics if someone should manage to break in.

None of those would be fun discussions. Then there was the issue of sex. He wanted to have some. He'd guess that she did, too. But during sex they'd be incredibly vulnerable. No telling what this nutcase would do if he broke in and found them going at it.

Despite Will's efforts not to dwell on worst-case scenarios, he couldn't seem to help himself. The media were always reporting on bad things happening to good people, people who had never done anything to deserve their fate. This latest threat might be enough for the police to get involved, but Will couldn't imagine what they could do unless something more overt took place. He could hardly expect them to park a squad car outside Amanda's apartment building every night.

As the four of them climbed off the bus, Will became aware of the deserted street, the dark shadows, and the overgrown bushes surrounding Amanda's windows. He wished she hadn't taken a first-floor apartment. None of this felt safe.

Either Amanda was putting on a good show for Mavis and Chester or she didn't feel the ominous presence. She was chattering away as if nothing was bothering her.

"We can all go back to Geekland on Monday night." She fished in her purse for the entry key.

Will thought he heard a noise. He glanced over his shoulder to make sure no one had come up behind them. Amanda seemed to be having trouble finding her key.

"Monday night suits me," Chester said. "They have half-price drink specials on Monday, so I wouldn't have to use up my coupons."

"Honestly, Chester." Mavis shook her head. "Does everything have to have a coupon or be fifty percent off?"

"Not everything." He wiggled his eyebrows at her.

"I'm going to pretend I didn't hear that." Amanda finally came up with the key.

Will could swear the bushes rustled. "Come on. Let's get inside."

Her hand on the doorknob, Amanda glanced back at him. "Will?"

The rustling sound came again and panic gripped him. "Just open the door."

"Something wrong?" Chester looked from Amanda to Will.

"Probably not." Amanda opened the door and waved Mavis and Chester inside.

Will practically pushed her through the door and closed it behind them. The security lock clicked into place, and he sighed in relief.

As Mavis and Chester started down the hall together, Amanda hung back and lowered her voice. "What was it?"

"I thought I heard something. It might have been the wind."

"There was no wind."

"I know."

Mavis and Chester passed Chester's door, which was once again decorated with the red heart Mavis had put there. They both paused at Amanda's door and Mavis turned. "Thank you for a wonderful evening. I especially liked the singing. It was like old times."

Amanda smiled at her. "I'm glad you had fun."

"We did. Come along, Chester."

"Only if you promise not to cook me anything."

"Don't be silly. Eating at this time of night is very bad for you. Ruins your digestion. Good night, kids."

Amanda stared as the two of them disappeared inside Mavis's apartment. "I can't believe it. You should have seen how they used to fight."

"Maybe the red vibrator broke the ice."

"Maybe." She opened her door and walked into the dark apartment. "Shoot, I forgot to leave a light on."

"Stay right here." Leaving the door open in case they needed an escape route, Will moved carefully into the living room. Adrenaline flooded his system.

"Will, you're scaring me."

"I'm scaring myself, but I don't want to be stupid about this, either." Listening for any sound — the scuff of a shoe on the carpet or a cough — he made his way over to the end table and turned on the table lamp. No one was in the room.

Then Amanda gasped. "The window."

He looked, and there, outlined in white spray paint, was a giant heart. Heart pounding, he walked over to touch it. "It's on the outside."

"I . . . forgot to close the drapes."

Will reached for the cord and took care of that. Then he turned to her. "There's no reason to stay here like sitting ducks. We can go to my apartment for the night."

Pressing her lips together, she shook her head.

"Why not? I'm on the second floor. He may not have any idea where I live."

She took a shaky breath. "Because that will only prolong it. He's not giving up, so that means we have to wait until he shows himself. Then we can deal with him."

"I'll bet we could outwait him. If you

moved in with me for a couple of weeks, he'd probably get tired of not knowing how to get to you and go away." Will wasn't sure of that, but it sounded better than hanging around this apartment with its overgrown bushes and easy access.

"He'd only track me to your place. He knows I work for Gloria and he knows I work at Geekland." She clenched her fists at her side. "I'm sick, sick, sick of the suspense. I want him to make his move. Then, one way or the other, it will be *over.*"

"Let me check out the rest of the apartment, and then we'll talk about it." He started toward the bathroom.

"We can talk about it all you want, but I'm staying here."

And if she did, so would he. But they had to come up with some defensive strategies. He looked behind the shower curtain in the bathroom and then made sure nobody was hiding in her bedroom, either.

He almost tripped over a thick book lying beside her bed, and underneath the bed he found the wand for her vacuum cleaner. She was too neat to have them there by accident. As effective weapons, though, they left something to be desired.

Continuing on to her closet, he discovered that she didn't have a lot of clothes, but the ones she had were hung up neatly. Her shoes were arranged in a tidy row on the floor. He was reminded of the humming-bird's nest he'd seen.

Someone was trying to destroy that nest, which created a fury in him that he'd never felt before. Not even Helen's betrayal had affected him like this. He wanted the son of a bitch to show himself, too.

Maybe Amanda was right about staying here and drawing him out into the open. The jerk had been toying with her long enough. Judging from the escalating threats, he'd make contact with her soon. When that happened, Will wanted to be ready.

"Nobody's here." He walked back into the living room, shrugging out of his coat on the way. "At least he didn't try to break in tonight."

In his absence Amanda had locked the door and taken off her coat. She stood gaz-ing at the red numeral glowing on the answering machine. "Before I play this, tell me what was in the valentine."

He dug it out of his pocket, unfolded it and handed it to her.

She read it and glanced up at him. "Okay, we can go to your apartment if you want. I didn't realize he'd targeted you, too."

"That's not why I suggested it. I'm not

worried about myself. I'm worried about you."

"Whatever. Let's go. Give me five minutes to get a few things together. And I think we should call a cab instead of hanging around the bus stop and making ourselves easy targets." She started toward the bedroom.

He caught her arm. "Wait."

"I'm not putting you at more risk, and that's that." Determination gleamed in her blue eyes.

He'd never wanted to kiss someone so much in his life. But this wasn't the time for kissing. It was the time for a logical approach.

Still, he wasn't above using touch to bolster his point. He took her other arm and brought her in a little closer, within range to be convinced, one way or another. "I thought you wanted to give the guy a chance to show himself?"

"That was before I found out he's offering to get rid of you."

"Maybe that's only a scare tactic."

"Well, it worked. There's more security in your apartment. I think you even have better locks."

"With all we had going on, you noticed the locks?"

"Yeah." Her expression softened. "I'm capable of focusing on something besides condoms, you know."

"I'm sure you are. So let's focus on catching this guy. We can do that better by staying here."

She shook her head. "Not if it puts you in more danger. I dragged you into this, and I can drag you out again."

"I don't think so. Not anymore."

Her eyes searched his. "Just because we had a little sex doesn't mean —"

"In the first place, it was a *lot* of sex. And in the second place, I have these powerful protective instincts to deal with."

"You need to disconnect those instincts immediately."

"Sorry, no can do." He caressed her arms. "They come hardwired in most guys, and it's quite often activated once you let them have sex with you."

"Is that right?" In spite of everything, she smiled.

"Do the research. You'll discover that the same instincts which prompted the cavemen to fight off the saber-toothed tiger are driving me, now. After eons of human development, there's no stopping the process."

"You are so full of bullshit." But her eyes

told him she was loving every nerdy word of it.

"Let's stay here and man the barricades."

"Or woman the barricades, whichever makes more sense at the time. I demand equal barricade time."

"I knew that." He was falling for her. After eons of human development, there was no stopping that process, either.

TWENTY-SIX

If Amanda had heard the song on the answering machine before making her decision to stay in her apartment, she might have chosen differently. But she'd committed to staying and catching the guy and she knew that was the best course of action. Still, hearing Michael Jackson's "Smooth Criminal" rattled her more than she wanted to admit.

"Forget what I said," Will said. "We're going to my place."

She reminded herself that this kind of mental torture could go on for a very long time if she didn't make a stand. She looked Will in the eye. "I'm staying."

"But there's stuff in that song about blood on the carpet."

"You said it yourself. He's trying scare tactics. He might be angry that you're on the scene."

"Might?" Will blew out a breath and

pushed his glasses more firmly on the bridge of his nose. "That's like saying Michael Jordan might be the best player the Bulls ever had."

"Okay, so he's angry."

"He's more than angry. He's furious because you have a boyfriend."

"Good. Then he'll want to do something, something that will draw him out where we can see him."

"We need a strategy session."

"We need coffee." She walked into the kitchen and grabbed a can of Folgers out of the cupboard.

"Good idea. You got anything sugary, to jump-start our brains?"

"Ding-Dongs." She gestured toward the counter. "They're four months old."

"Ding-Dongs? Really?" He picked up the package. "I haven't had these in years."

Amanda dumped the coffee in the basket and ran water in the carafe. "One bite and it'll be years before you have another one. They're a gift from Chester. He had a coupon."

"Maybe they'll work as weapons." He took one out. "Still too soft. We could freeze them."

She punched the button and started the coffee. "Great plan. When the valentine guy shows up, we'll have him wait in the living room while we get the frozen Ding-Dongs to pelt him with."

"Seriously. We need something." Will bit into a Ding-Dong. "These are incredibly stale."

"I have a vacuum cleaner hose and a copy of the collected works of Freud."

"I know. I almost tripped over them, but it's not enough. Got any knives?"

She shuddered. "I can't picture myself stabbing anybody." She saw his expression and reconsidered her answer. "But I'll work on that. I realize that when the time comes . . ."

"It probably won't get to that. He's only one person and we're two. But still, I think a knife would be good to have handy. Which drawer?"

"To your left."

He opened the drawer, took out the biggest, baddest knife she owned, and laid it on the counter.

She looked away. "Yuck. I wish I knew karate or something."

"Me, too. Some protector I am, huh?"

That got to her. He'd willingly interrupted his life to deflect this threat, and it was turning out to be much hairier than either of them had thought. Walking over to him, she put her arms around his waist and gazed up at him.

"What?"

"I won't have you minimizing what you've offered to do for me." He felt so good that she pressed closer, which naturally caused him to put down the Ding-Dong so he could wind his arms around her, too.

"I haven't done much," he said.

"Yes you have. You've been wonderful, and I'll never forget it."

A gleam came into his green eyes. "Are we talking about my bodyguard abilities or something else?"

"I'm talking about your friendship."

He smiled. "Thanks. You're pretty darned friendly, yourself."

She rubbed against his crotch and felt him respond. "We can't have sex tonight, can we?"

"Not if we stay here. We'd be too vulnerable." His gaze grew hotter. "Are you sure you don't want to go back to my apartment?"

"Of course I do." She stood on tiptoe so her hips aligned perfectly with his. "You'd think I'd had enough, but I feel as if we just got started."

He cupped her bottom and pulled her in tight. "Then let's call a cab."

"Nope." She rubbed against him, tormenting herself as much as she was tormenting him. "And don't think I don't regret that choice. You have an amazing effect on me."

He leaned down to nibble on her mouth. "Same here. And you taste a hell of a lot better than Ding-Dongs."

She accidentally began kissing him back, and before she knew it, his tongue was in her mouth. Things went downhill from there, or uphill, depending on what perspective a person had on the situation.

Kissing her with increasing enthusiasm, Will edged her out of the kitchen and toward the living room. "We shouldn't do this." He unbuckled her belt.

"No." She unzipped his fly.

"We'll be quick."

"A quickie." She reached inside his pants and found exactly what she was looking for. He was silky smooth and rock hard — the exact components that made her heart race faster and her panties become wetter.

He shoved those wet panties down around her knees about the time she engineered the release of his penis. By nudging one shoe off, she could pull one leg free of being trapped in her pants leg.

He'd propped her up on the arm of the couch, which meant he only had to reach around to the seat cushion where his laptop case lay. She suspected he'd planned it that way. In seconds he scored the last piece of the puzzle, a shiny gold packet, and ripped it open.

She was gasping with eagerness by the time he steadied her on the couch arm, spread his stance slightly and thrust in deep. Clutching his shoulders, her head thrown back, she closed her eyes and held on. Nothing beat the sensation of Will pouring on the steam, and she gloried in it.

He pumped fast. "Just . . . once . . ."

She could live with that. And her once was about to happen. She announced the fact with one long, lusty cry. He quickened his pace, milking her for every last tremor. Then he shoved home one more time with a groan that seemed to fill the small room.

Struggling for breath, he held her tight. Slowly she lifted her head and gazed at him through heavy-lidded eyes. If any orgasms deserved to be described in purple prose, it would be those created by Will Sloan. But apparently every time he made her come he fried a couple thousand brain cells, because all she could say was, "Good."

"Yeah." So he was no silver-tongued devil afterward, either.

She liked that about him. She liked quite

a few things about him, as a matter of fact. He could give her a quickie any old time.

So they were doing it, right under his nose. Hidden in the snowy bushes outside Amanda's living room window, Harvey shivered as a breeze whipped around the corner of the building. He was so cold he'd bet his nuts were the size of grapes.

Moving around to stay warm was out because someone might hear him. So he had to hold still, and his fingers and toes were practically frozen. He wouldn't be surprised if he ended up with frostbite, and it would be all Amanda's fault.

He'd listened to them talking in there, talking about him. That Michael Jackson song had been perfect, and they deserved it, too, after the way they were acting. When they hadn't started having sex the minute they'd walked in the door, he'd hoped, like a dummy, that he'd been wrong and they were only good friends. Ha.

He'd kept that hope alive when they'd gone into the kitchen to make coffee. Except they hadn't stayed in the kitchen. Before long they were back, and Harvey had known exactly what was going on in there. He'd recognized those sounds — the heavy breathing, the moans, the steady creaking of whatever piece of furniture they were using, probably the couch.

Then he'd heard them both come, and that had made him so mad he'd been ready to go in there and do something drastic. Except he hadn't brought any of his tools tonight. He hadn't thought it was time.

Now he knew different. Next time he was bringing everything — the glass cutter, the knock-out gas, the gas mask for himself. Next time Amanda would find out what it was like to do it with a guy who knew what a woman liked and how she liked it.

How could she treat him that way? He'd had it all planned out. He was pretty sure that until today, Amanda had been going without.

The way Harvey had figured it, Amanda would be starved for a good poke. Nothing like a woman who hadn't had any for a long time. Harvey liked to think Amanda had been saving herself for him.

But here came this nerd, taking advantage of Amanda being sex-starved. It wasn't fair, when Harvey was supposed to be the one giving her what she really needed. He'd thought of enjoying Amanda for a few nights before arranging it so Louise would find them together and be properly impressed.

With the nerd around, that plan was in the dumper. There was no point in waiting until Valentine's night, either. Amanda had ruined everything because she just couldn't wait. Now he'd have to change his plans.

The nerd shouldn't be all that much trouble. Harvey could gas him into unconsciousness along with Amanda. Then he'd get her in the Mercedes and have some fun with her, except she probably wouldn't be all that much fun, now that she'd already had sex.

He might as well drop some hints to Louise, too, because he might have one chance to make Louise sit up and take notice of how studly he was. To be on the safe side, though, he probably should hide the shotgun shells.

Those two were acting so cozy in there, all nice and warm while he was out here freezing his ass. He would go home soon, but first, they deserved another scare.

Over coffee and Ding-Dongs served in her little dining nook, Amanda tried to help Will brainstorm ways to make the apartment safer. The brainstorming wasn't going well, because she didn't have much on hand that would be useful. No little bells, no thin wire, no rope, and no bungee cords.

"I've been denying that I had a real problem," she said. "If I'd admitted it earlier, we could have gone to the hardware store today and picked up a few things."

"Don't blame yourself. We'll go tomorrow." He glanced at the clock. "It's already after two. It'll be daylight before you know it."

Despite the coffee, Amanda could barely keep her eyes open. She'd had a busy day, including some powerful sex. Now she was ready for sleep, but Will had wanted to go over their options for jerry-rigging an alarm system, and that seemed easily as important as sleeping.

She forced her tired brain to come up with another suggestion. "We could line a bunch of cans along the windowsill, so they'd make noise if someone tried to come in." She covered a yawn.

He put down his coffee mug. "I'll do it. You go on to bed. And take that knife on the counter with you. Leave it on the bedside table where you can reach it."

All thoughts of sleep disappeared as her tummy started to churn. "Uh . . . how about you being in charge of the knife? I'm more into beating someone over the head with the collected works of Freud."

"I doubt the collected works of Freud will

scare anybody."

"That's where you're wrong. Freshmen psych students quake in their boots at the sight of it. Some have been known to faint."

"Very funny. You need to take the knife."

"I'm really good at swinging a vacuum cleaner wand, too. You should see me. Just like Tom Cruise in *The Last Samurai*." She made a chopping motion with one arm. "Hee-*ya!*"

Will laughed. "Come on, Amanda. I can't see that thing doing much damage, either."

"I'm not good with knives. Once when I thought I might actually cook something, I bought a whole chicken to cut up and fry. Couldn't dismember the chicken. Fried the whole thing, instead, which didn't work out all that well."

"The thing is, I planned to sleep on the couch, so you need some sort of real weapon."

"The couch?" She didn't like that idea at all. "Why?"

"You even have to ask after what just happened? There's no way I can lie quietly next to you all night. It would start with one little touch, and then we'd be kissing, and then —"

"I get it." All he had to do was talk about it and she was primed for liftoff.

"Yes, you would. Passionately and often. I can't seem to help myself."

She leaned her chin on her fist. "That's not all bad."

"It is when I want to keep my attention on something else, like this valentine wacko. There's no telling . . ." He paused. "Did you hear something?"

"No."

"There it is again."

Dread trickled down her spine. She held her breath and listened. Then she heard it, a steady tapping, like a woodpecker was clicking his beak on the living room window. But it was night, and besides, all the woodpeckers had flown south for the winter.

"That son of a bitch." Will shoved back his chair and headed for the front door. He grabbed her keys and jerked the door open. "Morse code."

"Will!" She raced after him. "Don't! You —"

"Lock the door!" He slammed it behind him.

Sick with fear, she ran back to the kitchen counter and grabbed the knife. The handle felt so cold and hard. But Will was out there, alone and unprotected.

She sprinted down the hall while hysterical laughter bubbled in her throat. Her mother had taught her never to run with knives. It was dangerous. Someone could get hurt. No shit.

Wrenching open the front door of the building, she stepped into the freezing night air and gasped with the shock of it. She whipped her head around at the sound of running feet and ice cracking on the pavement. Will was tearing down the sidewalk, arms pumping.

At the corner he slowed and looked both ways. Then he leaned down and braced his hands on his knees. Heart thudding fast, she hurried down the steps and started toward him. As she drew closer, he turned and spotted her.

He began to jog in her direction, and his breath fogged the air. "Hey!"

She stood next to a street lamp and waited. No point in meeting in the middle, like a couple in a movie slow-motion shot. Damn, it was cold out here.

When he reached her, he was breathing hard. "What in hell do you think you're doing?"

She didn't need a degree in psychology to figure out he was very angry. She held up the knife. "Coming to your rescue."

"That's crazy." His eyes glittered in the light from the street lamp. "I told you to stay there."

"No you didn't. You told me to lock the door. You didn't say anything about staying put. And you ran out with no coat and no weapon. Don't talk to me about being crazy."

He looked at the knife in her hand. "I thought you didn't do so great with knives."

"Yeah, well." She shrugged.

His angry scowl eased. "Thanks."

"I'm not saying I could have stabbed anybody."

"It's the thought that counts." Putting an arm around her shoulders, he steered them both back toward the apartment building.

She'd been all prepared to be brave and stuff, but walking back to the building with Will's arm around her was more her style. "Did you see him?"

"Only from the back. He had too much of a head start on me. When I got to the corner, a bus was pulling away about a block down. I'll bet he was on it."

"So maybe . . . he won't be back tonight." The adrenaline rush was gone, leaving her weak and shaky.

"Let's hope not."

"Could you tell anything at all about him?"

"I'd say maybe five ten, a hundred and

eighty pounds or so. But that's about it. He was all bundled up. Couldn't see his hair, let alone his face."

She sighed. "So he could still be anyone."

" 'Fraid so. Damn it, I was too slow! That's what I get for letting myself get fat and lazy."

"You're not fat, and after our various physical activities today, I can also testify that you're not lazy."

He was obviously not going to be mollified. "I'm not talking about sex."

"I was."

"Sex is easy."

"If your talents lie in that direction."

He blew out a breath. "I used to be able to run faster than that. Five years ago I would have caught the bastard."

"And then what?"

"I would have punched him out."

She gazed up at him. "Do you do that kind of thing a lot? Because somehow I can't imagine you punching someone out."

"I didn't think you'd come to my rescue with a knife, either. You're a psychology major. You tell me what makes us act out of character."

Love. That wasn't the scientific answer, but it felt like the right answer. She and Will had accidentally fallen in love. It might be a temporary infatuation that would burn itself out, or it might be something deeper, something that would cause her a whole lot of trouble in the end.

She might have found the love of her life, and she wasn't ready for that yet. Someday she would be ready, but Will wouldn't be around then. No guys these days waited years for a girl to make up her mind.

But she chose not to say any of that. "Fear of loss can make you act out of character."

"Hm."

She wasn't sure how she'd respond if he asked her to elaborate on her answer. If they were each afraid of losing something, or more specifically, *someone,* that pointed to that very emotion she'd rather not discuss.

So she changed the subject. "The Morse code thing, would that be any kind of clue?"

"I wish, but I doubt it. Some guys learn it in the Navy, but lots of kids pick it up in Scouts or just for the fun of it."

"I never did."

He gave her shoulders a squeeze as they started up the steps of the apartment building. "Just as well."

"Why? What did he say?"

He fished in his pocket and pulled out her keys. "Never mind."

"After all this, I think I deserve to know."

"He said *I will fuck you.*"

"Oh." Her shaking got a whole lot worse. Maybe she shouldn't have insisted on knowing, after all.

Twenty-Seven

Between lying on Amanda's lumpy couch and worrying about some loony-tunes coming in the window, Will didn't get much sleep. He wore his dorky flannel pajamas to remind himself he wasn't supposed to have sex with Amanda, in case he sleepwalked his way into her bed.

No such luck. He stayed on the couch like a good boy, tossing and turning. Toward morning he finally conked out. The phone interrupted an outstanding dream that featured Amanda lying naked on a deluxe king-sized bed.

His reflexes weren't completely shot, because he made it to the phone before the answering machine kicked in. He had no doubt who was calling this morning, and he decided to use some intimidation tactics of his own.

"Listen, you asshole. Forget about playing one of your creepy songs, and stay the hell away from this apartment, because the next time I'll beat the shit out of you. I have a black belt, and I know how to use it. Got that?" The part about the black belt was a lie, but the rest was absolutely true. He'd had it with this jerk.

"Will Sloan, you lying nerd! Justin says you're having sex with *my intern!*"

It took him several seconds to get his brain around the fact that Gloria, not the valentine weirdo, was on the line. "Justin doesn't know what he's talking about." Amanda was going to kill him.

"Oh, yes he does. She was the mystery girl who gave you that hickey!"

Amanda was *really* going to kill him. But if Amanda let him live, he would make it up to her by killing Justin. "Was he drunk? Because he's been drinking a lot lately, and you can't believe a guy who —"

"He wasn't drunk. He didn't want to tell me, but I had something he wanted desperately, especially after I'd teased him for about an hour. Confessing your sins was his only way of getting it."

The apartment was cool on this winter morning, but Will began to sweat. "Look, none of this is Amanda's fault. She needed someone to scare away the stalker, but I'm the one who came up with the idea of staying here. Then I took advantage of her vulnerable situation."

"But why? She's not nearly as attractive as I am!"

Will felt a headache starting at the base of his skull and working its way up his scalp. What to do, what to do. Admitting to his attraction wouldn't go well for Amanda.

He grasped for something to say that wouldn't get Amanda thrown out of Gloria's office. "For one thing, she's not a client."

"Oh, for God's sake. I can see it all, now. I aroused your sleeping libido and she got the benefit because she's *not a client*. Well, I'm leaving you so we can have sex. Deal with it."

"What about Justin?"

"My social calendar has room for *at least* two men."

Will sighed. This was turning into a nightmare. "I won't be one of those two men."

"Ooo. Now that's sexy. You're demanding exclusivity, then? I usually don't agree to that, but for you I might make an exception."

"I don't want exclusivity, Gloria. I don't want to get sexually involved with you at all."

There was a long silence. He wondered if

she'd quietly hung up. That would be fine with him, but he was very worried about how this nasty little scene would affect Amanda's relationship with her boss.

"So," Gloria said at last. "You've started this affair with Amanda, and now your conscience won't let you drop her."

"It has nothing to do with Amanda. I just —"

"It has everything to do with her. Put her on."

Will closed his eyes. He had a bad feeling about how this would turn out. "She's asleep."

"No I'm not."

He turned to find Amanda standing there looking like an angel who'd been forced to buy her robe at a thrift store. "Just a sec, Gloria." He covered the mouthpiece. "Justin told her we had sex."

"Justin? How did he —"

Will felt like a worm. "Last night it sort of . . . came out. I mean, he knew I was staying here, and he saw the hickey. So did Gloria, but she didn't guess it was you. Justin did."

"Hickey?" She walked over and peered at his neck. "I did that?"

"Uh-huh. Yesterday morning, before we made it to the coffee table."

She took a long shaky breath. "Then I guess I did this to myself. Might as well give me the phone."

He handed it over reluctantly.

Amanda tucked her hair behind her ear and placed the receiver against it. "Good morning, Gloria." After that she did nothing but listen and nod. Finally she cleared her throat. "I understand. Consider it done." Taking the receiver from her ear, she pressed the disconnect button.

He didn't like her resigned expression. Whatever she'd agreed to couldn't be a good thing. "Consider what done?"

She gazed at him, her eyes revealing no emotion. "Either you move out, or she dumps me as an intern. You're moving out."

Amanda should have known that something would come along to destroy her new-found happiness with Will. The hell of it was that she'd been tripped up by her own enthusiasm the first time they'd had sex. Now that he'd mentioned the hickey, she could see it, but she hadn't noticed it before. It wasn't very big, smaller than a thumbtack, but big enough for a hawk-eye like Gloria.

After she'd delivered the bad news, Will shook his head as if refusing to accept her edict. "You need someone here."

"Maybe, but it can't be you." She sounded calm, but inside she was screaming at the unfairness. "Gloria said that if I told you to leave, you'd be released from all feelings of obligation."

"I hope you know I don't feel obligated to stay."

That touched her, but she couldn't afford to be touched. Her future was on the line. "I would assume you don't."

"You don't have to *assume* anything." He grabbed her, ugly bathrobe notwithstanding, and administered a toe-curling kiss.

She did her best to stay objective, but once he started using his tongue, objectivity took a back seat to lust. Soon she was clinging to him and wrapping one leg around his. They still had a lot of flannel obstructing their progress, but the goal was clear to both of them.

He pulled away and dragged in a breath. "So if you don't throw me out, she'll say you behaved unprofessionally to justify dropping you as an intern."

"Bingo." She dived in again, holding his head so she could kiss him with the kind of dedication he deserved.

By the time he came up for air again, he'd divested her of the bathrobe. He tossed it on the floor. "How will she know if I've left?"

"She'll be here in an hour." She finished unbuttoning his pajama top and shoved it down his arms.

He unfastened the tiny buttons at the neck of her granny gown. "I could leave, and then come back."

"Nuh-uh. She'd quiz me in the morning, and I'm horrible at lying." She untied the drawstring of his pajama bottoms. "Once you leave, you have to stay gone."

"But you'll be alone! What if he comes back?"

"I'll buy all the things we talked about today. And he might not come back after the way you chased him." She gave his pajama bottoms a push, and they fell to the floor. "Now stop talking, get a condom, and come into the bedroom. We have a time crunch, here."

"Give me a key to your apartment. I could sneak in here after you're asleep. Technically, you wouldn't know I'd been here."

"Technically, I would probably bash you in the head with the collected works of Freud! Don't sneak, please. Just come to bed with me right now. We've never done it on a mattress before." She turned and walked toward her bedroom, pulling her granny gown over her head as she went.

"Don't think I haven't noticed."

In her bedroom, she threw back the covers and stretched out on the bed. Life would be hell once Gloria arrived, but that wouldn't happen for another hour. She glanced at the bedside clock. Correction, fifty-five minutes.

Will arrived, naked except for his glasses. He was bearing a shiny packet in one hand. He paused in the doorway. "Just let me take a mental picture to sustain me."

"Good idea. Me, too." She cataloged his thick dark hair, which fell untamed over his forehead after a night's sleep. How she would miss those green eyes, even the horn-rimmed glasses. And his mouth. She'd loved his mouth from the beginning.

He was no muscle-bound weight lifter, but he had decent pecs sprinkled with dark hair, a respectable six-pack, and then came the *pièce de résistance* as they probably said in French bordellos. That magnificence was all hers until Gloria showed up in fifty-five minutes. She looked at the clock again. Fifty-one minutes.

She beckoned him forward.

"Yeah." He took off his glasses, put on the condom, and joined her on the mattress. "Ah." He gathered her close. "How is it that we've never tried it this way?"

"Circumstances." She wiggled against him.

He kissed her and brushed the hair back from her face. "How much time do we have?"

"Allowing fifteen minutes for you to pack up and leave, I estimate that we have approximately thirty-four and a half minutes."

"Spoken like a true nerd." He rolled on top of her.

She spread her thighs to give him access. "I am not."

"You are so."

Then he slipped deep inside her, and she was willing to be anything he wanted if he would only keep up that certain rhythm that was exclusively Will's. He had a gift, and she was the lucky girl receiving it right now. She wouldn't think beyond this moment.

Her first orgasm rocked her world. The second turned her into liquid fire, and by the third, she was ready to levitate.

"We're not finished, you and me," he crooned into her ear.

She moaned and lifted her hips. "I hope not."

"I'm not talking about coming."

He might not be, but he was the master at that activity, and she couldn't think while he plied his craft. "Okay."

"I mean it."

"Me, too." She meant every whimper, every cry. Beyond that, she saw no future for them. They were victims of bad timing. He wrenched one more climax from her thrumming body before riding her hard and letting go with a groan that was half blessing, half curse.

They sank together onto the mattress. This was cuddle time, pulling up the covers and basking in the afterglow time. They couldn't afford it.

She waited until his breathing returned to normal. Then she gave him a nudge. "You have to leave."

"This sucks."

"I know. But right now, she holds all the cards."

He sighed. "And she plays dirty."

"It's her game."

Rising up on his elbows, he looked into her eyes. "I'll find a way around this."

"Please don't take chances with Gloria."

"I won't." He gave her one last, lingering kiss. "But I will be watching over you, somehow. You're not facing that wacko alone."

"He could be gone, scared away." Because she couldn't cling to Will, she'd cling to that hope.

Will went home, although he would have loved to stay and tell Gloria what he thought of her high-handed tactics. But he couldn't jeopardize Amanda's standing with the university. So once he got home, he flipped through the phone book until he found the number he needed.

When Chester didn't answer, Will figured out that Chester and Mavis were still holed up in Mavis's apartment. Will envied them the luxury of spending their Sunday morning together, when he'd been summarily run out. Thank God for those last moments with Amanda, though.

He hoped she'd understood what he was trying to say, without saying it. If they let go of this special connection, they'd be making a huge mistake. He hoped she realized that what they'd found — the amazing sex, the easy conversation, the natural friendship — didn't come along very often. Sometimes never.

Sure, she had her goals, and he respected that. He only wanted to add to her list of things to want — a special person to share the life she wanted to create, a person who wouldn't drag her down, someone who would support and enhance her dreams. He could be that person, if she would let him.

Going further into the telephone book, he found Mavis Endicott and dialed the number.

Mavis answered immediately, sounding irritatingly cheerful.

"Mavis, this is Will, Amanda's friend."

"Will! Why are you calling? Why not just drop over?"

"I'm not at the apartment building right now." And he felt that acutely, as if the world didn't sit quite right on its axis now that he'd been banned from Amanda's place.

"That's a shame. Chester and I are having rooibos tea. It's that bush tea they talk about in *The No. 1 Ladies' Detective Agency* mystery series set in Africa. Chester doesn't much like it, but he'll get used to it. You should come over and try some."

"I need a bigger favor than sharing a cup of tea." Will hesitated, needing to know but not wanting to know. "But first I have to ask . . . how much can you hear through the apartment walls?"

Mavis didn't answer right away. "That depends," she said at last.

This was uncomfortable, but Will pressed on. "On what?"

"Whether Chester and I turn off our hearing aids."

"Oh."

"We turned them off last night," she said quickly. "Any noises that came through weren't clear. It could have been the TV, for all we knew."

"Right. The TV." Will didn't bother pointing out that Amanda didn't have a TV, so anything Mavis and Chester had heard had been a live performance.

As for Will, he'd been concentrating so hard on Amanda that he hadn't even considered the noise level. He'd thought about it in his own apartment earlier in the day, which told him his involvement with Amanda had escalated the longer he'd stayed with her. That wasn't the point of his question, though. The transfer of noise from one apartment to another was vitally important for another reason entirely.

Mavis cleared her throat. "Did you hear anything from . . . my apartment?"

"Didn't hear a thing." Amanda might have, although that didn't matter now. "I have to know whether, with your hearing aids turned up, you would be able to hear someone crying out in distress in the next apartment."

"Oh, my, yes. With our hearing aids turned up, we hear every little scuffle. I know how thin the walls are, so I'm careful to be quiet. Chester is, too. But it turns out we both had the same idea, not to tell Amanda about the thin walls. That way we can watch over her without her knowing."

"I see." He and Amanda had been playing to quite an audience, between the stalker outside the window and the neighbors with their ears to the wall.

"But we really didn't hear much of anything last night," Mavis said. "Honestly."

Will didn't believe a word of it, but he'd get over his embarrassment. That was chump change compared to keeping Amanda safe. "Circumstances have forced me to move out of Amanda's apartment," he said.

"Oh, dear. Please tell me you didn't have a fight. I was assuming the yelling had to do with — um, not that I *heard* much yelling at all. Maybe a teensy bit, but like I said —"

"It's okay, Mavis. We didn't fight." Will explained the situation with Gloria. "So I need to be there, but Amanda can't know I'm there. And I need a key, in case she has a problem."

"That's simple. I have a spare key Amanda gave me in case she ever locks herself out. She never does, of course. Very disciplined girl."

Until I interfered in her life.

"And you can hide out in Chester's apartment for as long as you need to," Mavis continued. "He's not sleeping there anyway. That way you can take one side of Amanda's place, and we can cover the other side. Chester and I can show you the best spots for maximum hearing."

"Okay." Will controlled the urge to laugh.

"Not that we *use* the spots to listen in on Amanda. But naturally, when you live somewhere, you notice these things."

"Of course."

"When do you want to set things up?"

Will gave thanks for snoopy neighbors. Mavis and Chester already had the surveillance thing down. "I'm sure Amanda will be going out sometime today. If you could call me when she leaves, I'll head over then."

"Perfect. Don't worry, Will. We won't let anything happen to that girl."

"No, we won't." And because Will wanted to be completely alert tonight, he'd take a nap after he finished this call. If that wacko showed his face, Will would take him out.

TWENTY-EIGHT

"I am furious with you, Amanda, absolutely furious. But I can't have you getting raped on my account." Gloria stood, hands on hips, and gazed at the white heart spray-painted on the window. "What were you thinking, renting a first-floor apartment? No single woman rents a first-floor apartment."

"It was cheap and available. It's right on the bus line. I have good neighbors."

"You mean Mavis and her boyfriend Chester, the ones I met last night? They were spying on me through a crack in the door as I came down the hall. I call that nosy, not neighborly."

Amanda had the right to call them nosy because she loved Mavis and Chester, but she'd be damned if she'd let Gloria diss her friends. "They're concerned about me. And they're good-hearted."

"Apparently everyone on this floor is good-hearted. I've never seen such a valentine frenzy in my life."

"It helps bring the tenants closer together."

"That's all well and good, but you need something more than sappy sentiment. You need motion detectors and Mace. Why didn't you tell me this guy was leaving creepy songs on your answering machine?"

Amanda shrugged. "I thought it was my problem."

"So you solved it with Will, is that it? You're damned lucky I haven't terminated your internship. You betrayed me, Amanda."

"It wasn't meant to turn out like that. It was a temporary situation." And if saying that made her heart ache, too bad.

"All men are a temporary situation. Monogamy was created by a patriarchal society. It's up to women like me to battle that concept." Gloria pushed back the sleeve of her fur coat to consult her jeweled watch. "Grab your coat. By the time we get there, the hardware store should be open."

Amanda couldn't imagine a more bizarre activity than shopping in a hardware store with Gloria. She'd probably spend all her time examining the ropes and chains.

"Come on." Gloria tapped her watch. "We're burning daylight."

"I really appreciate that you're taking an

interest, but I can do this myself. I realize that I need some sort of personal protection and I was planning to get a few things today."

Gloria let out her breath in obvious exasperation. "Lord give me strength. You're on a limited budget, right?"

"I can manage this expense." And Gloria was the last person she wanted giving her charity.

"I can picture it, now. You'll buy the inferior, on-sale item that will fail you at a critical moment. That's how you ended up with this death trap of an apartment. Get your coat. This shopping trip is on me."

"No. I mean, no, thanks." Amanda had her limits. Gloria could get away with banishing Will because that was probably in Amanda's best interest. She'd been getting too involved, too attached. But Gloria was not buying her protective hardware.

"You don't want to argue with me." Gloria's gaze was filled with haughty confidence. "I'm still holding the big club."

Amanda's jaw dropped. "You'd give me a bad review over *this?*"

"You bet your sweet little tush I would. A good psychologist keeps an open mind when confronted with a problem. You have a problem, but your mind is closed tight against the possibility that I might be of some help. You're allowing stubborn pride to skew your thinking."

Amanda tried to stare Gloria down, but she couldn't do it. Gloria was right. That was a humbling revelation. Gloria could be criticized for many things, but having a closed mind wasn't one of them.

Besides that, Gloria shared one quality with Amanda — she was incredibly tenacious. Admitting that they were even slightly alike was tough, but if Amanda believed in being open-minded, then she had to look at Gloria honestly. She wasn't completely bad, not by a long shot.

Amanda took a deep breath. "Okay, let's go to the hardware store. And thank you."

"You're welcome." With a smile of triumph, Gloria headed for the door. "We'll also pick up razor blades and solvent so we can take that damned heart off your window. It's creeping me out."

When Harvey came back from Starbucks all caffeined up, Louise was waiting for him. She stood in the living room, smoking a cigarette. It sagged, like it was still sort of soggy, which meant it was one of the ones he'd frozen.

Because he'd convinced her that she'd put

the cigarettes in the freezer, she refused to buy a new carton when she still had this one. With all her money, she was weird about the little stuff, sort of like Scrooge. She had trouble keeping the thawed cigarettes lit, though. She had to smoke with one hand and keep her lighter handy in the other.

"You've been gone a lot." Louise took a drag on her cigarette. "Shit." Flicking the wheel on the lighter, she relit her cigarette.

"You know I go to Starbucks, butter buns."

Louise drew in a lungful of smoke. "I'm not talking about Starbucks in the morning, like now. I woke up in the middle of the night and you were gone. What the hell were you doing roaming around at two in the morning?"

"Something."

"You pencil prick. It better not be a girl."

"Okay."

Louise advanced on him, her cigarette in the corner of her mouth and smoke coming out the other side. She looked exactly like a fire-breathing dragon with tits. "It is a girl, isn't it?"

"I can't help it, lemon lips. You know I'm a bad boy."

She blew smoke in his face. "You little

turd. Tell me her name, *now.*"

"Amanda."

"That's a lie. Amanda Detmer's a famous actress. She'd never go for a twerp like you. You're making this up." The tip of her cigarette stopped glowing. She swore and flicked the lighter over it again.

"Not Amanda Detmer. Amanda Rykowsky."

"I don't know any Amanda Rykowsky!" Louise puffed on her cigarette and coughed like she was about to hack up a lung.

Harvey waited for the light to come on in Louise's brain. He'd told her about Amanda last week. She would remember if she thought about it long enough. He knew the minute she'd made the connection, because her eyes started shooting sparks.

"The *receptionist.*" Louise began to quiver.

"She's so pretty."

Louise got right in his face, and her eyes glowed like the tip of her cigarette. "If I catch you messing with that girl, I'll glue your dick to a train track."

A thrill of excitement ran through him. "I'll try to stay away, jelly joints, but I can't promise. She's in love with me."

Louise's jaw worked. "In love with you?"

"She wants me real bad."

"The *bitch.* So she thinks she can steal

another woman's husband, does she?"

Harvey sighed dramatically. "Guess so."

"We'll just see about that!" Louise glared at him. "From now on, I'm keeping an eye on you, buster. A very *close* eye."

That was exactly what he wanted. He'd make his move tonight. Louise had taken him for granted for years, but if she saw that he had someone else, if she thought she might have to fight to keep him, things would change around here. Finally he'd have the upper hand.

For the first time since he'd become involved with Amanda, Will had to buzz the apartment intercom to get inside the building. Mavis had called mid-afternoon, after Amanda had taken off for the library. She'd told Mavis she wouldn't be back until dinnertime.

It wasn't a very good intercom. Mavis's voice was crackly and hard to hear. Will spoke with exaggerated clarity. Between a bad intercom and her dicey hearing, she might not have the faintest idea who he was. "It's *Will Sloan.*"

Her response came through loud and clear. "Goody!"

The door lock buzzed, and he was in. Walking down the valentine-infested hallway made him grumpy. He'd tried to call Justin and ream him out, but Justin hadn't picked up. Will didn't blame him. If he were in Justin's guilty shoes, he wouldn't pick up, either.

Hell, maybe it was for the best. He'd wanted to believe he could be an asset to Amanda and not a distraction, but in reality they'd spent too much time having sex. While she was near, his hormones kept him from admitting the bitter truth — they couldn't seem to control their urges. Because of that, he could be a huge distraction, one she didn't need at this time in her life.

Mavis and Chester came out of Mavis's apartment. Mavis looked as if she'd won the lottery. Chester wasn't exactly smiling, but he looked less disgruntled than usual. Will tried to feel happy for them, but instead he was irritated and jealous. A few more hours of sleep and he might be able to dredge up some better emotions.

"This is the second time she's left," Mavis said as she came to meet him. "Here's the spare key I keep for her."

Will pocketed the key. "I hope the first time she left included a trip to the hardware store for something to discourage an intruder."

485

"Yep," Chester said. "She went to the hardware store with that Gloria person, the one who broke you two up."

"You're kidding."

"Nope." Chester unlocked his apartment door and ushered them both inside. "They came back with a boatload of stuff. Mavis and me, we went over later to find out about it."

"Well, and to return the vibrator," Mavis said. "That seemed only fair, with you being gone and . . . and . . ." She paused, her cheeks pink. "You know."

Chester closed the door. "She's trying to say that she doesn't need that thing now that she has a live model."

"Right." Will didn't want to think that he could be replaced in Amanda's life by a red vibrator, but it could be true. How totally depressing. "So what kind of supplies did they get?"

"Motion detectors and pepper spray," Mavis said. "They also got some wire and strung up a series of bells in case the motion detectors fail somehow, like the guy figures out how to cut the electricity or something."

"Good."

Chester hooked his thumbs through his belt loops. "Much as I hate to say it, Gloria seemed to know what she was doing."

"But Amanda's never going into a hard-ware store with Gloria again," Mavis said. "Gloria asked the clerks all kinds of embarrassing questions about ropes, and pulleys, and counterweights. She made it clear she was building a sex gym in her guest room."

Will groaned. More bait to keep Justin enslaved. But the way Will was feeling about Justin at the moment, he was willing to abandon his buddy to whatever fate he'd chosen.

"So, this is the place." Chester swept an arm around the living room, which was very similar to Amanda's except that Chester had a TV in one corner and an American flag tacked on the wall.

"Thanks for letting me hang out here, Chester."

"No problem. You're welcome to sleep in the bed." He gestured toward the bedroom.

Will noticed that the floor plan was a flipped version of Amanda's, with the living room on the right and the kitchen, bed-room, and bath on the left. "If I sleep, I need to be close to the common wall be-tween the apartments, so I'll probably stay here in the living room."

"The middle of the walls seem to be the best for hearing anything," Mavis said. "I think they skimped on insulation there."

"They skimped on insulation everywhere," Chester said. "But it's worst in the middle of the wall between apartments."

"But we don't listen," Mavis said.

"I'm sure not." Will didn't care if they spent all day and night with their ears to the wall, if it meant that he had a way to keep Amanda safe.

"There's beer and frozen pizza in the fridge," Chester said.

"I could bring you a nice meal if you'll give me a few minutes," Mavis added.

Chester gave him a nudge. "I'd advise you to stick with the beer and the pizza, my friend."

Will held up his duffel bag. "Thanks for both offers, but I brought sandwiches."

"Sandwiches." Mavis rolled her eyes. "I could make you something hot."

Chester steered her toward the door. "Leave the poor boy alone. You can make me something hot."

Will pretended not to understand the meaning of Chester's remark. His life sucked enough without being reminded that the seniors were having sex and he wasn't. "Thanks again for the loan of the apartment, Chester."

"Make yourself at home." With a wave,

Chester maneuvered Mavis out the door.

Prowling the living room, Will decided to rearrange the furniture so that he could sit in an armchair and look outside. Unfortunately, his view was limited by snow-covered bushes. He'd have to rely mostly on sound, but maybe he'd get lucky and catch a glimpse of the slimeball sneaking around Amanda's window.

He put his sandwiches in the refrigerator, opened one of the Cokes he'd brought, and settled down with the book he'd grabbed before heading out the door. It had been handy, but it might not have been the best choice under the circumstances. With a sigh, he opened *Titillating Trivia.*

Amanda's dedication to her goals had abandoned her. She'd hoped that by immersing herself in academic surroundings, she'd regain her sense of purpose. Instead she'd wasted hours sitting in the library thinking about Will.

If only she'd taken an acting class sometime in her college career, she might have a better grasp of this lying thing. Then she could have been comfortable sneaking Will into her apartment, because she would have been able to convince Gloria he was no longer there. Instead she was forced to walk into an apartment that felt emptier than she ever remembered.

She'd picked up a fast food hamburger before heading home, so she ate that without enthusiasm, only because she needed to keep up her strength. She wondered what Will was doing right now. Maybe watching a basketball game with Justin. Sure, he might be angry with his friend, but they'd known each other a long time. They would have patched up their differences by now.

Then again, Gloria might be keeping Justin busy constructing the apparatus she'd described to a very embarrassed hardware clerk earlier today. Will might be alone and missing her as much as she missed him. That thought should cheer her up, but it didn't. One of them should be happy.

At least the apartment was more secure. Two motion detectors would alert her if anyone came through one of the two windows. Wires threaded through little bells crisscrossed the windows, in case the motion detectors failed. If someone came through one of those windows, Amanda would know about it.

Gloria had advised her to run out the front door if that happened. Amanda thought it was good advice, but she would love to catch the guy, and running away wouldn't make that happen. Running was the wisest choice, though.

Maybe she wouldn't have to make that choice. So far as the guy knew, she still had Will staying here, a man willing to chase a prowler down in the middle of the night. The guy might think twice about taunting a determined protector like Will.

Except Will wasn't here. She had only a backpack full of books to take to bed with her. And she might as well. She'd hauled them home from the library in hopes that she'd become inspired to study eventually.

Changing into her flannel granny gown, she picked up the backpack and carried it into her bedroom. The place reminded her of sex with Will, but that was just too bad. She wasn't likely to change residences in the next four months, so she'd have to work through those hot memories.

Propping pillows against the ancient headboard, she settled in with her laptop and her backpack full of books. She would get something accomplished or know the reason why.

His heart beating fast, Harvey assembled his equipment. Louise had told him she was going out for coffee, but he didn't think she had. She'd taken the keys to the BMW, leaving him with the Mercedes.

She'd left with her oversized gym bag, and Louise wasn't the type to work out. Harvey knew what was in it. He'd emptied the shells out earlier, to be on the safe side. She'd never think to check if it was still loaded.

Now he pictured her parked in an alley where she could see if he left the house. He was definitely yanking her chain and loving the power he had over her. She would soon find out that he was man enough to get someone as hot as Amanda. Maybe Amanda and Louise would fight over him. That would be awesome.

Not every guy would go this far to have sex with a new woman. Even Amanda should give him some credit for making this kind of effort. She'd taken the easy way out by jumping into bed with the nerd. Harvey was doing all the work in this relationship — in both relationships, come to think of it.

Feeling virtuous, he carried his supplies out to the Mercedes.

Twenty-Nine

At first Amanda thought the buzzer that woke her up was her alarm clock. Groggy and disoriented from falling asleep during her study session, she fumbled for the clock on her bedside table. In the process, she knocked something on the floor. Muttering, she leaned over and picked it up.

Pepper spray. And the buzzer wasn't my clock.

She tried to focus, but something was very wrong. Instead of becoming more alert, she was getting sleepy. Was she dreaming that she'd heard the motion detector? Was this a nightmare or was it real? *I have to stay awake. Have to . . .*

Will jerked awake at the sound of a buzzer in Amanda's apartment. It could be her oven timer, except that she didn't cook. What did a motion detector alarm sound like? Damn it, he had no idea! He'd imagined that he'd know when something was happening next door, but now he wasn't sure.

Anxiety flooded through him like hot oil. The buzzer kept going. He leaped from his chair and felt in his pocket for the key Mavis had given him. Better to charge into her apartment and find out he'd made a mistake than screw up by not doing anything.

Last of all he grabbed the butcher knife he'd brought from home. It was dull because he never used it, but it was the closest thing to a weapon he owned. Then he charged out the door and down the hall. By the time he put the key in the lock, the buzzer had stopped.

But he'd come this far, so he might as well go in. The lock was balky, like always, and he stuck the knife under his arm so he could use both hands to jiggle the key. The apartment was very quiet.

What if she was in there making taffy and the buzzer was to remind her when to quit cooking it? Or she'd bought a frozen pizza like the kind Chester had offered him, and the buzzer had simply been signaling its doneness?

Then he heard the tinkle of a bell. Mavis had said Gloria and Amanda had strung bells across the window.

He went very cold and very still. Although his body felt frozen, his mind heated to the boiling point as a thousand scenarios played out in his fevered brain. Whatever was going on in there, he had to stop it.

He still had the element of surprise going for him, and if he kept making all this noise with the key, that would be lost. He twisted the key slowly and silently. The lock gave way and he edged the door open.

The living room was dark, but he felt a blast of cold air. The drapes flapped in the breeze, and he could see the large hole cut in the window. Wires and little bells dangled where they'd been cut. Something about the air in the room didn't seem right, either, so he held his breath.

The only light came from Amanda's bedroom. He crept toward the doorway. The room was empty.

At a noise behind him, he spun around, knife raised.

"Yikes!" Mavis, dressed in a frilly pink nightgown, jumped back and almost dropped the rifle she was holding. "We thought you were him!"

Chester stood behind her in his red plaid pajamas. "Where is she?"

Breathing hard, Will stared at them. "Gone." He felt dizzy. Something was definitely wrong with the air in here. But he had to find Amanda.

Shaking his head to clear it, he hurried over to the large hole in the living room window. The light from the street lamp shone on the shiny exterior of a Mercedes parked by the curb. Someone was shoving something floppy into the back. *Amanda.*

"No!" Will climbed through the window, the knife clutched in one hand, the broken glass cutting into the other as he steadied himself. Then he dropped to the ground and ran across the snow toward the street, toward the maniac wearing a gas mask who was climbing behind the wheel of the Mercedes.

Just as he reached the car, he heard the locks click into place. Raising the knife he still held in his hand, he stabbed the nearest back tire. Then he ran to the front and stabbed that tire as the engine growled and the car started to move.

The car veered away from the curb. Will threw down the knife and jumped onto the back bumper, grabbing the short rubber radio antenna for balance as he wedged both feet against the back fenders. The car swerved, either on purpose or because of the lacerated tires. He gripped the antenna with all his might and prayed for the strength to hold on.

As the car skidded sideways, Amanda's head banged against the armrest. The pain jolted her out of the fuzzy half-sleep she'd been drifting in and she opened her eyes. When she tried to move her arms to steady herself, she discovered that her wrists were tied behind her back. Her ankles were tied, too. She realized this was not good news, but she still felt too loopy to get excited about it.

From this angle, she could see in the rear-view mirror, and her chauffeur seemed to be a space alien. Besides that, some guy was trying to play Spider-Man by clinging to the back of the car. She couldn't see his face, but his body looked a lot like . . . Will? Oh, God, not Will!

The car veered off the road. The space alien fought the wheel and got the car back on the asphalt, but a loud thump from the back window suggested Will had just smacked his head against it. Panic overrode the fog in her brain. She opened her mouth to yell, but only a squeak came out.

The space alien ripped off his face, which turned out to be a gas mask. "Are you awake, Valentine? That's good. I tried not to give you too much gas, so you'd wake up quick and we could have some fun."

She cleared her throat. "Stop this car!"

"I can't, my sweetheart." The car lurched again, and there was a clunking sound coming from the vicinity of the front and back wheels on the passenger side. "I have to drive until that Wall Street guy falls off."

She couldn't let that happen. Her muscles weren't cooperating very well, but she managed to gradually scoot around until she was sitting on the seat.

"I can hear you *moo*-ving," the driver said in a singsong voice. "I'll bet you're ready for some good sex, aren't you, cuddle-umpkins?"

Amanda bent her knees and eased her feet up in front of her while trying to identify the voice. She'd heard it before. "Stop the car and see if I am or not."

"Can't. Not until the nerd lets go."

The car careened wildly and Amanda lost her balance. Slowly she inched her way back into position. If only she had on shoes. Shoes would make more of an impact than bare feet, but she had to work with what she had.

"Did you like my valentines?"

She stared in the rearview mirror, trying to place him. "Harvey Kenton?"

"That's me." He sounded proud as punch

about it, too. "And we're finally alone. Well, except for the nerd on the back of the car."

"I think you have a couple of flat tires, Harvey." *And a few screws loose.* Rocking back on her spine, she bent her knees and brought her feet up gradually so he wouldn't see what was coming.

"I know. Louise is gonna kill me when she sees the rims on those tires. But you're worth it, Amanda. I've been waiting for so long."

"And now I'm here." She brought her feet up. Almost ready. *Hang on, Will.*

"Yes. It'll be so good. But we don't have much time. I'm pretty sure Louise is somewhere behind us."

Ducky. Taking a deep breath, Amanda slammed her heels into the base of Harvey's skull. His head bounced forward, hit the steering wheel with a sickening crack, and the car bounced off the road and rammed into some bushes.

Amanda was thrown facedown on the floor, and the hump in the middle knocked the breath out of her. As she lay there gasping, Will pounded on the front passenger window.

"Amanda? I'm going to break this."

A moment later he'd shattered the window and unlocked the door.

"Oh, *Will.*" She'd never heard a sweeter sound than his voice. "Are you okay?"

"I'm fine." But his fingers shook as he worked on the ropes binding her hands. "How about you?"

"I'm good. Check Harvey. See if I killed him."

A moan from the front seat answered that question.

"He's alive," Will said. "Who did you say it was?"

"Harvey Kenton. One of Gloria's clients."

"Ex-client," Will said. "Once I get this rope off you, then I can tie him up nice and tight for the cops."

"Good idea." Once her wrists were free, she pushed herself to her hands and knees and took her first look at her protector. "Oh, Will. You're hurt." His glasses were gone and his shirt was ripped. He had a bruise on the side of his face and both hands were bleeding.

"I'm fine." He crouched down and gazed into her face. "Are you?"

"Yeah."

Harvey moaned again.

"Go tie his hands to the steering wheel," she said. "I can get the rope off my ankles."

"Right." He started to open the front passenger door.

"Don't move, either one of you."

Amanda had never looked into the business end of a sawed-off shotgun, but she recognized immediately what she was seeing. She almost peed her pants. Those double barrels had a mesmerizing effect, but eventually she lifted her gaze in order to identify the owner of the shotgun. "Louise?"

She sneered at Amanda. "Yeah, *Louise*. It's bad enough that you lured my Harvey into your trap without wrecking my Mercedes!"

Will swallowed. "Look, Amanda didn't lure this guy anywhere, so you can put the gun down."

"Don't worry." Harvey lifted his head and wiped the blood from his eyes. "It isn't loaded."

"Oh, yeah?" Louise sighted down the barrels. "Let's see."

Will dived for Louise and knocked her sideways as the gun roared.

"Damn you!" Louise struggled to her feet and pointed the gun at Will. "Look what you made me do. You made me shoot the side of my car!"

"I unloaded that gun!" Harvey yelled.

"Surprise! I reloaded it! Looks like I have to waste this interfering bozo before I can take care of the husband-stealing bitch in the car."

"Just try it, sister. Make my day."

Amanda blinked to make sure she wasn't seeing things, but sure enough, there was Mavis in a frilly nightgown holding a rifle that looked to be at least a hundred years old. "How did you get here?"

"Chester has an old Honda Civic. We followed you." Mavis shoved the barrel hard against the back of Louise's jacket. "Drop that gun. Now."

Will cleared his throat. "How about if Louise sets the shotgun down slow and easy? Not to interfere, Mavis, but I'm thinking if she drops it, the thing might go off again."

"Good point," Mavis said. "Set it down, slow and easy. Don't try any funny stuff."

"I'd do it if I was you," Chester said, coming up behind Mavis in his pajamas. "That's her great-granddaddy's gun, and she's dying to find out if it still works. She might pull the trigger out of pure curiosity."

"It's not *fair,*" Louise wailed. "She was trying to seduce my Harvey."

"Yeah, right," Mavis said. "That's why he had to gas her and tie her up. Now put it down before I get the urge to test-drive Granddaddy's thirty-thirty."

With a moan of frustration, Louise laid the shotgun on the frozen ground. "I wanted to shoot them."

"And I wanted to shoot you, but sometimes we don't get what we want. We have to delay gratification. That was always an important lesson for my third-graders."

Amanda was so fascinated by the sight of Mavis toting a gun that she hadn't noticed Harvey reaching for something under the seat. But Will had. He lunged at Harvey and wrenched the tire iron out of his grip.

"Thanks for the backup, Will," Mavis said.

"No problem."

Amanda couldn't stop staring at Harvey and Louise. To think she'd considered them just another couple who paraded in and out of Gloria's office. Although they were temporarily subdued, she wouldn't relax until they were in handcuffs and headed for jail. "We need the cops here ASAP. Who has a cell phone?"

Will shrugged. "No telling where I dropped mine along the way."

"I don't have mine," Mavis said.

Chester threw up both hands. "I never bought one."

Amanda glanced at Louise. "You know what? I'll bet Louise has a cell phone. Will, want to check?"

"You're gonna use my phone to call the cops to arrest me?"

"Sounds about right." Mavis pushed the barrel of the rifle up against Louise's jacket again. "Now don't move while Will gets that phone."

Will found the phone inside Louise's jacket and dialed 911. "Anybody else we want to call?"

"I want my lawyer," Louise grumbled.

"Sorry," Will said. "That won't be happening until much, much later."

Amanda couldn't resist. "See if she has her therapist on speed dial."

Will glanced at Amanda and a faint smile crossed his lips. "Yeah, let's see." He consulted the contact list. "What do you know? She has Gloria's cell number right here." He punched the button and handed the phone to Amanda.

When Gloria answered, Amanda relished telling her what had happened.

There was a moment of shocked silence. "I'll be right there," Gloria said. "We're only a block or two from there. Justin thought we should check on you, so we were on our way over. See you soon."

Amanda closed the flip-top phone. "She'll be here any minute."

"You bitch!" Louise's mouth curved in a

snarl of contempt. "You think you have everybody dancing to your tune, don't you? Well, I'm not through with you. I'll get you sooner or later, and I'll —"

"That's enough!" His expression thunderous, Will stepped in front of Louise.

"I'll tell you when it's enough, mister. She thinks she's so hot, but I —"

"Louise." Gloria stepped from a cab in a swirl of mink. Justin followed close behind.

Like a little kid caught stealing cookies, Louise cowered at the sight of Gloria striding toward her. "Wha-at?"

"Remember our little talk about boundaries?"

Louise's shoulders slumped. "I guess so."

"And what did we say about boundaries?"

"To . . . uh . . . respect them?"

"Have you done that tonight?"

Louise sighed. "No, I haven't, Dr. Tredway, but your receptionist was trying to steal my Harvey."

"Did Harvey tell you that?"

"Yes."

"Is Harvey a reliable source?"

"Maybe not. But, Dr. Tredway, they —"

"It's my professional opinion that you and Harvey need more help with this issue of boundaries." Gloria glanced at the shotgun holes in the Mercedes. "Quite a bit of help, actually. We'll see that you get it."

Louise nodded. "Thank you, Dr. Tredway."

"Now let's all get more comfortable and wait for the nice people to come and straighten everything out. Amanda, you look cold. Justin, give her your coat."

Once they all made it back to the apartment, Will convinced Amanda that the frozen microwavable dinner that Mavis brought over would be adequate first aid for the bruise on the side of his face. A couple of teeth felt loose, but he didn't mention those. They'd firm up in a few days.

He also managed to talk everyone into leaving so he could be alone with Amanda. Even Gloria agreed. She had to be feeling a shitload of guilt over this whole episode. Once the police had taken Louise and Harvey away, Gloria had suffered a minor meltdown.

Interestingly enough, Justin had been the only one able to comfort her. Will thought he might have to reevaluate his position on that relationship. After tonight's events, it seemed to Will that Gloria needed Justin almost as much as Justin needed her.

So everyone was coupling up. And Will needed to have a heart-to-heart with the woman who had captured his. She might not like what he had to say, but it was the only decision he could live with.

He'd brought his stuff over from Chester's, and Amanda might think that was because he was moving back in. Quite the opposite. And a temporary separation wouldn't work — they'd both try to find ways around it.

She'd made coffee and hauled out the last two Ding-Dongs. They'd taped cardboard over the hole in the living room window, so the apartment was warm again, but not exactly cozy. The violent memories would have to fade before the place felt like home to Amanda, and he hated to add more sadness. But now was the time.

His duffel sat next to his chair. Reaching down, he pulled a red envelope out of it. "I wanted you to have the real thing."

She opened the valentine with a smile that trembled around the edges. "You could have waited a couple of days."

"I wanted you to have it now." The valentine had a single red rose on the front. Inside it said, *I'll remember you forever, Valentine.* He'd signed it *Will,* resisting the urge to add the word *love.*

She reached across the little dining table and took his hand. "I still can't believe you hid out in Chester's apartment so you could come to my rescue."

"I couldn't leave you here alone." His whole body ached from what he'd been through, but his whole heart ached worse as he thought of what was coming. He drank his coffee too fast and scalded his tongue.

"I think Gloria's dropped her objections to us."

He nodded. "I think so, too."

"So, what do you say? Can we make it work?" The light in her blue eyes told him that she expected him to say yes.

He would rather take a beating than say it, but he had to. "I don't think so."

Her hand stiffened in his. "Why not?"

"You know why. I wouldn't want to keep you from your studies, but we've discovered neither of us are very good at delayed gratification." He tried to make a joke out of it. "I guess we both needed Mavis as our third-grade teacher."

She looked stricken. "We can do better! Maybe if we made up a chart, and marked when we could afford the time. You know, schedule it, so that —"

"Schedule our sex?" If he hadn't been so filled with grief, he would have laughed. "Amanda, do you remember how we are together?"

"I know, but we'll develop better discipline. We'll —"

"No. I know myself, and I think I know you pretty well by now, too. There's one way to guarantee that you'll graduate with honors, keep that spot waiting for you at Harvard, and become all you want to be. I have to butt out of your life."

"I don't want you to!"

"I know." He gave her hand a squeeze. "But I'm doing it, anyway." His heart broke as he pulled his hand from hers and stood. "Goodbye." He couldn't look at her, couldn't bear to see the tears that he knew would be there. Grabbing his coat and his duffel bag, he walked out of her apartment, out of her life.

THIRTY

For several weeks, Amanda allowed herself to hate Will for being so damned noble. Then she went through a period when she tried to convince herself he must not have cared very much if he'd let her go so easily. That argument didn't last long, because she kept thinking of the look in his green eyes when he'd left her that night. He'd looked as horrible as she'd felt.

Basically she had only herself to blame for laying out her program so well in the beginning. The worst part was — Will had been right. If he'd hung around, she wouldn't have studied very much. Without him there, she poured all her sexual frustration and longing for Will into her class work, and her grades showed it.

Every day she expected to run into him in the hallway going to or from Gloria's office. She practiced what she'd say and imagined what he'd say back. Those imaginary conversations changed as her mood changed.

Amazingly, a real meeting with Will never happened. He had to be deliberately avoiding her. In that case, she could assume that the breakup had hurt him as much as it had hurt her, and he couldn't deal with only casual contact.

They'd never had a real shot, anyway. If they'd planned to reunite after the semester was over, reason told her he'd want marriage. A guy like Will deserved a family, too, and he couldn't be expected to delay that gratification for an unknown number of years. She wasn't ready to commit to motherhood. She had too much to do first.

Finally she arrived at her last day of working for Gloria. Graduation was at ten the next morning, and Gloria couldn't be there because Amanda had given her only two tickets to Mavis and Chester. Gloria was meeting them afterward, though, for lunch and a party at Geekland.

Justin was coming to the party, too. He and Gloria were inseparable these days, which meant Amanda saw him often. They were each careful not to mention Will's name.

As Amanda cleaned out her desk, Gloria appeared with a gaily wrapped package. "Here." She plopped it in the middle of

Amanda's desk. "I know this won't make up for sabotaging your relationship with Will, but it's the best I can do."

Amanda stared at her. Gloria had never mentioned the breakup, and Amanda would never have guessed Gloria felt any guilt whatsoever. "You didn't sabotage us," she said.

"Of course I did. If I hadn't made it clear I didn't want you around as competition, you'd still be together."

"No, we wouldn't. We both knew after that wild night of the break-in that you wouldn't care if we kept seeing each other. You'd obviously bonded with Justin."

A dreamy look came into Gloria's eyes. "I did. And I have."

Because it was her last day, Amanda decided to be bold. "You should marry him, Gloria."

Gloria snapped out of her trance. "What made you say that?"

"I've been thinking about it for weeks. I finally decided to say something."

"Oh. For a minute there, I thought you might be psychic."

"Nope." If she were psychic, she'd know what was going on with Will, but she had no idea. "Why, are you considering the M word?"

"Just last night, as a matter of fact. I expect it's because you're leaving and I'll . . . oh, hell, I'll miss you like crazy."

To Amanda's surprise, she got a little choked up. "I'll . . . miss you, too." She'd never thought she'd speak those words, but there they were.

Gloria cleared her throat. "Anyway, last night I decided that it was time for me to admit that I'd found something special with Justin. I'd told you that I would never get married, but I figured after you left, you'd never know if I went back on my word."

"You wouldn't invite me to the wedding?" Now she was hurt.

"Honey, I wasn't planning to invite *anyone.* It would be too embarrassing. But now that the secret's out, I might as well make it a big bash, huh?"

"Might as well." Amanda saw only one problem with that. Justin would ask Will to be his best man, which meant she'd see Will at this wedding, whenever it took place.

"So you're saying it really wasn't my fault that you and Will broke up? That's a huge relief."

"It wasn't your fault."

"Then whose was it?"

"Mine."

Gloria sighed. "Still choosing your studies

over your love life. Then I'm glad I got you what I did. Call it a single girl's survival kit."

Amanda untied the red bow and lifted the lid of the sturdy box. She wasn't surprised by what she found inside. She counted at least three different kinds of vibrators, lubricants, a calendar of nude men, and a couple of videos. At the rate her life was going, she might need all those things.

"Don't go giving any of that away, either. I was going to give you a massage with Thor, but that's only an hour of pleasure. This could last you for years."

"I won't give any of it away, I promise." Amanda closed up the box. "Thank you, Gloria. I'm sure it's exactly what I'll need."

"I wouldn't doubt it. No telling what you'll find over there at Harvard. I know they'll have plenty of nerds, but you can't expect them to be like Justin and Will. Those two are special. Not to bring up a sore subject, but they are."

"I know." Amanda sighed. "Bad timing on my part."

Amanda woke on the day of graduation expecting to feel joyous that she'd finally reached her goal. She felt plenty of satisfaction, but joy was elusive. The last time she'd felt joy had been . . . with Will. And not only because of the outstanding orgasms, either. They'd clicked in a way she hadn't with any other person. He had the potential to be that much-talked-about combination, both a lover and a best friend.

So if that was the case, why in hell was she running off to Harvard? Was the prestige of getting her graduate degree there worth losing somebody like Will? Once she'd asked herself the question, the answer was obvious.

She could get her graduate degree right here in Chicago, and go into practice here. Why had she thought an Ivy League school would make so much difference? Will made the difference. With him, her life glittered. Without him, her life was perfectly fine, but a lot less shiny.

As for marriage and kids, plenty of people managed both a career and children. She might not get her graduate degree as fast, or build her practice in record time, but she'd be happy. Finally she realized that she would never be like her mother. For one thing, she'd have Will, someone who supported her dreams.

Dressing quickly in the casual outfit she planned to wear under her cap and gown, she gulped down an energy drink and ran to catch a bus down to Will's office. She had just enough time to see him before she had to be on campus for the ceremony.

Walking into the building felt strange, because she hadn't thought she'd be back here after cleaning out her desk yesterday. She felt a little bit like an interloper. Her desk didn't belong to her anymore. Gloria had hired a temp for the summer and would have a new intern in the fall.

But she wasn't going to visit Gloria. Passing the office where she'd spent such a tumultuous few months, she continued on to the offices of Cooper and Scott.

The receptionist put down her mug of coffee when Amanda walked in. "How can I help you?"

"I need to see Will . . . uh, William Sloan. It's urgent."

"Oh, I'm sorry. William doesn't work here anymore. Perhaps one of our other brokers can be of assistance."

The news took a few seconds to register. "How . . . how long ago did he quit?"

"Let me think. It's been about three weeks, now."

Three weeks? She couldn't believe that he'd been physically gone from this building for three weeks and she hadn't somehow sensed it. She was so far from psychic it was pathetic.

Despair threatened to swamp her, but she made one last attempt. "Did he move to another firm in Chicago?" She wouldn't have time to go there, now. Maybe she shouldn't go at all, if he'd leave the building without telling her. She could decide that after the ceremony.

"No, William has left town. But Jonathan Creighton is an excellent broker, if you'd like me to page him."

"No. No, thanks." Stunned, she turned to go.

"Are you sure?"

"Absolutely sure." He'd left Chicago without saying a word. No matter how many times she tried to get her mind around that, she found it impossible. Had she meant so little to him, then, or so much? Regardless of the answer to the question, he was lost to her.

Will stood still as the crowd of graduates leaving the ceremony eddied around him. He hoped to hell he wouldn't miss Amanda. Three times he'd thought he'd spotted her, only to have the blonde turn around and be somebody else. What evil, lost-in-the-mists-of-time impulse had decreed that all graduates wear the same black robes and mortarboards?

As it turned out, she found him. If he'd reasoned out that she might, he would have worn red, even if it was a bad color on him. The green polo shirt probably blended in with the grass he was standing on.

"Will?" She approached cautiously.

Before she reached him, Gloria swooped in and gave her a hug. "Congratulations! This deserves a round of Chi-Town Lakefront Breezes, and I'm buying!"

"I'll take you up on that." Chester walked up behind Gloria.

"And then you'll buy a round, right?" Mavis linked her arm through Chester's. Then she glanced over at Will. "Will! I didn't know you'd be here."

Gloria spun around. "Will? What are you doing here?"

Justin stepped into the group. "I'm probably the only one who knows, and I was sworn to secrecy." He gave Amanda a hug. "Congrats. We'll all meet you at Geekland. It's up to you if you want to bring that guy over there, the one with the hopeful look in his eyes."

Amanda stole another glance at Will. She wasn't convinced he looked hopeful.

"Come on, everybody," Justin said. "Let's

make ourselves scarce."

Throughout the commotion of their leaving, Amanda continued to stare at Will. "They said you'd left town."

"They said right." He waited until Justin had herded everyone away before stepping closer. "I left three weeks ago."

"Without telling me?" Her voice quivered, and she hated that, but what he'd done seemed like such a betrayal.

"You were finishing up, taking finals, doing all those last-minute requirements. I wasn't about to get in your way."

"But you should have known I'd want to know!"

"Well, now you know."

"Three weeks after the fact!" She was losing control of herself, and people were staring, but she didn't care. "Why bother? Why not just disappear, never to be heard from again?"

"Because —"

"Never mind that I went to your office this morning and asked about you."

"You did?" He began to smile.

"Yes! And never mind the shock to my system when I discovered you'd left the firm and you'd even left *town.* Never mind that I —"

"Amanda, I love you."

"Never mind that I expected to run into you, and for these last three weeks you weren't even there to run into . . ." She paused. "What did you say?"

"I love you."

She would not cry. She would not. "So what good does that do us? You left town."

He moved closer. "I didn't just leave town. I moved to Boston."

Boston? "You moved to Boston? But that's where —"

"Uh-huh. I was able to transfer to a Cooper and Scott office there. Last week I found an apartment in Cambridge. I had to wait until the students started moving out at the end of the semester."

"Oh." Her brain didn't seem to be functioning quite right. It sounded as if Will had moved to the very place she was going next week.

He gazed at her uncertainly. "Amanda, if this won't work for you, then I understand. I made some assumptions, and maybe I was wrong."

"If what won't work?"

"Getting married. See, I thought if we had the summer to get used to having sex all the time, then maybe by the fall semester we'd settle down enough that you'd be able to study."

Finally she figured out what was going on. She'd had to make a complete one-eighty from her previous belief, and the shock of seeing Will suddenly appear had been too much to assimilate all at once. But she had it, now.

With a whoop of joy, she flung herself at him, knocking her mortarboard to the ground. "It works for me." She grabbed his face in both hands and laid one on him. After a few minutes, she realized they might be into it a little too thoroughly when someone nearby let out a wolf whistle.

Will lifted his mouth a fraction. "We need to continue this somewhere more private."

She wanted to. Oh, how she wanted to. But people were expecting her. "I have a party at Geekland."

"I have a hotel room two doors down from Geekland. And I told Justin that if everything went well, you might be a little late."

She nibbled on his lower lip. "Everything's going exceedingly well."

"So the marriage thing is a definite?"

"Definitely a definite. I love you, William Sloan."

Smiling, he eased away from her, wrapped an arm around her shoulders, and steered her toward a cab waiting at the curb. "Then come with me, Ms. Graduated-with-

Honors. It's long past time to celebrate."

Yes, it was. As Will helped her into the cab, she marveled that he'd cared enough about her future to leave when he had to and come back when she was ready. Finally she'd found someone she could trust with her dreams, and that was worth a gigantic celebration, one that would only require two people, a bed, and an adequate supply of condoms.

ABOUT THE AUTHOR

Vicki Lewis Thompson is uniquely qualified to document the nerd experience and has the National Honor Society pin to prove it. Long before brains were cool, she made passes at guys who wore glasses. She eventually married one. Being a smart man, he recommended she write romances. Being a smart woman, she wrote about romantic nerds. When *Nerd in Shining Armor* hit the *NYT* bestseller list, it validated her secret passion and confirmed what she's always known — nerds are hot and getting hotter! The runaway success of Vicki's nerd books indicates that we have officially entered an era of nerd love, which suits her perfectly.

Visit her Web site at: www.vickilewis thompson.com

The employees of Thorndike Press hope you have enjoyed this Large Print book. All our Thorndike and Wheeler Large Print titles are designed for easy reading, and all our books are made to last. Other Thorndike Press Large Print books are available at your library, through selected bookstores, or directly from us.

For information about titles, please call:
(800) 223-1244

or visit our Web site at:
www.gale.com/thorndike
www.gale.com/wheeler

To share your comments, please write:
Publisher
Thorndike Press
295 Kennedy Memorial Drive
Waterville, ME 04901